NEW WORLD

"Where am I?" he asked.

The woman did not answer.

"What place is this?"

Recovering, the woman unwrapped his fingers from her wrist and picked up the empty bowls. He could see well enough that she was no Celt, nor of any race of Europe. A slave, perhaps. A captive from another land.

Aengus stood to survey the line of rocky islets, full of morning and sunlight. Were those the fingers and fists of stone that had ended his long voyage in a rain-slashed, midnight instant? Were they the black spikes that had punctuated his nightmares? He found it hard to believe, so peaceful they looked, standing in mild sunshine and a gentle blue sea.

Approaching the village, he could see smoke seeping through roofs and long boats drawn up on the beach.

Suddenly, people poured out of the houses: men, women, hordes of dogs and children—or so it seemed to Aengus then. They came forward hesitantly.

He noted their bronze skins, their long, black hair and broad faces set with bright, black eyes.

These were not people of any part of the world Aengus knew.

BLOCKBUSTER FICTION FROM PINNACLE BOOKS!

THE FINAL VOYAGE OF THE S.S.N. SKATE   (17-157, $3.95)
by Stephen Cassell
The "leper" of the U.S. Pacific Fleet, SSN 578 nuclear attack sub SKATE, has one final mission to perform—an impossible act of piracy that will pit the underwater deathtrap and its inexperienced crew against the combined might of the Soviet Navy's finest!

QUEENS GATE RECKONING   (17-164, $3.95)
by Lewis Purdue
Only a wounded CIA operative and a defecting Soviet ballerina stand in the way of a vast consortium of treason that speeds toward the hour of mankind's ultimate reckoning! From the best-selling author of THE LINZ TESTAMENT.

FAREWELL TO RUSSIA   (17-165, $4.50)
by Richard Hugo
A KGB agent must race against time to infiltrate the confines of U.S. nuclear technology after a terrifying accident threatens to unleash unmitigated devastation!

THE NICODEMUS CODE   (17-133, $3.95)
by Graham N. Smith and Donna Smith
A two-thousand-year-old parchment has been unearthed, unleashing a terrifying conspiracy unlike any the world has previously known, one that threatens the life of the Pope himself, and the ultimate destruction of Christianity!

Available wherever paperbacks are sold, or order direct from the Publisher. Send cover price plus 50¢ per copy for mailing and handling to Pinnacle Books, Dept.17-538, 475 Park Avenue South, New York, N.Y. 10016. Residents of New York, New Jersey and Pennsylvania must include sales tax. DO NOT SEND CASH.

PASSAGE to EDEN

VERNE WADE

PINNACLE BOOKS
WINDSOR PUBLISHING CORP.

PINNACLE BOOKS

are published by

Windsor Publishing Corp.
475 Park Avenue South
New York, NY 10016

First printing: June, 1991

Printed in the United States of America

PROLOGUE

Five centuries after Christ's time on earth, His sprawling Church was rent with heresy, schism, and disorder. Bishop Turfu, a spare bundle of rectitude and compassion, of zeal and heartache for the afflicted communion of the Son of God, began to despair that the ancient faith would survive its troubles. With young Aengus to aid him, he set forth from old Armorica—from the district lately styled The Lesser Britain—to go into other parts of Europe and beyond, to warn and salve fractious Christendom. His mission was not favored by God. Its effect was nothing. Within a year, Turfu was dead.

In his final moments, he had clutched Aengus's hand tightly and whispered, "Love Jesus." His heart's last beats were for sixteen-year-old Aengus, now stranded without friends in a town on a river that ran to a sea with no European shore, but the only earthly service he could offer him was the admonition to "Love Jesus."

If Aengus had no friends in that land, at least he met with occasional kindnesses. Turfu's remains were taken away and the boy was put on a strange boat made of the skins of animals. Its master was paid to take him to a Christian community downriver.

There was no such community in the place he was put ashore, nor in the next town to which he was directed, nor in any other that he could find. He stayed awhile with people who lived in reed houses in a great marshland, and then with others who lived in tents in the desert. Eventually he came to Siraf on the sea, on a gulf of a southern ocean, where he found the mariner Hektor of Tarsus.

Hektor wanted nothing to do with the responsibility and trouble of taking a boy home. "Find your own way," he said brusquely. "I was on my own when I was your age."

That was the first day. The next day, Hektor sought the boy out and took him to a ship that had just come in from Africa. Hektor called it a "mtepe." Its prow was made like a camel's head with a little bell hanging below it, just like a real camel. Aengus's unaffected curiosity about the fanciful craft touched a responsive chord beneath the mariner's gruffness. Soon the sailor was showing him how its planks were sewn in place with a rough kind of rope rather than held together by pegged tenons, and how its sails were made from folded and plaited palm leaves. Then Hektor talked with the men of the mtepe, dark-skinned men, in their language. Just when Aengus was beginning to suspect that it all was something more than an improbable lesson in shipcraft—that some arrangement was being made for him—Hektor said, "No good. This isn't the ship for you," but he would not say why.

Nor would he say why he rejected the next ship they examined, nor why none of the ships that came to Siraf was suitable to start Aengus on his journey home. In the end, the boy found his own objections to this ship or that one. The only ship that finally satisfied him—delighted him—was the one he sailed in with Hektor. Eastward.

Eastward they went in a meandering, discontinuous odyssey that neither of them wanted to end.

They came, after two years of wandering—maybe three—to Muziris in the land of the Chera people, a place Hektor called Kerala. Not only Cheras lived in Muziris. There were Sericans, the first Aengus ever saw of that remote race, and people from a place called Tanah Malayu, which had a fine sound to his ears. There were Africans of several races. And, most remarkable of all, there were men from Europe that the Cheras called

6

Yavanas. Those Yavanas were merchants from Greece and Italy who traded in silks and spices and precious stones. The Church of Christ was there also, vying for the people's attention with other religions, some local and some from other places.

Muziris was a wonderful place, beautiful and exciting, the crossroads of the whole world, it seemed. Aengus and Hektor would have stayed there for many years, perhaps forever, if Aengus had not fallen in love.

The girl was Jasleen. He met her in her aunt's garden, a private walled place that he had stolen into because its fruit trees and dim pathways through flowered tunnels were more temptation than he could resist. Aengus and Jasleen literally stumbled into each other's arms. He returned every day, even though the girl told him she was already married. That marriage had taken place when she was five years old and the prince who claimed her was forty. Soon, she was to join his household.

Aengus stole her away before that came to pass. He and Hektor stole her away. They smuggled her through the streets of Muziris and onto a boat Hektor had acquired. They sailed many days to another land that Hektor said must be Taprobane. But they had not gone far enough. After almost two months of lovers' bliss, Jasleen, on a morning walk alone, was snatched from the street of the village that was their refuge. The prince himself had found her, as Aengus came to believe. However, when Hektor and he returned to Muziris, the prince was not there; nor did he ever return, although his great, empty house and servants waited for him.

A year later, when he had given up his search, Aengus saw Jasleen's jewelry in a market stall in a small island town. Several pieces. There could be no mistake. He and Hektor traced the jewelry to its source nearby: a pirate village in a small cove whose entrance was blocked by a sand bar at low tide. The pirates boasted that they stole valuable things but did not take slaves. More mercifully, they said, they always killed their victims.

The two friends exacted consummate vengeance. They

7

went back to Muziris, persuaded the prince's family, and Jasleen's too, to provide a force of men, then returned with them to the pirate's cove and watched the burning of the pirates' ships and houses and the slaughter of all the men of the village. Aengus and Hektor only watched the destruction from a distance because they suspected that their own deaths had been ordered also, once they had led the Cheras to the pirates. They slipped away as the attack began. It was ten days before the Cheras gave up their search for them and sailed away, ten days before Aengus and Hektor could leave the forest, reclaim their own boat, and set their course eastward again.

There were other adventures, although none so sad for Aengus. There were glorious exploits and incidents of pure terror. And then, suddenly, it was all over. The years with Hektor were done.

The two friends had lodged in the house of a man who owned ships while they waited for that man's return from a voyage of his own. Then came a great dying, a plague that swept across the city in a day and was gone in ten with the lives of almost all of its inhabitants. Hektor and Aengus were among the first to succumb to convulsions, vomiting, aching delirium, and unconsciousness.

When Aengus awakened, he was alone in the house and almost alone in the city. The first to die had been buried in communal pits, burned on pyres, or simply cast into the sea from boats. The recently dead lay everywhere. None of the few dazed survivors knew what had happened to Hektor or to the other dwellers in the shipowner's house. It was as if Aengus inquired about people who had never existed.

The carrion-filled city was soon abandoned. Some people went up the river to go to relatives in other towns; others just vanished into the tropical forest. Aengus found a boat and took to the sea again, alone.

For five years, he was alone. *With* people often, but without Hektor's gruff tutelage and steadfast friendship, without Jasleen's lilting loveliness, without Turfu's mad, blessed love for the hidden best in men. Five desolate years

8

of solitary wandering, oppressive toil, and bleak imprisonment.

And then Hsin. Seven years in Gau—in Serica—with Hsin, whose face creased in a great, irrepressible smile whenever he saw Aengus. Yen Hsin, who showed him that a friendship grounded in honor and gratitude could be no less staunch or deeply felt than any other. Seven years of service to Hsin's father and his family of craftsmen and traders, years in which his work was approved and he was granted a place, although not a home with land and a family, in Gau.

Seven years that ended in an instant.

While Aengus was away from the town, his return delayed by unseasonable winter rains, Bah men had come south along mountain trails from the great Yahng plain. Bah men: dispossessed farmers and vagabonds with neither hope nor homes of their own who gave their allegiance to a butcher, a self-styled general—the Eighth General, he called himself—even though he gave allegiance to neither king nor commandery. When Aengus came back to where Gau had been, he found only ashes, ruin, and death. And danger for himself, for the Bah men were everywhere.

He fled downriver from Gau. Down the Little Ou to the Great Ou, then past the city of Luh to the sea. Near Luh, he took a small fishing ch'uan from two Bah men who had stolen it only recently themselves. They had run it aground on a sand bar. After Aengus helped them to release it, he threw the two men overboard, for he was a tall man, strongly built, and they were unsuspecting by then.

I

The fishing ch'uan had meant no more than deliverance from the Bah-infested valley of the Ou when Aengus seized it. He did not think beyond escape until he was past the estuary of the Ou and the mud shoals there, past the offshore rocks and reefs, and among the coastal islands. He knew those islands, and the Jo-shans north of them, from two years, nearly, that he had worked with the Jo-shan fishermen. Now, while his mind was still filled with thoughts of flight and refuge, he considered briefly that he might return to those people. He had only been a toiler on their boats, though, and that was a long time ago—before Gau, even before his imprisonment. He did not feel drawn to the Jo-shans.

He thought of other places he knew in Serica, and places of which he had only heard. In all of them, he saw Han men who rejected him for his alien appearance, Yueh men who were so fearful that they would never speak to him, and Bah men—who were Han men, too—washing back and forth across the vast land, destroying everything.

Then another idea came, one born of a yearning that had stirred in him more than once during the past months. It came while he was at night anchor in an island cove, listening to the sea slap against the hull below him. Deeply weary and despondent, yet fretful, he tried to ease his mind by reflecting on that sea, contemplating that it was part of the same world ocean that touched all the

11

places he had ever known. He thought of it tumbling, even then, against a distant European shore: Armorica, his childhood home—rolling woodlands and fields and rocky headlands jutting into the western ocean that he had not seen for . . . what . . . seventeen years? No, eighteen. Eighteen years. Over half of his lifeyears ago. And suddenly he knew that Armorica was where he must go. Home. He did not know whether his parents thought about him often, or rarely, or not at all anymore, or even if they were still alive, but he knew that he would make his way home again to Armorica.

"Tellacloute," he murmured. The sound of that name, the village where he was born, soothed him. "Tellacloute," he said again. "Tellacloute."

The name and the decision to return there renewed life and purpose within him, and raised another question of direction: should he go south and westward, retracing the long route he had followed years before, or should he take his little ship eastward, into the empty ocean, as Hektor would have done?

Hektor had not been the first to say that the earth was a great ball; others had told Aengus in times before that it was true, but those people made unreliable assertions about many things, in his judgment. Hektor was the first to *prove* it to him.

He and young Aengus had been lazing atop a low hill on a soaring, clear day that beckoned minds to dwell on wonders. A tropical sea below them spread away to the horizon. They had been following the progress of several coasting ships when Hektor drew Aengus's attention to another, very distant and sailing almost directly away from them.

"Tell me what you see," Hektor said.

Thinking that his friend was challenging him to a contest of eyes, Aengus replied, with only a bit of invention, "I see a trader with a high stern gallery and two sails, one cocked. It has a circular device marked on it. There are two men at the tiller—"

"Enough!" Hektor broke in, laughing.

Aengus, though confident that his eyes, twenty years

younger than Hektor's, were the sharper, nonetheless felt remorseful that exaggeration might have won the contest for him.

"I don't really see two men," he said.

"I know," Hektor replied, clapping him on the back. "The small one can't be any more than a boy."

They talked of other things awhile, until Hektor pointed to the ship again and said, "What do you see now?"

Surprised that Hektor wanted to renew the competition, Aengus looked carefully, then said, "Only the sails. They look like one sail now."

"And the hull?"

"The sails hide it."

"No, not the sails. What hides it?"

Aengus stared hard. "I don't know. I only see a sail— only the top of a sail, I think. Is the ship sinking?"

"No," Hektor said with the air of one who has a great revelation to impart. "It's not sinking. We're like a fat man who has to put his hand on his pizzle to know if it's still there. The ship's hull is hidden behind the round belly of the sea."

"I've never seen that before."

"You've never looked for it before. In truth, though, sea mists make it hard to see, most often. But what does it mean?"

"It means the ship is *not* sinking."

"No, no. What does it mean about the whole world?"

"That it's . . . like a fat man's belly?"

"Good enough. A fat man's belly and bum all together. It's a great ball. Have you ever thought of that before?"

Another time, when pangs of nostalgia were dulling Aengus's appetite for new lands and new adventures, his grizzled friend had said, "Which way, then, to the sea at the navel of the world and to Rome? Which way to your Armorica?"

Aengus pointed westward.

"Yes," Hektor said, "but maybe closer this way." He pointed to the east.

"Do you think so?" Aengus asked.

13

"Yes. I'm sure of it. We'll fetch Europe sooner by heading eastward. Always to the east."

Hektor never lied to Aengus. Sometimes he exaggerated. Sometimes he was a bit artful when he wanted to persuade his cautious young friend. But he never consciously lied. And he had promised Aengus that he would never desert him. So eastward they had wandered.

And now, off the mouth of the Ou, Aengus pondered the hardships and terrors of the lands and seas he had already crossed. Then he tried to imagine the size of the earth's sphere, which Hektor had not been able to tell him. If a ship's hull could disappear while its sails were still seen, and if the stars were very distant as Hektor had said, and yet a few days sailing north or south could displace their tracks perceptibly, then perhaps it was not such a large ball after all. The distance he had come from Tellacloute—how much of that was easting and how much wandering? He wished that he had paid closer attention when he was a boy. He remembered it as an immense distance. Perhaps the distance remaining to complete a circling of the earth was much less. Perhaps he was now on the far side of Europe's great western ocean, an ocean that might be not so daunting as Europe's seamen imagined it to be.

By such reasoning, and trusting still the judgment of his long-dead friend, Aengus looked to the eastern horizon, saw stars rising there that rose over Armorica, and made his decision: He would set his course eastward.

The ch'uan was small, even for a fishing vessel: no more than twenty-five feet from its high, open stern to the flat water bruiser—the stem—that closed the space between the flaring wings of the bow. There was one large compartment amidships, a very small one just behind the water bruiser, and a family space aft under a housing that was raised a little above the deck. Access to the family space was through a small cockpit between the housing and the rudder post that divided the space between the wings of the open stern. The tiller extended across the top of the

14

housing, where the steersman stood when the tiller was not lashed.

There was one poor sail and little else. The Bah men had stripped their prize of everything of value, including whatever good nets had been aboard. In the small bow compartment, he found some old netting, good only for chopping up for caulking. Two long fish bins in the main hold were empty. The family space seemed empty too, until he lifted a hatch cover on the house top and let light into the dimness. He found a clay stove, baked hard by years of use, some firewood, an iron pot, some cooking stones, bowls, mats for sleeping and one or two that would do for patching the sail, two balls of twine, two clay water jugs snug in woven rope carriers, a caulking mallet and several drivers, and a box of small things such as awls for repairing sails and a broken knife.

He had found neither food nor water aboard, so, after a day spent determining his needs and reconnoitering the islands, he let a falling tide set the flat-bottomed ch'uan onto a mud shoal behind one of them. Several dark-of-night forays into nearby hamlets gave him enough to start his voyage.

Aengus counted himself a competent ship handler, but he had rarely sailed out of sight of land and he had not been a seaman for almost nine years. He saw no more islands for six days after beginning his ocean crossing and welcomed the sight of one on the seventh day. Near the island were two ships not very different from his own. They were fishing together the way Jo-shan fishermen pair their ch'uans at sea. He knew that he was still nearer to Serica than to Europe. By then, he had devised a catchment for rainwater on the housetop and had learned to lure fish that swam beneath the ch'uan into open water beside it where he could sometimes catch them in a net he had woven from twine. He did not stop at that island.

The moon, full at the outset a week earlier, waxed full three more times and almost once again before his next landfall.

* * *

The first days of that crossing, before doubt and illness and utter despair became his companions, he kept himself busy remembering old skills and inventing new ones. He lowered the rudder from its shallow-water position and rigged a lashing for the tiller that he could reset quickly as winds or swell changed. He patched his sail and laced the old matting more securely to the battens. When he could not find the clay box in which coals are kept alive from fire to fire, he dried wood scrapings in the sun and kept a supply in a wooden box so that he could make fire more easily. Fire making took time and he was not always successful, particularly on damp days, but, while his rice and millet lasted, he never had to chew it uncooked.

He did those and other tasks and tried to suppress images born of rage and terror and grief that would flood his mind from time to time. He tried no less hard to overcome the bleakness that would seep through him when he scanned the black void at night and saw no land lights or ship lights, often not even starlight.

He grieved for Hsin. He saw his smiling face often and could not resist smiling back, although there was no one on his ship to see it and Hsin could not even imagine it because he was dead and his body was lost in the Ou. Then Aengus would hammer on the housing or the mast with his fist and bury his head in his arms. Of all the people in Serica, Hsin had least deserved to die. His family should not have died either. They were reserved people, often embarrassed by their son's enthusiasms, but they had been good to Aengus for Hsin's sake.

Aengus thought of Hsin and Hsin's parents and brothers and sisters—all dead now—and he thought of his friends of other times. Then he would fall to brooding: if Hektor was wrong about the world being a ball and if Turfu was right about another world awaiting men beyond this one, he might soon be in that world and with more friends than remained in this one.

16

II

The ways of ships and the sea came back to Aengus. The weather was not boisterous in those first days, yet it was relentless in having its way. The wind blew so steadily out of the north and west that he was soon too far from Serica to turn back if the seas should become angry and his little ch'uan begin to fail him. He was even farther from Serica than he thought because he rode a great eastbound current, although he knew nothing of that.

The ch'uan was a stout little ship for all that it was old and had only one poor sail. He tried to make out its recent history from the clues he found aboard, but the Bah men had left too little. He could not tell whether a single fisher-family with children had lived aboard her or a crew of men drawn from several families. He could not tell how long it had been since its rightful owners had possessed it. The fish bins were clean and dry.

After a while, he stopped trying to people his vessel—*his* vessel now—with ghosts from its past. He began to cultivate those who had inhabited it all along: the spirits of its every part to which the Jo-shan fishermen had introduced him.

There is a spirit—a god, the Jo-shan people would say—who can, if skillfully cajoled, prevent sails from blowing out; another who keeps hull seams watertight—but only if he is flattered as one flatters any human lord. Lies are often more effective with them than the truth. There are spirits to make anchor stones hold, to keep nets from tearing or ropes from breaking, or even teeth from aching.

"There is a god for everything you can name," Old Kwaidz had claimed.

Kwaidz loved to argue and, for once, had found Aengus in a mood to oblige him: "So there is a god for this wall, then."

"Yes."

"And that one too?" Aengus put his hand on the wall adjoining the first.

"Oh, yes. That one too. A separate god."

"And the floor below?"

"Yes."

"If there is a god for each of those, then," Aengus exclaimed triumphantly, "how can there be another for the corner they make? Yesterday you were talking about a god of corners. If you take away the walls and the floor, which have their own gods, there is no corner."

Kwaidz was not at all dismayed. He said, with irrefutable finality, "But a corner has its own name, so it has its own god. You might as well claim that there is no god of fornication when fornication is not taking place. That would be a stupid thing to say."

The logic of that argument had seemed strained to Aengus then, but he took comfort in it now, knowing that he could have the company of as many spirits as he could find names for things.

Old Kwaidz, who was not old at all and took his nickname from the fact that his eating sticks—his kwaidz— were in other people's bowls as often as they were in his own, regarded Aengus's alien appearance as more interesting than threatening, and his experiences as a source of entertainment whenever he could be induced to talk about them. Others among the Jo-shan fishermen shared Kwaidz's estimation of Aengus, and he made a place for himself in their rough fraternity, even though he never sailed in the same boat for long. In the families with which he sailed, there were always one or two who had misgivings about him. After a disappointing catch, those doubters, usually women, would convince their superstitious men that, even if Aengus could not be blamed directly, his presence aboard must have offended the family god responsible for their success or failure on the fishing grounds. Aengus would be taken to another ship and effusively recommended to its laodah for his strength and skill and willingness to work.

His life with the Jo-shan people was only sporadically homelike and cheerful, but it brought an end to the purposeless wandering of that year following Hektor's death. Hard work on the ch'uans was tonic enough for his low spirits.

And now he was on a ch'uan once again, and more at home than he had ever been in the Jo-shans because this was *his* ch'uan, and its spirits were his own to call up or ignore as he wished.

He did not think to keep count of the days of his voyage until too many had gone by to remember accurately, so he waited until the moon was near full, as it had been when he last touched land, then started his count at thirty. Already he was certain that he had crossed a greater reach of sea than any he had ever known.

On the forty-second day, his carefully rationed bits of dried fruit—eaten one every other day—ran out. But that same morning, three winged fish hit his sail and fell to the deck. And a fog bank ahead seemed to hide land. There was a darkness behind it where it touched the sea. He stared a long while and thought he saw smoke rising through the fog, and then a light—just a flicker, a little speck of brilliance. He began to believe that his long voyage on the emptiest ocean he had ever known was nearing an end. He wondered where in Europe he would come ashore. The hub of the wheeling stars, when he could see stars at all, was higher in the sky than it had been in Serica. There, early on winter evenings, he had watched the seven-starred Bear prowl along the northern horizon. Now the Bear remained skyborne all the time. Had it been so in Armorica? He could not remember. Since Serica, though, the weather had become markedly colder. He had

19

drifted into northern waters, without any doubt. Under the pile of old nets in the forward compartment he had found the remains of a palm-fiber coat and hat, the bad-weather gear that Serican fishermen wore. He patched it together with pieces of netting and then wore it constantly, looking like a dark miniature haystack on the deck of his ship.

That same day, the forty-second, the fog cleared by mid-afternoon and he saw that the land of the morning had only been hope and imagination, a trick of the mist.

In the days that followed, his disillusionment grew. The fish that had accompanied him beneath the ch'uan disappeared. Several times, clouds covered the sky without a break for so many days together that, when he finally saw sun or stars again, he was sailing far off the eastward course he intended.

During an unnerving few days, the ocean showed its immensity in a new way: the little ch'uan, while tossed still by wind-driven, white-capped seas from behind, began a slow lift and fall in response to a deep swell from the southeast. The swell increased over two days until it was greater than anything he had known or heard of before, then increased more. His ch'uan became like a child's toy boat in the vastness of its billows. He was reminded of a region in the barren mountain country he had passed through on his way to Siraf, the city where he found Hektor. Long, smoothly wrinkled mountains there had seemed like huge, frozen dunes and he and the people with which he traveled a column of ants. Now the mountainous swell impressed him as awesomely. In the troughs between stupendous walls of water, it seemed that he would be crushed. Then a surge would lift him swiftly to the sky, threatening to leave his bowels behind. For an awful moment, he would ride atop a crest crossed by spume lacework. In the breaking seas and howling wind there, he could look out over range after range of the same crawling ocean mountains. Then the fearsome plunge again and the appalling certainty of imminent destruction.

The little ch'uan survived two more days of that prodigious heaving and falling, with Aengus cowering in the house or venturing no more than his head and shoulders through one of the hatches. Then the swell diminished, and he realized anew that he was starving.

The seas were still too rough to try to net or spear fish. The millet and rice had lasted only a few days longer than the dried fruit. Several dark albatrosses appeared and swept the sea nearby for most of a day. During that night, one of them roosted on the tiller and watched with its head swinging foolishly from side to side while Aengus slowly came out of his compartment and stepped onto the housetop. He held a piece of wood in his hand and approached the bird, talking to it all the while as he had talked at other times to the sail god or the fish net god. The curious bird made no attempt to escape until he had seized it by the neck. He crushed its head against the tiller with the piece of wood.

Over days, he ate almost every part of that bird, even the feet, which he chewed slowly while he fashioned a new device from one of its leg bones. He split a long piece from the side of the bone, sharpened its two ends, and used an awl to drill a hole through it halfway along its length. He tied the bone piece to the end of a long length of twine, then wrapped it with gristle from the albatross so that one end of the bone was held against the twine. He hoped that he might entice a fish to seize the bone in its mouth. If he could detect, or even see, the fish do that, he would tug sharply on the line so that the bone would catch and turn sideways, toggle-fashion, and jam in the fish's mouth.

The first time he used it, he tied the other end of the line around the rudder post, then wrapped the line once around his hand and let the baited bone trail behind. He waited through most of the day. When the bait was finally taken, he felt only a slight twitch. He pulled in the line and found a broken end. The bone was gone. He counted that a success, though, for it meant that his device would work if only the cord would not break or be bitten through.

He had better luck with a second albatross, taking it the

21

same way he had taken the first one, before he had another stroke of encouragement—and disappointment again—with a new fishing bone. It came four days after the first strike. He felt a tug on the line, and, after he had jerked it to set the sharpened bone, he carefully drew it in against a lively force. His fish surfaced once; it was as long as his arm. As he reached for his net, he saw another swift, dark shadow. A message of brief violence traveled up the line to his hand. All he brought in was his fish's head, its mouth agape with the bone caught in it crossways and its startled eyes staring at him.

Two days later, he brought in a whole fish. As he chewed its raw flesh, he noticed that his teeth moved in their sockets.

The weather worsened again, but he paid little attention to it now. He left the tiller lashed in the same position all the time. He only raised enough sail to keep the ch'uan running before the wind whatever its direction might be. Most of the sail's matting was gone, blown away, but what remained was held flat by the battens and caught some wind.

He had become so convinced of his ch'uan's soundness during the days of great swells that he never worried about lesser seas any more. But it was those lesser seas, angry and sharply breaking, that eventually found the ch'uan's weakness. It happened while he was in the after compartment, struggling to make fire with a spindle and socket, the first fire he had attempted in more than a month. It was to be for warmth. He now ate the flesh he caught raw, believing that he got more strength from it that way. But he was weak and cold and sick and wanted a fire badly. The weather had worsened, but his mind was on making a fire.

Suddenly, above the steady slam—slam—slam of the seas, he heard a sharp popping noise, then a prolonged creaking of planks stressed beyond bearing. He looked around dully, trying to find the source of those new noises. When he turned back to his spindle and socket, he was holding the spindle firmly between his palms still, but the notched board was under water. He was kneeling in water! He wondered if it had been there when he started to make his fire.

A powerful sea hit the stern on the quarter and the ch'uan's hull twisted on itself. A great wrenching, rupturing din filled the compartment and a flood of water poured through the stern, washing Aengus up against the bulkhead separating the aft and middle compartments. He knew that his ship was breaking up and that he should do something, but he could not think what it should be. He pushed open the small hatch over his head and pulled himself up so that he hung with his elbows outside the coaming on either side. He looked for the sail, but it was gone altogether. It could have been torn away days ago. He tried to remember when he had last seen it. The tiller bar that should have been over his head was gone too. When he twisted around, he saw that the rudder post no longer divided the space between the wings of the open stern. The whole rudder must have been torn away, but he could not tell for sure from the hatch opening, nor dared he go aft to investigate because that part of the ch'uan was awash. Seas flushed through the cockpit and filled the compartment in which his legs dangled. Floating objects struck his legs or wrapped around them.

He hung in the small opening for a long while, afraid to climb onto the housetop because of the seas that washed over it—one of them taking his hat—and unwilling to drop back into the sloshing water beneath him. With nothing to hang on to in there, he would be battered against the hull and bulkhead until he was unconscious. He waited for his ship to break apart. He wondered if he could make a raft from its parts. In that churning sea? No, he concluded. He would be lucky to find a single piece large enough to keep him afloat. And that would be no luck at all; it would just put off his certain death for as long as he had strength to hold on.

But the ship did not break up. It settled by the stern and hung there with its bow uptilted. The water bruiser was now like the sloping roof of a shallow suspended nook.

23

The hammering seas slowly moderated. As the sky darkened, the clouds separated and he saw the bright evening star in the west.

While he still had light to see by, he pulled himself through the hatchway and up to the front of the housing. Braced against that foothold, he wrestled the cover from the midship hatch just abaft the mast. To keep the stiff coir fibers of his coat from catching on the coaming, he slid through the hatch headfirst.

There was no water in the compartment. The watertight bulkhead had held. He reached out and pulled the hatch cover over the opening. From below, he could only set it loosely over the coaming and hope it would stay. Between the two bins in the compartment was a narrow space—coffin sized—where he had thrown netting from the tiny forward compartment as he sorted through it for good pieces. Now he crawled into that space, burrowed into the netting, and pulled his coat over all. He did not think of it as a place to die, or even to sleep. It was just a place to keep warm.

But he did sleep. He slept and wakened and slept again. He did not know how long he slept, whether moments or days. He was no longer hungry when he woke.

Once, in an interval of mental clarity and purposefulness, he returned to the after compartment and found his satchel by feeling in the murky, sloshing water with his feet. He counted that a stroke of great good fortune. The bag held nothing that would serve any present need; it was just that its trifling contents had been his for a long time.

Returning to the midship compartment, he saw two of the winged fish on the deck. He almost left them there, but picked them up after all and took them with him because he remembered that, at one time, such a discovery would have been significant.

Back in his nest, he spent a long while cutting and slitting the strap of his satchel so that he could tie it snugly against his side. He made it more secure with twine painstakingly raveled from a length of rope. Only when he had exhausted that compulsion did he begin to chew on the little fish, eating them as an animal would: skin, guts, and all, except for the long wing fins.

He slept and wakened and slept again, with time running now backward, now forward, passing through the same dreams and hallucinations in one direction, then another.

He woke one time with his finger tracing around and into his empty eye socket, wondering how it had healed so rapidly. He felt the matted netting beneath him. Was there a new prison master? The easy rising and falling of the ch'uan did nothing to dispel his delusion of imprisonment; he believed that the motion was a trick of his tortured mind. He was in his low, dark, wet cell in the Fifth General's prison in the city of Yin.

With vivid clarity—so fresh was his vision, he was certain that he was reliving events of just the day before—he saw himself on his knees before the Fifth General's prison master. His wrists were bound to his ankles behind him, and the pole used to carry him pressed painfully against his calves. A man stood on the pole on each side of him; one had his hand wound into Aengus's hair and was forcing his head backward and forward as the prison master signaled with tosses of his own head.

Aengus had demanded to be brought before the prison master to protest the injustice of his confinement. He had hammered on the heavy wooden door of his cell. He had shouted for days, and nights too, keeping the guard awake. And now they had brought him to the prison master, but that devil did not want to hear his complaint. When his two men had reduced Aengus to silence by whipping his head back and forth, they and two others held him fast while the prison master unsheathed his knife, coolly tested the sharpness of its tip against his thumbnail, then pressed the lids of Aengus's left eye far apart and sliced around the ball, deeper and deeper, cutting membranes and flesh as Aengus gasped and screamed. The prison master plucked the eye forward with his fingers and cut behind it to release it. With the fingers of one hand, he rolled the ragged ball against the palm of the other until he was sure that Aengus

25

could see and comprehend what he was doing. Then he put it between his teeth, crushed it until the humors ran down his chin, and spat the rest into Aengus's face.

Now Aengus was back in his cell, without his eye, but its socket miraculously healed. Even the pain in his crushed calves was gone. And the matting—he could not understand that kindness.

His mind roamed over the events that had brought him there, and, in the curious way that time had now of sliding backward and forward between past and future, he saw also his coming to Gau. Hsin stood at both ends of his mind's wandering. He saw Hsin, a stranger to him then, running madly through the streets of Yin with the Fifth General's soldiers pursuing him. The Jo-shan fish boat Aengus worked on then had brought fish to Yin and was waiting to pick up new hemp nets, for the best and cheapest were made there. During that time of waiting, Aengus had found a young woman who was willing to trade a passionate hour for a coin, and he was finding his way from her house back to the ch'uan through dark streets when Hsin rounded a corner and slammed hard against him.

Aengus heard the shouts of the pursuing soldiers. Something about the young man's helplessness and terror made Aengus react swiftly. He pulled him through the door of a warehouse, pushed the door shut, and held his hand over Hsin's mouth until the running feet had passed.

To Aengus's questions, Hsin told him that he had brought valuable things from Gau to trade for coin—coin that had only recently become acceptable currency in his home district. He showed Aengus his bag of coins. The Fifth General's men had been pursuing him for that bag.

Aengus took Hsin to the ch'uan and persuaded the laodah to give Hsin passage to the mouth of the Ou for some of those coins. Hsin had come to Yin, which was the mainland port nearest to the Jo-shan Islands, by the Yahng trails, but he dared not return that way because the soldiers knew his route. The Fifth General's soldiers were disciplined men, not like the Bah rabble of later years, and the general himself was a true general who gave his allegiance to a king. But his soldiers paid themselves with what they could take from the lands and cities they passed through or occupied. They dealt harshly with anyone who denied them. Hsin was now a common criminal in their eyes.

Aengus did not tell the laodah all of that. He introduced Hsin as a friend from other days.

Eight days later, just south of the Ou's mouth, Hsin swam to shoal water and waded ashore.

A year after that, Aengus sailed up Yin's river again on another ch'uan, but for the same purpose. He had no reason to fear the Fifth General's men, for only Hsin knew what he had done. Most likely those soldiers were in some other place now and others had replaced them in Yin. Nonetheless, he stayed on board the ch'uan and kept out of sight.

The women of the ch'uan had already begun their machinations to have him put off the vessel. They blamed his presence aboard for a series of poor catches. But the laodah had taken a liking to Aengus. He called him "D'bairun": big, fair-skinned friend. One of the frustrated women may have inferred something from Aengus's reluctance to go ashore in Yin. She may have said something to a soldier. Aengus never knew what was said or who might have been bribed. He only knew that soldiers appeared on the ship one day and seized him. Without a word of explanation or accusation, they took him ashore and shoved him through the streets of the city to an old, long, and low building they used as a prison. There he stayed until his protests cost him his eye. There he stayed for a year, until the Fifth General's men vanished from Yin.

There he stayed for a few more days, until he realized that the guard was gone, that he was not being fed, that, when he pushed against it, the door of his cell swung open.

Hsin found him many months later. Word had come to Gau that the Fifth General had been called to the

Emperor's capital at Kin-ling. The Emperor, displeased—
for who knew what offense—at the king whom the Fifth
General served, had the general and his officers executed
and his army disbanded. The general's now-powerless
king yielded to another sent by the Emperor to replace
him. Hsin, hearing of this, decided that it was safe to
return to Yin with more trade goods and, this time, with
men to help him carry them.

In Yin, he heard of a gaunt, pale wraith of a man who
begged food in the back streets and slept wherever he was
not chased away. Hsin wondered . . . then he searched
until he found the beggar. Aengus did not know Hsin at
all, and Hsin could hardly believe that the wreck of a man
he had found was his stalwart rescuer of only two and a
half years before. Nor could he ever be convinced that
Aengus's duress had not been because of his service to him.

He took Aengus back to Gau with him—had him
carried in a litter most of the way—and told his father that
the Yen family could never fully discharge the debt they
owed the stranger for his timely aid and his suffering that
followed.

Aengus did not consider that a debt existed, but he had a
great need when Hsin found him. And, he soon realized,
he had a great friend in Hsin.

Hsin's parents believed that they understood what was
owed more clearly than did their son, but they tolerated
Aengus beyond honor's obligation for Hsin's sake. They
kept Aengus under their roof, even though their house was
a Sangha house and the Sakya Master, the Enlightened
One, was revered there, and Aengus was a disbeliever who
had once worshiped a phantom god and an unmeritable
Master Jesus, but was now utterly confused in such
matters. They endured, too, the disapproval of their
neighbors in Gau who felt that alien Aengus brought dis-
credit to their community, even ridicule from the common
Yueh people they were forced to live among.

In the dark compartment on the ch'uan, Aengus began
to see his prison cell every time he opened his eye and the
prison master's knife every time he closed it. At last, when

28

he noticed that no one was bringing him food anymore, he got up and pushed on the hatch. It lifted and slid aside easily. There was no guard outside. With great effort, he pulled himself onto the deck. It was cold there, but clean. The air smelled good. Even the stinging rain felt good. He had forgotten his coat, but he still had his satchel—a purse-mouthed small sack now—tied to his side. He wondered why his jailers had not taken that. He did not understand their oversight, but he was glad for it; all that he owned in the world was in it. He had difficulty finding a secure place to crouch on the sloping, wet, heaving deck, so he braced his feet against the coaming of the midship hatch and his back against the mast. Months ago, he had tied a rope around the mast to hold on to in rough weather. Now he wrapped several turns of that rope around himself and the mast. It took a long time to make it secure, but he was able to relax within its windings when he was done.

Darkness came, possibly more than once. The wind increased until it was a tempest. That may have taken hours or days. He did not know then or have much recollection of it afterward. In the end, his ship was smashed against a rugged shore and he was flung, nearly dead, onto a great, flat rock thickly matted with sea moss and stalked barnacles. Had he been aware, he would have been appalled and saddened to learn that the dark people who found him there knew nothing of Europe or of his own fair race.

III

Death hung about the rough shelter for many days, then withdrew slowly, reluctantly. Aengus's mind stirred: he contemplated huge rock pillars, black against a black sky, thrusting up through inky chaos; vast surges of water and wind swept his empty body through sea and sky; clamorous noise filled all the world and heavens.

Then came silence: storms raged in silence; a sail ripped without noise; his body tumbled endlessly, soundlessly.

When the roaring din had been gone some time, he suddenly understood that his hushed visions were not real. He struggled to grasp any part of consciousness, to learn, at least, whether his mind inhabited body or spirit.

He failed.

Adrift again, he saw the rock pillars standing now in a quiet sea before an indistinct coastline. Slowly the coastline vanished. The pinnacles became nothing more than the remnants of a lone island suffering its own gradual destruction in mid-ocean—ragged stone fingers reaching through the sea in final supplication to the god of islands. Desperately now, Aengus fought again for conscious awareness.

Minutes or days later, he was able to open his eye. His success came during the night. He could make nothing of the dim shapes he saw, the gradations of blackness. By a great concentration of will, he learned again to make his fingers move . . . then an arm . . . to discover that he lay among furs on fiber mats . . . to touch a bowl with water in it . . . another with soft food . . . berries, perhaps . . . or meat. . . .

His satchel! Where was the package of his poor treasures? Ah, there . . . still tied to his side as it had been for the last, dying days of his sea voyage.

The water bowl . . . He found it again and brought drops to his mouth on his fingertips. So began his return to life.

He lay in a bower fashioned crudely from old boards and fresh branches. He was alone; there was scarcely room for any other. Someone refilled the bowls at intervals, but always while he slept. He began to hope that he had fallen among a band of rude Celts, those in the west of Hibernia, people who spoke a language similar to his own, people who could help him make the last stage of his journey home.

One day he was awakened from a shallow sleep by a hand close to his face. He grasped its wrist and drew the hand away. An elderly woman's startled face stared into his.

"Where am I?" he asked.

The woman did not answer.

"What place is this?"

Recovering, the woman unwrapped his fingers from her wrist and picked up the empty bowls. Although her back obscured the light seeping through the opening, he could see well enough that she was no Celt, nor of any race of Europe. A slave, perhaps. A captive from some other land. He still held hope that he had made a European shore. If she had not understood his words, perhaps she would know the names of countries, of districts and towns. He tried several, saying them as a Brython would, then in the Roman tongue, and even, for a few of them, names he knew the Northmen used. The kneeling woman listened, but the words aroused no look of recognition or comprehension whatsoever on her wide face.

In frustration, he said the name of a large town near his home village: "Washlae."

The woman smiled broadly at that. She nodded her head and said, "Washalee, washalee."

Her intonation told him that she knew nothing of Washlae, but her friendly response heartened him. Frivolously, he put his hand to his chest and named the small village of his birth: "Tellacloute."

With a gasp, the woman fell back onto her heels, then turned and scrambled from the shelter.

Thereafter, his food and water were left no closer than the entrance opening.

One morning he woke to birdsong. Delicate fingers of sunlight probed the dim shelter, searching for him. Quite suddenly he felt more a prisoner than an invalid.

It's time, he thought. Enough of rest. Time to move—to get strong. But first . . .

He found a small leather pouch within his sack. From it he took the milky white stone with the right-sized dark mark that Yen Hsin had traveled to three villages to find, then had spent as many weeks shaping and polishing to glassy smoothness. Poor Yen Hsin! This eye—his gift— was very likely all that remained on earth to mark his life. That and the cherished memories of his friend.

Even well moistened, the eye seemed not to fit. "Just like the first time I wore it," Aengus thought. "And for the same reason." His fingers explored the gauntness of his face.

He crawled through the low entrance, then stood to draw in great, slow breaths of sea-washed air: hazy-bright, buoyant, inspiriting air. During those moments, he felt that his recovery advanced as much as it had in all the days he had lain in the shelter.

A quick movement drew his eye to his right. Two men, who must not have noticed him come out, now stood and rushed toward him. They were short, like Sericans only sturdier. One carried a spear held level in threat or warning. Aengus's instant thought was of Serica, of the long year of his imprisonment there. When the spear carrier was almost upon him, Aengus stepped forward quickly and snatched the weapon from his hands. He thrust its point into the ground and shouted, "No!" That swift reaction, his strange paleness, his yellow beard and hair, and the fearsome glare of his stone eye, now too large for his thin face, completely disheartened the men. They stood in shocked dismay as he walked between them and down the short path to the beach. After a moment's hesitation, they recovered their spear and followed him.

Their threat and his sharp response left Aengus weak and dizzy. He clambered over a tangle of beach logs slowly, carefully, then stood to recover and to survey the place to which the sea had brought him.

Several miles of broad beach lay between two immense, discontinuous walls of rock that, broken into fantastic pillars and arches, stretched out to sea for half a mile. The beach was backed for most of its length with masses of bleached, broken logs and roots, which in some places were loosely scattered, in others piled up like gigantic ravens' nests. Behind the logs was a narrow band of trees, then a bluff sharply rising and crowned with dense forest. In a cluster, about a half-mile along the beach to the south, he saw a number of long, gray buildings.

He could not long postpone meeting his succorers, but he was not ready yet. The two guards, now standing uncertainly behind him, confused him. Why had they been set over one as weak as he was? By the ease with which he had disarmed them, were they guards at all? Why had he been cared for so far away from their homes—if that was what the buildings were? He considered those questions while, minute by minute, he grew stronger and more accustomed to standing erect.

"Just like a butterfly newly emerged," he mused. Then, looking ruefully at the filthy remnants of his clothing and his emaciated body, he thought, "Butterfly? More like a fly from a dung heap."

Abruptly, impulsively, he untied his sack, dropped it to the sand, then dashed down the beach and threw himself into the surf. His warders rushed after him as far as the water's edge. There they looked at each other and at him unsurely. Aengus gave them a cheerful wave of his hand while he washed away the stink of infirmity. At that, the two squatted to wait patiently.

Full of morning and sunlight, Aengus stood to survey the line of rocky islets. Those bounding the northern end of the beach and the ocean before it were close by. Were those the fingers and fists of stone that had ended his long voyage in a rain-slashed, midnight instant? Were they the black spikes that had punctuated his nightmares? He found it hard to believe, so peaceful they looked, standing in mild sunshine and a gentle blue sea.

He retrieved his sack, then signaled the two men to accompany him as he started toward the village. Approaching it, he could see smoke seeping through roofs, long boats drawn up on the beach and a few people around them, and something like a white fence beyond the houses. Suddenly the two men, who had hung behind, rushed past him, waving their arms and hailing loudly to announce their arrival.

People poured out of the houses: men, women, hordes of dogs and children—or so it seemed to Aengus then. They came forward hesitantly and stopped altogether when they met his erstwhile guardians. He came up to the crowd with a confident mien and a smile to dispel whatever fear or enmity his fierce, alien appearance might provoke. He noted their bronze skins, their long, black hair, and broad faces set with bright, black eyes, the almost childlike expressions of many of them. These were not people of any part of the world Aengus knew. The women wore rough fiber skirts, the children nothing at all, and most of the men no more. A few men and women wore woven fiber cloaks or blankets. But the young men were robust and the young women comely; no one bore marks of want or war.

Suffused with optimism and geniality, he waited for someone among them to step forward, to speak. When none did, he said his own few words of thanks for the care given him and hope for their continued welcome, trusting that his tone would tell what his words could not. The people's reserve broke. They began to chatter excitedly among themselves and to him. A few came forward, then more, then all of them pressing close upon him. They touched his hair, his beard. One put his hand on Aengus's head, then turned around with the level hand still upraised to demonstrate to the others that the stranger stood taller than any of them.

Some small children had squeezed through the forest of legs and were being pushed hard against him. The crush became oppressive. He stooped and hoisted two of the little ones into his arms. They made a less offending barricade, he thought, than if he were to raise empty arms against the inquisitive mob. Reacting against his unexpected familiarity, the two children pushed away from him with straightened arms and stared fearfully into his face.

Suddenly a shout caught everyone's attention. Aengus looked over the bobbing heads to see who had spoken. Three men approached, slashing with their arms and bellowing to make the people move aside. The crowd did so reluctantly as Aengus knelt on one knee to permit the squirming children to escape.

One of the newcomers strode up to Aengus, then turned to face the crowd. He launched into a noisy harangue accompanied with expansive sweeps of one arm that seemed to indicate the whole length of the beach. His other hand held a paddle, its pointed blade punched into the sand. Occasionally he half-turned to glower at Aengus and speak a few angry words.

Aengus could not immediately make out the man's intention. At first he thought it must be to instruct his people in simple courtesy toward a stranger. But then he recognized a darker hue in the man's words. They seemed to assert some possession of him, some domination. His interpretation became certain when the speaker turned to face him and shouted a fierce, incomprehensible command.

The two who had come with this commander—this chieftain—seized Aengus's arms and made to propel him toward the houses. Though still weak and greatly aware of it, he threw up his arms and flung the men from him. Their chieftain raised his paddle to strike him, but Aengus tore the weapon from his hands and hurled it away. Then, to show his authority in matters of his own person, he strode past his startled assailant, through the crowd, and toward the houses.

A lifetime before, when a pack of dogs stalked them on the Washlae road, Aengus's father had cautioned him: "Don't run." Aengus heeded that admonition now. Waves of anger and apprehension passed through his weak body. He concentrated his will to suppress his trembling.

Before the plank-walled buildings, he turned to face the following crowd. By a gesture, he asked which house they wanted him to enter. Ignoring that, the scowling chief, who had stopped a cautious distance from Aengus, made his own query. Among the words Aengus heard "Tulukluts," spoken twice with emphasis.

Aengus remembered the woman's fright in the shelter. "Tellacloute," he said. He put his hand to his chest and repeated, "I was born in Tellacloute."

Everyone began to talk animatedly: the chief with his two lieutenants, and the others among themselves. In their gestures and alien speech, Aengus thought he could detect awe and fear, but also disbelief and mockery, even anger. He did not relax his own self-assured stance; he kept alert to seize whatever advantage might come from their misinterpretation of his declaration.

Abruptly, they all turned their attention back to him. It seemed that they expected him to know their conclusion, their intention toward him—or their leader's intention, for it had been a pronouncement from him that had ended their parley. Aengus repeated his gesture toward the several buildings. A woman—the same who had tended him in the shelter, he thought—came forward and took his arm. The others stood back to make a wide lane through which she led him into one of the buildings.

Aengus stopped immediately inside the door, his eye stinging and watering from acrid smoke and his sea-delicate nose wry from the fetid stench of drying fish, uncured animal skins, rotting bits of food, and sundry human odors. Recovering their boldness, those behind pushed past him and against him until the whole crowd was inside. They stood on benches along the outer walls; they sat on half walls that partitioned the interior; they stood to fill all of the floor space. In their midst, Aengus turned about, searching for the chief in the dimness. The only light came from the door opening, now blocked with people, and from gaps in the roof where planks had been slid back.

He became aware of persistent tugs on his elbow. Looking down, he realized that the woman who had led him to the building was now trying to direct him again. Together they forced their way toward a corner. Abruptly, the woman's firm hand on his stomach stopped him as he was about to walk into a clear space. He looked down and saw a small bed of mats and furs almost hidden by the swirling dust at their feet. Then he saw a face: one of their children, a little girl, lay there.

The woman had moved around the child and stood facing Aengus across her pallet. He knelt. The girl seemed to be asleep.

"Strange," he thought, "that the din doesn't waken her." Then a chill crept through him. "She's dead. And I'm blamed. . . . No. I'm to restore her to life. Is that what "Tellacloute" means to them: some kind of magician?"

Suddenly weak again, he dropped his head. If only he were back in the shelter. If only he had been prudent and had made an investigation through the branches and doorway of that refuge and then escaped by night. Now something impossible was demanded of him. He faced the fate of failed magicians: death or worse.

The discordant mutters around him became louder, more ominous.

IV

Aengus raised his eye to the woman across the child's bed. Four others, women and men, stood with her. They made a small group, somehow apart from the rest although the crowd pressed closely against them. Their bent heads shadowed their faces under the meager light, but he sensed something different in their interest. They seemed solicitous for the child, whereas the rest behaved like spectators at a trial.

Sadly, Aengus laid his hand on the girl's forehead to detect if her passing had been recent. To his astonishment, she opened her eyes and looked wanly at the faces above her. Another glance upward told him that this awakening had not surprised her people. They expected something else from him, then.

His vision slowly adapting to the poor light, he pulled back the coarse fiber blanket that covered the child. A surge of pity swept through him. Her little thigh had been badly broken. A splinter of her bone jabbed through scabbed flesh. He touched a pad of soft fiber that covered the worst part of her injury. It was dry. He bent down to sniff for putrefaction but could smell none. Then, as he raised his head, he saw a large, smooth swelling at her hip. Her leg made an unnatural angle there. It was disjointed.

Quickly, he examined her other limbs. They were scratched and bruised, but he could find no fractures or dislocations. When she rolled her head slightly, though, he discovered a great, swollen contusion below her right temple. Peering closely, he saw that her eyes were glassy and a little crossed. One pupil was larger than the other.

The poor child! She was not dead after all, but so close to death that no man could save her. She was quiet now. The worst of her agony must be over. She would pass quietly, he thought. But then how would her people vent their anger toward him? Though primitive, they were probably sophisticated in matters of prolonged torture and ferocious execution.

Aengus would not submit easily to being killed. He would fight. If he survived, though, he would still have to escape from their overwhelming numbers. But where? To sea? Along the shore? Into the forest? He had strength for none of those. The single sharp coups he had made earlier had left him weak and dizzy. A prolonged battle or flight were more than his diminished strength could sustain.

Then, full-blown in an instant, he had an idea that might avert violence altogether. His safe leaving might be bought with the child and whatever powers greater than their own that her people had ascribed to him. But he would have to act while she clung to her thread of life. And, though she seemed to be past pain, he must take care lest she cry out, for how might her unpredictable people react to that?

His scheme was simply to carry the girl away from the village under the pretext of taking her to a private place to work his magic on her injuries—whatever magic they supposed "Tellacloute" to possess. The barrier of strange tongues, he hoped, would foil their searching questions. His success would depend on a peremptory demeanor and their barbaric imaginations.

Aengus stood and looked for a mother he had seen earlier. The example of her swaddled babe, bound to a board for ease of carrying, would show what he wanted for the injured child. He saw the mother standing nearby, steadying the board with its precious burden on the top of a half wall. He pushed through the crowd, but before he made the short distance, the young mother realized that she was his goal. She slid her child over the wall into the arms of a man who quickly lost himself in the crowd. When Aengus looked back to find the mother, she too had gone.

Turning to search for another infant, he collided with the woman who had led him. Again she tugged his elbow to draw him back to the little girl. Revealing a perceptiveness that surprised him, she knelt among the close-packed legs, rolled up the edges of some mats, and showed him that the child already rested on a board. It extended beyond her head and feet to provide something to grasp for those who would move her. By his hands held to the child's head and feet, he told them he wanted a shorter board, and indicated that he alone would carry her.

His purposeful gestures seemed to fan some spark of hope in the small group—were they her family? he wondered. They responded eagerly. One of the men shouted across the mob. Those far from the focus had become boisterous; now they fell still. Some by the door began to remove a board that was part of the wall there. The wall was made of planks held in place between paired posts. Each plank was supported by cords tied between the posts of a pair and was set to overlap the plank below. The men slipped out a short board and it was passed over the heads of the crowd to those around the child.

Aengus slid the mat on which the little one lay from the long board to the short one placed beside it, then he began to pack furs and blankets to hold her injured leg in place. The others took his work from him. Soon not only those few who he supposed to be her family, but also others in the crowd brought forth all kinds of padding and cords to wrap and truss the child securely. Aengus rested.

When the pathetic bundle was ready, they helped him to hang it across his chest with bands over his shoulder and around his body. The child had made no sound. He looked down at her. Tears wet her russet cheeks. Gently, he folded the corner of a blanket to cover her face.

He had not seen the chief within the building, nor could he locate him when they all poured out into the light again. Aengus had thought at first to follow the beach until he was quit of village and villagers. He had even considered returning after nightfall to steal one of their boats. Now his sapless body said no. If he tried to clamber over the rocks at the end of the beach, he would spend his strength before he was out of sight of the houses. He must have one of their long canoes now. But where was the chief?

Aengus scanned the score or more of boats drawn up from the water's edge. A trickle of misgiving quickly became a flood of doubt. The canoes were much too large for a single man to handle. He looked for smaller ones but could see none. And those he saw were not crudely hollowed-out logs. Though they lay more than a hundred feet from him, he could see fine craftsmanship that told of weeks or months of work in the making of each one. Deception might persuade them to give up a dying child to him, but he did not believe that they would let him take one of their valuable craft. And if they were the seagoers that their capacious canoes signified, the ocean would have no secrets from them. They would know every foot of coastline. If they did not follow him now, they would know where to find him later.

For them, the dark forest behind must be the sanctum of obscure magic and mysteries. It was there he would have to go if he would not be followed. But the forest edge stood more than a hundred feet above the beach. If he had little strength for a beach hike, how could he scale that steep bluff and carry the child too?

There had been other times when he found a reservoir of stamina somewhere beneath exhaustion. So it must be again. And he must leave now, while the people were yet disposed to let him go—before they perceived indecisiveness in him.

A path behind the buildings angled up the lower, gentler slope and then, perversely, led straight up the remaining steepness. The crowd followed him between their houses and through the belt of trees behind. Only two continued with him as he climbed the lower path: two men, moving resolutely. One bore a basket on his back, hung from a tumpline around his shoulders. Aengus wondered if they intended to accompany him as far as he would go, if his escape was to be foiled after all.

When he paused where the path became steep, he saw that the two were of the group he had assumed to be the girl's family. The unburdened one pushed past him, then extended his hand to help him. Together, grasping shrubs, branches, and the exposed roots of trees, they pulled themselves to the top.

The uphill trail opened onto another that ran just behind the crest of the bluff, parallel to the beach. Aengus could go left or right, but ahead of him there was only dense forest with tangled undergrowth.

He turned to the men and put his hands to their chests to tell them that he would go on alone. He had expected them to object; instead, a look of ineffable sadness fell across their dark faces. They stepped back.

Knowing that he lied, but moved to give them whatever solace he could, he touched the child and then his own legs, and promised by gestures that he would have her walk again. He did not promise to return her to her home. Perhaps they would remember that . . . when she did not come back. They might believe then that she ran and played in some other village.

Before he left them, the man with the basket hung it on Aengus's back. For a strong man, it would not have been heavy. For Aengus, its weight almost staggered him. While he yet had any vigor at all, he turned and walked away from them. He did not give them even one last look at their child lest the delay become too long for him to bear. And lest she be dead already.

The path was shaded except for flashes of sunlight that flickered through gaps above as he walked. Spaces between the boles on his right held brief, bright vistas of beach and sea. He paused once to look back at the houses peacefully smoking in the mild sunlight. Most of the people had dispersed, but a small cluster of them still lingered on the beach in front of their houses. They were scanning the bluff top and pointing, but they did not see him. Some children and a dog raced through thin scallops of water, wave traces, that slid up the beach. Aengus looked for evidence of the savagery he had feared, of murderous caprice. He saw only sunlight and tranquility.

A half-mile or more along, the path descended where the bluff dropped to form a valley for the passage of a small river. A short, well-used path along its bank led to the beach.

"That would have been the way to come," he thought. "The men must have thought I would go north, not south."

He splashed through a shallow ford and was climbing again when he heard voices behind him—out on the beach. Something urgent in their inflection made him stop, but he could hear nothing more. Then he saw them: three men trotting as best the loose sand would allow along the highest part of the beach.

He had only glimpses of them through the trees. They were close to the short connecting path when he recognized them: the chief and his two henchmen. Each carried a spear and a heavy sword or club, white like bone. When they turned into the connecting path, Aengus plunged off the trail and into a leafy thicket.

V

The men spent little time deciding that Aengus had crossed the river. His wet footprints betrayed him.

He could not see his pursuers below, but he heard at least one start up the trail after him. That one was just passing the thicket in which Aengus crouched when a yell stopped him. The man turned to shout his reply. Aengus looked directly into his savage face, no more than ten feet from him.

The man and another below argued while Aengus held his breath and kept one hand barely above the blanket covering the child's face, ready to smother any noise she might make. He narrowed his eye lest its glisten or movement attract the man's notice. The voices ceased.

The one above started to rejoin his fellows, then stopped and peered directly toward Aengus. Aengus did not move, did not blink. Even hidden behind the leafy screen, his fair skin and beard must be a bright banner declaring his presence, he thought. Apparently his pursuer concluded that he saw nothing other than new spring foliage. He loped back down the path.

The three men returned to the beach. Aengus stood and saw them resume their rapid course along the sand, as if to intercept him farther along. The trail he had been following, then, was only another beach path, one used when the tide was high or storms raged, or, perhaps, used to cross the rock walls that blocked passage along the sand. He returned to the river, being careful to leave no track to tell that he had done so.

The short path from the beach crossed the trail and, though faint from little use, followed the river bank back into the forest. Aengus went that way, but not by the path. He splashed up the side of the riverbed, moving as fast as he could with his double load.

His mind veered desperately from anxiety about his weakness and the ruggedness of the course ahead, to doubt about the correctness of his perception of threat back in the village. Only the chief and his two men had shown hostility toward him there. Now only those three chased him. Why? Most of the others had seemed indifferently disposed toward him, only curious about him. Why had the chief not recruited a larger company of pursuers from their number? Was his influence weak, his leadership flawed? Why had he not slain him among them, if that was his intention? And the child's family: the men who had helped him climb the bluff, the old woman who had tended him while he drifted between death and life . . . He began to wonder whether his flight was a fearful and foolish reaction born of weakness. But, no. He did not know their customs or language. They had seemed to be a barbarous community, therefore unpredictable. He had chosen wisely. Only flight promised survival.

Suddenly exhaustion felled him. He dropped to his knees, then onto his hands. The foot of the child's pallet hung into the water. Tension and fear had carried him this far, but now his strength was gone.

"I'll leave her on the path," he thought. "I can make it alone."

She had been jostled often but had made no sound. He had not looked to see if she was still alive. He did not look now.

After long moments, he raised up on his knees and looked behind him. He expected to see the little river disappearing into dim forest behind him as it did ahead of him. He saw, instead, brilliant beach and blue ocean! He had come no more than two or three hundred feet.

Frantic, he scrambled to his feet. He could drop neither child nor basket here where they could be seen from the beach. Though it would have been only a matter of seconds to hide both in the dense shoreline greenery or back amid the great trees, his ragged mind cried, "Run . . . run . . . run!"

He kept to the river until its bed became too rocky and slippery for his unshod feet. Ashore, the path was more difficult to follow. It was no more than one that animals might have made. He was forced back to the river when the faint track vanished. Along the bank or in the water, he fought onward for a time he could not reckon. His legs moved as if they were something not part of him. One thought preoccupied his mind for a long while: "Don't fall!" If he did, he knew he would drown in inches of water before he could rise again.

"I'll go on until darkness comes," he told himself. Ages later, when darkness had not yet come, a roaring sound frightened him. He thought that he heard surf. Had the river turned back to the beach? Did it have two mouths and no source? No. It had to be the river's own noise. A rapid, or a waterfall perhaps.

Around a bend, the river's banks rose to enclose a bosky glen. At its head was a waterfall that descended in two stages over a mossy rock scarp. Verdant gloom closed around him. It was not the gloom of twilight, but he took it for that.

He found a clear, dry place among great trees and collapsed there, pushing the child past his face as he fell so that her pallet lay beyond his head, although its straps were still tangled about his neck. He shrugged the basket to one side. Then waves of weakness and nausea lifted him out of consciousness.

How many minutes or hours he lay there, he did not know. He thought it might have been days when he first wakened, except that he had not moved: the lashings about his neck and shoulders were no more tangled than when he fell. But the blue sky he saw through the branches confused him. If it had been late in the day when he came

46

there, had he slept through the night?

No, he thought as he struggled to untangle himself and stand, he was neither chilled nor stiff enough to have spent a night on the ground. This must still be the day he had returned to the world of men, although it did not seem to be the same day at all. His brief, deep sleep had broken connection with what had gone before. If it *was* the same day, though, he could not have come far enough from the beach to be safe. He must move on. He must buy distance with all of the time daylight granted him.

The basket, he discovered, held dried fish and other wrapped things that he presumed were food also. That would go with him. His own small package was still tied to his side. But the poor child—he could carry her no farther. He watched to see if the blanket over her chest rose and fell. It did not move. Her face was still covered. He did not want to see her dead. He slid the little pallet, now her bier, beneath great ferns that bordered the clear space.

The sides of the narrow dell were rocky, steep, and choked with growth. For many minutes, he examined them for the best route up and around the waterfall. His decision finally made, he dropped to his knees to sling the basket's tumpline around his shoulders. Doing that for himself this time, the faces of the two men who had helped him before came to mind. Sad faces. Distressed men. How long would they cling to hope for their little one? Surely they had known that she would die, that nothing could be done for her. But why, then, had they provided food for several days? Had they thought she might live that long?

Although he realized that he was revealing his route to any who might come this way, he pulled the child's body back into the open. Her family should know what had become of her. Their hope should not die a little each day through long months. Let his pursuers find her here, and he would take his chances.

The way up that he had chosen was not an easy path. It was, rather, the only way not completely barricaded by dense brush and perpendicular rock faces. Sleep had seemed to restore his morning strength, but the difficult

47

climb quickly exhausted it. When he realized at last that he was forcing his way through level forest, daylight was fading—truly fading this time. He returned to the river above the falls and found a secluded refuge close by under the low branches of a great tree. He decided to stay the night there.

He rummaged through the basket and brought out a deep wooden jug with a lid carved to fit closely and held with thongs. The jug contained a fishy oil. Dried pieces of a white fish dipped into the oil for condiment made a palatable meal. However, he found that he could not eat the food they had provided and keep the child's family out of mind. Their faces returned and returned again: the woman who had brought food and water to *him* when others might have thought he was beyond saving; the two men who had quietly accepted his insistence that they stay behind and entrust their child to him. He became irritated. He could see no reason for his feelings of guilt. He had saved his own life and taken no one's. But he felt, if not guilty, then ashamed that he had found no other escape than one that required him to act callously and perfidiously.

He continued to be troubled. His mind would not let go—would not let him rest. While there was still some light, he followed the river bank back to the top of the waterfall. From there, he could see the tiny clearing below and, dimly, the pitiable bundle he had abandoned. Others had taken possession of the space: ravens. They strutted about with awkward pomposity. One hopped onto the child and made a hoarse croak. Another seized the corner of blanket that covered her face and tugged at it. Clever birds. If her eyes had opened in death, they would peck out those glazed morsels first.

Aengus screamed. The birds looked up. He seized rocks from the river bank and hurled them down, although none reached the clearing. He screamed again. Several of the ravens croaked grotesque retorts. Another fusillade of rocks crashed through branches and into the brush below. The birds flew into trees and complained angrily. Aengus smashed through the riverside brake. Unsure of the way he had come up and with gloom fast thickening, he threw himself from rock to tree root to mossy slope, heedless of whether there was foothold or not. Sliding and falling, he descended into the glen in minutes, but not before the ravens had returned to claim their priority over the scavengers of the night.

He burst into the clearing with arms flailing to drive the obscene demons away.

"Ours! Ours! Ours!" they squawked.

"Mine!" he shouted back.

The birds had not attacked her face. Quickly he slid his head and shoulders into the makeshift harness of her pallet.

It took longer to climb out of the glen this time. He was weak and beyond exhaustion again. The child's pallet caught on branches; he had to twist awkwardly to pass it through narrow places. Darkness was complete when he came at last to the place where he had left the basket. He found it by touch, on his hands and knees.

He slept without dreaming until a shaft of sunlight on his face wakened him. Dried bits of grass, bark, and needles clung to his hair and beard as he roused himself.

"So late," he thought, noting the height of the sun. "But, good. I feel restored."

He dug another piece of dried fish from the basket, then sat as he chewed and reflected on the sad task ahead of him.

"I'll bury her—not leave her for the animals. Her people will know she's dead even if they don't find her remains."

Reaching, he folded the flap of blanket away from her face. Long strands of dark hair fanned across her forehead and still-closed eyes. Aengus recognized the same callow sweetness he had found familiar in little girls' faces the world over, no matter how alien their race. This one had been seven or eight years old—no more than eight. She seemed more asleep than dead.

Yen Hsin's grandfather came to mind. More than five years had passed since that quiet afternoon when Aengus and Hsin had collected the old man's scattered bones on the mountain ledge where they had been told to look. Days later, back in Gau, they spent hours carefully assembling the skeleton. They rearticulated each joint, then fastened each in place with cord to replace ligaments long decayed. When the skeleton, clothed in robes saved for that day, finally lay at rest in the Cave of Ancestors, Hsin believed that only then was the old man's soul released from earth to enter heaven.

The child's face still held Aengus's eye.

"I did nothing for this one while she lived," he thought. "The least I can do now is restore her hip and straighten her leg before I bury her—if she's not too stiff. She should appear more seemly when she meets her gods. Or *my* God, if He rules in this savage place," he considered.

When he unwrapped the body, her head rolled slightly under the touch of his hand. He stopped then, but there was no breath. He uncovered her narrow chest and watched for a long minute. It did not move. He put the back of his hand to her cheek but could not tell whether he felt the chill of morning or the cold of death.

Remembering as best he could the structure of the old man's hip joint, he gently manipulated the child's leg to find how it was bound to her pelvis. There seemed to be strong ligaments in front of the joint but not behind. He flexed the shattered leg onto her stomach. The leg did not yield freely at the place of fracture. The break must have been partial, like the one-sided rupture of a green twig. Using the intact ligaments as a point of rotation, a fulcrum of sorts, he put his hand under her hip and forced it into place as he brought her leg down straight again. The ball slipped smartly into its socket. Instantly, he heard a long, indrawn breath. The child's body stiffened and arched upward in agony. Aengus was astounded. Did she still live? Or was this some reaction of corpses that he had not known of? No—she exhaled with a long, squealing cry. He felt her heart pound in her chest. She lived. She lived!

VI

He put his hands to the girl's chest to hold her down if she were to writhe in pain or throw herself about. She did neither, but he could feel her heart race. Her breathing was rapid through clenched teeth.

Thinking that he could ease her agony, he swept her up, ran to the river, and set her into the chill water at its edge. She gasped twice, then took a great breath and held it. Kneeling beside her with his arm under her shoulders, he waited long, anxious moments until she began to breathe again, slowly and regularly. He spoke to her. She did not reply. He opened one of her eyes. She saw nothing.

Contrary thoughts raced through his mind: "Alive? Strong men die from less. . . . I can fix her leg, too. No— impossible. If she lives longer, she'll just suffer longer. She'll die no matter what I do. . . . If she lives, I could take her back. I could leave her near the houses, then yell and run. Or I could keep her until she's well. If I take her back healed, her people might help me. They'd be grateful . . . or they'd be afraid of my powers—whoever 'Tellacloute' might be. . . . But she won't live. She'll die. I shouldn't prolong her dying."

While his mind reasoned thus, fitfully and feverishly, his actions had a single purpose. He laid the little girl's shoulders against the grassy bank, then ran to his pack. He took his great knife from it, a knife that had once been a sword but, with years of wear, misuse, and intentional reshaping, had taken on more useful dimensions. He snatched up the blankets and padding that had wrapped the child then rushed back to her.

"There'll be no better time to fix the break. If she's past feeling now, I can't hurt her more. If she lives and I try this later, it'll kill her most certainly."

He padded and propped the child's slight upper body and head against the damp river bank. Her hips and legs lay in the water on a small patch of sand. He placed a stone under the knee of her injured leg to raise the top of her thigh above the water's surface.

A light film of rust coated his knife. He ran its blade through sand under water to cleanse it, then, grasping it near its tip, he teased away crusted blood where a spike of bone had broken through her flesh, and bits of wood fiber and what remained of an application of wood ash. ("So her people know at least that way to prevent suppuration. And I have no better.")

Kneeling in the water, he became oblivious to everything but the leg. Cold water kept the wound clean and seemed to staunch the flow of blood. He opened her leg, carefully cutting between strands of muscle rather than across them, until he could feel the erupted top surface of the bone. Then: force, gentle guidance, pulling, more force, lifting of bands of tissue, pressure on the great splinter beneath them, more force, straightening force under the knee and above the break. A tense and intensely focused half-hour passed.

Working rapidly, he raised her leg inches higher so that her blood would displace water when he closed the gaping wound. He reached for the bindings that would hold all in place. At that instant of broken concentration, voices close by froze him to the marrow. He had heard no one approach. Now the voices seemed almost on top of him. Listening closely, he determined that they were following the route he had taken around the waterfall, or nearly so. If they would come back to the river upstream from him, they might not see him. The sand on which he knelt had collected behind a spit from the bank. Tall grasses grew on the spit—last year's grasses, dry and withered, but they gave some cover at least. He could not move the girl now. His work would be undone. In any case, the voices were too close for him to risk making noise.

He stayed motionless, his hands wrapped over the girl's thigh to hold it together. If the voices belonged to men of the girl's family, there should be no trouble. They would help him. But he could not identify those he heard. If they were the chief and his two men, they might let him finish with the girl, but there would be a fight at the end. And he was not strong enough to best the three of them. Not yet.

The intruders spoke at intervals, and tersely. Between, Aengus strained to hear other sounds of their passing, but those were indistinct and difficult to locate. After a long period of silence, he glanced upriver. Two men walked along the bank there, moving away from him. They were looking carefully for signs in the mud and for broken reeds and branches. With intense relief, Aengus identified them as the men of the child's family. He half-stood and raised one arm. As he filled his lungs to call out, one of the men turned around. Aengus had been wrong! It was one of the chief's men. Aengus did not move, did not lower his arm, held his chestful of air. The man seemed to be staring directly at him.

But then the chief himself came from the woods to the riverbank. Seeing him, the man who had looked back turned again and the three continued upriver.

Before they were gone from his sight, Aengus returned his attention to the girl. He wrapped her leg with a thin, soft mat, then a stiff one which he bound firmly with the lashings that had held her to the board. He brought the board and bound her to it so that her hip and leg were held securely, but her other limbs and shoulders could be released for movement. Then he bathed her face and carefully carried her back to the secluded shelter under the tree.

He did not know whether the men would follow the river for days or would return before nightfall. He did not know whether their homegoing would be along this route or by some other of which they knew. The girl could not be moved far—should not be moved at all now. He went to the river and obliterated all marks of their being there. He collected fresh and dead branches and used them to weave a screen around their tree and into its lower branches. He inspected his work frequently from outside to ensure that he had not offended nature. Then he retired within to wait out the day.

He found a small wooden bowl or cup, no larger than a hen's egg, in the basket. He brought water for the girl. During the morning, she made no effort to swallow, so he only wet her lips lest she choke. In the afternoon, she swallowed a few drops, and he was greatly heartened by that.

Late in the afternoon, the men returned. They kept to the riverbank until they came to the top of the waterfall. He saw them pass. They stayed so long at that lookout that he became afraid that he had left some sign: perhaps fresh holes where he had plucked rocks to throw at the ravens. He might have thought that the men had made camp there for the night except that when he crawled from his concealment to investigate, his eye caught the backs of two of them taking the same shortcut down that he had taken when the ravens threatened the girl. He waited a long while, then went to the top of the waterfall. From there, he saw all three picking their way along the riverbank just beyond the mouth of the glen below.

During the following days, he moved upriver in short stages, a mile or two every day. He would carry the girl with great care, then return for the basket. He kept her wound moist with moss rinsed clean. When he saw that her skin would not draw together and heal, he contrived a needle and, with animal sinew, joined the edges. In time, she became conscious and increasingly alert. He held her against the chill of the nights and sometimes during the days when she felt weak and ill. Her pain, a constant companion at first, eventually became only an occasional visitor. And eventually Aengus's despair that she would ever be a healthy, vigorous, spirited child again began to subside.

Miles from the ocean, the river became a stream. He found a sheltered campsite up a small tributary rill. It was a level space on a hillside, embraced half around by a rock wall that arched over to provide some shelter. There was a view of the main stream through a leafy screen and full exposure to the inconstant sun. The rivulet trickled along one side and was caught in two deep, rocky pools before it dripped into a marshy area below the site.

Their second day there, when the girl sensed some permanence as Aengus continued to arrange things for their comfort, she became suddenly communicative. A hummingbird flew into their clearing, searching for early blossoms. The child pointed to the little jeweled sprite and named it: "kwetah-koots." Then she pointed to herself and told Aengus her own name: "Kwetah."

She had trouble with his name. She understood well enough that he was identifying himself, but she could not pronounce the word easily. It came out something like "Yahd-guss." Her face told him that she knew she had failed. Later, as he worked to lay in branches for a shelter against the rock wall, she called to him in her clear child's voice: "Akwahti."

He brought her a cup of water, which she drank eagerly, then he returned to his work.

Shortly she called again: "Akwahti."

He brought another cupful of water. She drank it more slowly. On the third summons, she refused the proffered cup with an uncertain look on her face. Suddenly understanding, he realized that she would know nothing of the language used between foreigners in Europe. His mind, preoccupied with his work, had heard "aqua"; she had intended something else.

55

"So *I'm* Akwahti then, am I?" he said with his hand to his chest. She smiled happily and snuggled down into her blankets.

Days later, he learned the fitness of his new name in her mind. A great white-headed eagle with glowering eyes and yellow beak took roost in a tall tree by the stream below their camp. It, also, was "akwahti." So Aengus, yellow haired, yellow bearded, his face made grim by a stone eye, became "Akwahti," hunter and provider for his little nestling.

Food was plentiful. A mile below their camp, the stream widened to make a marsh-edged pool that drew deer and other animals. Aengus learned to lie on a rock above their path to the pool. A hard blow to the neck with his heavy knife or, later, a stone-headed club would knock down a deer. He chose animals of a size that he could carry away to butcher so that others would not learn to fear that place.

Edible roots, too, were found in the marshy places: one kind that he selected by chance and, later, another that Kwetah recognized among several he brought for her inspection.

He grew stronger rapidly. Kwetah came along more slowly, but her improvement was steady. Though she relished the warmth of her bed, she would never flinch when he carried her to one of the deep, cold pools at the edge of their woodland home. When her wound had closed, she exercised her legs there every day, moving them against the resistance of the water with the motions he showed her. Afterward, he would rub warmth into her icy limbs, then flex and stretch them to keep them lithe.

He began to wonder how Kwetah would tell him that she wanted to go home to her family. With few words known between them, he looked for signs but saw none. Instead, she became freely affectionate toward him. That surprised him. He looked nothing like her solidly built, bronze-skinned people. He was markedly taller than they were, gaunt during those first weeks, and his face, to one unused to it, had no beauty in it. In his experience, children did not readily take to strangers, and not at all to strange-appearing strangers. But Kwetah was never shy with him. Often, for no reason apparent to him, she would hold out her arms for a hug. Aengus, who had known nothing of a child's affection since his own childhood, was enthralled.

He learned her language. She was an enthusiastic teacher. Even when she was still very weak, she would struggle to tell him meanings long after she had strength to do so. Then he would gently put his hand to her mouth or, if he was holding her, press her head to his tunic until she slept. He would repeat the new words she had taught him and compose sentences with them to please her when the next day's lesson began.

He resurrected skills long unused. From the skin of his first deer, he made trousers such as horsemen wear and a blouse for Kwetah. He prepared the hide as his uncle had taught him. He loosened the hair with wood ash; scraped, cleaned, and softened the skin using the sharp bone from the animal's foreleg that his uncle had said was provided for that purpose; tanned it with a mash of its brains and liver; then washed and smoked it and worked it to softness. When Kwetah saw the garments take form to her dimensions, her eyes sparkled with anticipation.

No child of Europe could have shown greater delight in a new gown than did dark little Kwetah when she was finally arrayed in her unfamiliar garb.

"A month ago, she was almost dead," he mused in wonderment. "Soon I'll be teaching her to walk again. Then what? Back home for her. But will I ever again know a home like this? I shouldn't become too attached to the child."

VII

Although Kwetah knew many useful or edible plants, even as far as their camp was from her home on the shore, she seemed unknowing about and fearful of many of the animals. Only the small birds and butterflies pleased her at first. From her bed or other places to which Aengus carried her, her eyes would follow those tiny forest nymphs glittering in the sun or almost lost in the darkness amid the leaves.

One morning as he started down the path from their ledge, he saw a mother and calf of a very large kind of deer. They were feeding on the sedgy growth along the rill that joined the stream below their camp. The mother looked up and gave him a long, frank inspection, then resumed her browsing. He returned for Kwetah. Her recovery was not yet far advanced and, although he knew few of her words then, her wan face and lusterless eyes spoke of her ache and weakness that morning. Hoping to cheer her, he held her and sat on the rocky rim of their ledge where it overhung low growth beside the descending path. He pointed to the spotted calf, thirty or forty feet away.

Far from being delighted by the pretty sight, Kwetah stiffened and clutched Aengus's arm. He held her more closely, but did not leave. He wanted to show her that there was no harm in the beasts. The calf—*fawn* would be too delicate a word for such a robust baby—left the boggy

58

patch for the path and began to nibble new grass and leaves along its sides. Although its mother raised her head for a moment, she did not object to her youngster's independent behavior. Kwetah's anxiety increased as the calf moved closer. When it became apparent that it was going to come up to them, she twisted around and buried her face in Aengus's tunic.

Aengus stripped some grass from a clump behind him and held it on his knee to entice the animal. Showing no fear, the calf deliberately browsed closer and closer to them until it required only the slightest lift of its head to extract the blades from his grasp. Its moist nose brushed Kwetah's leg. The girl became rigid with terror. Aengus pushed the calf's shoulder gently. Ignoring his gesture, or perhaps enjoying it, the calf turned to stand against his knee even as it nibbled the shrubs below his dangling feet. He whispered, "Kwetah," but she would not look or relax her grip on his clothing.

Many weeks later, when Kwetah was liberated from her bed and he knew more of her language, he heard her scolding, "Go away, old ugly! Go back to your people!"

He had been laying strips of venison onto a rack for smoking. His back was to the girl. He swung around to see her awkwardly hurl a stick of firewood into a thicket that bordered their camp on the side opposite the pools. A bear raised its head, startled by her abuse. Kwetah hobbled to the very edge of the clearing, rattled her newly made crutch against the scrubby stems there and, in her piping voice, once again ordered the bear to leave. The old sow snorted with annoyance, raised its forelegs from the ground, and swung its massive body away from the tiny termagant. She and Aengus watched the black back, awash in a sea of low shrubbery, until it disappeared amid the trees of the forest.

Such boldness struck Aengus as inconsistent with her timorousness before the deer calf. With that in mind, he asked, "Why did you do that, Kwetah?"

The child construed his question more simply.

"You have to do that with bears. If you don't chase them

59

away, they go into houses and destroy things. If you let them come too close one time, then it's more difficult to chase them away the next time."

Confident that she had properly instructed him in the ways of bears, she returned to the miniature figure she had been making of sticks and tied grasses.

To tease her, he said, "I thought at first that you were calling *me* 'old ugly' and telling *me* to leave."

The suggestion appalled her. If the bear had not frightened her, his careless humor had.

"No, no, Akwahti," she protested. "You're not ugly. I don't want *you* to go away."

She was uncertain that he knew enough of her speech to understand her meaning. She became agitated and the words tumbled out. He laughed aloud at her pretty discomfiture, not yet realizing how cruelly the thought of abandonment tormented her. Her special efforts to please him during the rest of the day informed him that he should not banter with her thoughtlessly.

They were visited by many animals. The large ones were generally content to recognize Aengus and Kwetah's claim to their sylvan home, while the small ones freely asserted their own right to share space and leavings. Kwetah's variable attitude toward those visitors and guests, Aengus learned, was determined by what she had inferred from the conduct of the people of her village toward them. She had seen her elders casually chase off bears, and it called for no special courage for her to follow their example with the lumbering brutes, who had always responded with lumpish obedience. The large deer were not unknown to her, but she had only seen them in sizable herds as they wandered out to her beach in the winter. They were always given way. They were not hunted for food—at least, not to her knowledge—and she had assumed that her people considered them to be fierce. The great racks carried by some of the stags had impressed her as terrible weapons.

During their first months together, Kwetah was a timid and dependent little girl, considerate and affectionate toward Aengus always, but fearful of what might lie beyond the verge of their campsite and sometimes tearful for little cause. As her strength returned, she became more self-reliant, mettlesome, and joyful—characteristics she must have had before her accident, Aengus thought, because she repossessed them so naturally.

Stages in her progress from timid uneasiness to a heartier, more confident disposition were marked by their several encounters with a pair of rowdies for whom the camp became a way station in their wanderings. Kwetah and Aengus were wakened early one morning by a chorus of whistles and yelps and the sound of their woodpile being scattered. Half awake, Aengus's first thought was that they had been invaded by a gang of unruly boys intent on mischief. With a shout, he sprang from the shelter he had built under the overhanging rock. In the midst of their havoc, a pair of bright-eyed otters stared at him with impudent curiosity.

Expecting them to run off, he started to rebuild the woodpile; to his surprise, they followed him like young dogs, even scampered between his feet and nearly tripped him. Still stiff and cheerless from the night, he could think of no more than to get rid of the boisterous intruders. He kept little fresh meat in camp because of the scavengers it would attract, but he found a piece left from the last night's meal. Passing it near the otters' noses, he threw it down the path toward the stream. They were after it before it hit the ground.

When he went to the head of the path to see whether they had found the meat, they were nowhere to be seen, although he could hear their chattering and burring noises above the splash of the stream. He soon put them out of mind as he attended to routine duties: preparing a morning meal and moving Kwetah to a sunny place as soon as the sun was high enough.

The child could not yet hobble about at that time, but could stand with her stomach or back against a rock table and move down the length of it, bearing her weight on her elbows as she swung her legs in crabwise steps. That exercise strengthened her and, more importantly, cheered her, for she felt that she was making her own contribution to her recovery. And she relished Aengus's praise as her movements became quicker and more proficient.

That morning of the otter's first visit, she was resting during her exercise, leaning forward against the rock and standing on her good leg, when the frolicsome pair reappeared from the path. In a lightning-fast circuit of the camp, they leaped to the top of the woodpile; they scampered madly along the length of it, again knocking several sticks to the ground, jumped to Kwetah's rock and ran past the startled child, hurtled to the pools and porpoised through each, then slid along the smooth, mossy course of the rill and dropped from view over the rim of the ledge. Though they had no more than brushed against her, Kwetah's flinching reaction to their sudden and unexpected nearness made her topple to the ground. She lay for a moment in shocked surprise then began to cry, partly from her sudden fright, partly from outrage, mostly because she was still physically and emotionally weak.

With otters, once is rarely enough. The two ruffians soon appeared from the path to repeat their foray. Aengus was beside Kwetah by that time, anxiously examining her to make sure that her injuries had not been aggravated. When the animals jumped again from the woodpile to the rock table, he shouted at them angrily, "Stop! Get away from here."

Stop they did, instantly, but they did not run away. To his surprise, they plopped down beside him and the girl and began to mewl and chitter and move around them in an ingratiating manner, alternately soliciting forgiveness and indulging their own curiosity. They showed no fear at all and were as familiar as a pair of house dogs. One even climbed Aengus's hunched-over back and peered down at Kwetah over his shoulder. They took no such personal liberty with her, but she was greatly frightened nonetheless and clung to his arm.

Harsh words and missiles would have driven the otters away, but their friendliness and almost childlike supplications for approval won Aengus over. He did not want them to become dependent nuisances so he gave them no food, but theirs was not a begging sociability. In fact, later that day he found the chunk of meat he had thrown for them to chase. It was lying by the side of the path, uneaten. They wanted no more than occasional companionship during the few days they foraged along that section of the stream.

Aengus could not understand the reason for their tame behavior. Certainly no others of their kind acted the same way, although he saw several. At first he believed that they must have been raised by people. Then he wondered if the camp had been their early home; perhaps he and Kwetah were associated with "family" in their minds. Later, he ascribed their madcap amiability to nothing other than youthful playfulness. When he finally saw the fully grown otters of that land, he realized that this male and female were probably only yearlings, and siblings because they were too young to be a mated pair.

They adopted the camp as a safe haven between their prowls along the stream. Hunting was mainly a nocturnal enterprise with them, and they spent much of the day on the ledge, often sleeping on Aengus's bed, to Kwetah's obvious distaste. He laughed aloud when he first saw the pair sprawled on his mats, lying on their backs with their forepaws folded against their chests like contented, well-fed babes asleep. Kwetah smiled briefly when he carried her near to show them to her, but she made no sociable overtures toward them. They, in turn, seemed to recognize her fearfulness and frailty. They became quiet when they were close to her, and they never forced their attentions upon her. That, though, was the only respect they showed for Aengus and Kwetah's home and few belongings. Whenever the mood came upon them, their hosts' things were peremptorily, often violently, rearranged for otter comfort or play.

Their departure was as abrupt as their coming. One day they were no longer there. Aengus missed them.

He had known other otters in streams near his boyhood

home and had tried, with scant success, to befriend them. This young pair resembled those so nearly that he began to hope he might be closer to home than he had believed even though most of the other animals of Kwetah's land were new to him or differed considerably from their European counterparts. He reasoned that the hunting territories of most animals, if marked on a map of the world, would resemble a random pattern of paving stones, whereas the riverine domain of otters would more nearly correspond to the net of crevices separating the pavings. Most kinds of animals inhabited local areas, while otters followed rivers and streams for great distances. This pair could belong to the vanguard of the otters of Europe, spreading westward across the world.

"Perhaps otter trails will take me home." The thought warmed him.

Sometimes, though, contrary notions seemed as compelling. If it had pleased God to create the prodigious variety of creatures and people that Aengus had met already, why should He have chosen to restrict habitable space by making the earth a ball? Perhaps the world was a limitless plane after all, to provide space for all the creatures of God's limitless imagination.

The otters were gone a month, almost forgotten, when they burst into the camp again, chittering wildly. After a brief, physical welcome, they took possession of Aengus's bed and slept from midmorning until dark. They must have made a long last stage to have become so exhausted. He was pleased at that indication that they valued his and Kwetah's company.

The pair found a different Kwetah than they had known. She was strong enough to assert her will, but not yet able to participate in their rampageous play. They accepted the new Kwetah as they had the other and obeyed her demands no matter how unreasonable those must have seemed at times. The larger of the two pools, to cite an instance, must have seemed to them more than adequate for one small girl and two young animals to occupy at the same time. Kwetah would have none of such communal bathing, though, and the otters cheerfully accepted their banishment while she used the pool.

The animals' third visit followed a more lengthy absence. Whether they instantly recognized subtle clues that told of Kwetah's recovery or merely had decided that she *ought* to be better by that time, their forbearance toward her was over. Aengus and she were just waking when the otters bounded into the shelter. Both of them pounced on Aengus in his bed, but, when the male nestled into the crook of his arm, its sister leaped the space between his bed and Kwetah's and promptly dived beneath her blankets. It made a quick tour of the warm space while Kwetah gripped the mats and furs to keep them from sliding off. The otter poked its head out on the other side of the astonished child, then thrust its nose under her chin and promptly fell asleep. Kwetah looked at Aengus in shock, then suddenly giggled and hugged the weary animal to her.

"I thought they would smell bad," she told him later, "but they don't at all. They smell new-washed all the time." Indeed, their fur, when completely dry and sun warmed, had a pleasant, spicy scent. Unfortunately, they loved water almost more than air, and only rarely was contact with their friends not attended with some degree of dampness.

Kwetah became their playmate, but not quite in the same manner Aengus was. A favorite game with them was to toss some object for him to chase: the dog-and-stick game, with Aengus taking the part of the dog. They would hold a stick or stone between their paws, then heave the forward part of their bodies upward to propel the object. Their aim was entirely haphazard. Playing the same game with Kwetah, they did not require her to always chase their missiles, sensing that she could not do so easily. Instead, they chased their own wild throws and only expected Kwetah to retrieve and toss back those that fell close to her. In other ways, too, they were gentle with her. Her hands and legs never bore the tiny scratches their teeth inflicted on Aengus in the abandon of rough play—those same

VIII

Summer in Kwetah's land was a glory. Aengus exulted in it. The forest essences reminded him of the smell of wine sheds or the scented interiors of temples. The quality of the sunlight gladdened him. It was never oppressive, never brassy. It seemed to flow through the forest like some ethereal fluid, a luminous balm for a one-eyed man.

But the season had changed since he was cast ashore. Thoughts of seasons to come began to press on his mind with growing insistence. They forced him to consider how his and Kwetah's summer idyll must end and what would come after that.

In their camp was a grassy nook that Kwetah favored. It was an angle between rocks that caught the sun and blocked the breezes. One morning Aengus idled there, his back against the warm rock and Kwetah between his outstretched legs. He watched awhile as she constructed a little tower of some sticks he had cut for her, then he asked her offhandedly, "Why are you called 'Hummingbird'?"

"My mother named me. The hummingbird is her favorite."

"What is your mother's name?"

"Hahpellpah."

"What's a 'hahpellpah'?"

"My mother." Kwetah's aspect became sly, teasing.

"No, no," Aengus persisted. "What animal or bird or other thing is called 'hahpellpah'?"

67

"No other thing. It's my mother's name."

She bent her head then to hide a fit of giggles and said in a deep, mocking voice, "What is a 'yahd-guss'?"

Aengus recognized her playful mood, shook his head, and smiled at her. At that, Kwetah fell back against him and reached to pull his hair or ears while he put his arms behind him and twisted and turned his head to frustrate her. That game would always end when he would suddenly wrap his arms about her so that she could not move. When he pinioned her so this time and she relaxed comfortably against him, he thought that he would never know greater happiness in this world. And that thought forced the next.

"Kwetah, we must begin to think of taking you home before winter."

"Home?"

"Yes. Back to your mother and father."

"We can't do that. There's no way back."

"Oh, child, we're not *that* far from your beach, and I know the way. If we start at sunrise some day, we could be there before dark."

"But that's not what happens. How could I get my bones back inside me?"

"Your bones are inside you *now*."

"No, no. My *real* bones. The ones in the woods behind our houses."

"What are you talking about, little one?"

Then slowly, slowly, Aengus began to understand her meaning.

"Kwetah, do you think you have died?"

"Yes. Both of us have." She paused. "I was afraid to die when I was first hurt, but it was easy. And then I was here . . . with you. I like it here. You don't have to try to take me back."

"But if we're dead, Kwetah, why are we alone here in this forest? Why haven't we met other dead people—old people you've known who have died?"

Kwetah looked at him sharply. Then, like a novice

68

responding to a catechist, she sought words to explain what she believed. "When people in that world die, Akwahti, people in this world come for them—or for the part of them that can come to this world. We'll stay here, near home, until my mother and my friends no longer think about me every day. Then we'll go to Hahtoppul where the other dead people are."

Abruptly, her solemn mien gave way before childish curiosity.

"Akwahti, you didn't wait until they put me out under the trees. You came into our lodge to get me. Why did you do that? Did you want my hurting to stop? Did the people there see you? They didn't run away—they couldn't have seen you. Or was I just dreaming that I saw you there?"

"Shush, child. Ssh."

Aengus held her against him while his mind roved over the implications of her misapprehension:

"So that's why my strange appearance didn't frighten her—or offend her. She believes that I'm a shade from her spirit world come for her. . . . If only that were true. I think I'd gladly give up my life for the promise of this kind of bliss. . . . But it's *not* true. . . . She'll *know* it's not true sometime. . . . And her family has more right to her than I have."

He spoke to her again: "Kwetah, if you were still in your village and not hurt, and you saw me walking on your beach, would you run away? Would I frighten you? Someone who looks like me—would that frighten you?"

"I *did* see you, Akwahti. When you were hurt and asleep on the big rock. I was the one who found you. Yes, I *was* afraid, but you were hurt so badly, I felt sorry for you."

"*You* found me? You alone?"

"Yes. I'd gone for barnacles beyond the hole-through-the-rock. That's where the most barnacles are—big ones—on the rocks past our beach. That's where I found you: lying on top of a big, flat rock, all tangled up in kelp."

The girl paused for a moment, then continued quietly, "I'm sorry you died, Akwahti. But I'm glad it was you who came back for me. I'm glad to have you as my friend here. I'd be frightened if I had to be here alone or with some very old person."

An urge to tell her that she was not dead, to convince her that she could return to her family, to see disbelief turn to jubilation, welled up in him. Immediately, however, a cautionary impulse intruded. As long as she considered him a trusted friend, she would be content to stay with him until she was healed and strong. He had more confidence in the care he was giving her than that which she would receive in her dim, dusty lodge. In the fellowship of the dead, she would confide in him; she would freely tell him whatever he might want to know about her land and the people in it. If he became something else in her mind—a captor, perhaps, who had stolen her from her family and held her in this forest by deception for some selfish purpose—how might she react to that? Would her affection turn to horror? He put aside the urge to reveal.

"Kwetah, how were you hurt?"

He had given the girl opportunity to talk about the cause of her injury before. She had always avoided the subject, and he had not pressed her. Now, in the face of his direct question, she fell silent. A tear grew in one of her eyes, then slid down her cheek. She seemed to withdraw from the question and from him.

"Never mind, never mind, little one," he whispered, drawing her back against his chest. "I don't need to know."

They were quiet then for a while. Kwetah nestled into the crook of his arm and laid her head against him. Long minutes passed. Finally, in low tones, she began to tell her story. It was punctuated with silences. He did not interrupt or urge her on.

"When I brought people to help you, they were afraid. Some thought you were a man who lived in the ocean like a fish. Others thought a bird had brought you from another world and dropped you there. Some wanted to push you into the sea or just leave you there, but Kobessa told Mahkalt and Sierka to make a place for you nearby,

70

and they carried you to it. Kobessa said she would look after you and that the others could kill her if . . . if you became something wicked."

Kwetah glanced up quickly to see if the suggestion of wickedness offended or dismayed him. Reassured by his smile, she continued:

"After a few days, my father asked me if I had seen your boat. I had seen nothing like that, but he asked me again and again. Then he took me to the high rock above the hole-through. It's very steep. He had to pull me most of the way to the top. He made me point to where I had first seen you, on the rock just below us. Then he pointed to this place and that place and asked me if I had seen anything here or there. He said you had come in a boat and that I must have seen it, or parts of it. But I had not seen anything like that at all! He became very angry and said I was stupid." In a very small voice, she concluded, "And then he threw me down."

Aengus bent his head to look into her face, his question written on his own.

"He picked me up," Kwetah said, "and threw me off the high rock where we were. He threw me onto the rock where I'd found you. That's how I was hurt."

Aengus tried to remember the end of the beach and the great, decomposing rib of the world that stretched out to sea there in a series of high, rocky islets. She must have fallen from a height greater than the tall trees of the forest. Her father must have meant to kill her. What had saved her? Perhaps ledges of rock interrupted her fall. Perhaps the mat of seaweed was deep enough to have cushioned her impact.

Though she paused often, Kwetah must have found relief in the telling of her story, for she continued it through the last hour of morning until the sun was past noon. For the most part, Aengus held back his urgent questions. He did not want to distract her; with patience they would be answered anyhow.

"I can't remember hitting the rock. I can't remember being taken back to my house. It's as if I were asleep most

71

of the time until I woke up here with you. It's not very hard to die at all. But I remember seeing you in the lodge. You were kind of blurry. And before that, I heard someone say that I had fallen. I wanted to tell them what really happened, but I knew I should not."

"Why not, Kwetah?"

"Because my father is the chief. If a ko-tlo says something bad about a chief, the ko-tlo is killed. And my mother would have been killed too."

Aengus did not understand that at all. He tilted his head back and gazed at the sky. Kwetah sensed his incomprehension.

"Some people are ko-tlo," she explained. "They come from outside. Some people are chiefs. They're called 'chabotta.' They belong to families of chiefs. All other people are between. Some are high; some are low. It depends on the family they were born into, or whom they marry."

Ko-tlos, then, must be captives or slaves, but Aengus knew no better how Kwetah could be a slave and her father a chief. He said nothing and waited to hear what she would say next.

"My mother came from outside. She came from a village so far away that the people there don't look like the people here. Her skin is white."

Aengus started. "White? Like my skin?"

"No. White like mine."

The little girl's skin was, in fact, lighter than the dark bodies he remembered from his brief hour in her village. For him, who had seen people of many lands, the difference was not remarkable. For Kwetah, who had known nothing of other races before his coming, it must have been enough for her to feel set apart. Her face, he observed now, was somewhat more narrow than those he remembered from her village, and her eyes had a cast to them that reminded him a little of Yen Hsin's people. She was a beautiful child, he had thought all along, but her beauty was of her own race, not his.

Kwetah continued, still speaking of her mother: "She was taken from her own village when she was a young girl. A chief in another place kept her for a while, then another chief took her from him. That one traded her to my father and she became his wife."

"So then she was no longer a ko-tlo," Aengus prompted.

"I'm not sure. I think she was not a ko-tlo at first, but then another ko-tlo came. A man. He was from far away also, but not from the village where my mother was born. Then my mother . . . did something. . . . Some old women I've heard talking about it say it was wrong. She and the man ran away and lived in the forest—like you and me, Akwahti. Akwahti, is it wrong that I live in the forest with you?"

He smiled. "No, child—"

"We're supposed to live here now, aren't we?" she interrupted to answer her own question. Then she continued her account:

"My father found them and killed the man. He didn't kill my mother, but she was a ko-tlo after that and didn't live in his house. She lived in the old people's lodge with Kobessa. That's where I was born."

Aengus mulled over the girl's revelations. Her people had seemed to be simple and savage and their chief ineffective, as if his people knew little of government. But there were hints in her story of complexities, of subtleties that he had not perceived in their society during his brief time among them. And the chief—if he had killed his wife's lover, why had he spared her? Because he loved her? Could such a cruel man ever love a woman? Could he continue to love her after she had run off with another? Even if she carried that other's child?

Kwetah remained silent for a long time, a faraway look in her eyes.

"So you were a ko-tlo then, too, Kwetah. Did you live with your mother?"

"Yes. My father . . . Sometimes he would speak to me or let follow him around our village like other fathers. Other times he would send me away and seemed angry. Some-times he hit me. One time when he had hit me, my mother told me not to call him 'father.'"

"But your mother loved you."

"Oh, yes. She would hold me close and sing to me. But sometimes she seemed not to know me very well, and she acted like a stranger. If I left her alone those times, then she loved me all the more later. She is very much afraid of my father. Sometimes I think she fears him more than she loves me. But Kobessa looked after us. She won't let my father hurt my mother. And Mahkalt and Sierka will look after her, too."

"Two men?"

"Yes. They're my friends."

Aengus saw that Kwetah was spent. Telling her story had been an exorcism of suppressed terrors for her. The silence that overtook her now spoke of exhaustion, not thought.

Her account left many questions for him to consider. Had the chief's assault on her been the impulse of a moment of savage irritation, or was it the culmination of long-smoldering resentment against the child of his wife's infidelity? What was his interest in Aengus's vessel? What did slavery mean in their village—some diminished status or a complete deprivation of all privilege and participation in their community? What would Kwetah return to? Could he intercede for her? For her mother?

"No!"

The word rang loudly only in his mind, but its sudden-ness startled him. From somewhere deep within, the word came again: "No! Not again. This is what happened with Jasleen. I thought I was doing the best thing for her. And for me. But it came to nothing. If Hektor and I had let the old prince take her, she might be alive now with many children. We rescued her only for death to find her.

"Whatever fate has intended for *any* of my friends, I've never been able to do anything to prevent it. Not for Turfu. Not for Hektor. Not for Hsin—maybe once for him, but not the next time. My wanderings have been for nothing—

for them or for me. If I'd stayed at home or had turned back early, I'd be a considerable man in Tellacloute or even Washlae now. Even here at the end of the world, only Tellacloute—only Armorica—holds anything lasting for me. Not Kwetah. Not her people. Not the life of their village with all their sufferings and whatever their primitive satisfactions are.

"No. I'll return Kwetah to her family. Once she's healed and strong, I can do nothing more for her except bring her more trouble than she's known already. So, home! I'll go home. There's a way. . . ."

IX

"I'm going to leave you tomorrow," he told Kwetah, "but only for two or three days."

She must have read that possibility in his restless stirrings about the camp for several days. She said nothing.

"I'll leave enough food and lots of wood for the fire."

Kwetah examined her hands lying in her lap.

"You'll be fine by yourself for a few days. You'll have everything you need. I'll leave my knife with you."

"When will you be back?"

"A few days. I don't know. Two days. No more than three days."

"Why must you go? Where are you going?"

"I want to see where the mountains and rivers are, and where the trees end."

"Can't you see those things with your magic eye?"

He laughed and sat down beside her. "It's not a magic eye, Kwetah. It's just a smooth stone to replace an ordinary eye."

Kwetah still looked at her hands while she spoke in a small voice. "It doesn't look like a stone."

She was silent awhile, then said, "What if you don't come back?"

"I will be back, Kwetah. I won't abandon you." He paused, but she said nothing. "The time will go quickly. You'll hardly know I've been away."

They both recognized the truthlessness of that, but it ended the conversation. For the rest of the day, he gathered things for her against his absence: berries and edible roots to add to their store of dried meat. He collected wood and made a huge stack against the wall of the shelter. It looked like a monstrous, tipped-up raven's nest when he had finished.

"Three days, Kwetah. I'll be back before the end of three days," he called to her as he started down the path from their ledge the next morning. Her woeful eyes followed him, but she said nothing.

He traveled eastward all that day, following streams upward. Then, when those dwindled to nothing, he found new streams in new valleys. He marked his trail carefully so that he could find his way back, but the unvarying nature of the terrain made him increasingly anxious. He began to wonder if he had been cast up on the shore of a country that was completely covered with forest: trees, trees, and more trees that would forever deny him any wide view of where he was or an open trail to cross to another ocean. He remembered the story of the rich man who became lost in his vast storehouse of gold coins. He was found days later, drowned in his wealth. Perhaps, Aengus thought, that might be his own fate in this forest of riches.

Kwetah . . .

Kwetah knew of a path from her village to another one, but nothing of how the coastline lay, where mountains might be, or how great her land was. She had heard of no community larger than her own village; she found the idea of "city" incomprehensible. She could tell him none of the things he must know after he would leave her at her village.

After he would leave her at her village . . .

Kwetah . . . Kwetah . . .

He could not keep the child out of his thoughts. Concern for her loneliness, fears for her safety, kept welling up in his mind. Each time, he would force his thoughts away from her. He would try to picture the high place clear of trees that he sought, the place that would show him how to start his journey home, but his mind would not hold to its purpose.

"She'll be all right," he told himself over and over again. "The forest has been good to us. It's safe. She'll be all right."

And if she became frightened—well, that, after all, would serve his intention well enough. It would satisfy his brief leaving's real purpose that he had not told her of, the motive that had been in his mind like a command on waking one morning. No, not to find a way to Europe; he could find that later as easily as now. This temporary parting was to prepare the girl and himself for the permanent separation to come; to begin to turn her mind away from him and back to her own people; to harden his own heart so that recollection of her artless affection would be just fond reverie and not a wellspring of constant yearning.

Throughout that day, his scheme brought him nothing but torment. For the first time in many years, he thought of an incident on a dusty road near Rome when he was conducting a holy brother to an audience with Bishop Turfu. They passed a swaddled babe lying on a patch of grass under a wayside tree. If the infant had been in shade when it was placed there, many hours must have passed because now the sun was full upon it. It made feeble attempts to cry, but these came as mere gasps. No mother, no one at all except the foul-bearded monk and himself, was anywhere near.

"A child of pagans," the monk explained with pious scorn, "or lapsed Christians. When their children become inconvenient to keep, they set them out to die like that. A little crowding, a little poverty, and the teachings of our Lord are forgotten."

Young Aengus kept looking back until his companion was moved to irritation. "It wasn't left for *us* to find, boy. Some childless woman may take it. Too many are abandoned that way for us to start collecting them."

But that was the only one Aengus saw during all the

78

months that he and Bishop Turfu made their way across Europe.

When night came to the forest, Aengus made a bed of boughs and ferns under the drooping branches of a great cypress—*his* name for those trees because they reminded him of the cypresses of Italy; "canoe trees," Kwetah had called them. He slept poorly and woke to a gray, cheerless sky. His mood was dreary as he climbed to the top of the hill he had slept below. And then his spirits leaped, for, through trees to his left—to the north—he saw another forest-clad hill and, beyond it, a higher one quite bare of trees.

He carefully marked this point of turning, then plunged down and through the thickly undergrown trees. He reached the second hill well before midday. Blackened trees there, standing and fallen, and new saplings thrusting through spikes of willow weed told him that fire had cleared the hill two or three years before. A lightning strike, he guessed.

As he climbed above the forest barrier, he turned often to search the prospect opening behind him, to the south and southeast. Each higher pause revealed only new hills behind those seen earlier, blue hills behind green ones. A dread that, from the summit, he would see no different view in any other direction slowed his pace.

His apprehension vanished with his first glimpse over the hilltop. Scrambling to the top, his heart soared. He beheld a magnificent strait, perhaps twenty miles wide, that stretched west and east as far as his eye could see. A range of mountains rose into sunshine beyond its far shore. Looking to the west, he was not sure that he could see the ocean he had drifted across. The leaden horizon there was quite indistinct. But the strait—a passage through this land, perhaps?—made him light-headed. He threw up his arms, pranced around like a fool, and sang one of Hektor's ribald ditties at the top of his voice. Did the water before him merely separate large islands? Did it connect with Europe's western ocean just beyond his view? He became drunk with excitement over the possibility.

Blue sky above and beyond the strait was reflected in its waters. The brilliant openness drew him as flames draw a night traveler. Had the sky been uniformly heavy, horizon to horizon, he might have turned back then. If he had followed his blazed track, mostly descending, he would have been back with Kwetah by nightfall or soon after. But brightness and color tipped his decision toward the promising strait. He thought that a quick sally along a stream he saw below might bring him to its mouth before dark. There he would discover whether broad beach or level littoral would permit him to travel eastward on foot, or an abrupt shoreline would require that he find a boat. He would see if people lived there and, from a safe distance, he might learn if they could help him or should be avoided. Then he would return to Kwetah on the morrow. With a marked path to follow and none of the groping along false trails that had robbed him of time on the way here, his return could be accomplished in a single day. And, if the hike to the strait proved longer than he supposed, or difficult, he could turn around at any point.

By the time he had resolved those considerations to his satisfaction and ease of conscience, he had bounded down the northeast slope of the hill and plunged through the thicket that edged the watercourse.

The hike downstream was difficult only in a few places where the stream bed formed rocky rapids or waterfalls that forced him to make his way through the woods alongside. Otherwise, he found easy walking along sandy or rocky edges, although he had to cross the stream often to pass obstacles on one bank or the other. The soles of his deerhide buskins became slick. He removed them and hung them around his neck.

A mile or two along, a faint path he had found became noticeably more worn. He was sure that he was yet nowhere near the mouth of the stream. He became watchful lest he come upon people by surprise, a vigilance that was particularly taxing for a man with a single eye. He stopped frequently to listen for new sounds above the splashing and gurgling of the stream—or little river, which it had become. Occasionally the path cut through the forest where the river bent away in large loops. One of those shortcuts passed through a small meadow of tall grasses and scattered shrubs. Movement along its far side caught his attention—a deer in the berry bushes there, he decided. He was so intent on that distraction that he almost collided with two dark urchins standing wide-eyed in the path.

Stopping abruptly, he looked around for their mother. His amazed eye saw many mothers, and other children too. Every bush had its berry picker, or several of them. They were all around him. He could not believe that he had come among them unseen and unseeing. They and he stood and stared, momentarily a garden of statuary.

Two of the women near him, no more than girls, moved closer to each other. When he glanced toward them, shy smiles illuminated their attractive faces. Heartened by that apparent welcome, he returned their smiles and took a step toward them. Instantly, all of the women and children took flight. Those behind him bolted past through grass and brush and joined the path where it disappeared around a turn just past the meadow. No one had spoken a word or cried out. The only sounds had been from swishing grass and pattering feet.

Aengus ran to the turn in the path, which was near the river's edge, but all of them had passed other bends beyond. River, path, all of the world that he could see was empty. The silent people seemed no more than a remembered fragment of a dream.

If his decision to investigate the shore of the strait had been impulsive and heedless of Kwetah, at least good sense prevailed now. He turned back along the path and made rapid strides to separate himself from those to whom the women would report their encounter. He doubted that their men would follow him very far, but the possibility of any pursuit at all persuaded him to abandon his exploring and return to camp.

And with that turnabout, the barrier he had tried to build in his mind to separate himself from Kwetah collapsed utterly.

"Stupid! Stupid! Stupid!" He railed at himself. "What kind of man leaves a child alone in the forest? It won't have made it any easier to part from her."

Far from easy, he realized as he thought of comforting her in his arms that night.

After crossing the meadow and before joining the stream above, the path passed through deep woods. In its gloom, his anxiety for Kwetah began to rise to panic. His loping pace became a run. Even the sight of rivercourse brightness ahead gave him no ease. He was running still when the brush on either side of him burst into life. His anguished voice rasped, "Kwetah!" as he ran full into a thrown net.

A dozen men brought Aengus into their rough camp a half-mile downriver from where they had overwhelmed him. They threw him onto mossy ground against a large tree at the back of the clearing, then returned to the riverbank to discuss their prize. Their women and children, watchful and silent, stood near several brushy shelters at one side of the clearing. They were the same people he had surprised earlier, he assumed. But they could not have warned the men who caught him. The men must have seen him pass unawares before he came to the meadow, then followed.

The conferring men became argumentative. They returned to him under the tree.

"Who are you?" they demanded brusquely in Kwetah's language, just as they had when they first took him. "Why are you here?"

As before, Aengus said nothing. Best they believe he could not understand them. They might discuss their plans for him more freely then, and in his hearing.

Two of the men held him, still seated, against the tree. Others bound him to it. As he had done when they wrapped ropes around the net after they first seized him, he held his legs slightly apart and his arms a hand's thickness from his body. The men left him again.

Apparently the group had finished their tasks for the day, or had abandoned them because they found discussion of the significance of their captive more interesting. The women set about building up a great fire over the smoldering remains of an earlier one at the center of the clearing. The men gathered around it, arguing and gesticulating.

Aengus could imagine what they were saying. Undoubtedly they were still preoccupied with the same questions he had overheard as they brought him here: Was he human or spirit? Why were his colors so peculiar? His eye—what living thing had an eye like that? Nothing human, certainly. He was bigger than men. Why? Why? All their talk had been of him. He was unable to learn whether they were part of a larger band, where their main camp was, whether they were people of the river or people of the seashore, or how long they would be here.

Cocooned like an insect, he watched the men eat, then the women and children. Afterward, as daylight waned and the women and children retired to the shelters, the men lolled about the fire, their backs against logs drawn up to it. No food was brought for Aengus. No one approached him, although occasional glances were cast his way. He could not decide whether he had been left without close guard because the men were confident of their mastery or because no one wanted to stay near him without the others for support. The women, he was sure, watched him from their bowers.

He began to work at his bonds as soon as he believed that his small movements were masked by the deepening gloom. His captors had trussed him inexpertly. They had wound cords over those that already bound him. They had been afraid to remove the net before they tied him the first time even though he had not resisted their numbers once he realized they were not going to kill him on the spot. The many ropes they had passed round and round the net did more to reassure them than to secure him. They had inserted a line through the net to bind his wrists but, seeming loath to touch him, had made a poor job of it. The net was long and narrow, made for trapping fish rather than men, and much of its bulk only hindered their subsequent attempts to trammel him more thoroughly.

As he freed his hands then worked to loosen the edges of the net drawn together and tied beneath his feet, he thought furiously about his escape. A cloudy sky and no moon tonight. Dark. Even so, he would have to move slowly and cautiously until he was well along the path. He would have to detour through the woods to find it. Or hide in the woods until daylight. But that would gain him nothing but certain recapture. He must escape by dark, then, and make no noise greater than any other night sound.

His blood raced but he remained clear-headed. More clear-headed, he thought, than at any time since he had planned this foolish expedition. He was confident that, some way or another, he would elude his captors. His lifetime of desperate escapes and miraculous survivals was not to end on this wretched spot and among these benighted savages. He was certain of that.

But another thought began to intrude. If an escape by stealth was successful, he would leave behind one more band of people he must avoid thereafter. First Kwetah's people and now these river people. If he continued to surround his forest refuge with people he had run from, he could be trapped there forever, like a cage-broken animal that runs from the terrors of freedom back to its prison. Sometime he would have to deal with the people in this land. Despite their churlish treatment of him, this band did not seem murderous.

By the time he had released the bottom of the net and found that he could wriggle out like an eel from an egg, he had a new plan, a more daring plan, but one that might, in the end, ensure his escape from the cloistral forest and savage coast.

X

Aengus kept a watchful eye on the men, now full-bellied and drowsy. They were gazing into the flames as if hypnotized by the flickering fire wraiths there. He replaced and reknotted the ropes so it would seem that he had flowed through them like water, then he stood and calmly walked up to the fire.

One man saw him approach, then another, then several, their widened eyes alone betraying their astonishment. The last to be aware of him were the two he stopped between. He folded his arms across his chest and stared into the flames while he sorted through fragments of legends from other lands and allusions Kwetah had made to local myths. Then he spoke to them in their tongue:

"What manner of hosts are you? You have eaten well, but you forget the brother of the wolf and the eagle. You take food from the forest and the river, but you do not recognize the spirit that lets that food be taken. I have come among you as a man rather than a raging demon, and yet you have abused me. You have not welcomed me."

The men's mouths gaped. None of them moved. They seemed to have stopped breathing.

"Inhospitable people!" he continued. "Shall I tell my brother deer to leave this forest, to go to other lands for other men to hunt? Shall I tell the fish not to swim up this river any more? Shall I command my whales to swim to the other side of the ocean?"

Several logs in the dying fire suddenly fell together, and a grand shower of sparks flew into the blackness above. The men started. Lest any one of them initiate a general mad flight, Aengus raised his hand to quell the flickering gust and sustain his spell.

"I have come among men as a man. Now I hunger as men do. My body is weary, as the bodies of men become. I wish to rest easily—not bound to a tree."

His audience continued to sit dumfounded. Emboldened by the apparent success of his masquerade, Aengus's next words were spoken before he gave thought to any consequences beyond the one he hotly desired.

"Men have women to comfort them through the hours of darkness. You have young women to offer a guest, and I am a guest you have treated badly so far."

Slowly, his eye swept the awe-struck circle; he looked into each lurid mask of primitive terror.

Raising his voice to the bellow of a bull, he roared, "Your guest grows impatient!"

Some of the men leaped up, others scrambled away on hands and knees, and a few rolled backward into the darkness. They were gone in an instant. Aengus stood facing the fire, his back to their bustling activity. In the poor light, his ears told him more than his eye, but also he savored the moment: it pleased him to flaunt his sudden ascendance. His fear of these simple people who were so easily cowed evaporated into the forest gloom and river mist. And so, when he thought about it, did his misgivings about meeting Kwetah's people again.

A woman brought a bowl and set it an arm's length from him. When she retired, he sat and took the bowl into his lap, tipping it toward the firelight. There were pieces of fish in it and something vegetable, all cold and oily. He chewed slowly and found they satisfied his hunger. Behind him he heard sticks being broken, brushy branches and other things being moved, and voices urgently muttering.

Then silence. He stood to see what they had provided for

him. It was an arbor much like their own shelters, but apart from them, near the tree to which he had been tied. The people stood in two clusters, one on either side of the new structure. When he had come close enough to see their expressions—very close, in the darkness away from the fire—he saw that they were those of anxious children hoping that they had done better than was expected of them.

"*Hoshyok,*" he told them. It was the word Kwetah used to express thanks and pleasure. "*Hoshyok,*" he repeated and motioned them toward their own shelters. The men retreated uncertainly, the women with a few smiles of satisfaction among themselves, and the curious children most reluctantly of all.

Aengus crouched to pass through the low opening, then lowered himself to his hands and knees while his eye adapted to the blackness within. He felt the edges of mats and crawled forward, then stopped with one hand hovering. He heard breathing—but from where? From which side?

Slowly, dimly, he made out *two* figures, one on either side of a center space left for him. Two women laying on their backs with their arms held tightly to their sides and their eyes fixed on the brushwork above them. They lay as soldiers would stand before an emperor. They had removed their only clothing, their fiber skirts, but then modestly used them to cover themselves.

Two of them! Both frightened out of their wits. To laugh would have been unfortunate. With difficulty, Aengus stifled his impulse to do so. But then he hardly knew what to do next.

Whimsically, he removed his tunic and trousers, lay down between the two women, arranged the garments over himself as they had done with theirs, and adopted their posture. Moments later a giggle, unstoppable, shook him. Both heads rolled toward him, then quickly rolled back again as he turned each way to look at them. He examined the profile of each one. They were very young—

they may have been the same two whose smiles in the meadow had put into his head the ardent notion that was responsible for their being there.

Concluding finally that to spend the rest of the night at that impasse made no sense at all, he considered the charms of each girl and decided on the one he judged to be the younger. At the moment of his decision, the older one slipped her hand into his and moved closer, still staring at the zenith. He never knew whether that initiative was intended to protect the innocence of the younger girl or to claim the elder's first rights. Perhaps it was merely to let him know that she was experienced in such matters.

His satisfaction with her was immense and immediate; hers must have been very little. Probably her experience told her to expect nothing else, for she abruptly turned her back on him and fell asleep.

The younger one had watched the whole performance with wide-eyed amazement and intense curiosity.

"Have you killed her?" she whispered.

"No. She's just asleep."

"What did you do to her?"

"I'll show you, but not right now. Is she your sister?"

"Yes."

Leaning on his elbows, he drew her closer.

"Where is your village? How many people live there?"

She answered those and his other questions readily and volunteered more than he asked. She seemed pleased to show off what she knew, although she could tell him little of the territory beyond the vicinity of her own village at the river's mouth and the few miles between there and this river camp. She did not know what lay at any great distance to the east along the strait. They talked at length, until he found himself becoming more interested in the girl than in her stories.

He was unhurried this time. She responded shyly at first, then warmly.

He slept awhile then with her in his arms.

*   *   *

"I saw you untie those knots then tie them up again," the younger sister confided to him later that night.

"You have sharp eyes. Who else saw?"

"My sister and a few others. We thought it was clever when you frightened the men."

"Do you like to play jokes on the men?"

"Sometimes we do, but we never let the men find out. We keep our jokes to ourselves or the men become angry. Mostly we give them names. We call one 'Skinny-Legs' and another 'Barks-Like-A-Seal.' One time we told Skinny-Legs that the wife of our chief's son loved him and wanted to run away with him. The chief's son is a very strong man. Skinny-Legs was beaten several times before he gave up trying to see her alone."

Her rapid, whispered chatter taxed his understanding of her language, but it delighted him nonetheless.

"Do the men not like jokes?" he asked when she paused for breath.

"Oh, they play many tricks on each other and laugh a lot, but that's with men. They don't like women to play tricks, although they tease us all the time. I think it's unfair that men and women should be so different." She paused and gave him a sly glance. "At least, I *did* think it was unfair. . . ."

He caught her up then, and conversation ceased for another while.

Still later, she asked him, "How long will you stay with us?"

"I'll leave in the morning."

"Won't you stay until Pugahlkuthl arrives?"

"Who is Pugahlkuthl?"

"He's a great magician of our village. He lives in a house with heads outside."

"What do you mean by 'heads outside'?"

"Heads of people. His enemies. They're stuck on sticks that he has fastened to the front of his house. They're very old heads because *he's* old and doesn't go on raids any more."

"Who were his enemies?"

89

"Other warriors, he says, that he killed on raids. *He* says that. My father went on a raid with him once, and all they did was sneak up on a fisherman fishing alone. They killed him and brought his head back."

"I think you don't like Pugahlkuthl very much."

She thought before making a careful answer.

"He's a powerful magician. He has killed people in our village by magic."

"Why is he coming to this camp?"

"Because he was sent for after you frightened our men. He understands the secrets of spirits. He'll know whether you mean us harm or not."

"I don't intend to harm any of you; but I'll not wait for Pugahlkuthl. I must return to my world."

With that, he fell asleep—a deep and careless sleep.

Pugahlkuthl must have sensed that Aengus represented a danger to his authority. He traveled during the night and arrived at the camp before daybreak.

In the twilight of dawn, Aengus was awakened by four men who pounced on him, pinning his limbs. Two others, crouched against the wall, held lances as if to pierce him where he lay. Except for his first startled reaction, he did not struggle, but tensed his muscles to pull one of the men onto him if the others were to use their lances.

The girls were gone. Pugahlkuthl stood just outside the entrance. Aengus knew him immediately by his trappings. He wore a long cloak decorated with a profusion of feathers, shells, animal teeth, and tufts of fur. Strings of long, thin shells hung from his neck. Bracelets of the same shells wrapped his wrists and ankles. He wore an immense wooden hat carved in the shape of a fantastic and monstrous bird's head. His own forbidding face looked out from under its massive projecting beak. He was older than Aengus, although not as old as the girl had implied. He appeared virile and strong, not frail with age.

Pugahlkuthl peered through the low entrance but did not come into the crowded interior. He commanded others still outside to find ropes and stakes, then resumed his glowering scrutiny of Aengus, an inspection that was hindered by the dimness within the shelter and the press of bodies between them.

Aengus considered making a sudden, fierce resistance, catching the men off guard perhaps, then escaping into the forest. He weighed his chances of success in that action against continuing his mystical pretense and saw less risk in the latter. Raising his head to look past his restrainers, he roared, "I've found you at last, you mocker of spirits!"

The shaman's eyes opened wide.

"You fool who claims to know the rituals, but knows nothing!" Aengus continued. "You killer of innocents! You have disgraced your people, and I have come for you. The longer you hold my man's body captive, the longer you mistreat me, that much more terrible will be the torture of your ghost. You will burn and burn forever. When I escape this body and leave this land, I'll take the animals of the forest and the fish of the rivers and sea with me. Your people will starve."

Those holding Aengus looked uncertainly toward their savage priest. He was not deceived at all, Aengus knew, but he would be blamed for every misfortune henceforth if he had Aengus killed on the spot.

"I will show that you are no spirit," Pugahlkuthl said with sour malevolence, "and then I will kill you myself."

Men had returned with four stout stakes the thickness of their arms. Mats were moved and the stakes were pounded deep into the ground around Aengus while six men held him down. Whatever uncertainty the men may have felt in their hearts, they found courage in their work; they made a thoroughly good job of fastening his ankles and wrists to the stakes. Stubs of branches had been left when the stakes were cut, and those stubs, angled upward, became barbs that prevented the stakes from being easily uprooted. The stones they used as hammers had smashed the tops of the stakes into flat heads so that the bindings could not be slipped up and off. Such confidence had the men in the fetters they had made that no guard stayed behind when they left with Pugahlkuthl.

Aengus could do nothing with his outstretched arms

and very little at first with his legs. Using his bound wrists to anchor his body, he pushed and pulled against the stakes that held his ankles. He worked with silent intensity until his wrists and ankles bled. He did not stop even then. He worked through pain until he felt the stakes move in the ground.

He paid little attention to sounds from outside other than to keep alert for footsteps nearby. The crackle of flames as the night fire was rekindled for morning made even that vigilance futile. The entrance to his shelter—his prison—faced neither the fire nor the other huts. He could not see what the people or their shaman were doing.

"An hour!" he thought. "If my pretense has bought me an hour, I'll be gone and a spirit no more."

Both stakes at his feet began to shift in the earth, one more freely than the other. He concentrated his efforts on that one, rocking it back and forth as he strained upward with his leg. At last it came up, scattering loose earth onto him, but he was exhausted for the moment and the muscles of his freed leg were cramped and aching.

He found that he could slide the loose stake under the ropes that bound his other ankle and use it as a lever. It was tied to his foot with enough length of rope between that he could twist his foot underneath its end to push.

He had worked the second stake almost loose enough to pull out when a yelp of pain drew his attention to what was happening outside. Squandering a precious minute to listen, he heard the shaman haranguing his people, but could not make out his argument. He seemed to be goading the others against Aengus, but to what action Aengus could not tell.

The second stake came loose, but he soon found he was little closer to release. He could exert no effective force against the stakes that held his arms outstretched. He could not maneuver the stakes still fastened to his ankles to force them under the bindings at his wrists. He tried to swing his legs over his head so that he would fall over face down and possibly improve his advantage, but he only managed to wrench his neck.

Listening again, he heard Pugahlkuthl still speaking. Aengus's heart plummeted when he realized the import of the priest's words. To prove that Aengus had no miraculous powers to save them, the man was demanding that the two girls who had been with him be slain. Aengus understood now that the lengthy tirade that was giving him the time he hoped for was also persuading the reluctant people to agree to Pugahlkuthl's cruel test.

Three lives now! Not only the child in the forest, but these innocent sisters depended on his escape for their lives. He lunged left and right. His hands became slippery with blood.

XI

"Ssst!"

Aengus lifted his chin to look behind him, then left and right. He saw no one.

"Ssst!" again. "I'm outside. Can you help my sisters?"

"The ones Pugahlkuthl would kill? Yes! Yes!" Aengus whispered urgently. "Bring a knife—or a heavy stick to pry me loose."

A moment later, a crawling youth forced his way through the wall of the shelter from the forest side. He pulled a stout branch after him, one that had lain against the base of the shelter.

"They would see me if I went for a knife," he explained.

"There, under the rope there . . . Pry up," Aengus instructed him.

The branch was flexible and not stripped of twigs and needles. It was almost too long to manipulate within the hut. Aengus twisted his leg up to plant his foot against the stake, but he could only touch it. He could not apply any force to rock it in its earthy socket.

From outside, they heard Pugahlkuthl's hoarse shout: "Come out, you false spirit! Save these women if you have the power. Show us your magic, you deceiver. You pretend to be a demon, but you are no more than a mouse. You have the blood of worms in you, and I will spill it back into the earth!"

The frantic boy lunged upward with his shoulder under

the branch. Aengus felt that his hand would be torn from his wrist. Suddenly the branch snapped with a loud report. The end of it struck the roof and the whole structure wobbled. But the stake was loose.

"Pull it up! Pull it up!" Aengus whispered, desperately ignoring his agony.

The stake was almost out of its hole when Aengus pulled sharply, snatching it from the boy's hands and from the earth, and rolled to grasp the one remaining. Seated, he pushed and pulled it with his hands and feet while the boy tugged upward on it.

The breaking of the branch and movement of the hut had silenced the priest for a moment, but he must have decided that Aengus's frenzied thrashing would be ineffectual except to make his own power seem greater by comparison.

"Your strength is nothing!" the shaman cried. "Come out! Come out! Save these women who lie with slaves, if you can!"

"Why doesn't your father stop him?" Aengus muttered vehemently.

"No father . . . just us," the boy gasped between heaves.

The two girls were huddled together on the ground before Pugahlkuthl when Aengus burst through the side of the shelter. The older one's hair was wound up in the priest's fist; his knife was raised over her. Aengus stood across the clearing from them, his naked, white body smeared with his blood and spattered with dirt. The four stakes hung from his wrists and ankles. Whatever image of awe and horror the priest had tried to evoke in his people, it paled before this huge new ghastly, bloody, earthy apparition.

In silence, dragging the stakes, Aengus walked deliberately toward Pugahlkuthl. The shaman's fist slowly relaxed and the girl's hair unwound and fell from his fingers. A fury grew within him. A lifetime of carefully nurtured witchery and guile, hoax and intimidation, was crumbling before this upstart menace. With a shriek, he threw himself at Aengus.

Aengus grasped the end of one of the stakes with both hands, drove it fiercely into the priest's crotch, and twisted aside to avoid the sweep of his knife. Pugahlkuthl doubled over. His wooden helmet tumbled to the ground. Aengus clenched the ends of both stakes with his hands and raised them over his head. As the shaman straightened to renew his attack, Aengus brought the double bludgeon down with all his strength. Pugahlkuthl's skull collapsed. He fell toward Aengus, who pushed against the priest's chest and sent him spinning onto the fire. There, he fell face down over the blazing logs. His body quivered; his arms and legs straightened then fell as if to embrace the pyre. The edges of his magnificent robe curled into flame.

Aengus sat where Pugahlkuthl's knife had fallen and used its sharp antler blade to saw through the ropes that bound the stakes to his mangled wrists and ankles. Then he went to the cold river and washed away blood, dirt, pain, and anger.

When he returned to the fire, the people sat or stood around it still, their terror-filled eyes fastened on him. The two girls were gone, perhaps to join their brother, whom Aengus had instructed to leave the shelter the way he had come without being seen. Aengus looked around for his clothing and saw a man hiding behind the others, taking off a pair of trousers. Aengus pointed to the man, then held out his hand. Shamefaced and afraid, the man brought them to him.

"I came for Pugahlkuthl," Aengus said. "I will not harm any of you. Return those things that are mine."

Two men went to their huts and brought back his tunic and buskins. He took them, then pointed to the priest's body, now burning with a disgusting odor.

"Do with him what you will," he said. "I have his ghost. His body is nothing. Hereafter, choose your magicians more wisely. Choose those whose magic serves you rather than enslaves you."

With that, he turned and strode out of the camp, back along the trail that had brought him there.

*　　　*　　　*

As soon as he was far enough from the river camp that he could not be seen or heard, he broke into a run, driven by a rising dread that he had left Kwetah alone too long. The effort soon made his ankles and wrists bleed afresh. He chilled them again in the river, then continued at a lope as fast as he could sustain.

On a chart, his track out from his forest home would make two sides of a rectangle, but he did not dare to attempt the diagonal returning. He could have become lost too easily and he did not know what obstacles lay that way. If he did not stop to rest or eat, he estimated that he would be back with Kwetah by nightfall or shortly after — within the three days that he had promised.

He snatched berries from bushes as he passed. He reached the bald hill and crossed over its shoulder, then came at last to the place of turning westward. The sun stood almost at noon.

The turning point was higher than the camp where Kwetah waited, but the ground between was so much up-and-down that, coming or going, it made little difference. Blazes he had made on trees and other clues that he had left were all that kept him from becoming lost. Even so, he had several anxious times when he seemed to be somewhere he had not seen before. He would turn around then, to see the place from the same aspect as on the first day, going out. Once, even that tactic did not help, and he became convinced that he was following the wrong stream. He crossed the stream to climb a rise that he hoped might give him some better view, when, miraculously, he put his hand on a blazed tree. His first reaction was that it was someone else's mark. Approached from the stream, the place did not seem familiar at all. Finally accepting that it must be his own sign, he turned downstream again and, to his relief, soon found other clues to confirm that he was headed aright.

Tired, hungry, bleeding, and impatient, he began to stumble and fell several times. Remembering stretches of slippery boulders ahead of him, he had wit enough, when he spotted a straight, stout pole lying where spring freshets had left it, to pick it up to use as a staff.

Daylight was fading when he came into familiar home territory. When he was close enough, he called out, "Kwetah, I'm back!"

There was no answer, so he called again. Hearing nothing, he ran headlong down the main stream and up the path leading to the ledge. Just as he spotted smoke from the campfire, he heard Kwetah call in her thin child's voice, "Be careful, Akwahti. Come slowly."

He stopped to listen, then cautiously climbed the last, steep part of the path. Looking over the rim of the ledge, he felt his heart stop, then pound furiously. Kwetah stood by the fire, leaning on her crutch and holding his knife in one hand and a flaming brand in the other. Facing her was a great, tawny panther, a beast he had not known to inhabit that forest. It had heard his approach and was watching him as he came into its view, its tail twitching with feline tension.

"Keep still, Kwetah," he whispered. "Let it come to me."

He dared neither to come up onto the ledge to face the beast openly nor to withdraw and leave Kwetah alone with the animal again. He wanted his knife, but, if she were to throw it to him, her sudden movement might provoke the great cat to leap onto her. His only weapon was the staff he still carried. Rocks and gravel had worn its end to a smooth, dull point. It was a poor lance, but nothing better lay within reach.

He began to make mewling noises, such as a small animal in distress might make. The panther had seen no more than his head, and had never before seen such a head as that: pale, with hair and beard matching its own tawny coat. Aengus hoped to convince it that he was some small prey. With little squeaks and small stirrings of the brush, he deflected its interest from Kwetah and drew the animal toward him. It crept and paused, crept and paused, its tail twitching more nervously as its excitement grew. Finally, when it was no more than twice its length from him, he ducked down out of its sight but continued to make the noises that attracted it.

The cat's rush was so silent that he almost missed it. It came over the edge with its paws close together as if to pounce on a rabbit. He shoved the lance upward between the paws, driving it against the panther's neck as he rolled to the side. The falling animal pushed the base of the lance into the earth and the blunt point into its throat. It hung suspended for an instant. Aengus leaped onto the ledge and turned to face the wounded animal, but it was badly hurt and wanted no more of him. It scrambled down the trail, the spear still caught in its neck and striking bushes as it ran, direly aggravating its injury.

He rushed over to Kwetah, who dropped the brand and knife and fell into his arms as he crouched down before her. She grabbed the neck of his tunic and twisted it into her fists as she buried her head under his chin. She trembled but did not cry. Nor would she let go, so he sat down and held her for a long while until she began to relax.

"Were you frightened, Kwetah?"

"No. I knew you would come back." She paused. "Yes. I was terribly afraid. I thought you had left me."

With that admission, the tears came and her small body shook with sobs as he caressed her and spoke softly.

That night and several thereafter, she slept in his arms, occasionally clutching him tightly when she was beset by nightmares.

XII

Kwetah's eyes followed Aengus warily whenever he approached the perimeter of their campsite. One morning when she was sleeping late, he went down the path to the stream to inspect a fish trap he had constructed there. He had seen fish in pools in the stream, but none had ever strayed into his trap, nor were there any there that morning. While he was pulling up stakes and resetting them to change the angle of the fences that led to the pen, he looked up and through the trees to see Kwetah peering over the edge of their camp ledge. Her eyes were averted at that moment, and she did not see his glance. She stayed there the whole time he remade the trap, but when he started back up the path again, he saw that she was gone.

She was back in her bed when he came onto the ledge, and she did not come out until he had a fire built and called her.

They ate slowly to stretch out their small morning meal. Kwetah's eyes darted again and again to Aengus's face.

Finally, to ease her nervous tenseness, he said, "I've been trying to catch a fish. You must be hungry for fish."

"I like fish, but I like what we eat here too."

"I thought you were hoping there would be a fish in my trap this morning."

Kwetah looked at him sharply, then lowered her eyes. After a moment, she said, "Did you see me watching you?"

Aengus almost said, "No," to avoid embarrassing her

further, but thought better of it. He had given himself away, and Kwetah would know that he was being untruthful.

"Yes. Were you playing 'peek-chick' with me?"

Kwetah shook her head, but said nothing.

"Kwetah, you don't need to be afraid that I'll leave you. I'll never leave you alone again. Not as long as we stay in the forest here, except when I have to get things for us to eat—nothing more than that."

"What if something happens to you when you're away?"

"Nothing will," he said.

But the next morning, he took her with him to the marshy pool rather than leave her in their camp alone while he gathered roots and bulbs. Regretfully, he considered the effect of his three-day absence. Far from inuring her to separation from him, it had made his eventual departure from her country only more difficult for both of them.

At the marsh, he lifted her onto the horizontal trunk of a fallen tree where the sun would warm her and she could watch him wherever he moved around the pond.

"There," she said, pointing over his shoulder as he settled her against a fan of upthrust roots.

"What?"

"Chowk-chebat. *Wi* chowk-chebat. Over there."

"Chowk-chebat?"

"Yes. A few days ago I told you."

Chowk-chebat! Little water mats.

"Yes. I remember now. I'll get some."

When she had first told him about chowk-chebat, he thought she was describing the mats of algae that collect on ponds in summer, but when she had told him that a poultice of the roots of chowk-chebat might ease the ache and soreness of her leg, he was confused, for the green mats he was familiar with certainly had no roots. Now he saw that she had been describing ordinary water lilies.

He worked his way slowly around the marshy edge of the pond, feeling with his toes for the firm cattail roots he

101

and Kwetah liked to nibble on whenever sudden hungriness struck them between meals. When he came at last to where the water lilies grew, he set his bowl-shaped basket, now partly filled, in an open space between shoreline bushes and waded into the deep water just beyond the reeds.

A few pulls showed him that he would have to dig for the roots because the long stems broke easily. A giggle from Kwetah, across the pond, made him glance up. He smiled, as much to himself as to her because he was pleased that the sun seemed to be warming her spirits as well as her small body.

The water was so deep along that side of the pool that his face was submerged when he leaned over to claw through the mud for the roots. Gasping for breath between, he pulled up one and then another. He held those against his chest with one hand and was reaching for another when Kwetah's chuckling stopped him. He stood up and she broke out in full-throated laughter. With her finger pointing toward him, she tried to speak but could not for laughing.

A grunt behind him told him that his struggles with the lily roots were not the reason for the girl's amusement. He turned to see a huge bear standing on its hind legs in the space where he had left the basket. Its forelegs were hanging as he turned, but its curiosity quickly gave way to crankiness, and it raised its great paws toward him.

With a shout, Aengus dropped the roots and threw water toward the animal with cupped hands. That sudden, frantic effort unbalanced him and he fell backwards. Just as the water closed over him, he heard Kwetah's shriek.

Kicking to free his entangled legs, he thought, "What a stupid way to die—eaten by a bear!" It was the very death his mother had threatened for him when he was half Kwetah's age and had wandered too far into the woods near his home. It was his earliest memory. The water around him grew dark as he stirred up mud—or as it was shadowed by something looming above. He rolled over and thrashed furiously, propelling himself toward the center of the pool.

With his legs finally clear and his lungs aching for air, he stood up in water only thigh deep. The bear was gone. He saw two black shapes—her cubs—scrambling and tumbling through shrubs and reeds along the side of the pool as they rushed to follow their snorting mother into the forest.

He turned toward Kwetah. Her place on the fallen tree was empty! The bear could not possibly have gotten to her and then back around the pool again during his brief submergence, but fear gripped him nonetheless. He splashed across the pool, through the reeds, and ran up the slope to the tree.

Kwetah had tumbled backwards from her perch and lay almost hidden in shrubbery. On his knees under the trunk, he found her motionless with her eyes closed and her face wet with tears. His concern vanished when he realized that her immobility and her tears were both from laughing. She opened her eyes and another fit of giggles shook her body.

"Kwetah!" Aengus said crossly. "That bear could have killed me. It wasn't funny."

"Oh, Akwahti . . ." she began, then struggled to suppress her mirth when she saw his vexation.

"Are you all right?" he asked curtly.

"Yes."

She fought to escape her leafy constraints, but finally Aengus had to pluck her up and hold her tightly to his chest with one hand as he crawled out from under the tree. He set her on top of the trunk again, then stepped back and looked at her seriously while he considered what he should say to her. Kwetah gazed meekly into her lap except for a few flickering glances up at him.

And then, after several moments of awkward silence, she giggled again. She choked it back and strove valiantly to recover her demure composure. But it was no use. Another giggle surfaced.

"Oh, Kwetah," Aengus said, shaking his head.

"Akwahti, you put the basket right under her nose and you didn't see her. She thought you had set it there for her. She ate everything—snooff, snooff, snooff—and then she stood up to see if you were getting some more for her. It was funny . . . it was funny. . . ."

"Not to me," Aengus said.

Rubbing her eyes, Kwetah replied between fits of laughter, "It *was* funny, Akwahti. When you splashed her and fell down, she was so surprised that she turned around and ran away."

"Bears are dangerous, Kwetah. You should have warned me."

"She wouldn't have hurt us. I was watching her children for her."

"You were—*What* were you doing?"

"Watching her children. She was behind those bushes all the time. When her children started to come around the pool toward me, she asked me to stop them if they wandered too far."

"She spoke to you?"

"Well, no . . . but she looked at me, and I knew what she wanted."

Aengus regarded her with some astonishment, then shook his head again and went to retrieve his basket.

That evening, as they sat by their fire watching for the first star to appear, Kwetah mentioned again their encounter with the bear, but Aengus did not respond. He wanted to make her understand the risk of being too familiar with bears without frightening her, and he did not know how to go about it. She took his silence to mean that the incident still rankled, and fell quiet herself.

After a while, she shifted to close the space between them and leaned against his arm. He wrapped that arm around her and said, "I guess it *was* funny to watch."

To himself, he thought, "And maybe she *does* know bears better than I do. Maybe the old lady *did* ask her to keep an eye on her cubs."

Kwetah reached her own arm halfway around his broad back in a conciliatory hug.

"Do you know any stories about animals?" she asked. "Stories with good endings. Not hunting stories where the animal is killed."

"Oh. Well . . ." he said, his mind searching furiously. Then he remembered the large deer that had frightened her, and an incident in Serica came to mind.

"There was a place I visited one time. It was called Luh, and it was near the mouth of a river called Ou."

"Those are very short names. Was it a small place and a small river?"

"No. Very large. Luh was a huge village with thousands of people in it and wide trails among its buildings to go from one part to another. And the Ou was a river so wide . . . so wide . . . You know how far it is from here to the bear pool? That's how wide the Ou is."

"Is this a power story?" Kwetah asked, suddenly suspicious.

"A power story?"

"The kind that people tell about how they get a power or a name or a special gift from the spirits. Those stories always have things in them that other people have never seen. Sometimes I think they're not true."

"No, this isn't a power story. And it *is* true. There really is such a place, and I was there. Well, then, *Luh* means deer—not the little bo-kwitch kind—it means the big kind that we saw down there with her baby. I don't know what *Ou* means."

"Why did they name the place after a deer?"

"Well, that's part of the story. A long time ago, when it was a smaller place with a different name, a white deer—a stag—wandered into that big village with a cluster of blossoms in its mouth. The blossoms were from a tree that doesn't grow here, called 'plum.' Now, the people of that place thought the white deer was an omen of good fortune, and plum blossoms mean good fortune too. So, when the deer came there carrying the flowers in his mouth, why, the people thought that was the best sign they could possibly have. Good things would happen to them."

"This sounds like a power story to me," Kwetah interjected skeptically.

"No, it isn't. Well . . . maybe if I had lived in that place and was telling you about the stag, I would think it was a power story. But it's not."

"Is that the end of the story?"

"Oh no, no. That's only the first part. Well, the people named their big village 'Luh' because of the white stag. And when I visited there, a long time after the stag came—"

"Was the stag still there?"

"No. I don't know what happened to the stag. Probably it came and went on the same day. Back to the forest. That was a very long time ago. I don't think anybody knows now what happened to the stag."

He looked at Kwetah to see if she was ready to let him tell his story his way. She gave no sign that her store of questions was exhausted, but her eyes glowed with pleasure.

"So . . . I visited that place. My friend Hsin and I came there to trade things we made in our village for things the people of Luh made."

Kwetah opened her mouth to ask another question, but Aengus's pleading glance quieted her.

"When we arrived, the people were preparing for a ceremony. Something like the ones you've told me about, but not inside their lodges. This was to be outside on the wide paths between their houses. It was in the springtime, a spring celebration when the plum trees were in blossom. The people were decorating carts"—here Aengus reached for the tiny toy cart he had made several weeks earlier for a fascinated Kwetah, who had never known of wheeled conveyances before—"carts something like this, but large enough to carry people. And they were making costumes for people to wear.

"Luh was so big by then that people in one part didn't know people in other parts very well. People in one part would think of their own part as if it were a separate

106

village that had been built up against other villages. Each part was like a separate village in the people's minds, even though, to a visitor, all the houses looked like one huge village. So the people in each part were decorating their carts and making costumes for their people, and trying to make their carts and people more grand and colorful than those from the other parts of Luh. The next day, all the people in costumes and all the decorated carts were to walk or be pulled along the paths, and the people who were not in that procession were to watch from either side."

He paused to see if Kwetah understood Luh's spring festival and the parade through the city's crowded streets. Whether the picture his words and her imagination conjured up was accurate or not, it certainly delighted her. Her eyes danced and she nodded for him to continue.

"So, when Hsin and I came there, the people in one part of Luh saw me. They saw that I was taller than they were, and that my skin was lighter than theirs and my hair and beard were yellow. My beard was short then. They grabbed me so eagerly, I thought I was being attacked. But they only wanted me to be in their part of the procession. They wanted to dress me up like the white stag. Did I tell you that the ceremony was to honor the stag? Well, it was. Each part of Luh would decorate a cart or a person or a group of people to look like the stag. Those pretend stags were the main part of the ceremony, the most important things in the procession.

"So, the people in that part of the great village of Luh where Hsin and I first came asked me to be their stag for the procession. I was honored to be asked and said yes.

"They made a costume for me out of that light fabric I showed you in my bag there, all in bright colors—strips of bright colors sewn together—and one of the men made a set of antlers from wood to put on my head."

Kwetah had shifted so that she was on the ground in front of Aengus with her hands crossed on his knee and her chin resting on them. She chuckled at the image of an antlered Aengus.

"The next day, the people dressed me and tied the

107

antlers onto my head with a cord that went under my chin. They tucked plum blossoms into my beard and held them in place with little drops of something sticky, like pitch. Then they made a long strip of that same light fabric—like a long cord—and fastened more flowers along its length. They tied the center of the flowered strip around my middle, and six little boys and girls held the ends and led me along the path.''

When Aengus paused as the memories of that long-ago spring day came flooding back, Kwetah prompted him to continue. "And was your stag the best? Better than what people from the other parts made?"

"No. The best one—the one that most pleased the people watching the procession—was made very differently." He picked up the toy cart again. "The people who made that one used a cart like this, except that it had only two wheels, at the front. Instead of wheels at the back, it had handles sticking backward like this. A man would stand between the handles and lift the back end off the ground. Then he would push the cart wherever he wanted it to go. But this cart I'm telling you about was so heavy that *two* men had to stand between the handles, one behind the other, to make it go.

"On the cart, the people built a stag of sticks and fabric, a stag with a big head—it was *mostly* head—big enough for a man to sit inside. He had a smoldering fire in a pot that made lots of sweet-smelling smoke. The smoke came out of the eyes and ears and mouth of the stag. And he could open and close the stag's mouth from inside. The men behind would push the cart from one side of the wide path to the other. When they came up to the people watching, the two men would lift up on the handles to make it seem that the stag was lowering its head to charge. The man inside would open its mouth and blow out a cloud of smoke. The people who watched would shriek with delight and move back as if they were frightened. It was very exciting."

"I've seen a head like that," Kwetah remarked. "A

magician wore it over his own head. It was made like a huge raven. And he could open and close its beak with cords. He rushed at us the same way too, but there was no smoke coming out."

"A magician from your village?"

"I don't know. Sierka told me how it worked, but he didn't say who wore it and I didn't recognize him. . . . Then what happened? In your story. What happened next?"

"That's all. That's the end of it," he said, and lifted her onto his lap with her back against him so her attention would be drawn by the fire. But Kwetah had seen the shadow come to his face and would not press him for more than he wanted to tell.

Aengus's thoughts clung to that day in faraway Luh that had started out with such gaiety. He had been too far back in the parade to see clearly the great silken stag on the handcart, but he had seen it when the parade assembled and had admired its clever construction.

From his place in the parade, he heard the excited shouts ahead and caught glimpses of the spectators pushing back against the buildings. Wisps of incense drifted back to him. For his part, he shuffled along, taking care not to break the children's ribbons and repeatedly pushing his crown of antlers upright because it kept sliding to the side of his head. The spectators fell silent as he passed. It was his first visit to Luh, and they had never seen anyone of his race before. They did not know what to make of him. People from the part of town that had sponsored the silken stag on the cart began to laugh and jeer, some good-naturedly at first, but others mockingly. Still others, those who confined their participation in the festivities to scornful staring and getting drunk, took up the ridicule. They began to deride Aengus's appearance as something ugly and freakish. Hsin, walking along behind the spectators to keep up with Aengus, finally could take no more. He pushed through the crowd, grabbed Aengus by the arm, and threw the antler crown to the ground. Then he pulled him away, leaving the six children in stunned and tearful dismay. Aengus refused to return to Luh for several years after that.

Kwetah, too, had been turning Aengus's story over in her mind. With her head against his chest and her eyes fixed on the flames, she said softly, "Akwahti."

"Mmm?"

"That's how any story can be made to have a good ending, isn't it?"

"How is that?"

"By not going past the happy part."

Aengus rested his chin on Kwetah's head, his own eye watching the flames, and considered that if he were ever to tell someone the story of Aengus and Kwetah, he would have to remember to stop it there, by the fire, to give it the happiest ending.

would have trouble getting here . . . but we could meet her partway."

"You have it all planned out, haven't you, little one?"

"Yes, yes. We could build a winter house right here. Mahkalt and Sierka would help us. There's time before winter. We have everything we need. There's lots to eat. You know how to make warm clothing. . . . Can we stay here, Akwahti?"

Baffled by her proposal, but enticed also, Aengus could only say, "We'll talk about it some more, Kwetah. Not now. I'll have to think about it—at least as much as you have."

Kwetah was wise enough not to press for a decision.

That afternoon, Aengus wandered out to a rocky hillside a quarter-mile from camp. Trees were sparse there, but one of them was a great, sprawling oak—the only oak he had seen in that land. He had climbed into its branches once to see if he could look out to the ocean, but it commanded only a bowl-shaped valley. From its upper branches, though, the world below was shut off.

During his first visit there, he had settled into a comfortable fork and watched a parade of cumuli drift in from Serica, just as *he* had done. He wondered if they might have come all the way from Europe, and then he wondered if they would pass over Europe a second time; if not the clouds, then the great sky currents that bore them.

This day, the sky was blue everywhere, a cerulean emptiness that drew his mind away and away, far beyond the world if he relaxed his concentration and let his thoughts escape. The tree was a place to ponder the whole of things.

Aengus pondered many things there, but he found the whole difficult to grasp. If he looked for reasons to stay in this Eden as Kwetah wished, he could invent more than enough to convince himself. Until, that is, he sought reasons against and found as many.

Be it said in his favor that his thoughts were more for Kwetah, with her life ahead of her, than for himself, his own life half-spent. He freely admitted to himself now that he loved the child too much to abandon her to an uncertain fate in her village. He would stay with her here in their forest home, or take her with him as he searched for Armorica, or stay in her village as her champion until her safety and happiness there were secure. But which would be best for her?

His uneasiness about her father was tempered by his perception that the chief seemed to command his people no more absolutely than had Pugahlkuthl. He had no disciplined army to rally against Aengus. A confrontation would be one man against the other, nothing more, and Aengus was confident now in his strength and sagacity.

He was more troubled by changes in Kwetah that he was responsible for and that must eventually estrange her from her own people. Already her speech would set her apart from them. One day she had recited for him all the names she knew for the wind: there were words for winds of the morning and winds of the evening, winds that ruffled the surface of the water, winds that turned over the tops of waves to make foamy crests, winds toward the shore, winds away from the shore, winds along the shore from the north, and from the south, dry winds, rainy winds, and others; words wonderfully evocative, and yet words that rendered talk of the wind precise and economical. In the forest, those seacoast distinctions mattered less. He tended to use a single word for any wind—*wakosy*—and Kwetah, her mind more malleable than his, had come to follow his usage. If she did not learn again to use her more extensive vocabulary, her thinking would reflect her verbal impoverishment, and her people would consider her stupid.

On the other hand, his own language had ways to indicate the time of any action, which Kwetah's seemed to lack except to specify the time with more words. Nor was that a childish imperfection in her speech, for the young sister of the river people had spoken with the same deficiency. With Kwetah, he had begun to add his own variations to the words of her language to place action in the past, or the distant past, or now, or after now, and their speech, in that and other ways, had become a private language between them, something that would be incomprehensible to her own people. Kwetah had even adopted his flawed pronunciation of her words, she omitted now the clucking terminal flourishes that he had found difficult for fluent speech.

He tried to imagine her as a village girl again but could not picture her in that barbaric setting. She had become a different child.

And yet . . . only scant months with him had been enough to bring about those changes. Why should not the same time or less restore her village speech and ways?

"And that's the whole of it!" came his sudden admission. "I just don't *want* to give her up. There must be a time for fatherhood in men's lives, and it's upon me mightily now, so I concoct reason upon reason to hold on to her.

"If I were to take her back to her mother and then continue my home-quest, I'd pass from her mind like a dream."

He recalled Father Turfu's metaphor for the easy learnings of children: "Mere scratches in sand," he had said, "that any new tide in their lives will erase. Hold back those tides for long, though, and all hardens like the sand of Puteoli."

"She belongs with her own people," Aengus decided. "I should do no more than try to ensure her safety there. And if that can't be done, then I might have reason to keep her, to take her with me while I wander more, or even to return here. But the longer we stay here now, the more difficult it becomes to end it."

A small maple of sinuous habit brightened the autumn gloom of the forest in Kwetah's country. Along streams and in open spaces where winds had toppled giant trees, its brilliant reds and yellows made fall the brightest time of the year; the flowers of spring and summer bloomed shyly and singly, there being no open fields among the hills for them to congregate. A cluster of the maples below their camp glowed in cheerful splendor as they prepared to leave.

114

Kwetah had accepted Aengus's decision without argument, as if she knew that a child's pleas would be futile against an adult's resolve and would only mar their last days in their sylvan home. He had been apprehensive about what her mood would be when the day of leaving came, but she remained in good humor, though somewhat pensive. While he made up a pack of their possessions, she busied herself with cleaning the campsite and putting things in order. Her work took longer than his, so he watched her as she finished. It had been his intention to tear down and scatter the poles and brush that made their shelter, for no other reason than to signify some kind of conclusion. Kwetah's notion was different. Not only did she clean up the litter he had left inside, she repaired and refreshed a decoration of twigs and leaves she had kept beside the entrance. Realizing that she was taking time they might need for travel, she watched him askance as she collected some firewood. Seeing no disapproval, she laid the wood for a small fire and set their spit stakes neatly by.

"Ready now, Kwetah?" he asked as she looked over her work.

"Just one more thing."

She went to the sunny nook and made sure that all the miniature logs and planks he had cut from twigs—her 'building toys'—were secure and covered in a bowl she had made by stacking some flat stones.

"You can bring those with you, if you wish," he told her.

"No, they belong here," she replied. "Perhaps someone else will live in our home."

Clumps of the bright maples marked the stages of their journey back to the ocean shore. Kwetah rode on his shoulders, humming gaily at times as she decorated his hair with leaves snatched from bushes they passed. The sky was softly blue, the sun richly golden, and their spirits were at ease.

They traveled most of the day in that light-hearted manner, although by late afternoon he was growing weary and Kwetah had become quiet. He wanted to come into the village at the beginning of a day rather than the end, so they camped that night above the waterfall. They made a very rough camp, but comfortable enough that they slept soundly from sundown to sunup.

They spent the first hour of the new day repairing their appearances. They scrubbed themselves with sand from a bar in the river until they glowed. He combed out Kwetah's long hair and put into it a coronet of late-season flowers and leaves. She trimmed his beard until he took his knife from her.

"Your beard is short enough," she had said with a giggle, "but your nose is still too long. I'll just take a small piece off the end."

They had mended their clothing during their last days in camp. "Your people may think we're dressed strangely," he had told her, "but at least they'll see that our garments are neat and clean."

Their overnight camp was closer to the sea than he remembered. Shortly after they started out, they heard the roar of the surf. The dense forest muffled that sound so well that it was heard only moments before the ocean was seen.

They followed the river path down to the beach and approached the houses from the south. The sunny tranquility of the village reminded him of so many others he had seen, including his own, Tellacloute. They arrived so early in the morning that the children had not yet been released from their chores to play. Out on the rocks, they and their mothers were gathering mussels and barnacles. A few women, the older ones, were around the buildings, some making basketry, one looming a piece of fabric. The men were fewer to be seen; two or three worked on their fine-lined longboats, and some in a boat fished along an offshore reef.

The building area seemed to be fenced off on the southern side with driftwood piled up with some attention to symmetry. When Aengus and Kwetah came closer, he saw that the fence was not made of wood at all, but of the huge bones of whales stacked rib against rib and vertebra onto vertebra like so many rounds sawn from the trunks of trees. Kwetah had tried to tell him once that her people killed the great sea beasts. He had thought she exaggerated. She had claimed that her father was the greatest whale hunter of all. He thought then that she was inventing a father to supplant the cruel one that haunted her memories.

On the other side of the long pile was the partially assembled skeleton of a whale. He wondered at the strength or numbers of men who could have dragged the beast that high past the beach. Later he learned that the skeleton was a ritual object constructed and reconstructed many times from the pile of loose bones and occasionally made twice as long as any real whale.

Coming up to the houses, he knew that he and Kwetah were seen by the workers and gatherers. He saw their glances, even those from out on the rocks. Although the children stopped to stare, none of their elders left their work to greet the newcomers. They merely shifted their positions so they could keep them in view. Not knowing whether their behavior was due to shyness or some other cause, Aengus ignored it and asked Kwetah where her mother would be found. She professed not to know and seemed shy and uncertain herself. He put her down and untied her crutch from the side of his pack.

"Hahpellpah!" he called out. "Kwetah has returned! Come see your daughter!"

His boldness embarrassed Kwetah and she hid behind him, but it drew several women from the building in which he had first seen the child. They stood for a moment, then, when Kwetah peered from behind him, one broke away and ran toward them. Kwetah was still shy and stayed back, so he moved behind her and held her by the shoulders in front of him. Her mother—the resemblance was unmistakable—fell to her knees before her, tears glistening in her eyes. Finally Kwetah dropped her crutch and threw her arms around Hahpellpah's neck.

While they clung to each other in tearful silence, the

other women came up to touch the child's hair, to pet her arms and back, and to make gentle cooing and clucking sounds. Aengus stood by, feeling both proud and foolish.

Eventually Hahpellpah stood up and lifted her daughter into her arms. She looked at Aengus for a long moment, too affected to speak, then turned toward her house. The others followed. One looked back to see him standing there. She returned and took his arm, then led him to follow the others.

In the house, all attention was on Kwetah. Aengus sat on a bench along the wall while they fussed over her, hugged her, examined her leg, and asked her many questions. Kwetah slowly became familiar, answering them with single words at first, finally chattering excitedly about their life in the forest and all that had happened there.

Aengus was mostly ignored, but he did not mind; the scene delighted him. He marveled that the house impressed him so differently than before. Healthy now and used to campfires, he found the smells inside redolent and varied, not uniformly offensive as he had remembered them. The drying fish were hung on racks outdoors now, which made the interior seem much roomier. He saw that it was partitioned by chest-high walls into eight or ten separate living areas, each with its own fire pit. Kwetah had told him that several families lived in each of the lodges. The ceiling was still a storage area for their equipment: nets; huge baskets; animal skins, including some with the leg and neck openings tied shut and partially inflated so that they resembled long, saggy balls; and other things of obscure utility. Beside him on the bench was a large box, beautifully carved and colored. One of its corners was stitched together; he could not see clearly how the other corners were made. They seemed to be folded like paper, but, when he tapped the box with a finger, it was solid wood. He saw other objects similarly decorated. Some were containers; others were huge planks emblazoned with fantastic creatures and designs, and hung on the walls. As a boy he had been told that, in Rome, the houses of ordinary people were furnished and decorated like palaces. He had found that not to be true at all, but here, so far from Rome that the name signified nothing, was a house at once homely and ornate. The dim, light-slashed interior was steeped in wild and lovely magic; and Kwetah had told him that no lodge was more grand than any other.

The women gave Kwetah a piece of dried fish and a bowl of oil. She took them and sat on the bench beside Aengus to share her meal. The women watched while she broke her fish in two and gave him a piece. Only when they saw him dip it into the bowl and begin to eat did they bring more and set it between them.

One of the women was bolder than the rest—the one who had tended him months before, he believed; the one Kwetah called "Kobessa." She touched him several times, purposefully it seemed, and appeared anxious to ingratiate herself with him. To her, finally, he spoke.

"Those outside didn't seem to recognize us. Have we changed so much?"

"They must have recognized you," she replied. "They're afraid of you, I think."

"Why should they be afraid of me? I've done them no harm. I brought Kwetah back, as I promised."

"We think you killed Pugahlkuthl."

At this accusation, Kwetah looked at him sharply. He had told her very little of his encounter with the river people, but the violent story must have been known in all the villages along the coast by now.

"Pugahlkuthl was an evil man, a false magician," he said.

No one replied to that. They sat in awkward silence for a few moments until the sound of voices outside distracted them, the voices of men. He went out to meet them. His sudden appearance through the door took them by surprise. They raised the spears and clubs they carried, as if afraid that he would attack them.

"Is this how you greet a guest?" he chided. "Put down your weapons."

Those closest to him did so, but the more timid, in the

back of the group, held theirs ready to strike, although they would have had to push aside their fellows to do so. The chief, who was among those in front, spoke.

"Leave our place! Go away!"

Aengus answered Semackul, for Kwetah had told him that was the chief's name, "I'll leave you in peace, but not for many months. I'm your guest for the winter."

"No! You will leave now. You can have one of our canoes. Go away!"

"You surprise me, Semackul. You treated me well half a year ago. Now I've brought Kwetah back. She'll not even be crippled."

"For that, we will let you go alive. Now go, before I change my mind."

Aengus's reply came from the time of his impersonation of a supernatural visitant in the camp of the river people and had been rehearsed often in the weeks since.

"No, Chabotta Semackul, I'll not go, and you'll not kill me, but for another reason. While I'm a man, while I live in this body, you can see me; you can talk with me, argue and reason with me; you know where I am. If you destroy this body I use, or if I tire of being a man among you, you will see me no more. If you were to call out, you would never know if I heard you. Then you would weep by your fires, all alone in a dark, empty world."

Semackul's face showed a tinge of uncertain surprise.

"Why should we call out?" he said. "Why should we weep?"

"You are great hunters, but the whales do not come to your spears unless the spirits are willing that they should. If no more whales came to this part of the sea, if the seals and fish left, *then* you would call out to the spirit world. If your people sickened and died—all the men, women, and children of them, one by one—*then*, while any remained, they would weep bitter tears through the long nights."

"Are you a spirit, then? Are you a messenger from the spirit world? Who are you?" Chief Semackul's speech was touched with a mixture of irritation and curiosity, but showed no hint of fear.

"For now, I am a man with a man's needs," Aengus told him. "I am here to do the things men do. One of those things is to protect Kwetah from harm."

Semackul took offense immediately. "I am her father. I will look after her."

Aengus looked him straight in the eye and said with a measured voice, "Kwetah needs more than the protection her 'father' gives. Every man and woman in this village will see that no harm comes to Kwetah or her mother. You call them ko-tlos now. Later you will honor them and be proud that they have lived in your village."

One of the other men asked, "Are you Tulukluts?"

"It doesn't matter who I am," Aengus replied. "Don't try to please me as a spirit. You don't understand, nor can you provide for, the real needs of spirits. I'm a man among you, and you'll treat me as a guest."

Ambiguity, evasion, and eloquence; such are the tools of the divine. That had been the caustic observation of a priest of Kerala, discussing his craft with Hektor and Aengus. They were Aengus's watchwords now.

"You killed my uncle's son," Semackul said. His tone did not so much accuse Aengus as it sought confirmation of rumor.

Assuming that Semackul referred to the shaman of the river people, Aengus responded, "Pugahlkuthl was an evil man, a false magician." His unvarying response whenever Pugahlkuthl's death was spoken of would come to resemble a litany: an expected and, he hoped, eventually reassuring repetition of an accepted truth.

"And where is his ghost now?" Semackul asked. He seemed to be testing Aengus to see whether his reply would agree with the report from the river people.

"It burns forever. It will never reach Hahtoppul," Aengus told him.

Quite abruptly, with a scowl on his face, Semackul turned and stalked away, leaving his men to stand about uncertainly then wander away to their own affairs.

XIV

Kwetah's people called themselves "Kweneechekats." The name identified them as "dwellers near the promontory" that marked where the open coastline bent sharply back on itself to become the southern shore of the strait. Other Kweneechekat villages, including that of the river people, were scattered along twenty miles of shore each way from that rugged cape. Near-shore trails and canoes maintained their loose tribal unity.

Kwetah's village was Appowad-u-sissa, as much description as name. It meant "midway along the beach."

During the first weeks of their return, Aengus was neither welcomed in Appowad, except by Kobessa and some of those who dwelt in her lodge, nor rebuffed, except by Semackul and the two who served him. Most of the Kweneechekats of Appowad did their best to ignore his presence. To them, he represented disruption and occult menace. They wished he would be gone but were afraid to offend him.

He salvaged planks from the shelter they had made for him months before and built his own house closer to theirs than the shelter had been, yet distinctly apart. Kobessa would have taken him in, but he did not want the people of that house to share in the disapprobation he sensed from the other Kweneechekats. Someone—Kwetah's friends Mahkalt and Sierka, he believed—left a stack of old boards at his site while he was gleaning house material among the drift piles farther along the beach.

The house he built was small and rugged. Much of its interior was taken up by a bed shelf, wide and comfortable for his large frame. He enclosed his fire pit with great stones so that a blaze large enough to provide generous warmth would not take his house in payment.

Kwetah was often with him, sometimes for more than a day at a time, and he had to remind her then of her duty to her mother. Sometimes the child would be in her own house at nightfall, but he would waken at dawn to find her in his, huddled close to him for warmth. He built a small sleeping bench then for her occasional use. Only a bit of sandy floor around the fire remained clear. His few possessions were hung from spurs of driftwood around the walls and ceiling.

One rainy evening, Kwetah, sitting on her bench with drawn-up knees, surveyed the cluttered cavity and the strange shadows that flickered along its walls. "If some animal had swallowed us and all these things, its stomach would probably look like this," she observed.

"The fire would give it a bellyache, I think," Aengus said.

"Maybe some animals *do* have a fire inside," she replied. "I've seen smoke come from their mouths in winter. From people's mouths, too. Even from my own." She shuddered in the grip of her imagination.

He laughed and handed her a bowl of water to "put out the flames so you can sleep."

Aengus hesitated to insinuate himself into the community of Appowad, but he appreciated the company of those who would sit with him and talk. At first, those were only good-hearted Kobessa and the two shy bachelors who lived in her lodge: Mahkalt and his nephew Sierka.

Kobessa was overtly friendly toward him from the beginning. She was an amiable meddler, a well-intentioned intercessor in everyone's public and private affairs. She reminded Aengus of his Aunt Hylla, the most conspicuous and vexatious lady in Tellacloute, but one of the best loved. He took to calling Kobessa "Aunt," which she recognized as a term of affection and took great pride in.

It was Kobessa who told him the story of Mahkalt and Sierka. Despite the difference in their ages, the men had courted the same girl. The girl resolved her dilemma by marrying another, and the two distraught men were collected by Kobessa. Though they were fond of the old woman, Aengus imagined that the example of her puissant personality had discouraged them from any further consideration of matrimony.

Mahkalt and Sierka, in their turn, often mentioned Kobessa in their conversations with Aengus. He gathered that she had been widowed when raiders attacked Appowad many years before; her only child was drowned soon after. Her family thereafter was a fluid affair, consisting of those in her lodge and others old, infirm, or without families of their own whom she brought under her roof. Her household became a refuge for the unfortunate of all the Kweneechekat villages. Her strong-mindedness and the charitable sympathies of their neighbors had ensured their survival. Besides Kwetah and her mother and the two bachelors, two women so afflicted with sorrow that they never spoke lived there during that time. They lost themselves in their work and in silent ministration to others in need. There was also an old man whose wits had left him. He sat on his bench most of the day, staring into the gloom of the roof corners. When he would go for a walk along the beach, the others kept an eye on him, and one would eventually lead him back home. The lodge provided a heart for Appowad that, according to Mahkalt, no other village had.

Aengus asked him, "If it's such an unusual lodge, will it always be there for . . . those who need it?"

"For Kwetah and her mother? Yes. The people want Kobessa's lodge the way it is."

Aengus thought, "And what does Semackul want? Are the people's wishes any safeguard against his guile?"

He wondered then and often if he would ever be confident enough of Kwetah's safety to be able to leave her with his conscience clear.

124

But he saw no evidence to substantiate the conception of herself that Kwetah had hinted at back in their forest home: that she was unwelcomed and unaccepted by most of the people of the village. The overwhelming importance of Semackul in her life—father, headman, enslaver, and abuser—and Hahpellpah's forlorn submission to his domination had convinced the child of her inferior status. Reinforcement of the notion, if any was needed, came from thoughtless and cruel remarks by some of the children. But the fact was that, as much as any child is paid notice by those outside her family, Kwetah was regarded with kindliness and sympathy by most of the people, and with great affection by those who dwelt in her lodge.

Indeed, the notion of a hierarchy of social rankings that Kwetah had described for him must have had very subtle expression in Appowad, for Aengus saw no sign of it— even very little recognition of Semackul's primacy, except at the time of the hunting of whales when his commands were undisputed. More typical was the lack of respect accorded the chabotta's traditional first claim on the castings of the sea. Only when Semackul found such prizes before anyone else was he certain to possess them. The people did not flaunt their own findings before him; they just hid them until they felt it was safe to use them: the planks shaped by unknown hands, the urns and pots made of strange woods, and particularly the bits of metal that they pried from wood scraps to fashion into durable blades and points. Mahkalt told Aengus about those things during a few moments of guarded confidentiality.

Of other things that he wished to know, Aengus dared not ask. A preterhuman visitor should know already how the shores, straits, and rivers of the land lay. He should not need to ask about other villages, other tribes. Most certainly, he could not ask the Kweneechekats about their spirit world—the one he had claimed for his own. Kwetah's understanding of that world and its demons and deities was confused and immature. From her occasional remarks, he had surmised that Tulukluts was one of the immortals who figured importantly in legends from the time of creation, but who now existed apart from people and served only their own ends. More present were the kwal-k'washa: tutelary spirits of woodland, shore, and sea that had to be appeased or contended with in the conduct of ordinary human affairs of well-being, survival, and war. But the child knew little of the mysteries of her people's religion. Such matters were the concern of adults, in her mind. To learn those things that an avatar from the shadow world should know already, Aengus had to keep alert for accidental tidings.

While warm weather lasted, there were few opportunities for him to observe the Kweneechekats' practice of their faith. It was an individual matter with them during that busy season, it seemed. Whatever communion they held with the kwal-k'washa was done in private and alone.

The communal ceremonies that Kwetah had spoken of were held in late fall and winter. From what she had told him and from allusions made by others, he suspected that those gatherings were only partly religious. They were also occasions for telling the old stories, for making the history of Appowad known to its people. And for sociable entertainment to enliven the bleak months. Perhaps that most of all for some of the people.

He wondered often how his presence and his occult pretensions would affect those traditional congregations. He worried that, when the people had time and reason to focus their attention fully upon him and his claims, they would recognize the truth about him and turn against not only him but Kwetah too, and all those who lived in Kobessa's lodge. For his part, he could become a fugitive again. Those others could not.

The approaching season of rituals weighed on other minds also. One day, Mahkalt came to Aengus's house and, for the first time, came inside to speak with him rather than call him out under the open sky, which was everyone's preferred place for conversing with him.

After polite initial talk of inconsequential things, Mahkalt said, "Some of the people wonder if we should conduct our ceremonies as we have always done."

126

"The people have sent you to ask me about this?"

"Some of the people have been asking *me* what I thought. I think they expect me to ask you."

Aengus looked into Mahkalt's impassive face. He longed to put aside his masquerade with this gentle man, to have a friend, a confidant, a mentor among the adults of Appowad; someone to guide him through the mysteries, to have a Hektor again. . . .

But he saw nothing in Mahkalt's expression to tell him how he would react if Aengus were to admit that he knew nothing of their gods and kwal-k'washa spirits. The older man had shown himself to be well-disposed toward Aengus, but he was a man of Appowad and must be no less when Aengus was gone. Concluding finally that to ask Mahkalt to participate in his imposture would be more an act of cowardice than friendship, Aengus said, "The people of Appowad should do whatever they would do if I was not here. My only concern is that no one harms Kwetah—or Kwetah's friends."

Mahkalt replied, "The people have many questions. Our ceremonies were given to us a very long time ago. Perhaps we do them wrongly now, or badly. The people don't want to offend—"

Aengus shook his head and held up his hand. "Tell the people what I told Semackul the first day I came back with Kwetah. Treat me as a guest. Treat me as a man, and don't worry about what else I might be. The ceremonies are for the people of Appowad. I'm only a visitor, and I'll neither intrude nor make judgments about what the people do."

"Will you come and watch?"

The question was one that Aengus had been wrestling with earlier and had not resolved. His mind raced to come up with the best answer now. The prudent solution was the easy one—to stay away—but Kwetah's safety could call for more than prudence from him.

Mahkalt's dark features might have been carved from wood, but his eyes showed perception. When he saw that Aengus's reply was slow in coming, he said, "The first gathering is mostly for the children. You'll be asked to come. If you intend to stay with us for Kwetah's sake, then you should come." He paused and looked carefully at Aengus. "You should come, but . . . be watchful. Take care."

Saying no more, Mahkalt was out of Aengus's house and gone. There had been no time for Aengus to ask a question or even to thank him for his cautionary advice.

The children's assembly took place a week later. Its purpose was both to draw the young people into the religious life of Appowad, and to arouse their elders to eager anticipation of the more serious ceremonies of winter. The invitations—or summonses—to attend were made by the children. Aengus heard their drumming and their piping shouts when they were still at the far end of Appowad. He went down to the beach in front of his house and watched their slow progress from lodge to lodge. There were perhaps twenty-five of them, a few younger than Kwetah but most older. They gathered in front of each of the lodges in succession, with a handful of adults standing some distance behind them to offer encouragement and to see that none of their charges abandoned the responsibility they had been given. The invitation began with beating on shallow drums that were held in one hand or on hollow cylinders of wood suspended from cords. When that noise drew people out of their lodges, the children began to chant and shout, but hopelessly at variance with one another. The older boys called out names that Aengus had never heard before. They must have been the names of heroes of other days, for the boys then claimed to be as fierce and brave as those they had named. The girls and younger children chanted, "You come, you come, you come . . ." over and over again.

When finally they came down the beach toward Aengus's house, he saw some of the young people break away from the group, as if they did not want to come to his door, but the adults called them back and made them stay together. He went inside and waited.

The drumming began rather tentatively at first. He waited until the beating became loud and steady before he went out to meet them. He did not smile—to do so would have ridiculed their efforts, declared them to be childish. The children's faces were marked with broad lines of red ochre and black charcoal that had been mixed with grease and applied with flat sticks. Sprigs from canoe trees had been fastened into their hair. Some had extended their facial markings to their bodies. Others wore pendants, belts, bracelets, and anklets of various kinds of shells strung on cords—adornments they had made themselves, to judge by the workmanship and commonness of the shells used.

He thought at first that Kwetah was not among them. The small children were in front and she was not there. It was only after he announced, "I will come," several times and the children were leaving that he saw she had been standing at the back, hidden by those taller than her. He wanted to call her back, to see how her face had been painted and the ornamentation she wore, but he knew she would be embarrassed if he did so.

The gathering for the children's ceremony lasted only one evening: the one following the invitation. Later ceremonies, those of midwinter, would be more complex and take several days, with some days devoted to very sacred rituals involving only the elders of the village, and other days given over to general feasting and merriment. The children's ceremony was only a prelude to those others, although no less significant in the minds of the children and their parents.

Aengus had expected that it would be held in Semackul's lodge, the largest, but it was not. Was that because the chabotta felt it would demean him to offer his lodge for such a minor function? Or was it because the people of Appowad had not granted him primacy in religious affairs? Aengus wondered about that as he went into the lodge alone and found a place against a wall as far as he could get from the central fire. He did not sit with the people of Kobessa's lodge. If trouble was to find him that evening, he preferred that it find him alone.

He had delayed his coming to the lodge until he thought

that most of the people had preceded him, but he had misjudged the purposefulness of their comings and goings. Others wandered in after him, but almost as many of those already there wandered out again to return later. That ebb and flow went on for so long that it seemed to him most of the evening was being wasted and the children would be too tired for their ceremony to continue long.

The lodge was divided less completely into separate living spaces than the others, or else some of the interior half walls had been removed. Aengus felt awkward as the building began to fill up and no one chose to sit near him. Eventually, however, choice did not matter. As people jostled for room, some were, little by little, forced into the space that had been left around him. Those nearest did not speak to him, nor did he encourage them to do so with glances and smiles, but he was relieved that he was not as conspicuous among them as at first.

The children, newly adorned much as they had been the day before, came in with their parents. Kwetah arrived between Mahkalt and Sierka, her small hand enclosed by Mahkalt's huge, gnarled one. Aengus felt a pang of exclusion when he saw her thus, so small and arrayed as he had never seen her except for that glimpse the day before. He felt like a stranger to her, as he was to her society, and imagined that she might not even acknowledge him if he spoke to her. He tried to picture himself in Mahkalt's place but could not. Only Mahkalt and Sierka could lead her through ceremonies such as this and teach her what she needed to know to live in Appowad without him.

Semackul came in with Ubussuk and Butchasid, the two who, like some dogs, seemed to have no life apart from their master. They took a place near the entrance, which surprised Aengus because he had been told that was the kotlo place, drafty and farthest from the warming fires. It appeared that they were holding themselves aloof from the society of Appowad, that they did not want very much to be at the children's initiation. No one else seemed to find anything unusual or amiss in their chabotta's choice of place.

A sudden drumming and shrieks from outside startled Aengus and silenced the confusion of noise within the lodge. A group of adolescent boys burst through the entrance and into the space around the fire. They—or their parents—had scarified their arms, legs, and bodies with sharpened shells: they had made long incisions from which blood oozed as they leaped and pranced in a dance that they seemed to be inventing as they performed it. Before coming in, they had smeared their blood all over their bodies and faces, spoiling the carefully applied red and black lines. Their shouts and out-of-breath chants were mostly declarations that they would be fierce and fearless warriors against whom no enemy would dare raise a hand. Girls of the same age stood at the open entrance to the lodge, trying to find some common measure with their tambourine drums. None of the boys were following their beats, but the girls persisted gamely as long as the boys continued their dance.

A long and confused interval followed the boys' dramatic overture. Several people would initiate chants in divers parts of the lodge, each of them repeating a different name over and over and enlisting those nearby to join them, until finally one group would prevail over the others and the whole company would take up that name, chanting and clapping for a while. Then the contest of names would begin anew. Sometimes, when the noise abated a little, someone would rush forward to stand by the fire and excitedly begin to tell a story about the name being chanted. The names might have been those of the heroes that the boys had shouted during the invitations the day before, and the stories seemed to be the power stories of which Kwetah had disapproved, at least for intimate fireside telling in a forest camp. Here, she clapped her hands as gleefully as the others, and her face glowed with happiness. But the stories were rarely finished before another clash of chants would begin and another name won out. Most often, no one took up the challenge to tell the stories attached to those names. It was a daunting milieu for storytellers. Aengus guessed that the demonstration was meant to be no more than a foreglimpse of the solemn ceremonies of midwinter when the stories would be told and heard with proper reverence. Those who stood now to tell them may have intended no more than to lay claim to their rights to tell particular stories. Or perhaps they were usurpers trying to steal the stories. Aengus did not know, but it did not seem to be a serious matter to the people there.

There was a dance for the younger ones, too. Women of middle years and older began it, circling the open space with shuffling steps—two forward, one to the left, two forward, one to the right—and clapping their hands. Then some men of that age joined in. Mahkalt was one, Aengus noted, but apparently Sierka was still too young. In a single file, making a complete circle, they went around the fire with that simple step, and then beckoned the little ones to join them. Some came readily, others held off for a circuit or two, and a few finally had to be tugged with gentle hands to draw them forth. Kwetah came as soon as Mahkalt held out his hand to her. Aengus's eye followed her fondly. Though she still limped from her injury, she did not use her crutch. With Mahkalt holding her outstretched hands from behind, her movements were the most lively and delightful of any of the dancers. Others there may have watched other children and held other opinions, but that is what Aengus saw.

Later in the evening, a horde of "mosquitoes" swept around the lodge—young children armed with short sticks that had thorns stuck to their ends with pitch. Whining to mimic the insects, they ran and pranced around the fire, and made dashing forays into the crowd, attempting to sting those who could not move aside quickly enough. Most often, the thorns broke off against the blankets raised against them and the children ran back to their parents to have new ones affixed, but a few scratches were inflicted. The people who were stung would cry out and roll their eyes back as if they had been mortally pierced. Aengus noticed Kwetah running around the fire with the others, but he never saw her try to sting anyone.

132

The older boys were not in the lodge while their younger brothers and sisters were so engaged. They had run down the slope of the beach and washed themselves clean in the surf. Earlier that day, they had brought a basketful of yellow-gray mud from a claybank near the river mouth. Now they spread it on themselves in a pattern of bands encircling their limbs and bodies. They became hornets. When their buzzing noises were heard approaching the lodge, the small children ran back to their parents. The boys came running and leaping into the lodge with bark fringes hanging over their faces from headbands. They pretended that the fringes blinded them, but their swift motions showed that they could see well enough. They carried sticks, as had the younger children, but these did not have thorns on their ends; instead, the sticks themselves had been sharpened into long points and fire-hardened; they were scorched and then scraped clean with shells.

Aengus noticed something else when they came in. One boy lagged behind his fellows, then dropped his stick as he passed Semackul's group. Ubussuk reached out, quickly swept the stick beneath his crossed legs, and handed the boy another that he took from under his blanket. If others saw what Aengus had seen, they gave no indication of it; no one pointed or leaned over to whisper to his neighbor, at least that Aengus could see. But Aengus marked the boy and followed his course around the fire.

Mahkalt had been watching the boy too, it seemed. When the boy approached the group from Kobessa's lodge, Mahkalt lifted Kwetah into his arms and carried her away from the front row of spectators. He worked his way back so that there were many people between him and the fire.

Seeing that, Aengus chose to make himself more conspicuous. He raised himself slightly and shifted forward between those in front of him until he was in the front row. The boy circled past Kobessa's people and came toward Aengus, his covered face tilted toward the wall where Aengus had been sitting. When suddenly he saw Aengus

133

closer than he had expected, he became flustered and moved away.

On the other side of the fire, he composed himself, glanced toward Ubussuk, then began another high-stepping, zigzag advance toward Aengus. Aengus looked at the boy as little as possible, seeming instead to concentrate his attention on the other hornet dancers as they dashed into the crowd, stabbing lightly with their wooden stingers and pulling them back quickly. The people in the audience, though, had become aware of the new element in the performance. Their voices quieted to whispers. From their smiles and nudges, Aengus surmised that they believed they were only watching a boy playing bold before a stranger whom his elders held in some awe. Apparently few or none besides Aengus and Mahkalt had observed the switch of stingers and suspected something more sinister.

The boy became aware of the hush and the people's eyes upon him. He hesitated. When he saw that Aengus's attention seemed not to be on him, he began to approach him again, although he no longer made buzzing noises.

Aengus pretended to be bothered with vague itches, as if bugs were crawling on him. He reached behind to scratch the small of his back, then under one arm. Then he bent his head sharply downward and scratched under the hair at the back of his neck. Finally, with his head still bent down and his hair obscuring his face, he put his hand to his stone eye and deftly removed it. When he saw the boy's foot very close, he abruptly raised his head and thrust his hand forward. He clutched the stone eye between his fingertips and directed its baleful glare into the boy's face. The boy stopped, frozen with fright. Aengus held him so for a long moment, then made a little thrust with the stone eye. The people gasped. The boy squeaked in terror and backed away.

Finally, to break the awful tension, Aengus lowered his hand and forced a bantering laugh. A few people took it up immediately, then many more, and finally all of them, pointing derisive fingers at the boy and elbowing their neighbors in good-natured relief that they had only been observing sport and not some awful magic that might be turned against them next. The poor boy dropped his stick, turned, and ran out the door.

Aengus looked to see how Semackul was reacting to the turn of events, but his place was empty. He and his two kept men had slipped away.

The incident had disrupted the evening's ceremony beyond resumption, at least as long as Aengus remained in the lodge. He rose from his place and picked up the boy's stick. Carefully, he ran his finger up the tip of it. It was coated with a sticky substance that, when he held his finger to his nose, smelled like rotting meat mixed with something pungently vegetable. He wiped his finger clean against the side of the stick while he looked around at the people, all of them staring back at him. Silently, he dropped the stick onto the fire and left.

For many days after that, he kept to himself. He had much to think about. If Semackul had not managed to kill him with his poison, he might yet have made it impossible for him to live in Appowad. The people would not want him at their ceremonies if his presence meant disturbance, even though the trouble would be Semackul's doing. And if Aengus did not attend the ceremonies, Semackul would be encouraged to stir up disapproval and resentment against him in other ways.

Seeing Kwetah with Mahkalt had unsettled him also. He had seen that she was comfortable with the older man, as trusting and loving as she had been with Aengus in the forest. But this was not the forest. Mahkalt was the one who knew village life and traditions; he was a more fitting mentor for the child here. Aengus's influence over her would only make her less suited for Kweneechekat society.

The continuation of his pretense of having spirit power disturbed him also. He preferred to be straightforward and open in his dealings with men. Fraudulence had never been his way, certainly not with friends. He was afraid that, once started on that course, there would be no way back, not in Appowad. He sometimes had qualms that, even when Appowad was only a distant memory, deceit might remain a part of his character.

And Kwetah stayed away from his house. For days, he was alone with his thoughts. When he picked his solitary way along the beach, foraging, he caught distant glimpses of the people of Appowad, but Kwetah was never among them.

XV

During those days alone, the conclusion that his time in Appowad was drawing to a close became inescapable. He would never be able to make a place for himself among the Kweneechekats. Mahkalt and Sierka were better surrogate fathers for Kwetah than he could ever be, and she seemed to be as devoted to them as she had been to him. And if Semackul was so cowardly and lacking in authority over the people of Appowad that he only dared strike at Aengus through a gullible boy, then Mahkalt and Sierka should be able to cope with him.

He could think of many reasons why no one came to his house, but the one that rose in his mind most insistently was that the Kweneechekats had come to the same conclusion he had: he should leave Appowad soon. Mahkalt and Sierka—even Kobessa and Kwetah—must think that now.

On the morning of the sixth day after the children's evening of dance and masquerade, he began to select those things he would take with him. He pondered over which of his poor possessions would be suitable gifts for Kwetah and those who cared for her. He thought of what he would say to them, for he would not slip away without telling them.

Preoccupied thus, he was unaware that someone approached his house until he heard his name called. It was spoken with diffidence; he did not recognize the voice. He moved his door aside and saw one of the men of the

137

village there, a man he did not know well.

The man did not respond to Aengus's invitation to come in out of the chill. He held his place some twenty feet away.

He said, "Kwetah . . . uhm, she's gone to the river."

"To the river," Aengus repeated, trying to comprehend the man's concern. "The river down there?" He pointed toward the mouth of the river he had ascended with Kwetah.

The man nodded.

"Is something wrong? Is Kwetah all right?" Aengus asked.

"I don't know."

"Did she go alone?"

"Yes, but Kobessa went after her."

"Kobessa? Why did Kobessa go?"

"Because Mahkalt and Sierka are away." The man pointed out to sea.

Aengus saw nothing there. Probably the two men and others had taken advantage of calm weather to go to the deep reef some twenty miles out where they fished for shoo-yult, a huge bottomfish.

"Why have you come to tell me this? Is Kwetah all right? Is Kobessa all right?"

"I don't know. I came because . . . uhm . . . you said . . you said that all of us in Appowad must look out for Kwetah."

"So you've come to tell me she's in trouble. There's some danger. What is the danger?"

The man shifted his footing and looked away in agitation. Facing almost away from Aengus, he said, "Ubussul found her footprints on the beach, the mark of the stick she uses when she walks. . . ."

"And followed her," Aengus said, "and then Kobessa followed both of them."

The man nodded as Aengus rushed past him down to the firm sand at the water's edge, then along that strand toward the river's mouth.

If it had perturbed the man so greatly to approach

138

Aengus and yet he had done so, his fear for Kwetah's safety must have been more than idle. Aengus wondered how long ago Kwetah had left and when Ubussuk had followed. He would have asked except that the man yielded his information so painfully.

At the river and past the intersection of paths near its mouth where he had eluded the pursuing Semackul months before, he saw Kobessa ahead of him. She was rushing up the edge of the riverbed, slipping on rocks in ankle-deep water and grasping bushes alongside to keep from falling. Aengus soon overtook her.

"How far are they?" he gasped as he came up to her.

She only pointed up the river, having no breath for any better answer.

"Go back, Aunt Kobessa," he told her.

Pushing on, he kept watch along the shore for signs of Kwetah's or Ubussuk's passing. The wet spots he saw on shoreline rocks could have been made by anything, even the river's own splashing. The few broken twigs told him no more; they could have been snapped by animals hours or even days ago.

When the man who came to his house finally made known his message, Aengus had rushed away without his knife. Though he realized his oversight moments later, he did not return for it. Rocks, fists, and rage would be weapons enough against Ubussuk. Haste had been more important. Now the thought occurred to him that Ubussuk might have armed himself with bows and arrows. If he heard Aengus's approach and hid beside the river. . . . But, no. If Ubussuk had seen Kwetah heading for the river and had been taken with the impulse to harm the child while she was out of sight of anyone in Appowad, he would not have encumbered himself with needless weaponry.

Aengus rounded the river bend and came into the dim glen with the waterfall at its far end. Kwetah would have been slowed by the dense shrubbery and broken rock if she had continued that way. Why would she have followed the river this far? he wondered. Perhaps he had already passed her playing somewhere in the forest, unaware that others were looking for her.

He left the river and looked among the trees and in the clearing where he had almost abandoned her when he thought she was dead. He could find no footprints or wet spots to mark someone's passing.

Returning to the river's edge, he scanned the waterfall and the open places on the scarp it fell over. On the other side of the river, an easy climb led to a ledge that separated the two stages of the river's plunge, but the way to the top from there was blocked by the perpendicular face of the scarp, damp and mossy with no footholds that he could see.

He would climb to the top of the falls by the old way, then. From there he could see farther, and the sandy patches along the river above the falls might show him the footprints for which he was looking. He was just turning to act on that decision when a movement on the ledge on the other side of the waterfall caught his eye. Behind some rocks there, he saw the top of a head, enough to show him that it was Kwetah's.

He splashed across the river and began to climb through the trees. The route that had seemed so easy from the other side of the river soon revealed some hidden difficulties. There was a deep gap so overgrown with brush that he almost fell into it before he saw it. The rotting log he used to cross it sagged ominously beneath his weight. Then he came to a wedge-shaped opening between rocks that was so narrow at the bottom he could not squeeze through. He had to clamber up and straddle the gap with his feet pressed against opposite sides while his hands clutched branches that hung from above.

When he had passed through the gap and jumped down, he found himself on the ledge, but on a part of it hidden from below by huge rocks along its outer edge. And Kwetah was not there. Spray from the waterfall just ahead blew onto him; the fall's noise silenced all others.

"Kwetah!" he called.

The girl stood up, startled, from behind a rock just beside him.

140

"Akwahti!" she cried. "You frightened me."

"You frightened *me*, little thing. And Kobessa, too. What are you doing up here?"

"Hiding from Ubussuk."

"You saw him?"

"Yes. I was up here already when I saw him."

"Why did you come up here?"

"Because I thought it was an easy way to get to the top. Easier than the way you took me when we came back to Appowad. But it wasn't. I was just starting back down when I saw Ubussuk—You're getting all wet, Akwahti."

He took her hand and they picked their way through the jumble of great rocks that had fallen onto the ledge from the cliff above. They moved around the bulging rock wall until they could no longer see the waterfall and the pool it fell into.

He found a sheltered spot and sat on a mossy rock there. When Kwetah began to pull herself onto his lap, he lifted her to his knee and turned her to face him. He looked at her earnestly, not knowing whether to scold her, question her, or just hug her to him.

Kwetah resolved his dilemma when she said softly, "I've missed you, Akwahti."

"I've missed you, too. Why have you stayed away from me?"

"Because Mahkalt said I should stay inside—in our lodge—until he says it's safe for me to go out again."

"Did he say why it's unsafe for you to go out now?"

"He said I should stay away from Ubussuk and Butchasid. He said he was going to talk to the other men and I could go out after he talked to them."

She paused and her eyes brimmed with tears.

"Mahkalt said you might go away, Akwahti. Are you going away?"

"Why did he think that?"

"He wouldn't tell me. I heard him talking to Kobessa and Sierka. He told them that he was going to talk to the other men. Sierka said that there would be no reason for you to stay in Appowad after that. When I asked Mahkalt if you were going away, he said he didn't know. When I

141

asked him why you would go, he said he couldn't tell me. Are you going away?"

"I don't know, Kwetah. I think that I trouble the people of Appowad. If Mahkalt talks to the men and the men say they'll make sure no harm comes to you or your mother or the people who live in your lodge, then there would be no need for me to stay."

"Yes, there would be, Akwahti," the girl cried, her fingers clutching his sleeves and tears now spilling down her cheeks. "I love you. I don't want you to go away. Ever."

Holding her tightly to him now, he said, "There are more people in Appowad than just you and me, Kwetah. If I disturb them, if the winter ceremonies are disrupted because of me—"

"*You* didn't make that trouble, Akwahti. Ubussuk did . . . and my father," she added in a low voice. "*Some* of the people want you to stay. I *know* they do because I've heard some of the women talking."

"The women in *your* lodge."

"Yes, but others too. I've heard some of them say you'll make Appowad a better place."

"Did they say how I would do that?"

"No, but I know they want you to stay."

Aengus thought, "Do the women want me to stand up against Semackul because their men won't? Don't they know that Semackul will always stir up trouble if an outsider like me is the only one to oppose him? Their own men must do that."

To Kwetah, he said nothing for a while. He held her and rocked gently from side to side.

He remembered the man who had come to his house that morning.

"Why did you leave your lodge when Mahkalt told you not to, Kwetah? Kobessa was very worried. She came part of the way up the river looking for you."

Kwetah considered that for a moment, then said soberly, "I didn't think Kobessa would follow me. I didn't think about Kobessa at all. Was she very worried?"

"Yes, she was, but she knows you had a reason for

leaving the lodge. I'm sure she does, even though she probably doesn't know *what* that reason was. Nor do I. Are you going to tell me?"

"Partly I just wanted to go away because everybody seemed to be so worried and sad, and I thought it was about me. About you and me. So, when my father and Mahkalt and Sierka and the other men went away to fish for a few days, and my mother was lost inside herself, I thought I would go back to our camp.

"And then I thought you would come to find me, and we could stay there for a while. And maybe you wouldn't go away after that."

"That wouldn't be fair to Mahkalt and Sierka and Kobessa, to go without telling them where we had gone. It wouldn't be fair to your mother, even if, for a while, she would not seem to realize you had gone."

"I know."

"So we'll have to go back."

"I know. . . . Are you going to go away?"

"I *was* going to go away, but I'll stay awhile now. I'll talk to Mahkalt and see what he thinks."

"Do we have to go back to Appowad right now?"

"Kobessa will be worried. We can't stay here too long."

"Will Ubussuk be there when we go back?"

"In Appowad? Probably. Where did he go when you saw him?"

"He went up the other side of the falls—the way we came down. He slipped once and hurt himself. I heard him curse the kwal-k'washa of this place. When I saw him a little higher up, he was holding his side and there was blood on his leg."

"But he never saw you."

"Oh, no. I hid and kept quiet."

"Good. Mahkalt was right. You should keep away from—Sh!"

He held his hand up to Kwetah and listened. From the beetling lip of the stone wall over their heads, they heard, "Kwetah! I've come to take you home. Answer me, Kwetah!"

"Ubussuk!" Kwetah whispered.

"Yes. Shh. Keep still."

"Kwetah!" Ubussuk called again. "Answer me, Kwetah. Kobessa sent me for you."

At that, Kwetah looked at Aengus. He shook his head.

A few pebbles rattled down from above, falling just in front of them. Aengus waited briefly, then, cautioning Kwetah to remain, he moved back toward the waterfall, to where he could watch Ubussuk as he descended through the brush on the other side of the river.

Shaking foliage marked sturdy Ubussuk's progress down the rugged slope. Aengus caught several glimpses of him through the trees and brush, and then he saw him cross the narrow flat at the bottom and return to the river.

"Strange that there's no trail along the river," he thought. "The people of Appowad must get everything they need or want from the sea and never come up here."

While he watched Ubussuk recede down the glen, other thoughts formed in his mind. Or rather one thought—one plan—with two consequences: the threat to Kwetah that Ubussuk represented might be diminished, and perhaps Aengus could spend a day with Kwetah away from Appowad. During the last few days alone in his house, his mind had returned again and again to their months together in their summer camp. His longing had come to fill his waking hours just as it pervaded his dreams at night. A single day—there could be no harm in a single day.

He waited until Ubussuk was out of sight around the bend of the river then rushed back to Kwetah.

"Kwetah, perhaps we *can* spend a day up here, but I'll have to go back and tell Kobessa. Will you be all right if I leave you here? Are you hungry? Are you cold?"

"I'm fine," the girl said. "I brought some food with me." She pointed to a small package at the base of a rock.

"You won't be afraid here alone if I'm gone for a while?"

"No. I'll go back where the bones are. They'll keep me company."

"Bones?"

"Back there." She pointed to where the ledge narrowed, pinched between the rock face behind them and another that curved in from the side of the glen where he had climbed up to the ledge.

He followed her and discovered that the ledge did not stop where the rock faces almost came together. Instead, it became the floor of a narrow recess between them, then widened again in a dim grotto beyond. Kwetah slid through the gap easily; Aengus had to get down on his hands and knees to crawl beneath the place where the rock faces almost touched.

The grotto within was not a cave, just nearly so. One rock face—the one they had followed from the waterfall—arched over them and the other bent away from it so that a narrow gap of sky showed above, but off to one side. Several huge rocks had broken loose and were jammed precariously in the opening above; others had fallen through and shattered on the floor where Kwetah and Aengus stood. The wall that received falling rain was rank with moss and ferns. The other was so shadowed that Aengus saw nothing there at first until Kwetah took him by the hand and led him up to it. There, she touched a crumbling human skull that was the color of the rock shelf it sat upon, and was as ancient, it seemed.

Aengus's eye became accustomed to the gloom. He soon saw not just one skull, but many of them, some set in crevices in the wall or on natural shelves, and others fallen to the floor and broken. There were ribs and long bones too, all very old, lichen covered, and eroded by decay. It was like Gau's Cave of Ancestors, but abandoned for hundreds of years.

"Oh, Kwetah, I can't leave you here."

"Why not? It's dry and safe. Ubussuk can't find me here. There are lots of places to hide."

"Ubussuk's gone. I saw him just now going back to Appowad. But all of these dead bones—don't they frighten you?"

She looked at him in surprise.

"Why should they frighten me?"

"The ghosts of these people. . . ."

"These are very old bones, aren't they? The people who used them must have gone on to Hahtoppul a long time ago."

"I'm sure they must have," he muttered, turning to survey the whole length of the wall.

"Ah," he sighed. "Look at that."

The prow of a canoe, barely recognizable, lay tipped on its side. Behind it, where the rest of the canoe had been, was a jumble of rocks. Along one side of that fall, where there had been sufficient moisture and light, the rocks were covered with lichens and moss. Leaning on the rocks, he peered into the crevices to see if anything else was visible of the ancient sepulcher. He saw only blackness.

Kwetah pulled herself up beside him, clutching his arm for support, and looked where he had been looking.

She said, "Once, an important man of Appowad was laid into his canoe with many of his things and was carried back into the woods when he died. Do you think an important man's bones are under these rocks?"

"Very likely. Who was that other important man?"

"I don't know. Sierka told me about him one time. He was someone Kobessa knew. That's what Sierka said."

"When people die in Appowad, are they brought someplace near here?"

"No. Away down the beach, where the bluff isn't very high. In the woods behind . . . that's where they're put. Except children. When they die, they're put in the woods behind our houses on top of the bluff."

"Did you know about this place before today?"

"No," she replied. "Nobody comes here."

"I guess this is as good a place as any for you to wait, then—as long as you don't mind."

"I don't mind. The kwal-k'washa know that this is a people place. Nothing will happen to me here."

146

XVI

Ubussuk was a powerfully built man with a perpetual
scowl on his face. The scowl was not as much an expression of truculence, Aengus had thought, as it was a mask
to hide his slow wits. Semackul's other man, Butchasid,
"the flea," was a different type: intelligent, devious,
implacably cruel, hate-filled—a man that even Semackul
had to watch carefully. But dull Ubussuk was no more
than his name implied: as unpleasant as a sour smell. He
spoke to no one and no one but Semackul spoke to him.
He was, Aengus believed, full of superstition and vague
fears that could be played upon.

Hurrying downstream, Aengus watched for Ubussuk,
but did not overtake him. At the intersection with the trail
that led along the bluff top behind Appowad, Aengus
turned and raced up its slope, then past the village to a
place where he could descend to the beach unseen.

Keeping to the trees and brush at the foot of the bluff, he
went back toward the village as far as his house, collected a
basket there, then retreated some distance from the village
again and went out to the beach and into the calm water
up to his knees.

Prodding and prying with a stick, he gathered mussels
from rocks as he approached the village once again. He
saw several people around the lodges, but could not
recognize Ubussuk among them. Not at first. Not until he
was directly below the houses, where the few canoes not

taken by the fishermen were pulled above the tide line. Then he saw him coming out of Semackul's lodge with a cord in his hand, probably to collect a bundle of firewood.

Aengus left the water and headed back toward his own house, angling up the beach so that he would pass close to Ubussuk.

"Ubussuk," he said when he was almost upon him.

Ubussuk looked up startled, for Aengus had never spoken to him directly before. "What do you want?" he said, recovering his dour look.

"Your heart is not good toward me, Ubussuk. That doesn't bother me, because you can't do me any harm. But your heart is not good toward Kwetah, either. Or toward the people of her lodge. I may soon tire of watching you to see that you do *them* no harm."

Ubussuk's reply was slow in coming.

"You don't watch me. I come and go as I please, whether you're around or not."

"I'm *always* around, Ubussuk. Every time a thought of harming Kwetah or her people comes to your mind, I'm there—watching you, ready to stop your heart the instant you raise a hand against any one of them."

"I've never seen you near me. I haven't seen you for many days."

"Because I've wanted it that way. But I've seen *you*. I saw you put the poisoned stick under your blanket at the children's ceremony."

"You were inside then."

"So it seemed, but I saw you. And I saw you this morning."

"I haven't been near your house. You've been collecting mussels along the shore. You haven't seen me."

"I was with you, right beside you, all the way up the river. I was there when the kwal-k'washa caught your foot—there by the waterfall, when you hurt your leg and your side. When you cursed them, they were going to harm you worse, but I stopped them. I was with you when you tired of trying to find Kwetah by stealth and began to call out for her. My ears ached with your lying shouts—that you had come to take her home, that Kobessa had sent you."

Ubussuk's eyes opened wide and his mouth gaped as Aengus spoke.

"You've been here all the time," he said, his voice low and hoarse. "You were in your house when I left. You've been shore hunting while I was gone."

"Yes, I was working in my house. And I was shore hunting after that. But, while I was doing those things, I was with you, too. All the time.

"I can't change your heart, Ubussuk. Only you can do that. However, I can kill you in an instant if your bad heart leads you to do something I've forbidden."

Aengus left the stricken man and returned to his house. There, he put a few things to eat into his sack, snatched two blankets from his bed, then went to Kobessa's lodge.

"Kwetah's all right," he told the somber woman. "She's waiting for me near the waterfall. Ubussuk is back in Appowad. He may say some strange things to the people. Let him believe what he wants to believe. I'll bring Kwetah back tomorrow."

Kobessa seemed old and careworn. She had no smile for Aengus, only a nod or two of her head. He paused, looking into her creased face with concern. Was she finally becoming overwhelmed by the responsibilities she had taken upon herself? he wondered. Or dejected because Kwetah had been thoughtless and Mahkalt might find fault? Was she just feeling old that day, as Aengus himself sometimes felt although he was little more than half her age.

Or—a sudden thought as he left her lodge—was she despondent because soon he might be leaving Appowad forever, abandoning her and those who lived with her? He turned and looked back through her door for a long moment. In the dimness, he could make out no more than her stocky shape standing where he had left her. Her features, like her feelings, were hidden from him.

Returning to the river and the grotto where he had left Kwetah, he wondered what Ubussuk would tell Semackul—if he told him anything at all. Aengus was certain that Ubussuk would say nothing to anyone else in Appowad: not to the man who had come to Aengus's house, nor to any of those who had seen Aengus running along the beach afterward. The poison he had put in Ubussuk's mind would fester there because Ubussuk had no friends in Appowad to bring his fears to and have them explained away.

"If only Semackul and Butchasid could be cowed as easily," Aengus thought.

Because of the noise of the waterfall, he approached the narrow entrance to the place of the dead without Kwetah hearing him, although that was not his intention. When he dropped to his hands and knees to crawl through the cleft into the grotto, though, he heard Kwetah's voice and stopped to listen. She was singing, but used no words that he could understand. Her voice became faint at times, perhaps because she was moving around, he thought, for he could not see her. When he was satisfied that she was alone, he called out, "Kwetah, I'm back," so she would not be startled by his sudden appearance.

Inside, *he* was startled by what he saw. Kwetah was seated on a rock at the center of eight or ten other rocks—quite large rocks—that she had arranged in a half circle about her. On each rock, she had set a skull, each one on a bed of moss and all facing her. She had selected whole skulls; some still had the lower jaw attached. At her feet was a pile of materials she had brought in from outside, collected from the forest just below the ledge. Some of the skulls wore coronets of leaves or thin withes that bore red winterberries. Most of their eye sockets had been filled with carefully matched fir cones or dry, prickly husks of some kind of seed pod. Under a few, she had put pairs of thin sticks that stuck out on either side and ended in branches broken off to resemble fingers. Suitable sticks had not been easy to find, apparently; only three of the skulls were fortunate enough to possess those arms.

"Kwetah!" he exclaimed. "This is a sacred place. You shouldn't treat these bones so disrespectfully."

She looked at him in surprise. "These are *old* bones,

Akwahti. The people who used them don't care anymore. And the people who put them here must be dead too. A long time ago. I was just trying to make these heads happy—make this place happy."

"What were you singing to them?"

Embarrassment colored her face and she looked away. Then she smiled and said, "That was the song Frog sang to her babies to make them feel better, to make them stop crying. And then to get them to talk to her. Frog talk."

He sat on a taller rock behind her and contemplated her work. It reminded him of the Day of Ancestors that had been observed every year in Gau, when flowers were carried into the Cave of Ancestors. He recalled the few days before that observance, when the old women of Gau, and some of the younger ones too, would work by lamplight in the cave, repairing or replacing the decayed robes of all those who had died recently enough that there were still people in Gau who remembered them. And how the older bones were stacked reverently in deep alcoves, and the skulls were set around in niches or on ledges to keep silent vigil over their dead descendants.

"I guess the people wouldn't mind," he said at last. "They probably *would* be happy to see what you've done."

"Can you tell which ones were men and which ones were women?" she asked.

"No," he replied. "That little one, though—I think must have been a child."

"I thought it was, too. I tried to find something colorful for it, but all I could find were those bright leaves."

She had tied the stems of the leaves together with grass and set the construction onto the skull like a little pointed bonnet, the tips of the leaves hanging down all around. With its fir-cone eyes staring brightly ahead and its lower jaw set slightly askew, the small skull seemed the likeliest of all of them to break out in frog talk. Or perhaps something more intelligible.

Kwetah said, "I wish I could do what Toop-kollay did when she found her husband's bones."

Toop-kollay was a small ring-tailed animal that walked

like a bear and wore a black mask over its eyes. Aengus had never seen one until he came to Kwetah's country.

"What did Toop-kollay do?" he asked.

"She got some mud and covered his bones with it and patted it into shape with her hands until he looked like he did before Wolf ate him. She wanted him to be gray colored like he was before, but she could only find light-colored mud from a river bank and black mud from the bottom of a pond. So she mixed the two kinds together until she had the right color of gray. Except she was in such a hurry to have him back with her that she didn't mix the two muds completely. That's why he had black rings around his tail and a black band across his eyes when she was finished."

"I wondered why he was marked that way," Aengus commented. "Who told you that?"

"My mother. A long time ago. Kobessa said it was true."

"And Toop-kollay's husband was alive after that?"

"Oh, yes. That's why she did it. That was in the old time when things like that could happen. If only I knew how she did it, I could find some mud and make this little girl alive again."

"You've decided it was a little girl?"

"Or little boy."

"You'd have to find the rest of the bones first. I don't think she'd want to be alive if she was only a head."

"Well, I don't know how to do it, anyway. But it would be interesting to hear what she would tell us. About when she was alive, I mean. Alive the first time."

"I'm going to get wood for a fire, Kwetah. Everything's so damp, though, I don't know if I can get one started."

"Oh," she said, digging into the pile of material at her feet. "I thought you would make a fire, so I got this."

She held up a handful of stringy dry tinder that she had peeled from under the bark of a dead canoe tree.

As he crawled from the grotto, Aengus tried to remember what he had thought about when he was her age. Did he know many stories then? Did he have an imagination as vivid as hers? Would he have thought to find tinder for a fire? He concluded that he must have been a very dull child. He could remember almost nothing from that time.

The fire was not easy to start. A spark was a long time in coming. Kwetah waited for it on her elbows and knees, her fingers pushing the tinder ball close to the notch in the piece of dry wood that he knelt on while he spun a stick between his palms. The first spark died, but she caught the second one in the tinder and gently blew it into a flame.

They had moved the rock Kwetah had been sitting on when Aengus returned from Appowad and laid their fire there. Expertly, Kwetah tucked the tinder ball into a pocket of shavings and dry twigs under the wood—expertly, Aengus thought proudly, because *he* had taught her how to make fires.

When the larger sticks were crackling merrily, he shifted more rocks to make a comfortable place for them to sit: across from the skulls, with the sheltered rock wall behind them. He gave her a blanket to wrap herself in, then wrapped the other around both their shoulders. The afternoon was half gone now, and the failing light from a sky clouded over barely reached them.

Aengus's eye wandered over the fern-covered wall opposite them, behind the skulls. He looked up to the great rock chunks jammed in the opening above. He scanned the whole interior of the grotto, as much as he could see, from the entrance where the rock faces almost touched to the far end where they finally met, unseen now in the gloom. He tried to read the history of the place in what he saw, but the ancient rocks and bones told him nothing. Beyond the reach of the firelight, the gloaming from above outlined mossy stone masses, washed the crowns of mouldering skulls making them look like boulders from the river, and touched the forlorn fragment of canoe, feeling in vain for any trace of the brilliant color that once was there. The only images those shapes stirred in his mind were from his own past. He knew too little of the customs of Kwetah's country to imagine what might have taken place here long ago.

Kwetah concentrated her attention on the circle of skulls, looking earnestly at one and then another as if will alone might make them speak. They seemed to take life from the quivering firelight—she breathed a startled "Oh!" once—but, in the end, they spoke no more than anything else around them.

"I guess there's no way to ever know what happened in long ago times, is there?" she mused.

"There are stories, like the ones your mother and Kobessa tell you. And pictures, like those in that cavern on the beach, up past the hole-through."

"The pictures just show animals. They never show them doing anything. And the stories . . . Well, if one person changes the story, then, ever after, it's never about what really happened, is it?"

He thought of telling her that, in his own country, stories could be written down so that priests and other people who knew how could read them ever afterward. But then he remembered Hektor, who could not read, insisting that the priests would unroll the scrolls and pretend to read, but say whatever it pleased them to say; and Turfu, who could read, deploring how easy it was for kings and generals—and even bishops—to have lies recorded and then claim them to be true just because they were written down.

Kwetah looked up at him for an answer, but he only pulled her closer against him while his mind clung to memories of Hektor and Turfu. Kwetah became lost in her own reveries for a while, and the last of light from outside seeped into the darkness.

He kept their fire small so that the wood he had brought in would last the night. He felt cold and guessed that she did too, although she would not admit it. The food he had brought was dried-up meat of sea duck, old and tasteless and not enough. The stone floor they sat on and the rock they leaned against became harder; he caught himself thinking about the padded bed in his house.

154

"This isn't like our summer camp, is it?" he said.

She snuggled up against him and said, "If we were going to stay longer, we could make it comfortable. But I don't mind. I'm glad to be here with you."

Suddenly realizing that his comment might have been an expression of his own feelings rather than commiseration with her, she turned to him and said, "Are *you* cold, Akwahti? We could go back to Appowad if you are."

"No, no, birdie. I'm all right. I just meant that . . . this isn't like our summer camp."

"No," she sighed. "Already that seems like a very long time ago."

Their conversation after that was desultory. He asked her if she could remember any more stories that her mother had told her. She started one, but seemed to tire of it before it was done. She said his stories were better than hers, and asked him to tell her of strange things he had seen. Noticing the prow of the canoe nearby, which still bore the eared wolf's head where some long-ago whale hunter had rested his harpoon, he began to tell her of another craft with an animal's head at its prow: the African mtepe Hektor had taken him to in Siraf. Kwetah seemed to understand a plank-hulled ship, although that made it seem more like a house to her than a watercraft, but the idea of "camel" gave her trouble. He told her about the hump on its back that people sat on. Her glance expressed her reservations about that. He described the bell around its neck, but she understood neither "bell" nor "brass." During his diffuse explanation of musical instruments and metals, he was suddenly aware of her silence and her weight against him. She had fallen sound asleep.

Seated beside him still, her head slid onto his lap. It was an awkward position for anyone but a sleeping child. He contemplated her artless profile while he gently combed her hair with his fingers and pondered again the conflict between what he wanted—to stay in Appowad with Kwetah or take her with him—and what the welfare of the child and her village seemed to require—that he leave without her. The staring skulls across the fire put selfish

155

thoughts into his mind. If, too few years from now, he and Kwetah and all the people of Appowad would be no more than mute bones, their lives unremembered, what would it matter if he gave greater consideration to his own desires than to the guessed-at needs of others. But then he began to focus on those others. Besides Kwetah, there was Kobessa. He knew before any deliberation that he could never place himself ahead of that selfless soul. Then there were Mahkalt and Sierka, who had been for Kwetah all of her life what he had been for only a few months. And Hahpellpah. Even though he did not yet know Kwetah's mother very well, he knew that he would not willingly add more hurts to the many she had suffered already. Even the man who had come to his house that morning—who was to say whether he came out of fear or retribution if he did not warn Aengus, or because of sincere concern for the people of Kobessa's lodge. Very soon, Aengus's mean, self-indulgent mood passed.

Something moved in the darkness near the entrance to the grotto. He listened and heard nothing for a while. Then the sound of another furtive movement, this time on the rockpile that had collected at one side of the gap. And another noise in the gap. Animals, but what kind of animals? He thought he caught a glimpse of firelight reflected from eyes, but he was not sure. Finally, a low, throaty growl suggested to him that they were most likely wolves, but still he was not sure. He leaned forward, squeezing Kwetah's head, and slid a brand from the fire with one hand while he put new sticks on it with the other.

The wolves he had seen in Kwetah's land were small, gaunt, doglike, and he was not afraid of them. If two or three lived in that shelter, he would not dispossess them of their home—not as long as they accepted him as a guest. He held the brand for a while, ready to hurl it if their investigation should bring them too close. Before long, he put it back on the fire.

He may have dozed himself for a time. If he did, something aroused him. Probably Kwetah's stirring. He listened in the dark, suddenly alert for some new sound half-heard when he was half-awake. Pebbles. Pebbles falling from above. Were the wolves prowling along the edge of the opening high above? A few more small stones fell, rattling against bare rock between the ferns on the wall behind the skulls, then tumbling onto the floor nearby. He put a few small sticks onto the fire to produce quick light and looked up. Following the smoke, he saw where it struck the overhanging bare wall and flowed up its bulge until it disappeared. And then he saw another cluster of little rocks fall, followed by larger ones that bounced from the wall and hit the rocks beneath the skulls.

Carefully, so as not to waken her, he pulled Kwetah up against his chest and got to his feet. While the fire still flared, he worked his way through the broken rock to the end of the grotto farthest from the entrance—farthest from the wolves, he hoped. When he could go no farther, he crouched into the crevice between the two walls and waited.

His wait was not long. More pebbles fell, then a rush of crumbling rock followed by a great, crashing mass that buried the fire and plunged the tomb into darkness.

Kwetah wakened but did not cry out, or say anything at all at first. With Aengus's arms around her, she felt no fear.

When he did not move for a long while, though, she asked, "What happened, Akwahti?"

"The fire disturbed those rocks somehow—the rocks that were caught in the opening up above. The ones above the fire came down."

"What are we going to do?"

"Nothing now. We'll have to wait until morning."

They waited. Aengus slid his back down the wall until he was seated with his feet jammed against a large rock and his knees pushed up to make a warm pocket for Kwetah. She soon fell asleep again and he did too. He wakened several times during that long night; each time, he heard nothing other than the gentle soughing of the wind in the

157

trees outside. Several times, it occurred to him that the thunderous fall of rock might have been only part of a dream.

He was awake when the blackness began to turn to gray, before he could even make out the shape of the mound of newly fallen rock. And then, with more light, he saw that it had fallen in just one place: their fire and the half circle of skulls was completely buried. On the green wall, there was a broad slash of black and gray where the falling rocks had cleared away the ferns and moss. The rocks had washed across the floor of the grotto and piled up against the other wall.

When there was enough light to find his way, he stood and worked the ache from his legs until Kwetah awakened, then he set her down and rolled up their two blankets. Anxiously, she surveyed the opening overhead, then grasped Aengus's hand as they started away.

The floor where their fire had been was completely blocked by the fresh rockfall, and they had to climb over the pile. On the other side, Aengus searched along its edge and then began to pull rocks away from one place. Soon he reached into the hole he had made and pulled out his sack.

When he stood again, Kwetah held up a fragment of wood. "This is all that's left," she said sadly. The wood was from the canoe.

Aengus just shook his head. He wanted to be gone from that place. Kwetah was not quite ready to go; he knew that she was looking for some sign of the skulls she had been trying to coax back to life the day before. She found nothing of them at all, not even a shard. But, just as she turned to come back to him, she cried, "Oh, Akwahti! Look at this."

One of the wolves had been sleeping against the back wall, probably in its accustomed spot. It lay there still, with its head crushed by a large rock and a pool of darkening blood under it. Kwetah was moved both to pity and practicality. "Poor choochukst. Do you think he even woke up before the rock hit him?"

When Aengus shook his head, she added, "What about his fur? Are you going to take it?"

"No," Aengus said. He did not want to possess anything that would remind him of that place. "Come, Kwetah."

Returning to Appowad, Kwetah sensed Aengus's gloomy mood. It matched her own. Their stay in the grotto had become disturbing for both of them. The strange discoveries and the events of the night seemed to be elements of a message, perhaps from the forest kwal-k'washa, but its meaning was obscure.

"Do you think we're not supposed to go back to the forest, Akwahti?"

"I don't know."

"The rocks wouldn't have fallen if we hadn't been there, would they?"

"They would have fallen sometime. Our fire just made them fall sooner."

"But the choochukst wouldn't have died if they had fallen later. And the skulls wouldn't have been broken if I hadn't moved them."

"It's too bad the choochukst was killed, Kwetah, but we had no way of knowing that our fire would do that. It was just something that happened."

A little later, she said, "The last time we left the forest, I didn't want to go at all. It was the best time in my whole life, there in our camp. But this time . . . this time, it seems that the forest doesn't want us to live there. I'll be glad to see Kobessa and my mother again."

"And *that*," Aengus thought, "gives purpose to this dismal adventure. If there must be a reason for things, there it is. It has made her prefer her home to the forest."

XVII

Aengus stood in the doorway of Kobessa's lodge while Kwetah hesitantly approached her mother and Kobessa. Her mother did not recognize her for a moment, then abruptly swept her into her arms as if they had been separated for months.

Kobessa came up behind Hahpellpah. Kwetah, her chin on her mother's shoulder, said, "I'm sorry, Kobessa. I shouldn't have made you worry. I won't go away like that again."

Kobessa touched the child's head gently, then went back to her bench.

Neither woman paid Aengus any notice. He returned to his own house and slept until midday.

The fishermen returned late in the day, paddling furiously to reach shore ahead of darkness and rain sweeping in from the west. Their luck had been good. They had spent a night on the ocean far from land and had suffered no hazard despite the lateness of the season. Their canoes were filled with slablike shoo-yult.

The women had been watching for them from their lodges. When the canoes approached shore, they were waiting at the water's edge with their fish knives. The men heaved the great fish onto the beach, where the women swiftly eviscerated them, wiped the skins clean with handfuls of ferns, then sliced the meat into strips to be carried back to the lodges by the older children and anyone not occupied with other tasks. The job was finished just as gusts of wind hurled the first raindrops at them in the failing light.

Aengus had watched the activity from the beach logs below his house. He was too distant from the people to see clearly, but he knew about their work. When he was first learning Kwetah's language in their forest camp, she had described for him the preparation and preservation of the shoo-yult he had seen draped from racks under the roof of her lodge. Another time, he had come upon Sierka as he was fashioning the hooks used to catch shoo-yult. Modest Sierka, when he realized Aengus's interest, took great pride and pleasure in explaining how he selected splints of curved wood from around pitch-free knots—odorless to the fish—and bent them to shape. Encouraged by Aengus's attentiveness, he then told him how fragile kelp could be stretched and made into strong lines. He talked of other particulars of their fishery, seeming to forget that the spirit visitant would surely be familiar with everything he described.

Aengus had watched the people at their work and had matched what he saw with Kwetah's and Sierka's words. Now the people were gone from the beach, the doors of their lodges were drawn over, and he was left alone in the wet darkness.

Back in his own house, he saw in his imagination the scenes inside the lodges. The summer's catch of shoo-yult had been taken indoors when the dry weather of early fall had passed. Now he saw the women taking down some of those dried strips and storing them in baskets to make room on the racks for the new catch. The men were carefully coiling their kelp lines before they dried out and became brittle. Then, resisting insistent fatigue, they would talk. The men would be around one fire and the women and children around others, listening to the men's voices discussing the events of their two days on the sea, comparing this catch with others, telling story after story of fishing and gear and canoes, of acts of daring, acts of foolishness, acts of pure waggery. The women might

161

begin to talk among themselves about the size of the catch, about the unaccountable audacity of the men in challenging the open sea at this time of year notwithstanding there was fish enough already hung or stored in the lodges to provide for the whole village until the summer to come. Then, to assert their own indispensability to the venture, the women might speak of those things about which they knew more than the men: shaping and sharpening mussel-shell fish knives on surf-rolled tablets of sandstone that they found in the backs of shoreside caverns nearby; cleaning the skins of fresh-caught shoo-yult by wiping them with ferns and grass rather than scouring them in fresh water so that, after drying, they would cook up crisp rather than hard; and making women's prayers and observing women's rituals when the men were at sea.

Kwetah had wondered about the long-ago times and what had happened then. She need only look around her lodge, Aengus thought. What she saw now would be what other children had seen thousands of other times in thousands of other years. And, he reflected, what she saw was what he would likely never see. Because of his otherwordly pretensions, the people would always be reserved and fearful in his presence, they would always wish him gone, they would never accept him as one of them. He could never hope to have a home in Appowad, be a part of their society, work with them, fish with them, hunt great whales with them, have his own lodge and his own family among them. To survive his first days in their land, he had had to set himself apart from them. By arrogating to himself powers from their spirit world, he had forever separated himself from their humanity.

As he waited for sleep to come that night, he let his mind wander in a realm of fantasy where he was a fisherman, a teller of stories, a man with a family, a hunter of whales, a maker of tools and beautiful things, a Kweneechekat.

In the days that followed, he watched for Mahkalt. He wanted to talk with him alone, perhaps to begin to release himself from his imposture, but mostly to learn what Mahkalt and the people of Appowad expected of him. He saw Mahkalt several times going purposefully from one lodge to another. Aengus never had opportunity during those days to speak to him alone, but what he saw told him what he needed to know. Undoubtedly Mahkalt was reasoning with the men, arguing that Aengus could be persuaded to leave Appowad only if all of the men assumed responsibility for Kwetah's safety and well-being, only if the ko-tlo child and her mother were given protection that no ko-tlo had ever been given before: safe-keeping from the impetuous wrath of the highest-ranking man in the village.

Finally, Aengus realized that he would have no private conversation with Mahkalt. Mahkalt must talk with his fellows as a man of Appowad and not be seen as Aengus's intercessor—or pawn. And Aengus must maintain his dissembling pose to give credibility to Mahkalt's arguments. All that remained was for him somehow to let Mahkalt know that he accepted the men of Appowad's assumption of responsibility for Kwetah, and to say when he would leave.

Kwetah and her mother appeared outside Aengus's house one morning bearing a gift: a basketful of shoo-yult from the latest catch. Aengus beckoned them to come in, but Hahpellpah merely set the basket down and returned to the village alone. Kwetah's eyes followed her sadly. In a quiet voice, she said, "My mother knows that you're our friend, but . . ."

Then she turned to Aengus. "These have to be dried some more. We'll have to make a place in your house."

Together, they found three poles amid the clutter of logs at the back of the beach and fastened them under his roof, then carefully hung the strips of fish over them. The pieces had been hanging long enough in Kobessa's lodge to be dry to touch.

When they were finished, Aengus built up his fire from

coals and Kwetah made herself comfortable, sitting cross-legged on the bed shelf he had made for her as if she had been a visitor every day.

"Mahkalt says that I can come to see you now," she said, "but you should watch me from your door when I go back to Kobessa's lodge."

"Just as he watches you from his own door," Aengus thought. By that clue—that they would both watch out for the child in the same way, with the eyes of men—he suspected that Mahkalt was aware that Aengus was no spirit presence in Appowad.

"Tell Mahkalt that I'll watch you all the way back to Kobessa's lodge. Tell him—" He hesitated, and Kwetah looked at him expectantly. "Tell him that I've seen him go to the other lodges. Tell him that I'll stay here through the winter, but I won't come into the village unless I must. I won't interfere with the winter ceremonies."

Kwetah said nothing. Aengus knew that a question burned in her mind, but she understood that his message to Mahkalt was important and that she must carry it exactly as he had told her. She held her own question for a better time.

The fish she and Hahpellpah had brought required more drying and was food enough to last several weeks. From that, Aengus inferred a message from Mahkalt and Kobessa: the time to go is not yet. He hoped that they would be relieved when Kwetah brought his word to them.

Late one day when heavy rains and blustery winds announced the onset of winter and everyone was inside, Kwetah came to his door leading a thoroughly wet and bedraggled young woman.

"Leeaht says that she knows you," Kwetah declared.

He brought them inside, then turned the woman to face the light from the doorway and brushed her wet hair back from her face. It was the young sister from the river people. He hardly knew what to say. He had not expected to see her again and felt embarrassed. He made a seat for her by the fire and, when she took off her wet clothing, he hung it on the wall to dry. He gave her one of his blankets for warmth. Kwetah, meanwhile, perched on his sleeping bench like an inquisitive sparrow.

Leeaht had come from her winter village to visit friends, she said, but Aengus heard afterward that she asked for him at the first house she went to: Kobessa's. She had walked more than twenty miles along damp and gloomy trails. It was now growing dark. He was moved by her ordeal and by the girlish devotion she must have nurtured through all the weeks since he had known her; he was attracted by her comeliness; but, most of all, he was shaken by her sudden appearance and the threat of a responsibility he did not want.

He asked about her village, about her brother and sister. It took some time for her to stop shivering and converse easily. He fed her and Kwetah, but he was still unsure about how to put a limit to his hospitality. Kwetah finally sensed his disquiet and said, "Leeaht will stay in our house tonight. We have room."

Poor Leeaht looked dismayed but did not object.

During the night, Aengus was awakened by Leeaht back in his house, getting into his bed. The ardor of his welcome surprised even him.

In the morning, he was embarrassed once again, this time to find Kwetah in her bed in his house. He had not heard her come in and wondered when she had done so.

Kwetah showed great solicitude for Leeaht that day, leading or following her everywhere. When they were alone, she told Leeaht that Aengus was her, Kwetah's, true father, that all the ladies of the village took turns sleeping with him, and that he was committed to marry her mother just as soon as Semackul would permit that to happen.

Leeaht stayed with Aengus that night. By his fire, she was mostly silent. With a swing of her head and sweep of her hand, she brought her long hair forward over her shoulder and began to comb it very slowly, working out with her fingers the few tangles she found. Aengus vacillated between ignoring her and being awkwardly attentive.

A glint of firelight reflected from her comb and caught his eye.

"That's a pretty comb," he remarked.

Her shy smile was as fleeting as the glittering ray had been.

"It was my mother's," she replied, holding it out for him.

He took it and ran his fingers over the design cut into the horn surface. A small disk of iridescent shell was set into each side; it was one of those disks that had caught the firelight.

He held the comb overlong. The desire was strong in him to sit beside her, to lay her head against his shoulder, and to take for himself the warm pleasure of combing her lustrous hair. As he hesitated, she looked at the comb and then at him. Flustered, he handed it back to her, wondering as he did so why it was so easy to hold her close to him in passion in the dark and yet so difficult to yield to the sweet allure of domestic intimacy. Why should there be only noncommitting bliss in the one and entrapment in the other?

For her part, Leeaht could not find the words she wanted to say to Aengus. She was unable to ask the questions that troubled her; they surfaced only as obscure allusions that he did not understand except to suspect that Kwetah would know what he did not.

Both of them felt relieved to retire to his bed, where he could hold her close to him and no words needed to be spoken.

In the morning, he was astonished to find her squeezed against the wall and Kwetah between them, in his arms and smiling sweetly.

Poor Leeaht left for home that morning, Kwetah hobbling along on her crutch beside her to escort her part of the way. Aengus upbraided himself for letting the child get away with her duplicity, but she had solved a problem

166

for him as well as the problem she perceived for herself, and she knew it. Very likely, he told himself, seeking exculpation, very likely there would be several young men in her village who would be glad to see the return of lovely Leeaht.

"Kwetah," he chided when she came back, "I thought you always told the truth. Did you mislead Leeaht?"

She looked somewhat abashed, but only mumbled, "I knew you first."

For his own untruths, Kwetah gave him no reproof. She only referred to them once. Man and child had been sauntering along the beach, silence between them, their thoughts following solitary paths, when Kwetah said abruptly, "Kobessa says that I shouldn't tell people how you were different in the forest than you are here." She looked up until she caught his eye. "So I won't."

He picked her up then and carried her awhile with her arms around his neck and her chin on his shoulder.

XVIII

One day in midwinter, the men were gone from Appowad. They had been engaged in unusual activity during the week before. Unseen, Aengus had watched them from the trail atop the bluff while they took apart the great skeleton that had lain undisturbed on the far side of the village all the months since he and Kwetah had returned. Then the men constructed a new whale. One of them would select a bone from the piles with great care, touching first one of a particular kind—a rib, perhaps— then a second and a third of the same kind, eventually selecting one which he would fasten or lay into the growing skeleton. Through the time of his indecision, he would chant and move about with a shuffling or a high-stepping gait while his fellows provided a wailing accompaniment. Then it would be the turn of another man, and another after him. So they had rebuilt their great, empty leviathan. And now they were gone.

They had not taken to the ocean, though, for their canoes were still there, drawn up near the lodges. He came upon Kobessa on the beach near his house. She told him that the men had scattered to various rocky places up and down the coast, and to rivers and lakes in the forest. Each one, alone, was making himself spiritually ready for the dangerous trial to come by cleansing and scourging his body and by prayerful chants. By such means, the men would make themselves strong-minded and would prove themselves worthy in the eyes of the kwal-k'washa that dwelt in those places.

Aengus recognized the rituals she described. Heroes of his own race used to so mortify their bodies and strengthen their minds prior to battle in the days before Roman and Christian influence erased such primitive practices—at least in the civilized parts of Europe. Although his people had disdained their outlandish Hibernian and Caledonian cousins for still holding to those barbarous customs, their accounts of such ritual purifications before great undertakings had recalled to his youthful mind the story of Christ's forty days in the wilderness.

"They consider the task ahead of them to be so great?" he asked the old woman.

"Yes. They always prepare themselves this way before the hunt, but this isn't the time of year to go for whales. When they swim north in the spring is the time, not in midwinter when they go south. It's dangerous out there now."

"Then, why?"

"Who knows why men do crazy things. Why did they go for shoo-yult when our racks were groaning with the summer's catch? They're bored. They want an excuse to make a feast, perhaps. They don't tell women why they do such things. At least they don't tell me."

The next day, the canoes were gone. They were away all day and night and most of the next day. Late in the afternoon, they returned ahead of heavy clouds and a rising wind. The men had not taken a whale. They retired to their lodges and Aengus saw none of them for several days while they recovered from their fruitless ordeal.

Some days later, he was summoned from his house.

"Come out! Come out!" a voice commanded.

Aengus found Semackul waiting for him. The chief was alone, which surprised Aengus, for he had never seen him without his two sycophants. Semackul's scowling expression, the only one Aengus had known, was softened a little, although the rows of scars across his nose and

169

cheeks, each mark boasting of a whale he had killed, rendered his visage forever fierce.

"It's not right that you should live apart from us and have nothing to do with what we do," the chabotta began.

"If you're inviting me to live in your lodge, then I thank you, but I prefer my own house."

"No. I didn't mean that. I meant that you should join us in what we do. If you will be here until spring, then be part of Appowad, not a stranger living beyond our houses."

Semackul spoke with apparent sincerity, but Aengus remained wary of his intentions.

"What would you have me do, Chabotta Semackul?"

"We'll go for a whale again soon. Come with us. Join our hunt."

"Of what use would I be to you? You and your men are skilled hunters, but I've never hunted the whale. I would only be in the way."

"You said yourself that you call the whales to our spears. You said that you're responsible for our success in the hunt."

Aengus answered cautiously. "Then you heard me wrongly. I spoke only of keeping whales *from* your spears, not calling them forth. Your success is your own doing. If *you* perform the rituals properly, if *you*'ve learned what hunters must know, if *your* hearts are strong, then your hunt might be successful. It's a contest between you and the whale then, not between you and the spirits . . . unless you've offended the spirit world, and then there would be no whales and no contest at all."

Semackul pondered Aengus's words for a long minute before speaking again. "The men say you've driven the whales from us already."

"If the men say that," Aengus replied, "it's because you said it first. And it's not true. You've seen whales from the high rocks, and you saw them from your canoes a few days ago. If the spirits had driven the whales away, you wouldn't have seen them at all."

"Do you say that *we*'re to blame, then for coming back with nothing?" the chief asked querulously.

"I didn't say that at all. I said the hunt is a contest

between men and whales. The last time, the whales had the good fortune to escape your lances."

Semackul fell into his usual bellicose silence then, but he did not leave. He just stood before Aengus with his eyes turned away. It was not the habit of the people of his land to lock eyes with those to whom they spoke privately.

Finally Aengus said, "As long as I'm a man among you, neither can I help you in the hunt, nor will I drive the whales away."

He turned back to his house, but Semackul cried, "Wait!"

"Wait!" he repeated. "Come back. We've not talked the way I intended. I came to make my invitation to a man, not a spirit. Men shouldn't live by themselves, apart from other people. Come with us on our hunt. See how we do it. Enjoy the chase with us, and the battle if we're favored. Then we'll have stories to tell afterward."

Semackul had made his voice earnest and sincere, but Aengus perceived venom beneath his words. He thought: "Perhaps I only see the reflection of my own feelings toward him, but I don't trust him."

He considered possible motives for the chabotta's entreaty. Semackul, the whaling chief and sea master, wanted the men of the village to see that, in moments of violence and danger, Aengus would be as fearful as any ordinary man. Or he intended to show them that Semackul knew the kwal-k'washa of the sea better than the false stranger did. Or perhaps it was something else: Semackul might have sensed that *he* was becoming the outsider in Appowad. He would know that Mahkalt had been talking to some of the men. Maybe Semackul wanted no more than to close a breach that threatened to isolate him in his own village. Whatever the purpose, Aengus began to suspect that his own continued influence for Kwetah's welfare would diminish if he were to hold himself aloof now. It seemed that something significant must come to pass between himself and Semackul, and whether it was accommodation or violence, it could only happen in encounter, not separation.

"I'll come with you, then," he told the chief. "At least

171

I'll be a strong arm on the paddle for you. When will we go?"

"The men will take another day to prepare themselves. Then watch the stars and listen to the surf. When the stars shine steadily without flickering and when the surf calms, we'll leave that morning before dawn. I'll send for you."

Two days later, Kwetah came to spend an afternoon with Aengus. She was quiet the whole time, but, when he looked up occasionally, he saw her watching him with solemn eyes. He thought he saw a tinge of apprehension there, as if she was haunted by some presentiment or was troubled by talk she had overheard. He did not question her. When time came for her to leave, he held her close to him for long minutes.

That evening, the clouds drifted away, the wind died, and the stars shone placidly until the moon rose and drowned most of them in its light. Aengus took his knife and a few other things he feared might be stolen if his absence were prolonged and climbed the bluff to the path above. No one except Kwetah had seen the knife. He did not want to reveal that he had something better than the Kweneechekats' shell, stone, and bone tools and weapons lest they covet it. He went some distance north, away from Appowad, then into the forest and hid his things in a place he had chosen days before. He hid his stone eye there, too, and covered the empty socket with a leathern patch.

In the dark stillness, every noise seemed amplified. Small animals, busy at their night's work, stopped Aengus's work several times with their rustlings. A fragment of cloud cast a darting moon shadow across the ragged bright patches out on the path. Certain that he had seen some more substantial movement, he froze in place for a long moment. Then, as he stepped onto the path to return to his house, he heard rapid footsteps to his right, away from Appowad, and saw a moving shadow that could not have been made by a passing cloud. He was sure that his quickened senses had not fooled him. But, though he waited for a long time, then sat on his heels and waited even longer, he saw only stillness and heard only the softly booming surf.

"A solitary wolf," he concluded at last. "Nothing more."

Even so, he stopped and turned quickly more than once to see if anyone was following him home.

Before dawn, he heard someone slip on the beach logs below his house.

"I'm coming," Aengus called out. "I'll meet you by the canoes."

The blankets on Kwetah's bench were pushed up in a heap, making him think that the child had come in during the night while he slept. He bent to find her, to kiss her forehead or cheek, but the little bed was empty. He felt a pang of disappointment, then a sudden thin wash of depression, so that he could not direct his thoughts wholly to the trial ahead until Semackul spoke to him as he came up to the men gathered on the beach.

"You will come in my canoe." The chief pointed. "There, ahead of the steering paddle."

Aengus took his place alongside the canoe, one man behind him and six ahead. Great stones had been moved long years before to make a rough breakwater and a safe launching lane that angled through the surf. A rocky reef farther offshore subdued the greatest waves. Two canoes went ahead of Semackul's, then Aengus and the others half-slid, half-carried theirs over sand and cobbles into the wash of the spent rollers. When sea surges lifted the canoe, the men leaped into it and paddled mightily to keep pace with the retreating water.

One canoe followed theirs; four canoes in all, holding more than thirty men. Aengus looked around for Mahkalt and Sierka, but theirs were not among the moonwashed faces that stared back at him. Many other men were missing too, including those few who had ever been openly friendly toward him. He pushed against lines, baskets holding more lines coiled within, and inflated sealskin floats until he had his feet planted firmly and, seated on the thwart assigned him, could paddle handily. The four canoes traveled directly out to sea, breasting great smooth swells as the sky brightened. Aengus looked back several times to see inland hills rising behind the bluff against the red sky. Later, the canoes angled northward, and soon the houses of Appowad could not be seen at all.

After several miles of steady way, the heaving water became suddenly clotted against their paddles. He looked down and saw long, limp blades of kelp lying along the surface or just below.

"A reef down there," he thought. "That's where fish would gather, but would they draw whales?"

He knew little of whales then. He knew that there were different kinds, but he could identify none of them; he did not know that they bore live young and suckled them, making them kin to animals ashore rather than to fish; he assumed that they ate fish and perhaps large animals— seals, other whales, men. It was Kwetah who had first told him that the Kweneechekats were whale hunters, but she knew only what a child sees and hears.

The canoes stopped along the seaward edge of the long, rank kelp bed. Those in the bow of each boat stood, their eyes scouting north, south, and westward out to sea. The others pulled bearskins over their shoulders as their bodies cooled.

They stayed there through the long day, except for one canoe which was sent farther offshore, far enough to disappear from their sight for an hour or more.

After midday, a small basket holding pieces of dried fish was handed back from man to man. The one ahead of Aengus took his piece and reached around to pass it to the man in the stern. Abruptly angry, Aengus seized the passer's wrist and snatched up the single piece of fish that remained. He broke it in two and gave the steersman a portion. If the men's silence through the day had not made Aengus wary, that incident did. Perhaps the man behind him would have shared the last piece. Perhaps Aengus had misunderstood the apparent slight—but he did not believe that he had.

Very shortly after that trifling meal, the two canoes still keeping station with Semackul's drew closer. The men in them made desultory motions with their paddles, as if to free their boats from entanglement with the long kelp fronds, but Aengus sensed that the slow convergence of the three canoes was purposeful. The waists of the other two canoes came up on either side of Aengus's position near the stern of Semackul's. When one of them bumped and men in each reached to hold their boats together, he seized his paddle and shoved that canoe away, then stood to jab the pointed paddle blade against the man behind him. Aengus wanted his more defensible stern position for himself. But he was not quick enough. As he turned, the man ahead of him threw himself onto his shoulders and men from the other canoes tumbled into his, wrapping strong arms around his legs and body. Their weight forced him to his knees, then prone onto the clutter in the bottom of the boat.

Their assault was made with fierce shouts, but Semackul's commands quieted the men once they had overpowered Aengus. At sea, the chabotta's authority was undisputed. The men bound their captive, using many ropes and pulling the lashings tightly around him, against his straining efforts to keep his chest swollen and his arms and legs slightly apart.

In the end, the only weapon left to him was his voice. With that, he thought he might arouse the Kweneechekats' barbaric fears, their dread of ghosts from the spirit world—the very dread that he guessed had kept them from killing him outright lest they release his spirit in their midst. Twisting his head so that he could call out clearly, he shouted to the whales they had come for:

"Cheddapoke! Come for me! Ched-da-poke! Aengus calls you!"

The men flipped his thoroughly trussed body onto his back. Semackul's evil face glowered down at him.

"Soon enough," the chabotta muttered. "Soon enough."

XIX

Even bound, the sight of Aengus unnerved the whalers.
They threw a mat over his face. Now he could not see what
they did, but neither could he work against his bonds
unseen by them.

Sometime later, the fourth canoe returned. The scouts
had not seen any whales. They made no comment about
Aengus's subdual that he could hear. From that, he was
convinced that the attack on him had not been provoked
by his taking of the piece of dried fish. All of them must
have been privy to Semackul's plot against him.

The whales came late in the day. "Che-che-wud!"
someone whispered. Demon fish, he had said: beasts from
the primal world before there were men to hunt them. Fear
was in the man's voice. Did the whales belong to some
fierce species that the hunters had not expected, or were
their nerves overtaut from the long wait and from their
mistreatment of Aengus, who might yet prove to be allied
with irascible gods? He could not tell from their tense
mutterings.

One of the men said nervously, "They're coming
directly toward us," and several others hissed, "Shh!"
Aengus, listening as intently as the whalers were watching, suddenly heard two vast expirations close by. Immediately, the canoe lurched forward. Aengus raised himself.
The mat slid from his face, but he could not see over the

side. The furiously stroking paddler behind him shoved him down with a foot to his chest. Then, far forward in the canoe, an arm was raised higher than the straining backs. Aengus saw the fist and the end of the harpoon shaft above it frozen against the reddening sky as the canoe lurched and plunged beneath.

Semackul's voice exploded, "Now!" and the upraised shaft disappeared. At that same instant, the paddlers near Aengus seized him to heave him overboard. He had not been aware of the heavy line that was tied to his ankles and led forward over the thwarts, but he saw it now and knew its purpose immediately. He thrust his feet beneath the thwart ahead of him and bent his toes sharply to entangle the legs of the man there. In a mad instant, the man kicked to free his legs and toppled backward, and the line, bent sharply around the thwart, snapped taut and tipped the canoe violently as the craft swung about end for end. There were screams, and some of the men leaped or fell into the sea. Aengus saw the whale's great flukes raised against the sky, a frothing cataract spilling from their trailing edges. The tail smashed down onto the center of the canoe; men and pieces of the boat were thrown everywhere. Aengus was snatched through and away from the chaos by the line that linked him to the struck whale.

Then suddenly there was nothing—no pulling, no noise, nothing but water enveloping him, pressing him, cold water that was light above and dark below. The harpoon had pulled free, probably loosened when the line had snapped tight around the thwart and jerked the canoe's weight around.

Aengus was a strong swimmer, but, wrapped around and around by many ropes, he could only make cramped movements, convulsive thrusts like those of a dying fish, to propel himself. His lungs ached for air, although he had drawn a great breath before he was pulled under. Most threatening of all, long kelp stems brushed against him on all sides. If he thrashed too violently, he feared that the line from his feet might become entangled among them.

Writhing like some ponderous snake, he began to rise. If he reached the surface, he knew that only his expanded lungs would keep him afloat.

"Little breaths," he cautioned himself. "Little breaths of fresh to mix with the stale. Don't let it all out at once or you'll sink forever."

He grew dizzy for want of air, and cold—very cold.

When his upturned face finally came into the air, he was not at first aware of it. Fronds lay heavily over his head, telling him falsely that he was still submerged. Then he heard men shouting far behind him. His resolve became nothing—air exploded from his lungs; then he snatched a great breath, expelled it, and took another while he thrust desperately with his feet to keep from sinking.

When his gasps subsided, he warped his body half around to see what the Kweneechekats were doing. Daylight was fading. The winter sun had set. Aengus's eye would not focus properly at first, and he could only see any distance when the great, smooth swells lifted him. He cleared his vision by blinking furiously and was able to make out three canoes still afloat some two hundred feet away. He began to toss his head to shake off the kelp, then thought better of it.

Men were being pulled into the canoes. He guessed that no more were in the water because the shouting had given way to urgent argument that he could not hear well. The canoes moved toward a black shape that he thought must be part of the smashed canoe. He heard the probing blow of a paddle against it. "No. No good," someone said. Then the canoes moved a short distance toward the fiery west, to the edge of the kelp bed apparently, for they all turned south at the same place and began to range along that boundary slowly, searching. Their course took them within twenty feet of Aengus, but the light was poor and he hoped that they would not see him.

The whalers were looking for gear from the broken canoe. Twice there were shouts of discovery. They found a line of sealskin floats and then several harpoon shafts together. As they drew closer, Aengus heard that their primary object of search was the basket that held the harpoon heads. The lanyards attached to them might have caught on the kelp or wreckage of the boat, the men thought, but they were having no luck. When they were very close, Aengus eased his head below the surface. He was afraid that the kelp atop his head was pushed up and would signal his presence, or that his yellow hair floated out from his head like a bright banner. The canoes were slow in passing. Even underwater, he could hear the paddles dip and probe into the kelp. He could hear the men's voices when they spoke loudly. And he became aware again that he was chilled to the marrow. So cold, in fact, that when he concluded it would be safe to come up, his swimming motions were convulsive and awkward. He began to think that the miracle of his survival thus far was of no significance after all, and that he would die very soon.

Surfacing, he looked for the western brightness to orient himself, but he could not find it. Then he saw it, faint and high in the sky. Too high! Something blocked the horizon. One of the canoes! No—there was no sound. Kelp! Just a blade of kelp tipped up. He shook his head free of the fronds that had concealed him and again looked for the canoes from atop the passing swells. The boats were well beyond him now. One had started across the kelp bed, or had found a lane through it, and had turned for home.

Aengus put his mind to his more urgent peril. But what to do first? Try to loosen his bonds, at least to free a hand? Make his way like a dolphin to the canoe fragment that still jutted out of the kelp a few hundred feet north of him? Attempt to pull up the trailing line that might yet drown him—or that might have the harpoon head with its cutting edges still attached? Or pray?

Pray? Pray to whom? To Turfu's God? To the kwalk'washa, if the God of Christ had abandoned this savage place to them? No. Prayer had not saved Turfu and *he* had prayed often. Hektor, who had faced greater physical dangers than the good priest ever had, had said that prayer came only when nothing else could be done, and he

179

claimed that he had never had to resort to it.

Those were thoughts of an instant, a background to action, and did not paralyze Aengus. He worked to free his hands, which were tied at the wrist and bound against the sides of his legs. Other cords were wrapped around and around, over his arms and hands. The ropes had become slippery and, if anything, tighter than before. Or perhaps he had become weaker and too cold to work at them effectively.

Finally he was able to thrust his fingers—and then one hand—from beneath the lashings. Then the other hand. They stuck out from his legs like miniature flippers.

Hardly daring to attempt the maneuver because his muscles were so cold, but knowing none better, he somersaulted underwater so that he could catch with his hands the line that drifted down from his feet. The somersault was awkward because there were so many ropes wrapped around him that he could not bend much at his waist or knees. He made one cumbersome rotation end over end, then another, then a third, and at last he caught the line with one hand. Twisting onto his side, he found the line with his other hand also.

He passed the rope through his hands, inch by inch, until he felt it tighten against his leg and he realized that he was working it in the wrong direction. Cursing softly, he drew it the other way, passing it from left hand to right with cramped pushes and pulls. After long minutes, he felt the harpoon head brush his feet, and then it was against his hand. He felt for the barbs. One was gone or broken, the other twisted out of position. But it was the sharp shell blade he wanted, although he knew that he must exercise great care in handling it. As cold as he was, he could slice through a finger and bleed to death without being aware of it.

The same caution was necessary once he had his hand fitted carefully around the remaining barb and lanyard and had begun to saw the only cords he could touch: several together around his leg just below his hand. He could not tell when the blade would finish with rope and start on flesh except by stopping often and feeling for loose strands with the back of his hand.

Those first ropes yielded suddenly. Then others as he could reach them. There were many more wrappings than knots, so each severed rope released many turns. Finally he cut through the ropes before and behind him that had held his wrists to opposite sides of his body. With his hands free, he soon cut away the rest. The last, those binding his bare feet together, had to be cut by holding the sharp blade in his hand because the wrapping and gum that had held the pieces of the harpoon together gave way, and the barb and lanyard fell off.

Darkness had come. He had become disoriented. There was not even a glow along the western horizon to give him direction, and the moon was still hours from rising. He looked for lights ashore, or where he thought shore should be, but saw none. He looked for stars, but clouds seemed to cover them. Wiping seawater from around his eye, he scanned the sky more carefully. Stars were there after all, but only in some places. Clouds were coming up. Then, not where he had expected them, the seven stars of the Bear appeared, and the mariner's Star of the North. Now he knew where the edge of the kelp bed was and where to look for the shard of the canoe.

He breasted over the kelp and then rolled onto his back to paddle along its verge. That easy way of swimming was slow in the heaving water, but he was very tired. Very tired, but no longer achingly cold. Just numbly so. And tired— so very tired. Unpredictable swashes of water across his face began to torment him. It bothered him to have to think when to breathe. One wave broke over him and forced him under. Comfortably holding his breath and drifting, slowly sinking, he wondered how long he could put off returning to the troublesome surface. Then he realized that he did not have to struggle upward at all if he did not want to. He had only to choose when to expel air, draw in water, and begin to sleep forever.

Sleep . . . forever . . .

No! That was death's seduction; the soul grabber's easeful suasion. Aengus groped for the surface, for air and sky, unsure now where they were to be found in the blackness.

At last an arm pushed against nothing. He thrust down hard with the other. Water exploded from his mouth and nostrils. Piercing cold returned. Cold and air and pain and life!

He felt a blade of kelp against his face. He grasped it to stop his drift while he searched for the canoe. He did not know where it lay. Even if the stars could give him direction again, they would not tell him if he had swum far enough, or too far. So his eye followed the summits of the rolling swells—first to his left, then right, then those that surged beneath him and swept grandly shoreward without him—until he saw an angular blackness thrust up against the lesser black of the sky. He recognized the upended stern of the canoe.

When he put his hand on it at last, he saw that the stern paddler's thwart was still in place, and the one he had used also, but the one ahead of that was gone and the edge of the canoe was broken above its shallow sockets. That thwart and the canoe must have taken the shock that would otherwise have snapped his legs when the whale plunged. The canoe was broken off somewhere forward of that, but the shattered part hung deep underwater and he could not find it with his feet. It was caught in the kelp. The current which combed the long blades from their swollen bulbs was unable to move the canoe.

He pulled himself under the thwart that he had used and hung his arms over it, with the bottom of the canoe at his back. Paddling with his feet, he moved the wreck slowly from the kelp's grasp into the freely flowing current. Then he pulled himself up under the stern thwart, hung his arms over it, and drew his legs from under the thwart below so that he could sit on it. The canoe tipped back, his weight being mostly out of the water now, but it held him as a cradle would, and he rested easily—even slept awhile, rocked gently by the great swells as the current bore him along the edge of the kelp bed, then off to the north of it.

XX

The thunder of surf startled him out of his torpor. In the first confused moments of rousing, he saw clouds scudding across the moon, now halfway up the sky, and spindrift torn from the crests of sharp waves thrown up by a new wind. He pulled himself up and over the thwart to hang out and survey more widely. He saw that the current was bearing him close along a precipitous shore, but it was on his right side—to the west, if he judged the moon's position rightly. His first thought was that he was being carried into a cove. When he twisted to look past the canoe's side, though, he saw no beach there to receive him, just open sea. The surf was breaking against an island, not the embracing arm of a cove.

"Chardi . . . Chardi," he muttered, as if saying the name would force the confusion of water, rock, noise, and darkness to fit Mahkalt's description of a rock and cliff island that he said stood a half-mile off the cape at the entrance to the strait. Aengus drew himself up to see all around. All he saw as his weight toppled the uplifted stern of the canoe was the island's shore falling away and empty darkness in the direction the current was taking him. He leaped into the sea and swam frantically.

The current's strength frightened him. It swept him past rocks that seemed to be just beyond his fingertips. His desperate strokes and an eddy behind the island finally brought him ashore on its north side in a tiny cove enclosed by huge blocks of rock that must have fallen away from the cliff eons ago. A beach had formed at the cove's inner end, and there he collapsed until cold and discomfort distressed him more acutely than his exhaustion did.

When he stood, he saw buildings—rude houses—among the rocks around and above the patch of beach. This *was* Chardi, then: the only island with buildings, according to Mahkalt. He had said they were used during the summer's fishing. Even when the moon shone briefly between the darting clouds, most of the houses were in the shadow of the high island. They were whitish gray, dim with age, and planks were missing from the walls of all that he could see.

"Ho!" he called. "Ho, there! Is anyone there?"

No one answered.

Fire was his first need. Within the soundest house, he spent most of an hour searching for dry tinder and working up a spark. To feed his small blaze, he sacrificed boards from the walls of other houses, fully aware of the labor required to make them, but too cold and tired to care. He hung his clothing from stakes to dry, covered himself with a piece of matting and even a few boards, and fell asleep in the dirt beside his fire.

He was trapped on the island for several days by stormy weather. Out from the abandoned village, he foraged for mussels and other food amid the shoreline rocks, and explored with the hope of finding a boat—a vain hope in the end.

He set about making a crude boat from a straight log that had one end roughly pointed. He fastened a smaller piece to one side on poles as an outrigger.

During the night after his third day there, the howling wind died. At dawn he was on a high rock lookout, scanning the stretch of water between island and cape. The sea's surface was smooth except for the long swells that never ceased to roll in from the west. Lines of fog hid parts of the shoreline opposite Chardi, but the cape rode above them, a sure beacon to warn him if vagrant currents should carry him into the strait or south and west out to sea.

Gulls and other birds wheeled overhead or shot past like arrows, squawking their exhilaration at respite from storm and hunger. Aengus's heart was light also. Though he was anxious about what he would find at Appowad and had made no plan other than to attempt to find Kobessa or Mahkalt and Sierka alone and inquire about Kwetah and Hahpellpah's safety and well-being, he found reason enough for joy in the thought of release from his island prison. Ineffectual waiting had been hard to bear.

Turning to descend the rock, he glanced north and west—and his breath stopped. Ghostly in the pallid mist, a great, gray ship stood a quarter-mile off.

"Ch'uan!" he gasped. A Serican ship in these waters!

Frozen with astonishment, he stared at the silent hulk, listening and watching for movement, for life. The ship struck his heart as something ancient and evil, from a time he had put out of mind.

A Serican shipmaster had told him once of long voyages eastward. Although he had not known how much credence to give to the shipmaster's descriptions of his wilderness landfalls and the primitive populations he traded with there, the stories were convincing enough to persuade Aengus anew that his lost friend Hektor had been right: that Europe could be found by sailing eastward around a spherical earth; that the terrors the two had endured and left behind them need not be risked again. Aengus had thought that the unfamiliar people and lands described by the Serican mariner might have been in the wild northern parts of Europe. But he had never expected to see a Serican trading ch'uan again, and certainly not in midwinter.

The ship moved slowly; it seemed to be drifting on a course that would pass the island closely. Soon Aengus counted five masts, two of them bearing sails. The sails had lost almost half their area of matting, blown out or rotted away, although what remained would still draw because of the way Serican sails were secured to horizontal battens to keep them flat. But those tattered sails, backing and slatting in the light airs as the ship rolled; its unstayed masts groaning, creaking—even the three bare poles complaining as they shifted in loosened sockets and cases; the weatherworn gray wood and frayed ends of lines hanging everywhere; all of those suggested some long-dead thing from the bottom of the sea.

Then Aengus's eye suddenly resolved dark lines in the water ahead of the ch'uan: they were canoes filled with men straining at their paddles. Lines ran from the canoes to the ship. In the absence of wind, they were towing it. He counted eight canoes, each with fifteen or twenty paddlers. The canoes had swept-back sterns, unlike the vertical heels of Kweneechekat craft, and long, high prows above vertical cutwaters. They seemed less like working boats—whalers or fishers—than vessels made for long journeys, ships themselves to carry many men and heavy loads. He could even make out planks sewn on to raise the edges: wash strakes to deflect waves, they must have been.

The strange scene became familiar, but the menace it represented to Aengus did not diminish. He had finished with Serica more than a year ago; it was a cosmic injustice, an eruption of primal chaos, that Serica should have followed him here.

Why *was* the ship here? Were its men no more than innocent traders? Were they captives of the canoemen, or had the canoemen merely picked up a derelict? Nothing that he imagined gave him ease. More than ever, he wanted to leave this coast, to plunge inland and find his way to the western ocean of Europe. His concern for Kwetah's safety began to be tinged with this selfish yearning.

Then the ship, moving away now into the misty strait, began to vanish like a dream fading. Aengus shifted his eye toward the cape, but it had disappeared also. Fog had moved in and was thickening everywhere.

Foreboding gave way to depression. He slumped against the rock and stared into the mist. His mind refused to form thoughts, to make plans. The universe seemed suddenly incomprehensible and his part in it of no more significance or purpose than a stick adrift in the ocean.

He sat there for an hour, waiting out the fog. The birds had gone. Rafts of them off in the mist held muted, whistling conversations. Something must have disturbed one flock for, from afar, he heard them calling wildly, like desperate, lost children.

"It's not that far to the cape," he told himself at last. "Waiting when I want to leave, and *can* leave, is stupid. I'll take my direction from the swell and risk the current."

As if to encourage such decisiveness, the air brightened as he shoved his log vessel from shallow water, straddled it, and paddled out of the cove. Soon he could see clouds against a blue sky overhead, and then the top of the cape.

The heavy log did not respond readily to his powerful strokes, and eventually the great rollers loosened the outrigger's fastenings. Several hundred feet from his goal, he slid from the log and swam the rest of the way.

Swells broke against great rock pillars offshore and boomed thunderously into caverns under the cape where he came ashore. Large seals lazing on a broad rock table protested his arrival with irritated barks. Then more of them, sprawled on a small adjacent beach, took up the raucous chorus.

He climbed above the herd and found his way to a little-used path atop the cliff, followed it southward for several miles, skirted a village—another empty summer fishing village, it seemed—and came at last to a point of land that fronted a bay with a broad beach and an extensive low, marshy reach behind it. There were houses back of the beach, and the smoke of fires. Aengus retreated and waited behind the point until night fell.

The moon did not rise until after midnight and gave little useful light until the hour or two before dawn. He rose then, when the moon was up and fog had not yet thickened in the bottom land, and crossed behind the village and another one several miles south of it.

The light of the new day was seeping through the trees as he cautiously approached Appowad along the bluff-top

187

trail. Several times, he stepped off the path to look down between the trees to the beach and the headlands to see if one of his friends might be out early and alone. He did not really expect such good luck, but he had formed no better plan to contact them. As he turned from one of those futile surveys, he heard soft footsteps and hid behind a tree.

Through a screen of branches, he recognized the one who approached: Kobessa!

"Aunt Kobessa," he called softly while she was yet a little way from him.

The stocky figure stopped and turned, then turned again. "What? . . . Who's there?"

"It's Aengus. Don't cry out."

"Why should I cry out?" she demanded, a hint of quaver in her voice.

He stepped into her view. Kobessa's eyes widened.

"The men said you were dead."

"But I'm not, you see. I was lucky."

"Something looks after you. Washalee? You told me 'Washalee' once."

"The wind from the sea? Perhaps. Has Kwetah been told that I'm supposed to be dead?"

"No. She was away when the men came back. I'm going to bring her home now. I'm glad I won't have to tell her."

"I'll go with you, then," he said, turning back to lead her the way he had come, for the path was too narrow for him to walk by her side. "Where did she go? Why has she been away so long?"

"She went to see Leeaht. She thought she'd offended you by her treatment of the woman, and she wanted to make up with her."

"That's a long way for the child to walk—all the way to Hokodah."

"She didn't walk. Sierka took her in his canoe. He was to return for her on the second day, but the weather was too bad. Then Semackul forbade him to go."

"Semackul forbade him? I didn't think your people paid that much attention to what Semackul says."

"It's not the same now," she replied, speaking carefully. "Semackul is not a great chief descended from chiefs. He just became the headman of our village because he was the most skilled in hunting whales, the most daring sometimes. But now—the last few days—he claims that he's a true chabotta . . . because he sent you back to the spirit world. He claims that he has saved our village from an evil spirit."

Aengus turned then and put his hand on Kobessa's shoulder.

"Kobessa, you know that I'm not a spirit, don't you? That I'm just a man from a place so far away that I look different."

"There are others like you?"

He smiled. "Yes. All the people of my land. But we're not spirits."

"No. I didn't believe you were," she said, not altogether convincingly.

Walking again, he asked, "What will Semackul's claim mean for you and the people of your lodge?"

"Hah!" she snorted contemptuously. "I'm not afraid of Semackul."

Her resolute response thwarted the inquiry Aengus had intended to pursue. Any questions he might have asked about Kwetah and Hahpellpah's continued safety in her lodge would probably have offended the doughty old woman. Any suggestion that the mother and child might have a more secure place in some other village—Leeaht's village, perhaps—would surely have been taken as an affront.

Instead, he asked, "Why didn't Semackul kill me outright, if the men were willing to do his bidding? Why that foolishness of tying me to a whale?"

"I think he believed that if you were killed among us, your spirit would stay and cause trouble just as you threatened. If you died among the whales, if a whale killed you, then you would go with the spirits that govern the whales and forget about us. But who knows what Semackul thinks. He's a schemer. His thinking is twisted."

Aengus thought, "Perhaps too much of a schemer even

189

for your toughness to handle. I hope not, but now that he has most of the men obeying him. . . ."

Then to the old woman, doggedly matching his pace: "Hokodah is a long way. Wouldn't it be better for you to go back to Appowad now and let me bring Kwetah home?"

"No, no," she protested. "I want to go there. I have friends to see. And I want to be away from Appowad for a while."

Later, after a time of silence, she asked him, "Do you intend to stay with us in our village?"

"I don't know. I worry about Kwetah."

"You needn't worry. She's our child. Mine, Mahkalt's, Sierka's, as well as Hahpellpah's. We'll look after her— just as we always have."

It would have been cruel to point out that their protection had not prevented Semackul's earlier assault on Kwetah. Perhaps Kobessa did not know his part in the girl's injury.

Still, the strong-willed woman's assurance was what Aengus had hoped for. Why, then, he wondered, did he feel suddenly desolate at being so summarily excluded from what he had never requested: a place in Kobessa's family? And resentful that she seemed to be snatching Kwetah away from him?

"But it's better this way," he thought resignedly. "I could only make a place for myself in Appowad by force. Even a temporary place. And I would only make Kwetah's and Hahpellpah's—and Kobessa's—situations worse."

"You go ahead," he told her. "I have to go back for some things I left in the forest by the path. I'll catch up and go on to Hokodah with you. Then I'll say good-bye to Kwetah and leave from there."

"You could help me bring her home and get your things then. You could carry her. Her leg is still weak."

"All right. We'll do it that way."

XXI

Kobessa was as careful to avoid the two villages as Aengus had been earlier that day, and a third village, also, that sat in a bay off the strait. He thought at first that her caution was for his sake, until she told him, "I have too many friends in those places. If they saw me, I'd have to stop and talk. We'd never get to Hokodah."

The trail did not go around the cape but followed a belt of low marsh and grassland that lay between one of the ocean villages and the village on the strait. Ten or fifteen miles became two because of that shortcut.

"All that"—Kobessa waved her hand toward the high ground that backed the cape—"was an island once. This"—she indicated the bottom land—"was under water. Then the whole earth shook tremendously and the sea fell away so that all the villages were left far from the shore. Three days later, the sea rose and drowned all the villages. Only the people who escaped in boats survived. Three days after that, the water fell once more to where it is now. That was a long, long time ago."

Lest he should doubt her, she said, "If you dig any place along here, you'll find sand and bits of shell. This was the bottom of the sea once.

"A bad time," she continued, muttering. "Very bad. So many people killed."

The Serican ship had brought back bitter memories.

"There are worse times," Aengus observed. "When *men* slaughter men."

Kobessa had her own painful memories. "Yes. That's worse. Those who are left are sick for a long time."

"Sick?"

"Yes. Sick from the hate that fills their minds. Until they're free from hatred, nothing is right. They suffer every day."

Poor Kobessa shook her head as if to clear it of some rancorous miasma.

"But that time when the sea rose," she went on, "so *many* were killed. Only a few are killed when one village raids another. Sometimes the raiders are bought off with gifts and no one is killed."

"Then your country is different from other places I've been." Aengus shuddered. "Thank your gods for that."

He had much to ask the old woman, but he did not want to fatigue her. She needed all of her breath for walking.

For the last ten miles, the trail wound along the shore: stretches of beach separated by rocky outcrops that had to be climbed over. Kobessa was clearly tiring. Certainly she could not have expected to make the return trip with Kwetah on foot, Aengus thought. She must have intended to persuade someone to take them by canoe—someone more sympathetic toward the stubborn, selfless woman than Semackul was.

They stopped to rest. Kobessa pointed to a headland. "Hokodah is just before those farthest rocks. A river comes out near there."

"Where the smoke is?" Aengus asked. "They must have a great fire going."

The sun, dropping now through bands of clouds gathering above the western horizon, illuminated shore and sea mist with the same ruddy light. The offshore rocks seemed almost to float: ethereal shapes of buildings, animals, ships—

"Kobessa, what do you see there—past the headland?"

She squinted for a long moment.

192

"A great canoe, I think. One like it came when I was a girl. They come to places north of here more often. That's what I hear."

"It's the one I saw yesterday, then," Aengus told her. "It was being towed by canoes like the ones of this country. Is that a strange thing?"

"I don't know. They come for ti-juk. They trade things for the skins of ti-juk."

"Ti-juk?"

"Yes. You've seen Semackul's robe—the dark fur."

"His bearskin?"

"No, no. The one he wears when he wants to be important. The fine, soft one. That's ti-juk."

Aengus had not seen it and shook his head. Kobessa attempted to describe the animal: "Ti-juk is what you'd expect from the mating of a little river otter with a great fur seal. It floats on its back in the ocean and uses its stomach as a tray for its food, or a cradle for its young sometimes. It has a beautiful, warm pelt."

Kobessa became flustered. Aengus had been following her rapid description closely, trying to picture the remarkable animal; she must have interpreted his intent look to mean disbelief.

"It's true," she finished lamely. "They live in the ocean."

"I believe you, Aunt Kobessa. Do you think that's why the great canoe is here now—for ti-juk?"

"I don't know. I don't know why the other canoes would be with it. You say they were like our canoes?"

"Like this." He traced an outline in the sand.

"All of them were like that?" she asked, suddenly alarmed.

"As nearly as I could tell."

"Wayabuks," she whispered. "From far north of here. Fierce warrior people. Bad trouble. They don't trade—they kill and take what they want."

"You know this? They've been here before?"

"Not here, that I know of. But places over there"—she

indicated the land across the strait—"and away down there"—her finger pointed eastward. "All those people fear them greatly."

"I think we should get to Hokodah as fast as we can. If I go ahead, can you follow?"

"Hah!" she snorted, and scurried down the beach ahead of him.

He arrived many minutes before her, his heart pounding from apprehension. The smoke had seemed to come from many fires before he ever saw the village: thinning, twisting strands of smoke, becoming more white than black, like the smoke of dying fires. Then he saw a canoe upturned in the sea and soon after, as he climbed over the last rocky point before Hokodah's shallow cove, more canoes broken and scattered along the foreshore. At the back of the cove, where houses should have been, was smoldering ruin and no life at all.

He dashed madly up the sandy slope. He passed the bodies of men who had been struck with sharp weapons many more times than would have taken their lives. He ran from house to house and through the smoking rubble of each one, looking for Kwetah's small body and Leeaht's, and then for any body with life yet in it. He found Leeaht's sister, dead on the sand in front of the lodges, although he did not recognize her at first with her hair burned and her body smeared with blood and ashes. He found a few babes, slain with their mother's arms about them, but no other children.

He looked up once and saw poor Kobessa seated on the rock from which she must have first seen the terrible sight. She seemed numb with horror. He looked for the ship, but the headland hid that part of the strait. The raiders would have been lost in the gloom of approaching evening in any case.

He returned to his melancholy task, going through the wreckage of the few houses, and through them again. The village had been smaller than Appowad. He searched the wooded area behind the buildings until it became too dark to see, then he returned to Kobessa and slumped down beside her, his elbows on his knees and his head buried in his hands.

"There's no one alive, Kobessa."

She did not respond.

"I couldn't find Kwetah. I couldn't find any children at all, except babies. And very few women."

"The women, the old ones, are back in the forest," she said.

"You saw them?"

"No. But that's where they would go."

"With the children?"

"Some, maybe, but not all. Not many children. Or young women."

"What are you telling me, Kobessa? Where are they?"

"With the Wayabuks. They're Wayabuk slaves now."

"You don't know that. You're just guessing."

Again, the old woman was silent.

"You told me that raids aren't like that here," he insisted, "everybody slaughtered or taken slave. It happens in other lands, but you said not here."

"Now it's happened here," she said bleakly.

Aengus searched the old woman's face for some sign of hope, but all she said was, "Evil spirits drive the Wayabuks. Now they've driven them here. The Wayabuks have always taken slaves, and young people, even children, make the least troublesome slaves."

"Are you sure they're Wayabuks? Have you ever seen Wayabuk canoes?"

"Yes." She pointed across the strait. "The Didotah people had one when I was over there once."

Aengus looked along the foreshore at the dark shapes there.

"There are no Kweneechekat canoes left," he said. "They're all broken."

Kobessa seemed to withdraw into herself. Aengus went

195

among the canoes. Their fragile sides had been staved in with stones. They had been overturned and smashed again and again.

Back with Kobessa, he asked, "When will the old women come back?"

"Tomorrow, I suppose."

"What will they do? What will happen to them?"

"I don't know. There's never been anything like this before. Not here. Some will just want to die. There's no food. Their oil was used to burn the buildings, probably. They'll have no heart, no spirit. They'll want to die."

"We could take them to the villages we passed."

Kobessa looked at him as if he did not fully comprehend the catastrophe.

"The old ones? No. They'll be like Hahpellpah is now: hopeless and unable to do anything for themselves. I don't think they could get to the next village unless we carried them."

She thought for a few moments, then said, "We'll see how many come back, then we'll tell the other villages. They'll send canoes for them—for the ones that can be persuaded to leave."

"Can we get enough men together to go after the Wayabuks, do you think?"

"From the other villages? It would take a long while to get the men aroused enough. Hokodah wasn't an important village. Semackul's father came from here, but most of the people here weren't close to the other Kweneechekats."

"Then perhaps Semackul will—"

"Semackul? Hah! He'd be the last one to help another village unless he could find some advantage in it for himself."

The people drifted back throughout the next day: some alone, some in pathetic pairs or small groups. There were seventeen in all, only four of them children and none of them Kwetah or Leeaht. By evening, Aengus was sick at heart; he had clung to the hope that Kwetah and Leeaht would return, even after one of the old ones told Kobessa that the two had started to flee but had run back to help Leeaht's sister. No one had seen them since. So desolate was he that he did not even raise his arms to ward off the blows that a frail old man rained onto his chest.

"This is your fault," the old one wailed. "If you had not killed Pugahlkuthl, his magic would have saved us. He would have stopped them. He would have stopped them. . . ."

His thin voice trailed off and he sank to his knees, weeping dry tears, his arms wrapped around Aengus's legs.

Aengus and Kobessa left the next day after securing the survivors' promises that they would look after the four children, at least, and perhaps themselves. Kobessa promised to send help.

She went into each of the three villages on their way back to Appowad. Each time, she counseled Aengus not to accompany her, to stay hidden until she rejoined him. His appearance would be confusing; his presence would require much explanation and dispose the men to inaction until his significance was understood. Each time, she returned to tell him that the men had promised to send canoes for the survivors, but only when they had been convinced that the Wayabuks and Sericans no longer threatened.

"That's how much help you could expect from *them* if you were to go after the Wayabuks," she cautioned.

Aengus wanted to say, "*If* I go after them? I *will* go after them, by myself if I have to!" but he stifled the impulse. Even to doughty Kobessa, he did not want to show himself intemperate or given to unconsidered actions. *Especially* to Kobessa. If he was to secure the cooperation of Mahkalt and Sierka, and of any of the other men of Appowad if there were any there with stouter hearts than the men of these villages, Kobessa's advocacy would be more persuasive than empty bravado from him. Better to go against the Wayabuks with whatever few wise and brave men she could influence than with a wild, impetuous mob that would lose all.

Kobessa stayed overnight in the second village and Aengus slept against the trunk of a tree, dry enough under its tent of low-hanging branches although the sky wept all night.

Appowad lay below them about noon of the following day.

XXII

Once again, Aengus stayed behind when Kobessa descended to the village. Once again, Kobessa would carry the dolorous news of the sack and rape of Hokodah, but, before she returned to tell Aengus of their reaction, she would not mention what would disturb the men of Appowad more: his survival of Semackul's plot. From the bluff, Aengus watched her go first to her own lodge, then to another while Mahkalt and Sierka went far south along the beach and returned with Semackul and his two followers, Ubussuk and Butchasid. There was much activity in Appowad for a while with people coming and going, but eventually the men and many of the women gathered in the largest lodge—Semackul's—where a cloud of heavy smoke billowing through roof openings told of a fire being built up.

A warm fire on a gloomy day meant a long stay indoors, a long telling and retelling of the events at Hokodah, and a long discussion of their significance for Appowad. Aengus went back along the path and found a place where he could look down onto his own house. Although the light in the grove below was dim, he could see boards scattered about and he knew that he no longer had even that refuge in Appowad.

He went farther along the path and collected his package of belongings; then, suddenly overcome by despondency, he slumped to the ground, his back against a sodden, rotten stump and his hair rain-plastered over his face.

"Oh, God!" he cried to no god in particular. "Is this all I've got to show for half a lifetime?" He contemplated the ragged pouch in his lap, the handle of his sword-knife protruding. "No home. No people to call my own. Nothing but this handful of . . . things."

He brooded on memories of his dead friends, a trail of them that lay across the world with a lost child at this end and, at the other, a family who had grieved for him once, no doubt, but now must have forgotten him altogether. He did not reproach himself for that string of tragedies. It was hopelessness that overwhelmed him, not guilt. Besides, he knew well enough that the demons of calamity had no special affinity with him. Disaster and grief were the lot of the whole world and *all* the people in it. It had been so forever. He recalled the time when he first heard his grandfather relate how *his* generation had come to Armorica, displaced from Britain by Frisian marauders who had destroyed their town and killed most of its people. Aengus had wondered then, when he was a small boy, why his own very ordinary family should have been chosen for such rare and remarkable misfortune.

The years since had taught him about the world, that such catastrophes as his grandfather had described were neither rare nor very remarkable. "Even Tellacloute may not exist now," he reflected gloomily. "Armorica may have been overrun years ago and Tellacloute burned like Hokodah."

He dropped his head onto arms crossed over his knees and gave himself up to depression.

Some illnesses must deepen almost to death before the body rouses to heal itself; so with despair—at least this time for Aengus. For a while, his mind was consumed by utter hopelessness. Then, as if there was nothing left to sustain it, the hopelessness slowly dissipated and was replaced by . . . nothing. Empty of emotion, empty of thought, he wandered back to the place where Kobessa had left him.

Waiting, he occupied himself with small tasks. He restored his stone eye to its socket; he found a patch of the abrasive rush that grew in that country and scoured away the thin rust patina that had formed on his knife; he examined for wear the buskins he had made in the forest months ago. Since returning to the Kweneechekats, he had adopted their more practical barefooted way, but overland travel would require better protection than callused soles so he had kept his footgear.

Rummaging through his sack, his fingers touched something he did not recognize. As he fished it out, he saw a small rainbow flash of reflected light.

"Leeaht," he breathed. It was her comb.

His first suspicion was that Kwetah had played some mischief on the girl she had seen as her rival. But, no. If the child had taken Leeaht's comb, she would not have hidden it in his sack for him to find and be reminded of the one she wanted him to forget. Nor had Kwetah been in his house when he had admired the comb. Leeaht herself must have put it with his things. But when? He had emptied and repacked the sack the day before he hid it in the forest. Then he remembered that night—the noise on the path, the shadowy movement—and he wondered.

The image in his mind of Leeaht on the dark path was too vague, too unbelievable to hold for long against a stronger vision of her in his house, lovely and gentle by his fire. He was suffused with warmth . . . and regret. And then with sorrow almost beyond bearing. Leeaht and Kwetah—where were they now?

The rain had turned to a misty drizzle. Through its quiet, he became aware of noises from below: shouts of men. No. Shouts of *one* man. Semackul, he thought. But what had aroused his anger?

Concern for Kobessa stirred in Aengus. As he listened intently, his dismal apathy began to slip away. He hid his sack, except for the knife, and climbed down the bluff behind the houses. Crouching near Semackul's lodge, he tried to comprehend what he heard, but he could make no sense of it. He crept closer to hear more clearly.

"*You* are not the chabotta. *I* am the chabotta," Semackul was declaring. "Your lodge remains only because I permit it. If you and those in your lodge cause trouble, we will turn you out and take your planks. The men of this village and I got rid of one troublemaker—we can do the same with any others. You are not the chabotta. You don't even belong to Appowad any more, except that we let you live here, no better than slaves."

Aengus found a gap to peer through and saw Kobessa, Mahkalt, Sierka, and one of the silent women seated apart from the others, a forlorn group of near-outcasts. Apparently Kobessa had spoken earlier, but now she had nothing to say. In the poor light, she seemed downcast, very tired, very old and small.

"Enough of Semackul!" Aengus decided.

He knew that the dark Kweneechekats regarded his whiteness with awe and dread but considered his clothing only peculiar, so he removed it. He went around to the door. It had been left partly aside for ventilation. He stepped inside and stood while his eye adjusted to the dimness.

The decrease in light as he blocked the opening drew the attention of those on the floor nearest to him. They were aghast; their eyes and some of their mouths were wide with amazement. Awareness of his presence spread through the silent crowd, from those sitting on the floor and benches near the fire to those standing in the shadows farther back. Semackul stood with his back to him, declaiming, "If other villages are attacked, it's because their men lack courage. No one dares attack Appowad."

Then his words faltered. He saw that those before him were not listening. They were staring past him. He swung about irritably . . . then he stiffened, his words frozen within him.

"You accuse the men of Hokodah of cowardice," Aengus began icily. "They fought until they died. The Wayabuks were too many. The only cowards are their brothers who will not avenge their deaths."

"They were not my brothers," Semackul whispered.

"No man is your brother, Semackul. You were born of a serpent, not a woman."

"I'm not afraid of anyone. I'm not afraid to kill."

"I know *your* courage," Aengus replied sardonically. "It's the courage of a man not afraid to throw a child from that crag above the hole-through."

Semackul's eyes became desperate. He scanned the faces of those closest to him. Some of them stared back as if, Aengus thought, a suspicion had been confirmed.

"Kill him!" Semackul shrieked to Ubussuk, who stood against the wall near the doorway. "Kill him!" His pointing finger swept from Ubussuk to Aengus.

Ubussuk raised his weapon, a bone saber, and leaped toward Aengus. Aengus lunged and swung his heavy knife in a fierce, slaughterous sweep that almost severed Ubussuk's neck. His head rolled over onto his shoulder as his body plunged to the floor.

Aengus's eye caught Butchasid's movement on the other side of him, but when he turned, Butchasid slid down the wall and cowered on the floor, Aengus's gleaming knife over him.

"Hayektoyak," several people whispered. "Hayektoyak." The word passed through the crowd.

Aengus did not know the name, if name it was, nor what it might portend for him. He drew his knife back and held it before his face. "Skeinah," he told them in the Brythonic tongue. *Skeinah:* the word his own people used for such a weapon.

Instead of calming the people, his declaration terrified them. "Skeyna!" some near him squeaked as they pushed back among their fellows.

Aengus had not noticed Hahpellpah before, but he saw her now, moving out of the shadows and through the throng toward him. Her eyes were dull. They seemed empty of present awareness. He stood aside and she walked through the doorway. Her shoulder struck the wide plank that partly blocked it, but she did not seem to notice.

Turning to Semackul, Aengus saw that he now sat on the floor in abdication and abject submission. No one sat near him. Some had moved to avoid him. They pushed into the space that had separated Kobessa's group from them, although the old woman still seemed alone in their midst.

"Kweneechekats have been killed," Aengus declared to all of them. "Kweneechekat women and children have been taken by Wayabuks. I'm going after them to bring the captives back and to punish the Wayabuks so their people will know not to come here again. If men of Appowad want to help me do this for their brothers, be ready on the beach at daybreak."

The people continued to stare at him, none giving any sign that his words meant anything to them. In a more reasoning tone, he said, "If the Wayabuks go unpunished, this land will forever be their hunting ground for slaves and slaughter. Next year it may be Appowad that lies in ashes."

The people sat in numb silence, paralyzed with shock and fear. He saw that he could not reach their minds with words, not now.

Winter's chill began to seep through him. He left the lodge and found his clothing. He spent a while examining the canoes drawn high up on the beach or stored behind the buildings and watched askance as the people left Semackul's lodge in small groups.

Kobessa saw him and came over. "You will stay in our lodge tonight." It was an invitation, not a summons.

"I'll bring trouble to your lodge, I'm afraid."

"There will never be trouble in our lodge while you're there. The people are terrified of your powers."

"Even Semackul?"

"Semackul is finished. The people will no longer listen to him."

"Then, yes, I'll stay in your lodge. But I want to watch out here for a while. I'll come later."

When she had gone, he noticed something strange happening at Semackul's lodge. Two men had come out and were removing boards from a wall at the end of the building. As soon as the opening was large enough, something wrapped and bound was handed out from within. It could only have been Ubussuk's body. The boards were replaced and two more men came around from the door. The four carried Ubussuk down the beach past the river's mouth.

Following them with his eye, Aengus saw Sierka standing close by.

"Why . . . ?" Aengus asked, pointing to the wall of Semackul's lodge and to the retreating men.

"It's always done," Sierka answered. "Whenever someone dies in a lodge, his corpse is never removed through the door that the living use. The Hahtoppul ghosts are greedy, some say. They'll follow the dead man's trail back so they can seize another soul. If they meet a wall instead of a door, they're thwarted."

"Those ghosts can't be very clever, then."

"It's only a superstition," Sierka said, a little embarrassed. "Didn't you notice, when we gave you a wall board to carry Kwetah away? Some of the women in the back thought that she'd died and were protesting that a board shouldn't be removed so close to the doorway."

"I didn't understand your language then," Aengus replied simply.

Winter's late afternoon gloom had begun to close in on the beach, now empty, and on the dripping houses and trees behind. Sierka started toward his lodge, Kobessa's, and Aengus followed but stopped when he saw Semackul come out of his own lodge and walk sullenly down toward the water's edge. A small canoe was there, the kind one man would use for fishing. Sierka came back to stand by Aengus as they watched the fallen chabotta.

"That's his canoe," Sierka whispered.

"Is he running away?"

"I don't know. Perhaps. More likely, he's just going to bring it up above the tide line for the night."

Suddenly someone who had been lying in the canoe got up and stepped out to confront Semackul.

"That's Hahpellpah!" Aengus breathed.

Before the two men could decide whether the woman

205

was in peril, she lunged at Semackul with something held in her hand. Without a sound, he collapsed onto her, but she rolled him off and toppled him into the canoe. He did not rise.

Aengus started toward them, but Sierka seized his arm. "It's between them now," he said. "Don't interfere."

Aengus glanced at the man's hand firmly grasping his arm. It was the grip of a friend giving forceful counsel, a hand not constrained by demonic fear of him. Sierka's unwitting gesture of fellowship frustrated Aengus's compulsion to rush to Hahpellpah. Instead, he watched as she launched the canoe through the gentle surf and paddled slowly, purposefully, into the mist and darkness.

"We can't just let her go off like that," he protested. "She's not well. She's not safe."

"The kwal-k'washa lead her now," Sierka replied. "She wouldn't even recognize us. She's through with our world."

Aengus's unwillingness to accept that conclusion was written on his face.

"She's through with our world," Sierka repeated softly but insistently. He left Aengus and went to his lodge.

When Aengus followed him there, he was greeted with awkward silence. He knew no more what to say to his hosts than they did to him. One of the silent women brought him food. Only one fire burned and all of the people of the lodge warmed themselves around it, except for the witless old man. Aengus was half-afraid that no one would join him on the beach in the morning, yet he was more afraid to have that possibility spoken of now, even among these friends, lest the prediction, once uttered, would spread from lodge to lodge like some contagion and harden all the men against him. Perhaps, he thought, even the men of *this* lodge would be unwilling or somehow unable to join his pursuit of the Wayabuk raiders.

Finally, to initiate some talk among them, Aengus asked, "Was Semackul Kwetah's father?"

All their eyes lowered at the question. No one spoke at first, as if Kwetah or Hahpellpah stood to lose something by a truthful answer. Then Mahkalt said in a low voice, "Semackul was Hahpellpah's husband. . . ."

And Sierka finished what Mahkalt was reluctant to say: "But he could not have been Kwetah's father. Semackul killed that man."

"Why didn't Semackul kill Hahpellpah?"

Mahkalt answered. "He wanted her for his wife again, I suppose. She was very beautiful then. He loved her. But he was a jealous man and couldn't control his temper. He began to treat her badly, so she moved to our house."

"How did Semackul come to be the headman of Appowad?" Aengus asked.

Several of the people glanced quickly toward Kobessa. As if she had not heard, as if she were suddenly alone in the building, she got up and went to her sleeping bench. The others took her lead and left Aengus alone by the fire.

Deeply fatigued, he found the blankets Kwetah and her mother had used. He tried to imagine Hahpellpah out on the dark ocean with Semackul dead or injured, but he could hold no firm image in his mind. It was as if the kwalk'washa had already taken her from the world of men. He thought of Kwetah and the unremitting terror she must be suffering. Would she know that he would come for her, or believe that he could overcome her cruel captors? The thought that she might, even now, be dead flickered through his mind at the instant sleep overwhelmed him.

XXIII

Aengus waited alone on the beach a long while, hoping that "daybreak" signified some later hour for the men of the village than it did for him. Mahkalt and Sierka were still sleeping when he had come out early, impatient to be under way. Finally those two appeared bearing large baskets. They brought them part way down the slope of the beach, to where the rising tide would touch within the hour.

Aengus said, "At least you two believe we have a chance against the Wayabuks."

Sierka looked around the empty beach. "I didn't think we would ever see Kwetah again when you took her away last spring—no one did, except Mahkalt. But you brought her back. I believe you will again."

Mahkalt added, "She's lived in our lodge since she was born. She's like our own child."

"Will any of the others come, do you think?"

"I don't think you'll find anyone else willing to travel with Skeyna," Mahkalt replied.

"Skeyna? . . . Skeineh! Skeineh is the word my people use for a fighting knife."

"Skeyna is a demon. He can take any shape, become any kind of man or beast or thing. He tricks our people into harming him, then he takes his revenge at his leisure."

"Your people believe that there's such a demon?" Aengus asked incredulously.

"Many of our old stories are more believable since you've come here."

"What is 'Hayektoyak'? Would it have been better to have them think of me as Hayektoyak?"

"Hayektoyak is Tulukluts's lightning fish," Mahkalt answered unhelpfully. "We'll take our canoe—Sierka's and mine."

Aengus helped them haul the heavy canoe from where it lay against the side of their lodge, then waited while they returned to the lodge. He pondered the unlikely coincidences whereby his fate had become entangled with the spirit world of the Kweneechekats. Tellacloute-Tulukluts may have saved his life on his first day in Appowad and again when he returned with Kwetah; now skeineh-Skeyna dashed whatever remained of the hope he had framed of assembling a sizable force to overpower the Wayabuks and Sericans. He looked for some sign in those misunderstandings, some manifestation of the purposes of his own God, but the only message they seemed to bear was: "You can do nothing for Kwetah. There is nothing for you among these people or in this land. Move on. Move on."

"There's nothing for me anywhere," he countered, "except Kwetah . . . and Leeaht . . . and perhaps Mahkalt and Sierka, even Kobessa."

He repeated the names, pulled them around himself like a cloak, drew them into his heart and felt despair subside within him.

"They, at least, mean something to me, and I to them. And Kwetah needs me. Kwetah needs me. And Leeaht, too. I can't abandon them."

Strength and resolve began to warm him.

The men returned with two more baskets and Kobessa bustling along beside them. When everything was stowed and the canoe's bow afloat, the old woman rolled over its side and made herself comfortable among the baskets. Aengus watched her with amazement, then cast a sharp glance toward Mahkalt.

"Kobessa is only going to the next village. She'll speak

to the people there again," Mahkalt told him.

Afloat and paddling strongly to drive the undermanned canoe northward, Aengus scanned the western horizon several times and looked into hidden places along the shore as they passed. Then, as he turned to look once more, his eye caught Kobessa. Her wrinkled cheeks were wet, but not from the wind-driven spray.

"You needn't look for her," she said quietly. "We won't see Hahpellpah ever again. Her journey in this world is over."

The doleful finality of her statement sent a pang through him. Had Kwetah been safe in Appowad, he would not have accepted Kobessa's conclusion. He would have spent days searching for Hahpellpah, if only to be able to tell the child that he had done so. But Kwetah was not in Appowad.

They put Kobessa ashore near the next village, the one she had slept in coming home from Hokodah. Raw, blustery weather had driven its people from the beach, and it chilled the three men into silence while they waited.

Kobessa returned after an hour. With her, carrying heavy-laden baskets, were two women: a young one, about Leeaht's age, and a wiry one whom Aengus guessed to be a few years older than himself.

"No one will come?" he asked.

"Sistohka and Chehassa will go with you," she replied, indicating the two women with a nod of her head. "The village sends this food and some things you'll need."

Aengus looked to the two men, but they busied themselves stowing the new baskets. They rearranged them several times, pointedly ignoring the two newcomers. Aengus helped them into the canoe, and Kobessa handed in four paddles that she had carried from the houses.

"No men?" he asked Kobessa.

She seemed embarrassed that her friendship was not as valued nor her influence as great in this village as she had hoped. She shook her head, then added, "Sistohka and her daughter will be better than men. You'll see."

When all was ready, Mahkalt and Sierka waited by the

210

canoe. Aengus did not know how to take leave of Kobessa, yet he did not want the parting to go unmarked as it seemed it would be by the others. Wordlessly, he wrapped the old woman in his arms. As if not used to such familiarity, she seemed only to tolerate his embrace.

He looked back just as a rocky point cut off their last view of the beach. Kobessa still stood where they had left her.

The five paddled strenuously all day, first north, then around the cape and into the strait, and came ashore finally a mile before Hokodah. It rained off and on and a cold wind blew gustily, so they made a lean-to shelter and built a great fire before its open side. While they were engaged in this work, Aengus found himself alone with Sierka for a few moments.

"Nobody talked much all the way here," he said to the younger man.

"It was a long trip and rough water," Sierka replied.

"But it seemed to be something other than that. Was it because of the women? Are they going to be a burden? Was it because you don't know them? Are they strangers?"

Sierka smiled. "Strangers? No, not strangers. Certainly not to my uncle. Kobessa brought Sistohka to our lodge one time—for Mahkalt. When they realized what Kobessa intended, they were both so embarrassed that they never spoke to each other. Apparently they still find it difficult.

"But Chehassa and Sistohka are good women. Strong, like Kobessa. Kobessa wanted to come with us, but she's too old. These two come in her place."

When the shelter was made and a meal was being shared, Aengus watched the others and saw that there was no ill will among them, although there were few words either. Everyone was tired. Too tired, Aengus realized, to decide on a course of action or discuss their preparations for it. "Tomorrow. Tomorrow," he sighed wearily as he rolled himself into a bearskin robe.

Perhaps he slept more lightly than the others, or perhaps he thought his name was spoken; he woke suddenly, before there was enough light to see anything more than dark forms. Two figures squatted by the remains of the fire, trying to blow life into an ember to ignite a pile of twigs they had stacked over it. The two were strangers, not of Aengus's party, but there seemed to be nothing hostile about them. They were just two chilled young men trying to start a fire without rousing the sleepers.

Aengus got up and found dry wood to add to their twigs. Soon the fire blazed and the two men warmed their backs against it. Aengus found food in the canoe and offered it to the newcomers. They ate hungrily.

One of them was not much more than a boy and the other was about Sierka's age. The older one had a withered leg but had lived with it so long apparently, that his movements were not the awkward ones of the newly lame. Both were grimy and worn, their faces haggard masks.

The boy spoke first. "You're too late to help us this time, Akwahti."

Aengus was startled to hear Kwetah's familiar name for him. He looked at the boy more closely. "You're Leeaht's brother!"

"Yes. I'm Pahdow. You helped my sisters once, when Pugahlkuthl was going to kill them. But now one sister is dead and the other taken. And many others with her."

"I know. I was here just after it happened. Now we're going to bring them back."

Life came instantly to the two faces.

"You can do that?" the older one exclaimed.

"We can try. I'm not who I claimed to be in your river camp. I'm just a man. But we're going after the Wayabuks. If . . . the kwal-k'washa favor us, we'll bring the girls and children back."

His declaration inspirited the two. They moved around the fire to be closer to him.

"We killed one of them. The one who killed my sister," Pahdow said.

"You killed a Wayabuk?"

"No, not a Wayabuk. One of the others from the big boat. Mowbit"—he nodded toward his friend—"carried

212

an empty basket, pretending that it held something valuable, and he caught the murderer's eye. Then Mowbit ran up the river trail and he followed. I fell on him from hiding. We hit him until he was insensible. We carried him farther away. The next day we killed him." The boy shuddered. "It took all morning. He wouldn't scream at first, but he did before we were done."

Neither Pahdow nor Mowbit looked as if the killing had given them satisfaction or ease of heart. Aengus saw it as an opportunity lost. If the Serican had spoken a dialect familiar to him, he might have learned their course; but he did not betray his disappointment to the two suffering friends.

The others had wakened and lay listening to the talk around the fire. Now Mahkalt came forward. Mowbit recognized him. "Mahkalt! Mahkalt! Are you with this man?"

"Yes, and Sierka, too. But we have need for more, and room in our canoe."

Pahdow responded eagerly: "Will we start out today?"

Mahkalt nodded.

Sistohka joined those around the fire. "So now we are seven," she said. "A war party of seven."

Aengus surveyed their "war party": two women, a cripple, a boy, Mahkalt too old for battle, and himself half-blind. Only Sierka would have been chosen by a war chief.

"I've heard of war parties like this before," Aengus said. "My grandfather told me of one: a company of only ten at first; later of several hundred. They defeated a force of thousands. It was strength of heart and mind, not numbers, that did it."

"The leader of those few men must have been a great chabotta, then," Mowbit said.

"No. He was just a fighter. He died a fighter. Another horde came against him in another year, and then another the year after that. Finally, his people were overwhelmed by the numbers of their opponents. Most of them were killed. A few came to live in the land where I was born."

"What does all that mean for us?" Sierka asked. "That

213

we'll get our people back, or that we can expect no more than death if we find our enemies?"

"It doesn't mean anything except that I've heard of what a few can do against many. If our will makes us strong enough, clever enough—"

"And if the kwal-k'washa are with us," Sistohka interrupted.

"The kwal-k'washa didn't save Hokodah," Aengus said with sudden bitterness, then wished immediately that he could take back his words.

"Sometimes the kwal-k'washa are occupied with other things and aren't aware of our needs," Mahkalt said softly.

Because it seemed to matter as much to his friends now as it had at other times to him, Aengus struggled to bring the world of mysteries into focus, to find some hope there of divine aid for their cause.

"The Sericans—the men of the great ship—have their own gods. They're notoriously inattentive to the needs of men. The Sericans are always trying to arouse them with gongs and drums. The God of my own people, though, is supposed to know every secret in our hearts, to be aware of every misfortune—of the fall of even the smallest bird and yet," he paused, "evil things happen whether the gods are watching or not.

"The Serican gods will take the side of anyone who calls on them loudly and persistently enough. I don't know what it takes to attract the favor of mine. Most often He listens to no prayers at all, and our priests merely tell us to accept His inscrutable will."

Mahkalt absorbed this, thought about it, then said, "We would call those spirits 'demons.' The kwal-k'washa understand our world better, I think. It's also their world—not a foreign place as it seems to be for the spirits you describe. Ours may neglect us at times or make mistakes, but they respond to the prayers of the best men and women: those who are strong in heart and soul. They try to understand our needs if they're satisfied that we're worthy."

Sistohka had been following the discussion closely. When Mahkalt paused, she spoke. "Our people pray only after they've shown that they're not afraid of pain and are not governed by pleasure and personal desires. When we pray, we don't think only of ourselves. We remember others, even the souls of the animals we hunt. The kwal-k'washa look for the best in people and give help according to what they find.''

The others looked to see the effect of Sistohka's zealous words on Aengus. That the spirits of this land could be compassionate and responsive to just appeals encouraged him, but the power of first learnings tinged his feelings with a sense of sacrilege. He said only, "I hope the kwal-k'washa are pleased with us.''

Mowbit and Pahdow had not returned to Hokodah until the day before they came across Aengus's party. They had found their ruined village empty. The survivors were gone—to the other Kweneechekat villages, they assumed. The dead had been laid out in the forest behind the village and covered with partly burned boards and their broken canoes. There had been nothing else left from the fires to mark their common grave except a few broken tools and charred remnants of their possessions.

Earlier, from a high lookout back in the forest, Pahdow and Mowbit had seen the Serican ship and its Wayabuk escort head east, angling across the strait. They had not seen them return to the open sea.

"But we could easily have missed them in the dark or behind rain and fog," Mowbit said.

"And wherever they've gone, they have five days on us," Aengus remarked.

They drew crude maps in the sand to help them plan their pursuit, but Aengus soon realized that his companions' knowledge of the region was fragmentary and, of certain places, contradictory. In the baskets they had brought, Mahkalt found a hide wrapper that had been scraped until it resembled parchment. With fine, charred points, they drew a careful map on it to take with them and add to as they learned more.

Smoke swirled through the shelter at times, driven by

chilly gusts. Brushing the smoke and tears from their eyes, they constructed their map as if each line drawn gave them a new advantage over their enemies. It took shape in meticulous detail here, broad outline there. The land across the strait from them was the end of a long island whose axis lay roughly northwest to southeast, parallel to the coast of the mainland. So large was the island that to circumnavigate it by canoe would take a month. The land of the Wayabuks lay at some remote, unknown distance beyond the island's far end.

The strait beside them continued southeasterly for two or three day's journey, then branched into a long reach to the south, island-choked and blind, and another to the north and west behind the great island. The entrance to that northwesterly branch was confused by smaller islands, but the passages through them soon opened onto another broad strait for several day's travel.

Mowbit took the stick from Mahkalt's hesitating hand. "I've been almost that far," the younger man said, indicating the top of the strait just drawn. "Beyond are a tangle of islands and narrow, twisting channels. It continues that way until the passage finds the open sea again at the far end of the island. That's what we were told."

"Too narrow for the Serican ship," Aengus suggested.

"I don't know," Mowbit replied. "It would be the safest canoe route back to the Wayabuks' country in winter, but for the big ship . . . I don't know. There's bad water there. Strong currents. That's what I remember the people we visited telling my father."

Aengus stood and gazed eastward along the strait. "We have to decide on one direction or the other," he said. "Right now, that one seems most likely to lead us to them, and, in any case, it would be the route *we* would take if we have to follow them back to their own country."

Young Pahdow's eyes opened wide. "To their own country?" he said, as much to himself as to the others.

XXIV

For four chill, rainy days, they traveled along the coast of the great island, first southeasterly and then north through channels between the smaller islands. Aengus marveled that they passed so many villages, both large and small. He had not thought the country to be so populous. Mahkalt told him that it only seemed so because the people there clung to the shore; inland was left for animals and spirits.

The searchers did not take shelter in any of the villages at night. They camped in deserted coves where their small fire would not attract attention. During the days, they were watchful for evidence of ravage but saw none. Those days on the water were long, beginning at first light and often ending after dark. They did not stop to prowl the intricate channels and bays among the smaller islands, but paddled with power and purpose to reach the open strait that lay like an inland sea between the great island and the mainland, the waters where their map and intuition told them they would have the best chance of finding their quarry. . . .

. . . Unless the ravagers had retreated unseen to the open ocean and were now heading north along the other side of the great island. That possibility tormented Aengus. During the days, he could deaden his worry by concentrating on each paddle stroke, making each one perfect and powerful. Ashore, there was no such relief. Long after the others had fallen asleep, he would sit by the fire, watching the flames that at times became writhing human forms. Faces of the lost ones appeared in the smoke: the two dear to him and others he did not know but who implored his pity and help no less urgently.

Once when he looked up, Chehassa's anxious face was there, watching him from across the fire. But it was not Chehassa he saw. The eyes were Kwetah's: sad, suffering, loving. He held the vision as long as he could, until the quiet girl became embarrassed and looked away.

At times he reflected on what had impelled his companions to commit themselves to this uncertain venture. Certainly it was hot anger and thirst for revenge in the case of young Pahdow; no doubt the same for Mowbit, although Aengus knew little yet about the lame man's loss at Hokodah; Sierka and Mahkalt loved Kwetah without question, but their reserved demeanor marked them as unlikely warriors; and as for the women—he could not fathom the reason for their participation at all. But personal motive seemed to be a private matter among them. It was something no one was disposed to ask about, and soon Aengus found that he thought about it very little. His own pain and rage were enough to bear.

The women paddled as vigorously as the men during the cold mornings, but they rested or slept among the baskets through the afternoons. That respite restored their strength for other tasks: ashore, they gathered and prepared food. Sometimes the men fell asleep before it was ready, but, when they woke later, ravenous, Sistohka or Chehassa would be waiting patiently by the fire. Mother or daughter often fished from rocky headlands during the night as they kept watch. Kobessa's estimation of the worth of the two women—". . . better than men. You'll see"—became more valid each day.

On the fifth day, they put in at a village that Mowbit had visited as a boy with his father. The people there were more suspicious than friendly at first, but some remembered the earlier visit and, when they learned that only information was sought, they were willing enough to tell

218

what they knew. Their language was foreign to the Kweneechekats' ears, but Mowbit knew some of their words and Aengus made a sketch of the Serican vessel with the covey of Wayabuk canoes attending it. His heart leaped when the people pointed northward through the islands. They had seen the flotilla two days earlier, the ship under reduced sail and towing the canoes. They were curious about what it meant. By means of pantomime, recruiting as many of their children and young women as could be enticed to play the parts of victims, Aengus and Mowbit told their story. The people understood well enough; their expressions and gestures were sympathetic.

The next day, the searchers passed beyond the small islands and onto the western side of the open strait. Although they could clearly see the mountain heights to the east, winter mist hung over the water and they could not discern the shoreline below the peaks. Over the nearer water, they could see no masts or sails.

At the end of that day, they camped in a little cove with a narrow entrance and a marshy place at its end through which a small stream flowed. While they ate, Aengus asked if any of them knew the Wayabuk language. The others shook their heads.

"They come from very far north," Mahkalt said. "They're light skinned. Not our people at all."

"Hahpellpah's people, then? Kwetah's people? Did Hahpellpah teach you any of her words?"

"No, and it's not likely these Wayabuks are Hahpellpah's people, her tribe. There are several tribes of them, and I think they speak different tongues. They have their own names among themselves for their tribes. 'Wayabuk' is just *our* name for all of the northern people—it says that they're bloodthirsty marauders. I don't imagine they call themselves that."

"So with the Sericans," Aengus said. "There are several tribes of them, too, with their own languages and names for themselves, but I first knew of them as 'Sericans' before I ever came to their country. I learned only one of their languages well, but I understand others."

To have said more, to have spoken of what a Serican prisoner could have told them that would have put uncertainty to rest, might have been perceived by Mowbit and Pahdow as reproach. Aengus let the matter drop.

Early the next morning, when first light showed little more than the shapes of things, Sistohka shook each of them awake, whispering that they must hide their canoe. Without asking why, they threw the few things they had used in camp into the canoe and slid it quietly into the creek, where marsh grasses, though winter-sere, hid it well enough.

They struck their fire, then followed Sistohka back along the shore of the cove to the rock-girt entrance and hid in the scrub there. No sooner had they done so than two canoes appeared, rounding a bend of the shoreline south of the cove. The paddlers made no noise. Two more canoes followed the first two, then a final group of four. Each canoe carried more than twenty men: Wayabuks, with a few Sericans scattered among them. Looking over the low foreshore of the blunt point from which Sistohka had made her discovery, Aengus and the others saw the mast tops of the Serican ship.

The canoes passed by before the great, gray hulk of the ship came into full view. A few men moved about on its deck. Aengus's heart pounded. Only the planks of that barrel hull hid the captives from them. Kwetah and Leeaht were there! And all the other terrified children and desperate young women. He tried to picture them within the dark compartments but could not. Their distress remained words in his mind, not images.

When the ship had passed the entrance of their recess, Aengus and the others backed out of the brushy screen and gathered where they had camped.

"How did we get ahead of them?" Sistohka asked.

"They've been scouting along here, going slowly," Mahkalt answered. "We just didn't see them. The big ship may have been hidden somewhere while the men explored in the canoes."

Aengus said, "Most of them are in the canoes now—

more than they have paddles for—and they're not towing the ship."

"They look like people of one village going to visit another for a celebration or a feast," Sierka observed, "but they're strangers here. It's another raid. It can only be that."

"We must warn the village they're going to," Sistohka said.

"It's too late for that," Aengus told her. "We can't attack the Wayabuks on the water. They're too many for us. And we can't get to the village before them. We don't even know how far it is or if there are trails hidden from the water. Unless Mowbit remembers . . ."

"No. It was a long time ago when we passed here. I was only a boy."

"We can steal the ship while most of them are ashore," Pahdow suggested.

"No. We couldn't hold it against them. Counting Wayabuks and Sericans together, there must be more of them than all the men in Appowad—many more," Aengus said. "The time to rescue our people will come later, when we can get well ahead of the ship and prepare a trap or find allies. Right now, we need to know their route and what they plan to do before they leave this country."

They collected small weapons from their canoe, then headed up the side of the marsh. They soon found a poor trail leading north, away from the stream and parallel to the shore. The path improved as they went along so that, before long, they were able to run on the level parts.

They had gone less than a mile when fearsome cries and the clamor of an attack rang through the trees. Before they ever saw the village, they encountered a group of women and children running toward them. When they saw the strangers, the fugitives stopped in confusion and terror.

"Friends!" Mowbit shouted in their tongue. "Friends!"

He motioned for them to go past. Desperately trusting that reassurance, they came forward again. The Kweneé-chekats and Aengus were arrayed along a steep, root-broken incline; they helped some of the women with young children to clamber up. Rather than go farther along the path and risk frightening those still coming, who might then run back to their village, Aengus's band stayed at that place until all had passed. They hoped to see pursuers, but the trail emptied and no enemy appeared. Telling Sistohka and Chehassa to go with the village women, the men continued on, moving rapidly but warily.

They were close enough to the village to hear the crackling noise of fire when another woman came stumbling along the trail. She had been injured; her legs were smeared with blood. They started toward her, but Sierka, in the lead, suddenly motioned them into the woods on either side just as her pursuers appeared far down the trail.

The woman collapsed as her enemies—eight Wayabuks and a Serican—overtook her. Five of the Wayabuks and the Serican swept past her and past the hidden men. When those six rounded a bend in the trail, Aengus and the others rushed the three who stood over the woman, prodding her unresponsive body with their clubs. The Wayabuks raised startled eyes to a whirlwind of men and weapons and died in the same instant.

Aengus's knife did not find flesh in the melee; his companions attacked so furiously that he was shoved aside. Now they turned and raced after the others as he knelt beside the woman.

"I want the Serican alive!" he shouted after them.

The woman was dead. He ran to overtake his friends, but even Mahkalt was faster than he. Coming onto a straight section of the trail, he saw the fight already joined and the women and children watching fearfully from a distance beyond.

The Wayabuks had been taken by surprise, but, in truth, no forewarning would have saved them from the fury of the Kweneechekats. As he dashed toward them, Aengus was amazed to see Mahkalt fling a Wayabuk's arm aside, slash his neck nearly through, then hurl himself onto the back of another who had pinned Pahdow and dispatch

222

him as quickly. Even lame Mowbit's opponent was like a leaf against his tempestuous ferocity. By the time Aengus came up to them—a mere instant it seemed—the Wayabuks were slain and the Kweneechekats had surrounded the terrified Serican, who turned and turned to defend himself on all sides. Aengus seized him from behind and took his wind with his fist. Throwing him to the ground, he sliced through the great tendons behind his knees so that he could not run.

"We can do nothing more for the village," Aengus told his companions, who stood over him, their chests heaving from exertion and excitement. "Take the women and little ones to the stream, then go up the trail there, away from the shore. I'll join you when I find out what this one can tell me. I may be a while."

He was a long while. He carried his prisoner into the forest, then up an old rock fall to a level place.

The Serican did not respond at first so that Aengus began to think his questions were not understood. The sight of his knife loosened the Serican's tongue a bit, but the wiry young man considered himself to be a warrior who should neither disclose information about his fellows nor be expected to. It took almost an hour of exquisite torment to convince him that Aengus acknowledged no such privilege.

From him, Aengus learned that the Sericans had come on a trading voyage the previous summer. An unexpected series of storms along their northern sea route had damaged or destroyed all of their stock of sails and much of the ship's rigging, forcing them to winter over with the Wayabuks. On two previous voyages, they had made good trade—mostly metal tools for ti-juk skins—with the tribe whose men now accompanied them. However, on this voyage, when those people saw the Sericans' vulnerable condition, they exacted a heinous price for their hospitality and matting for new sails. The Wayabuk chabotta hungered for power and influence among his neighbors. He framed a plan to spread holocaust throughout these southern lands, thus to magnify his reputation as a ferocious prince of men, an Attila among the wild nations of the coast; he then intended to return with a cargo of slaves, an extravagant number of them, to impress the other chiefs—as many girls and children as could be crammed into the compartments of the Serican ship.

Aengus's prisoner told him that, on their return, there was to be a grand concourse of villages during which the invited chiefs would select the slaves they desired, and, if any remained unchosen, these would be given over to rape and ritual slaughter. If the company gathered were sufficiently aroused by the bloody spectacle, then the visiting chiefs, each trying to outdo the others, might surrender, one by one, the slaves they had previously chosen until all had been tortured and slain. In all that the Serican told him of the intended disposition of the captives, Aengus believed that he was only repeating speculations of the Serican crew, who understood little of the Wayabuk tongue and who would be morbidly impressed by the wild splendor and ferocity of their coercers to savagery. If, indeed, he spoke the truth, then it seemed to Aengus most probable that, in the end, the Sericans would find their lot cast with the victims rather than the victors.

Of more useful information, he learned that the Wayabuks did not trust their Serican confederates, even those among them who, like the one he interrogated, had taken readily to rapine and slaughter. The ship was never left without Wayabuk guards; most of its crew were put on shore during raids and were taken into the Wayabuks' overnight camps. The raiders had descended on three villages before the one now under attack and had taken almost one hundred captives, all now held in compartments within the ship. They intended one more assault: against a village on an island across the strait; then they were to return north through the channels beyond the end of the open water. They had come south along the seaward side of the great island, but would not retrace that route going back because they feared that the men of other villages of the tribes they had raided would be lying in wait for them.

The Serican did not recognize Kwetah or Leeaht from Aengus's descriptions, but he said that none of those taken aboard the ship had been killed.

At the end, his proud body reduced to offal by torture, he looked only mildly astonished when Aengus sliced his throat.

Aengus had been so intent on extracting every shred of information the reluctant Serican could provide that he ignored all else. Voices from the foot of the rock fall startled him. Peering over cautiously, he saw four Wayabuks searching, apparently for whoever had killed their fellows. Freshly broken stems and trampled earth must have led them to follow Aengus's path away from the trail.

He waited until he was sure of their number, then hoisted the Serican's broken, bloody corpse over his head. With a short run and a mighty heave, he hurled it over the steep slope. Arms and legs flailing loosely, the hideous remains fell fully onto one of the warriors at the instant he looked up. He collapsed with a sharp grunt. The others ran to him in consternation. Aengus threw a rock as large as his head onto them, and then another before they gathered their wits. The second rock struck one of the men and knocked him down; the other two scrambled through the brush toward the trail as Aengus plunged down the rock fall.

The two stunned Wayabuks died under his swift knife, but the other two regained the trail and escaped. Either from confusion or because they imagined further threat where none lay, they ran away from the village. Aengus followed at a slower pace, expecting to meet them returning after they had realized their mistake or had seen the Kweneechekats ahead of them.

XXV

Aengus found his friends and the fugitives from the village at the top of a bluff that looked out over a mile of forest to the strait. He had not encountered the two Wayabuks and was surprised to learn that the others knew nothing of them. The village people sat huddled silently together, apart from the Kweneechekats.

"Have you talked to them?" he asked.

"Not much," Mowbit replied. "Their language is the same as that of the village yesterday. They're Kowmux people. We showed them that we intend to overcome the Wayabuks. I think they understood. But I don't think they realize yet that their village is gone."

"They seem to have quite a few of their young ones with them," Aengus observed. "Perhaps they won't have lost as many as the other villages."

"Did you learn anything from the Serican?"

"Yes. Many things. For one, their alliance with the Wayabuks is insecure. Some of the Sericans—that one, at least—have tried to prove their worth and bravery to the Wayabuks, but the Wayabuks still don't trust them."

"Did you learn their route?"

"Roughly. They have other business before going north. That gives us time to get ahead of them—"

"Look!" Sistohka pointed to the strait. Between the treetops, the five bare masts of the Serican ship showed now their tips, now much of their lengths, as the ship slid southward close to the shore. Had it not been moving, its masts would have been taken for dead trees if they had been seen at all.

"I hope Chehassa sees it and keeps out of sight," Sistohka fretted.

"Chehassa?" Aengus exploded.

"She went to our canoe to get blankets for the children. We thought we would be here for—"

"There are two Wayabuks down there. I asked if you'd seen them."

"You asked if I'd seen any Wayabuks. You didn't say there were any to be seen."

"There are—two of them."

Aengus bolted to the trail with the rest of the men close behind.

They ran downhill until they caught a glimpse of the small cove where they had camped. Approaching more cautiously, they saw that their canoe had been pulled from its hiding place amid the tall marsh grasses, but still rested with its bow on the muddy bank there.

"Where's Chehassa?" Sierka whispered. Then he saw movement on the shore beyond the rocks at the cove's mouth and he began to run, but Mahkalt seized him.

"No!" the uncle whispered fiercely. "We'll go together, and carefully. We don't want to lose anyone, and certainly not Chehassa."

In the bowl of the cove, they proceeded through the trees that enclosed the open space until they came to the screen of brush from which they had observed the ship and canoes earlier. Below them, on the shore outside the cove, they saw the two Wayabuks holding Chehassa between them. And, to their dismay, they also saw a canoe with six paddlers pulling up to them. There were other canoes too, but farther out and back toward the village. There was no wind, and a fine rain had begun to fall. The ship, not yet in sight, must have been drifting with the current while the canoes patrolled the shoreline, looking for their lost men.

Aengus beckoned the others back and away from the Wayabuks' hearing.

"Do they want our canoe, do you think?" he asked.

"Very likely," Mahkalt answered with a tinge of pride in his voice. "It's a fine canoe. Probably they would have taken it already except that one of them would have had to hold Chehassa, leaving only one to paddle."

"They might bring their canoes inside. . . ." Mowbit began.

"More likely they'll put Chehassa into their canoe out there and send men back for ours," Sierka speculated. "I'll watch there, and the rest of you stay hidden here to take whoever comes in."

He turned to the screen above the outer shore while the others hid where they could see his signals. These were long in coming. Apparently the Wayabuks on shore and those in the canoe argued. Aengus heard their shouts and worried for Chehassa's safety. Once, Sierka started up as if to leap onto those below, but then he settled back onto his haunches again.

Suddenly he signaled with three fingers and lay flat to the ground. His meaning became clear when three Wayabuks climbed over the rocks near his lookout and came onto the cove's small beach. Aengus gestured to his companions that they should kill the three silently.

But the Wayabuks separated. One stayed near the entrance while the other two walked through shallow water toward the Kweneechekats' canoe. Their path was too far from their would-be assassins to allow a quick and silent dispatch.

Frustration grew within Aengus and the others, and in young Pahdow most of all. He looked from face to face to see what his friends would do. Finally catching Aengus's and Mahkalt's eyes, he silently mouthed his own plan, but they did not understand. Pahdow shook his head, irritated by his elders' obtuseness. He waited another moment, then deliberately limped from hiding, dragging his leg as if injured.

"Oh!" he cried with a surprised voice, to make the Wayabuks believe he had only now caught sight of them. He turned to run but stumbled and fell—or made a convincing pretense of it.

The one nearest the cove's inlet ran toward him. Pahdow picked up rocks and hurled them at him, then brandished his dagger. The other two looked around quickly for others who might be with the boy. Seeing no one, they approached from his other side. Pahdow looked up at them fearfully and thrust his dagger at them, now to one side, now the other. The men laughed . . . then died, swiftly and silently.

Aengus and the others dragged the bodies into the bushes. Sierka kept his watch; the others had signaled him to stay. They hid the canoe in the tall grass again, then concealed themselves.

Pahdow looked at them questioningly.

"We wait," Aengus told him.

"Until the others come to find these ones," Mahkalt said.

"What if they don't come?" Pahdow asked.

"We wait until Sierka tells us they're not coming. Then we'll see . . ." Mahkalt said. Impulsively he put his arm around the lad's shoulders and squeezed. "Your quick wit gave us those three, but now we need your patience."

Pahdow grinned proudly.

They waited. The chill drizzle began to drip through the branches onto them. They rubbed their stiffening limbs and waited longer, watching for a sign from Sierka all the while. He remained on his knees, motionless.

Their attention began to wander until Mowbit's hiss drew their eyes to Sierka again. His arm was moving close to the ground to tell them that the Wayabuk canoe was coming into the cove. It appeared in the opening, moving very slowly as the paddlers peered cautiously past the rocks there. Chehassa was in the bottom of the canoe, only her head showing among the five Wayabuks seated above her on the thwarts. Her eyes searched the shoreline as intently as theirs, but with desperation rather than wariness. Each mind ashore sent the same message to her: "Wait, wait . . . Be still . . . We're here."

The canoe drifted down the center of the little cove, keeping some thirty feet from the shore on either side as it moved slowly toward the marshy end. The Wayabuks looked for their fellows, but they did not shout, just as if they suspected that something evil had befallen them and were afraid they would call the same fate onto themselves.

The paddler ahead of Chehassa stroked gently to bring the canoe to a halt, and the others, heeding his vague impulse, dipped their paddles also. The girl misunderstood their caution; she thought their movements indicated retreat. She lunged for the side of the canoe and pulled on its edge with all her might to throw herself into the water. From her cramped position, her action was awkward. The man behind her dropped his paddle into the water and grabbed her. She pulled away and toppled free, but he snatched again and caught her ankle so that her leg struck hard against the side of the canoe as she fell into the water. She twisted and fought to bring her head above the surface, but the Wayabuk held her ankle now with both hands while another raised his paddle to batter her into submission when the first should release her.

The men ashore could stand no more. They broke from hiding and raced for the water. The Wayabuks were disconcerted by the suddenness of the attack. They abandoned Chehassa and paddled frantically to propel their canoe backwards out of the cove. They did not even stop to recover the dropped paddle.

Aengus and those with him might have been content to let the Wayabuks go—it would be a reckless act for swimmers to attack a canoe—but Sierka reacted hotly. From his lookout, he ran the few feet to the rocks at the inlet and leaped into the stern of the approaching canoe. His knife took the man he fell onto, then he rocked the heavy canoe as violently as he could to keep the others unbalanced until his friends could run to aid him.

They came in a burst, wielding sticks, rocks, and their knives as they jumped from the rocks onto the hapless Wayabuks. Mowbit's wild swing with a large stick caught Aengus across the shoulders and knocked him to his knees, and Mowbit himself into the water. The Wayabuks, though, were too confused by the suddenness and ferocity of the attack to take effective advantage of that accident.

They fought wildly with their paddles, but they died none-theless.

Afterward, Sierka and Pahdow slumped onto the thwarts, but Mahkalt and Aengus roused them quickly.

"We're not through yet," Mahkalt said. "We may have attracted the others. Pahdow—quickly—onto the rock and keep watch. Tell us if they come."

They pushed the canoe to the rock. Pahdow scrambled out, and then the others paddled the craft into the cove again and onto the beach.

"Enough fighting for one day," Aengus said, and Mahkalt nodded agreement, "so we'll send them a message to stay away. We'll bring all the bodies here, to their canoe."

He suddenly noticed that Sierka was missing, then saw him kneeling near their own canoe, comforting a dis-traught Chehassa. The girl clung to his neck while he tried to wash and examine her bleeding leg.

Mowbit, Aengus, and Mahkalt recovered the bodies from the water and the woods and sat them in the bottom of the Wayabuk canoe. As Aengus directed, they broke four Wayabuk paddles and set the pieces upright between the legs of the eight corpses, with the shattered ends caught under their chins. The bodies slumped against the sides of the canoe but remained fairly well upright.

Aengus glanced toward Pahdow, but the boy sat with his back to them.

"We have to make these corpses more horrible," he said. "I'd rather Chehassa and the boy don't see."

Grasping one of the Wayabuks by the hair, he slid his knife between the dead teeth, sliced back through the cheeks and ligaments that held the lower jaw, then broke the jaw down so that its chin hung against the splintered paddle blade. The face resembled those gaping skulls, silently and eternally screaming, that rested in nooks around the Cave of Ancestors where Yen Hsin's grand-father had been laid out. He shuddered, but quickly mutilated the other bodies in the same way.

Although Mowbit looked dismayed that the dead

should be treated so irreverently, he suggested halfheartedly, "Warriors like these would dread losing their male parts."

"No time . . . no time. This is enough," Aengus said. "Help me now."

Carefully they slid the canoe off the beach and walked it through shallow water along the shore to the mouth of the cove. With a powerful shove, made smoothly so as not to topple the macabre cargo, they propelled the canoe between the rocks and into the open water still ghostly calm under the misty drizzle.

Pahdow scampered to join them when they returned to the beach within the cove.

"Did you see the Serican ship?" Aengus asked him.

"Yes. It's coming into sight around the curve of the shoreline. It seems to be just drifting."

"And the other Wayabuk canoes?"

"There's two of them down there"—he pointed to the southeast—"but they're coming back. The others are scattered, mostly near the ship."

"Then they'll find our message soon. Quickly, take blankets and things from our canoe—just for the night. And food—enough for the children."

During the whole of their flight, they heard nothing from the sea. Chehassa limped painfully and Mahkalt favored a bruised arm, rubbing or holding it when he thought no one was watching. Aengus's shoulders ached from Mowbit's misdirected blow, but he said nothing about it.

The Kowmux women and children were still atop the bluff. They seemed not to have moved at all in the time the men were away. They looked up mournfully as the few blankets were distributed among them and a basket of food set out for their use.

Aengus and the Kweneechekats watched the strait from the rim of the bluff. They could only imagine their enemies' reaction to the grisly discovery that they must have made, for the canoes were hidden by the trees. Only the mast tops of the ship showed.

Before long, however, the slow alongshore drift of the ship ceased, and it began to move as slowly out into the strait. After some time, it was distant enough from the shore that they could see to its waterline. For Aengus, the intervening mist and rain obscured all detail, but several of the others made out canoes ahead of the ship. Apparently they were towing it, for there was no wind to drive it.

Mowbit said, "It's a sore thing to have been so close to our children and now to see them taken away again."

"We couldn't have done anything more with our numbers," Aengus responded. "We took advantage of the Wayabuks' carelessness, but they won't send out small parties now—at least not for a while."

"We killed nineteen of them, and none of us were injured," Pahdow noted. "That's a good start."

"Perhaps," Sierka said carefully, "and perhaps not."

Mahkalt nodded, but the others looked at his nephew with astonishment.

To reveal his meaning, Sierka asked Aengus, "What do the people where *you* come from do when they're terrified?"

"The same as people anywhere, I suppose. They become uncertain, afraid, ineffective. They flee if they can. . . . Is that what you mean—that we've frightened the Wayabuks off? That they'll run for home?"

"No. They may do that, but I was thinking of something else. Do your people make sacrifices to the spirits?"

"Sacrifices? In a way, yes. Symbolic sacrifices to atone for wrongdoing."

"As barter for protection?"

"From disasters? No." Suddenly the import of Sierka's questions became clear to Aengus. "Sacrifices of people? The captives?"

"We've heard such things about the Wayabuks. They have a bloodthirsty reputation."

Aengus told them then what the Serican had believed to be the ultimate fate of the captives. "I thought he was just imagining wildly."

"He may have been," Sierka said. "But we've heard many rumors of Wayabuk cruelty. To impress visiting chiefs, one chabotta, who owned many slaves, killed some of them wantonly and used their bodies as rollers when his guests' canoes were dragged onto his beach. Another story is of a chief who had his slaves dig deep holes to set the posts for his lodge. He forced a slave to go into each hole and wrap his arms around the post, then he buried them alive."

Mahkalt appeared to be disturbed by the turn of their talk, as if dwelling on such horrors might distract them from rationality and steadfastness of purpose. "Some of them may treat their slaves well," he said, "just as in our villages, but nobody remembers those kinds of stories. I wonder what terrible things Wayabuk mothers tell their children about us."

Aengus, who knew well the contagion of cruelty that infects mankind—and that had possessed *him* after their victory in the cove—was not yet ready to set aside the subject that Sierka had opened. "Who would be sacrificed first?" he asked him. "Boys? Girls? Young or old? The strongest or . . . ?"

"If the sacrifices were made with honest intention, they would first offer the best to the spirits."

That opinion might have relieved Aengus's fears for Kwetah or intensified them for Leeaht, but, before it could do either, he was struck with dread when Mowbit added bitterly, "Lame ones like me wouldn't even have value as slaves, let alone as sacrifices. They'd have killed them already."

Aengus's desolate expression penetrated Mowbit's momentary self-absorption; he had forgotten, when he spoke, that the little lame girl who had come to Hokodah was everything to Aengus, just as his sister's two boys were everything to him. He turned away. The others stared bleakly out across the strait, where the ship and canoes were lost now behind rain and mist.

XXVI

Mowbit kept the map. At first he treated it as if it were a sacred object that the others might think was improperly in his keeping; he would have yielded it to Aengus or Mahkalt instantly if they had asked. When he saw that they were content that he should be its custodian, he began to handle it less circumspectly. He studied it each morning, and, when he finally felt that there was no wrong in it, he began to put his own marks on it: small lines to indicate the set of tidal currents, and crosses for their camps. He neatly erased shorelines that proved to be incorrect and redrew them, taking great care to make distances in the new parts conform to those nearer home.

The others came to depend on Mowbit's understanding of the sea's changeable flow. It was his judgment that determined whether they would seek countercurrents along the edges of channels or simply wait on shore when strong tidal races opposed them. It was he who discovered that they had passed the meeting place of the tides, where tidal flow through the strait from the south met that from around the northern end of the great island.

"Stop!" he had commanded them then. "Bring the canoe to a complete stop."

While the other paddlers merely slumped in their places, he checked the canoe's drift against a tree on the shore and another farther back.

"We're moving southward on a flooding tide," he

announced, "not to the north as before. This is a place my father told me about when I was old enough to understand. He said it was as far as we had gone on our voyage."

"Where to now?" Mahkalt asked wearily. His hands gripped the sides of the canoe and his straightened arms jammed his shoulders above his drooping head. From the time they passed the smoking desolation of the raped village, they had paddled hard for two rainy days and rested poorly during the cold, wet nights. Their fires, difficult to start, burned fitfully and threw off more smoke than heat. They had only their damp bearskin raingear for warmth; their blankets now warmed small bodies back in the ruined village. This new day was as cheerless as the previous two had been—worse because of accumulated fatigue.

"Where do we go?" Mahkalt repeated when Mowbit had been silent awhile.

"Where the islands and all the narrow channels between them begins is not too far from here, I think. I remember a bright place on the horizon. When I asked my father about it, he said it was a cape, a sandy cliff on one of the islands. It caught the sun and could be seen from a great distance."

All their eyes followed Mowbit's arm, pointing ahead, but they saw only dismal, fine rain and nothing through it.

"Do we paddle that way, then?" Mahkalt asked dully. He and Aengus had been the leaders when leadership was required, but now he was cold and tired; he felt old and peevish. He had strength only to take someone else's direction.

"There's a village on that cape," Mowbit said. "A large village, I think. I wish I could remember what my father said about it. When he told me what the bright place was, he mentioned the village as if it was special."

"Then we'll go there," Aengus said.

A thought had been like a worm in his mind: an insistent worry that they had spent all of their endowment of kwal-k'washa auspices in their single encounter with their enemies, and that the Wayabuks had been frightened into such sober prudence that there would be no other opportunity to rescue the captives. He had a persistent vision of standing with his six companions on some sodden shore, dispirited and helpless, watching the Serican ship sail past surrounded by Wayabuk canoes and as inaccessible as the moon. "We must find allies," he said.

They took up their paddles again and forged northward against a weariness that had come too early in the day. The shore on their left fell away until it was mere darkness in the rain. Then the sky became as dark as that shadow, and no shore could be seen anywhere. The rain fell more heavily. The world they paddled through, hour after silent hour, became like a vague spirit world, and they like ghosts on some endless journey that had lost its purpose.

Late in the day, when the gloom began to deepen into winter dusk, Chehassa glanced up as she emptied her bailer over the side.

"There," she cried, pointing to the right of their course. The men ceased paddling and scanned an indistinct shoreline. They could make out none of its features until, quite abruptly, they saw trees on a spit of land that projected toward them. They were instantly aware that a powerful current was bearing them swiftly northward.

"The tide's changed," Mowbit shouted. "We're in a channel."

Chehassa and Sistohka grabbed their paddles to help the men drive the canoe toward shore and then, in the weaker current there, to work it southward again. They had to paddle strenuously at first, but in time the shoreline began to bend toward the southeast, and the current lessened all the while. The land behind the curving beach became steeper and finally presented a rising cliff to the spent paddlers. But there were no signs of a village or people.

Watchful Mowbit eventually directed them to put in to shore at a place distinguished only by greater numbers of the huge granite boulders they had been seeing along the beach and projecting from the shoal water before it. As the canoe approached shore, Aengus's desultory imagination

237

saw the tall rocks as guardians placed to warn off intruders like themselves who came when bad weather has driven people from the beach or in the dark of night. He was not greatly surprised, then, to discover that many of the stones were carved into huge, somber faces of men, birds, and beasts with all of their blind eyes facing the sea.

"You knew of these?" he asked Mowbit.

"When I saw the rocks standing here, I remembered something my father said about the path up the cliff to the village being guarded by stone men."

Aengus looked but could see neither path nor village— only the sandy cliff, perhaps a hundred feet high and extending left and right as far as he could see through the drenching rain.

Mahkalt and Pahdow sagged, exhausted. Aengus, Sierka, and Mowbit climbed out of the canoe to pull it ashore. Chehassa sat with her arms wrapped protectively around her drained mother while her childlike eyes looked anxiously at each of the men.

Suddenly they heard a call from far back along the beach. Instantly alert, they waited until the call was repeated.

"I think he's telling us to bring our canoe back there," Mowbit said, but, responding to another possible meaning, he shouted back, "Friends! Friends!" in the speech of the people of that inland sea.

The three in the water threaded the canoe through the maze of boulders, looking in vain for their hailers. Finally, another call revealed a small group of men and women standing on the beach among rocks as tall as they were. They signaled to bring the canoe in. Two men came into the water to help while other men and women went high on the beach and brought back log rollers. The rollers, carried from stern to bow as the boat was dragged over them, enabled the men to haul the canoe to the top of the beach and then onto a ledge where other canoes lay side by side and upside down. The Kweneechekats' canoe became one more in that row; the things they did not take with them, they stored underneath.

Whether their welcomers had seen them from above or were already on the beach when they passed, Aengus never knew. The lack of a common language was soon known, however, although Aengus recognized Kowmux words. The newcomers were led to a narrow, slippery trail up the cliff, then to a large village on top where more than a dozen lodges, similar in construction to Kweneechekat buildings, stood between the cliff top and the forest behind.

One of their escorts took them to his lodge. His fellows went to their own houses at first, then came back with friends and families as their curiosity compelled them. The travelers, the five men of them, removed their wet clothing and shook out their bearskins before entering. They hung those things on a rack of poles inside the entrance, although the rack was too far from any of the several fires to dry them properly. Kweneechekat men—and Kowmuxes too, it seemed—regarded clothing as a cumbersome nuisance. If their blankets and furs became wet, they cast them aside no less readily inside their indifferently heated winter lodges than outdoors in summer. Aengus had become easy with the custom. He no longer felt immodest or embarrassed, but he never became as insensitive to chill as those who had grown up in that fashion.

Chehassa and Sistohka were taken by some women to another part of the lodge. He saw later that they had been provided with dry clothing: skirts of shredded underbark that covered them from waist to knees. Women were never seen without that minimum raiment.

Food was offered. Word must have spread quickly that the strangers spoke a foreign tongue since while they ate, no one ventured any question to them. The people of the village looked on them with curiosity—some shyly, others more boldly. The children were fascinated by Aengus's improbable color. First one, then several, finally all of the rest approaching him in a short file, each of them in turn rubbed a finger against his shoulder or back to see if their own rich hue lay beneath his paleness. The last, a little girl, put her arms around his neck, not from affection as it turned out, but as a pretext to give his yellow beard a tug to determine whether he had grown it himself or had stolen it from some animal. Their parents might have restrained the children, but they were as curious themselves, and they saw that Aengus was more amused than annoyed.

Pahdow began to shiver; someone put a blanket over his shoulders. Warmed and fed, the youth fell sound asleep while still sitting. The weary travelers were then given mats and blankets and places to sleep near the fire, which their hosts thoughtfully kept fed through the night.

That consideration stood in sharp contrast to the abrupt summons that came soon after their waking. Men armed with spears and clubs burst into the lodge and hustled Aengus and the Kweneechekat men outside into the rain. Aengus thought at first that they were being ejected from the village and that the Kowmuxes intended to keep Sistohka and Chehassa. But the armed men took them to another lodge where they were brought before a man of importance, the Kowmux chabotta, as they guessed then and soon knew with certainty.

The chabotta was Mahkalt's age, but taller than him, a man of grand and imposing mien, made more impressive by his ceremonial attire: an intricately carved wooden helmet bearing grinning, fanged serpents' faces on its front and back and a water fowl—a diver—with its head raised to call on the top; and a full robe of ti-juk fur randomly embellished with clusters of white feathers and bits of white fur. A small section of the roof of the lodge had been raised like a lid and propped open with a stick; from it, a diffused shaft of gray light glowed coolly through the smoky interior and fell full on the chief and four sturdy young spearsmen who stood with him. Against the dim background and confronting the five uncertain and raggedly clothed searchers, the chabotta and his retainers were a splendid and dramatic presence.

Aengus waited for Mahkalt to speak for their party, Mahkalt waited for Aengus, and all waited for the chabotta. The standstill was shattered when one of the men who had brought them shoved Pahdow from behind and sent him sprawling. Aengus and the others turned to the assailant, who made furious gestures that all of them should similarly prostrate themselves before his magnificent chief. A quick, hot impulse raged through Aengus to react violently against that suggestion of enslavement. But cool reason checked him. The man had pushed the boy Pahdow, not strong Sierka or elder Mahkalt or alien Aengus. And only one man had given offense; the other Kowmuxes stood quietly by. Aengus stooped and, with his hand under Pahdow's arm, drew the frightened lad to his feet. Aengus turned then to the one who had pushed, grasped his wrist and deliberately removed the spear from his hand. Facing the chief, he rested the fire-hardened wooden tip of the spear against a rock beside the firepit and snapped it off with the side of his foot, an act more symbolic than destructive because a new tip could be made easily.

The only weapon brought to this audience by any of the five men was Sierka's prized knife, finely carved from antler, that he never set aside. Aengus extended his palm behind him and said, "Give me your knife, Sierka."

Sierka pulled it from its pouch. Aengus took it and laid it against the same rock. A sharp blow with another rock shattered it.

The chabotta watched imperiously while Aengus placed the broken spear and pieces of knife on the ground between them, but he seemed inclined to let the brazen stranger act out his peculiar demonstration of conciliation.

Aengus placed his hand on Pahdow's shoulder and said, "This is Pahdow," emphasizing the name. A gentle pressure told Pahdow to sit. In similar fashion, Aengus introduced the rest of his friends and finally himself. The chabotta looked from face to face as if trying to decide what to make of them.

At last he spoke a few words. His expression and tone suggested: "Who are you?" or "What do you want?"

Aengus attempted to tell their story. "Kweneechekat"

241

seemed to mean nothing to the chief, at least he showed no recognition. But neither did his aspect change when Aengus identified themselves as "friends," although he used the Kowmux word, and these people were surely Kowmuxes. Only when Mowbit intervened and took a wide board from several which covered a storage box, placed it between Aengus and the chief, and began to draw on it with charcoal from the firepit, did the chief's curiosity begin to melt his haughty expression.

Squatting on the floor, Mowbit told their story intelligibly enough for the chief to nod his head whenever Mowbit raised his eyes to see if he was understood. Mowbit identified his own people by an outline of their distinctive canoe, although the chabotta's people must have described to him already its wolf's head prow and vertical stern. Mowbit drew a map—an abbreviated copy of the one hidden under their canoe—and gradually led the chief to recognize its significance and where his village was on it. When Mowbit indicated the extent of Kowmux territory as he knew it—from the first village they had stopped at, then northward along the side of the great island and across the channel to the chief's village—the chief took a spear from the man beside him and traced along the eastern shore of the strait with its point. "Kowmuckthwaybsh," he declared, doubling his tribe's territory.

From the chief's tone and glance, Mowbit understood that "Kowmux" was a disrespectful contraction, not to be used in his presence.

Mowbit put his finger on the board where he had drawn no lines, north of the entrance to the channel they had been swept into before they found this village. "Kowmuckthwaybsh?" he inquired.

"Quaquolo," the chief said with a scowl.

Mowbit turned the board over and drew a Wayabuk canoe. The chief understood. He swept his arm to indicate a great distance to the north. But he did not understand at all, at first, Mowbit's sketch of the Serican ship or its connection with the fleet of Wayabuk canoes. Aengus was tempted to break in, as if his own familiarity with Serica and Sericans could somehow breach the barrier of strange tongues, but he saw that the chabotta was pleased with clever Mowbit, so he kept silent.

Sketches and pantomime finally conveyed the story of the disasters that the Wayabuks and Sericans had visited upon Kweneechekats and Kowmuxes; the chief seemed unmoved, as if he did not believe the tale or, perhaps, thought that it told only of imagined dangers. But when he was made to understand that his seven motley visitors intended to vanquish the raiders, he burst into laughter. Even Mowbit's claim that they had already killed nineteen of them was treated with good-humored derision.

Mowbit turned to Aengus in dismay, but when Aengus stepped forward to convince the chief of the truth of Mowbit's account and to make their request for an alliance, the chief stopped him. Apparently he had decided that the entertainment had gone on long enough and that it was time to proceed with the execution of his own decisions concerning the visitors. He embraced Mowbit with warm affection, which astonished the young man greatly. With his arms still about him, the chabotta called to three women. When they came forward, he delivered Mowbit into their charge with lengthy instructions that brought smiles to their faces and set their heads to delighted nodding.

When the women led Mowbit away, the chief, almost as an afterthought, waved the boy Pahdow to follow them.

The chabotta considered Sierka for a long moment, then turned him over to several of the men who had brought them there. But he had only scowls for middle-aged Mahkalt and miscolored Aengus. He dismissed them with a wave of his hand.

Aengus raised his own hand and held the chief with his eye. In a voice loud enough for his dispersed companions to hear, he said rapidly, "This chabotta seems to think we are gifts blown to him by the storm for him to keep or cast aside. Listen, Kweneechekats. I'm speaking to you, though it seems I talk to him. When these Kowmuxes sleep, get away if you can. Meet me by our canoe. Tell our women, if any of you are near them. If any of you are left behind, don't despair. We'll come back for you. But kill no one. We don't need any more enemies."

The lordly chabotta simply stared at the pale giant who spoke meaningless words, then walked away.

XXVII

Rain had turned to large, wet flakes of snow when Aengus gathered the Kweneechekats' bearskins from the rack and set the door aside to leave. The people of the lodge had carefully ignored him since he had returned from the chabotta's lodge. Even when he approached Sistohka to tell her quietly of his plan, the other women moved away to avoid him. Now many eyes watched him go, but no one attempted to stop him or to say anything to him. Either because his alien appearance disturbed them or because word had come that the chabotta had said he must go, the people seemed glad that he was leaving. Relieved, also, that he was leaving without having to be driven off by harsh words or force that might expose them to hazard from powers as extraordinary as his appearance.

Aengus had seen little of Mahkalt during the day and nothing at all of him for the last several hours. He wondered whether the villagers would be as loath to mal-treat one of their own race, but he trusted Mahkalt's good sense to keep himself out of harm's way.

There was an hour or more of daylight left when Aengus descended the cliff trail, light enough for him to see if their canoe had been damaged or their pitful stores looted.

Nothing had been touched. The knives and clubs taken from the slain Wayabuks were there, including one as fine as Sierka's that he had broken. Mowbit's precious map was safe and dry, wrapped in waterproof gut. And their supply of food was still there: about enough for a single meal for one hungry man. Aengus intended to use the rest of daylight to replenish that stock with whatever the beach offered, but darkness came before he had gathered any more than a small basketful of mussels.

He crawled under their canoe to wait and made a nest of the bearskins. Without the great wheel of stars to mark their passing, he knew that each hour would seem like many. But when many times many seemed to have come and gone, his fear that the others would not come began to harden into certainty.

"*Cannot* come, or *will* not?" he asked himself.

Tilted onto its side because of its high prow, the canoe was more like a shallow cave than a roof. Huddled within its shelter, he could easily watch the foot of the trail even though the snow fell heavily at times and accumulated in slushy puddles before melting. But no one came.

"*I'm* here," he thought, somewhat querulously. "At least *some* of them should have been able to come."

But he knew that a descent of the steep path, mushy-slick in the black of night, was a daunting prospect that might have deterred even him. Perhaps the others were under close guard. He could do nothing but wait.

To shrug off his own low spirits, he tried to imagine Kwetah's terror and discomfort, but no image would come. It was as if the pain of such thoughts would be insupportable; his mind refused to consider them. But other painful thoughts came unbidden. Were his friends losing heart? If they remained separated from him, would they forget their mission? And if they did, what would he do then? What *could* he do?

He thought of the small canoes at the other end of the row: one and two-man crafts. "I could take one of those, but what then? Even if I managed to steal Kwetah and Leeaht from the Wayabuks, I could never abandon the other children to them. And I couldn't take the Serican ship by myself. I couldn't even sail it alone if I did."

A feeling of utter futility, of everything having gone wrong, seeped into his blood and bones, just as the dank

246

chill had seeped in hours before. In the dismal, dripping blackness, he began to feel all alone in the world—almost the feeling he had had during his last weeks on the great ocean.

"If I took one of the small canoes and left this place looking for trails across the land toward home, who would suffer because of it? Probably we would all live longer— those of us who are alive now. Poor Kwetah may be dead already if a lame child has no value. If she's not dead, the Wayabuks may have recognized her as one of their own— or will soon enough. Then our interference would only deny her a home with her mother's people—perhaps the best home for her.

"Leeaht. Lovely Leeaht. She won't be a slave for long. Some prince of those people will claim her for his wife. Some handsome, strapping young fellow . . . like I was ten or fifteen years ago. Oh, God! Have I become this old in so short a time?"

He peered again toward the foot of the trail, then leaned out and listened for many minutes. He heard only the heavy dripping of water from shrubby growth along the foot of the cliff. He looked up toward the village and saw nothing, not even the huge, sloppy flakes that splattered his face.

"The old chief seemed to want Mowbit and Pahdow. With their own village gone, they may have a better home here than any other they could hope for. And the others? A home here, too. If not, they'll find their way back to Appowad. With me gone, they would be rid of any obliga- tion . . . to me or to Kwetah. Raids and seizings have forever been part of their lives. They live with such things; they accept them."

As much to bring life to his stiffening body as to act on his darkling thoughts, he left his shelter and prowled along the line of canoes. He tested the weight of the smallest one at the end and found that he could move it easily. He tilted it onto the slope below the ledge, then went below and eased it onto the beach and out to the water's edge. Two paddles had lain beneath the canoe. He returned for them, then launched the little boat out among the guardian rocks.

Paddling out beyond those rocks, he looked back toward the cliff top, but his sight could not penetrate the streaming blackness, could not even make out the beach. Only the nearest rocks, standing hunch-shouldered under the downpour, loomed dimly out of the night.

Snow had become rain again. He paddled slowly past the place where the rocks stood, then closer to shore and along it, guiding himself by the phosphorescent glow where small waves lapped onto the beach. He went the only way he knew to go: west and north into the channel they had entered before. He did not know whether he was going only far enough from the village to avoid being seen by its men when daylight came or was beginning some longer journey.

Later, when he noticed that the water accumulating in the canoe had covered his feet, he realized that he had no bailer so he beached the canoe to tip it. That done, he sank onto a beach log, suddenly empty of resolution, a husk of a man, sodden, miserable with the desolation of purposelessness more than discomfort. He felt so drained that he would not have been greatly surprised, or even disappointed, if the spark of his life had flickered out then and the blackness of night become the blackness of eternity. That vagrant whim persisted in his mind for some time, until, quite abruptly, its significance appalled him.

"What kind of coward have I become? The last time my spirit was this low, I was truly near death and had no hope of survival. If I could have imagined then my situation now, I would have felt that I'd been delivered: land beneath me; friends nearby—probably in trouble and needing me; a child who loves me, and I her—who could have dreamed such a wonder; and Leeaht—sweet Leeaht who isn't repelled by my ugly face. And there are enemies who can be beaten. . . . They *can* be beaten!"

To send flying the darkmen who had nearly stolen his soul, he rose to his feet, threw his arms over his head, and roared.

He saw then the treetops above him, the first hint of dawn. And the drenching rain had become a luminous drizzle. In a flood of new resolve, he determined to explore the channel during that day and return to the village at dusk to see how he might extricate his friends from the Kowmuxes who detained them.

"Take one thing at a time," he told himself. "The kwalk'washa were just trying me. That's all. Just testing me."

He shook out his bearskin as if to ensure that no taint of his despondency clung to it. He swept his wet hair back from his face and clamped it in place with his conical rain hat. As if light alone bore warmth, he felt the chill within him vanish. He briskly launched the canoe and continued along the shore, rounding the bend into the channel.

It was a wide channel. More than a mile separated him from the indistinct far shore, which he presumed belonged to the great island. Both near and far sides of the channel disappeared into the drizzle ahead of him.

Suddenly, from a place onshore that he had just passed: "Akwahti! Aengus!"

Pahdow scrambled from beneath the ground-sweeping branches of a great cypress. By the time Aengus had put about and come ashore, the boy had been joined by Sistohka, Chehassa, and another woman of Sistohka's age.

Sistohka began to speak as he and Pahdow drew the boat onto the beach. "The cliff trail was watched, but Atsah showed us another way. We've been waiting for you."

"We were afraid we wouldn't see you in the dark if you were far offshore," Pahdow added. "But where are Mahkalt and Sierka?"

"We've all become very much scattered, it seems," Aengus replied. "What about Mowbit?"

"Muklanogh, the chabotta, won't let him out of his sight. Atsah says he intends him to be his son," Sistohka said.

"And this must be Atsah." Aengus beckoned with his hand to draw the stranger closer.

"Yes. Atsah is a Didotah—the people across the strait from our own home. She has lived with the Kowmuxes for a long time. We've promised to take her home with us and then to the Didotahs . . . if anyone there remembers her."

Atsah seemed embarrassed, as if Aengus might consider her an unwelcome intruder or an encumbrance. But he saw immediately the value to their enterprise of one who knew both the Kowmux language and their own, and who was familiar with this territory. And he believed he saw a woman cast in Sistohka's mold—in competence and character, that is, for her figure was as stout as Sistohka's was lean.

"Welcome, Atsah," he said with a smile.

"But you've had no fire and no rainclothes," he continued with concern. "Pahdow, come with me for our canoe. Then we'll get to where we can make a fire and a plan."

"I'll come too," Sistohka said. "I won't sink this little boat, and you'll need help with our canoe."

As they returned to the beach of stone men, Aengus asked Sistohka, "Is Chehassa becoming weary of all the danger and hardship? She's such a quiet girl, I never know what she's thinking. She's so young—"

"She's older than Pahdow. My daughter thinks she looks after me—and I suppose she does, more than I admit to myself. Wherever I go, she goes too and never complains. But also, I think that whenever Sierka notices her, she forgets about cold and danger."

"Oh, ho!" Aengus burst out with a laugh. "Sierka's a fortunate man, but he's as shy as your daughter. He may need encouragement."

"Let them be," Pahdow broke in with youthful irritation at the insensitivity of an elder. "Sierka knows. They just need time to become good friends first."

Sistohka, in the bow, turned to Aengus with a grin, and he responded with a wink. Pahdow, in the stern, bent his head and intently plied his paddle.

There was no paddle for Sistohka, so she had breath to answer more questions.

"Why is the chabotta so taken with our Mowbit?" Aengus asked.

"Atsah says that Muklanogh lost a son, killed by people

who live near here. Quaquolos, she calls them. He loved his son dearly. That son was lame from birth and very clever."

"So the chief thinks his son has returned."

"No, not his son, but someone to take his son's place in his heart and to accomplish what his son would have accomplished. Just as Kobessa thought *you* were to do things that her husband would have wanted done."

"Me? What do you mean? How am I like her husband?"

"One-eyed. Her husband was injured so when he was still a boy. *His* father was chief of all the Kweneechekats—a great chabotta, as Muklanogh seems to be for the Kowmuxes, not just a village headman as Semackul was. But Semackul's father and some other troublemakers said a one-eyed boy could not become a chabotta. He would be a flawed leader in the hunt and when fighting had to be done. When the boy became a man and had taken Kobessa as his wife, it was young Semackul and his father who provoked the men who attacked Appowad, and then they betrayed Kobessa's husband to them. No one in Appowad has ever accused Semackul, but everyone knows it's true. The old chabotta died a few years later with neither son nor grandson to follow him, and Semackul claimed his place. By then, Semackul was a great hunter—the best to find whales. But men in the other villages, and some in Appowad, began to regret that they'd let Semackul have his way, so he was never able to become a great chabotta, chief of all the villages. And he was forced to tolerate Kobessa. Kobessa made him angry at times, but he thought the people would turn against him if he hurt her or sent her away."

"So what did Kobessa expect of me? Did she think that I would become the chabotta in place of Semackul?"

"No. She just believed that you would stand up to him, that you would give heart to the men of Appowad who opposed him but were still afraid of him."

Carefully, Aengus said, "Only a few days ago, Kobessa seemed anxious for me to leave Appowad. Semackul was still the chabotta then."

"I think she was afraid for your life. She told me that

251

Semackul had tried to kill you and that she'd been afraid for you then, and afraid for you again when you told her that you weren't a spirit. But when you faced Semackul down in his own lodge, she began to believe that she had been right in the first place: that you could do anything."

"Kobessa is your good friend. Is that why you came with us?"

Sistohka did not answer for some moments. "Kobessa wanted someone to be with you," she said at last, "to make sure that you and the men come home if you're unable to recover the girls and children. She thought you might be ashamed to return without them. And if you're killed, someone should bring back the telling of how you die."

"Do you think that's how this will end—in defeat or death?"

"I've thought so at times. But not now. Finding Atsah was like a sign from the kwal-k'washa. And you never lose faith. You're always strong and confident. I know we'll succeed."

Abashed, Aengus fell silent.

Shortly after, as they paddled cautiously close along the shore, winding through the first of the stone sentries and keeping a careful watch on the beach and the cliff top above, Pahdow suddenly back-paddled. Aengus turned to him to see why. The boy pointed ahead, but Aengus saw nothing.

"Men on the beach," Pahdow told him.

They moved closer, then boy and man left the small craft and waded along the shore, moving from rock to rock to stay hidden. When Aengus could clearly make out what Pahdow had glimpsed, he saw three Kowmux men bullying Sierka. Mahkalt lay propped against a log behind him. The Kowmuxes were not armed, had not even bothered to pick up rocks or sticks, but they were pushing Sierka roughly on his chest and shoulders, shoving him back and forth among them.

Aengus shouted angrily and ran toward them. The Kowmuxes ceased their abuse of Sierka, but two of them

252

picked up paddles as if to defend themselves against Aengus and Pahdow.

Sierka, seething with anger, shouted to Aengus, "You said not to kill these shitty Kowmuxes, so I've let them push me around. Can I kill them now? You saw what they were doing."

"They weren't trying to injure you." Aengus put his hands on Sierka's shoulders and spoke softly to placate him. "They weren't going to kill you. They were behaving like children—like bullies. What was the fuss about, anyway?"

Sierka pointed an accusing finger at the Kowmuxes, now standing together a few feet from them. "They said Mahkalt stole one of their canoes. But he didn't. Poor Mahkalt has been all night here on the beach. He slipped off the trail up there and has lain here all night. His leg's broken."

The trail that started on the far side of the row of canoes, where their own still lay, angled up behind the row, and there, about a hundred feet from the canoes, was at least forty feet above the beach. Mahkalt had tumbled down a steep, sandy slope into brush at its base. Aengus rushed to him.

"Broken? Your leg's broken?"

"No, not broken. Just wrenched. But I hit a log hard and I've been dizzy since I woke up."

"You lay here all night?"

"Yes, but I wasn't aware of it. I'm cold now, though. More cold than sore."

"We'll get your bearskin, but we'll have to settle this quarrel first. Pahdow, go back and bring their canoe. Sierka, *I* took the canoe. I'm sorry it caused you trouble. Who are these men?"

"I was supposed to work with them. I think they were told to see if I knew anything about repairing canoes. Kweneechekats make the best canoes. Even Kowmuxes know that."

Aengus smiled, but nodded agreement.

"They acted like they would be my friends at first,"

Sierka continued, "but when they saw their canoe gone, they became madmen. When they found Mahkalt, they were going to kill him, and then me when I got between them."

"Calm down, my friend. They didn't use anything but their hands. They were probably more afraid of their chabotta than angry with you, if the canoes were in their keeping. Maybe they just wanted to ask Mahkalt if he had seen who took it, and you got in their way."

And, indeed, when the Kowmuxes saw Pahdow leading the canoe toward them, their quicksilver anger vanished. They ran into the water and, with Pahdow, pulled the boat ashore, then examined it carefully while Sistohka scrambled out.

"Why all the fuss?" Pahdow asked. "The canoe we left is far better than this one."

"Probably they had already decided to keep ours," Aengus replied, "and didn't think of their loss as a trade. Sistohka, stay with Mahkalt while we get our canoe."

Some minutes later, after Aengus, Sierka, and Pahdow had reloaded their own canoe and were hurriedly wrestling it down the beach over too-few rollers, the Kowmuxes came running up, hesitated, then began to climb the trail.

"If they want to keep us or take our canoe, there's three of them against three of us," Sierka noted contemptuously, "but yet they run for help."

Aengus smiled at Sierka's persistent resentment.

"Why don't they just yell for help?" Pahdow asked.

Sierka replied, "Because they're afraid old stone-eye might throw a lightning bolt at them."

Aengus's eyebrows shot up in astonishment. As ready as he had been to renounce the occult powers he had once claimed, he was startled, nonetheless, to hear them now spoken of so irreverently. He marveled, also, that gentle Sierka could be provoked to such dudgeon—or rise to battle as fiercely as he had against the Wayabuks.

"Less talk. Hurry," Aengus scolded, "or we'll have all of them throwing more than lightning bolts at us."

XXVIII

"There's water on the other side of that land," Atsah said, pointing to the eastern shore of the channel. "Wide water. That land is like a long tongue with Muklanogh's village a crumb on the tip of it. The island is wider farther up."

Atsah's half-forgotten Didotah words came flooding from her deepest memory. Except for a few, they were also Kweneechekat words, for the two tribes were of the same stock. She had put an end to Mahkalt's painful and feeble exertions by taking his paddle from him. She took his place on a thwart, but she could not suppress her excitement over what she regarded as a remarkable stroke of good fortune: deliverance from her captors, however benign their treatment of her, and the possibility of returning to her childhood home. She stopped paddling often to tell her new friends everything that crossed her mind that she thought might be of value to them.

Before midmorning, young Pahdow remarked, "The current's not as strong now. Will it change against us soon?"

"Yes, soon," Aengus said, pulling harder on his paddle.

"There's a good place to camp just ahead," Atsah said.

"Not far enough from Muklanogh," Aengus responded.

"Yes, it is. Yes, it is," Atsah contradicted him. "The current becomes very fast in this channel. If it's turning now, it will be against anyone who follows us until after

255

dark. If we go *too* far, we'll be among the Quaquolos."

"What about there?" Sierka asked, pointing to a ragged bay studded with large and small islets.

"No. Not far enough. There's a path back to the village from there. We'll soon be at the place I spoke of."

So saying, the rotund little woman began to paddle with short, rapid pulls that the men tried hard to ignore so they would not lose the rhythm of their own slower, more powerful strokes.

Atsah's "just ahead" turned out to be several miles distant, but the drizzle ceased while they paddled, and intermittently the sun broke through the low clouds to evaporate the mist that hung over the water and in the trees along the shore. Even Mahkalt began to stir and forget his aches as he became dry and warm.

Eventually the channel bent sharply westward to form a pocket about two miles deep. From roughly the midpoint of the north side of that pocket, the passage continued northward again through a narrows, although they only knew those contours then from Atsah's telling. Following the eastern shore of the channel as it bent westward into the pocket, Atsah directed them into a small bay that lay against an almost-island. Had they passed the island before turning, they would have been in the narrows. Within the bay, Atsah had them beach the canoe on a low neck that tied the small island to the shore. Over the neck, they could see shimmering swirls and lines of racing water in the narrows.

"I know this place well," Atsah told them. "We've come here often during the summer for clams and fish, and in there"—she pointed to a narrow entrance that led to an inner lagoon off the bay—"for reeds and things to weave with, and for birds and . . . and many things. *Most* summers, that is. Some summers the Quaquolos are here when we come, so we stay away and they use this place those years." A sudden remembrance brought a broad smile to her face. "One spring our men stayed back at that bay"—she pointed vaguely back down the channel—"and only the women came here the first day. We found the

Quaquolos here already—mostly women—only three old men were with them. So we stayed and worked and talked and laughed with them all that day, then went back to our men's camp. Every day after that, we found excuses to leave the men behind. At the end of summer, when they found out that we'd become friends with Quaquolos, they were very angry. But Muklanogh only laughed when he heard about it."

"You speak Quaquolo?" Aengus asked.

"A few words," she replied. "Some of the other women know more, and some of the men speak it easily. But you don't need to know each other's words to have a good talk—women don't . . . at least *I* don't," she finished with a laugh.

In a pocket of beach enclosed by an arc of rock ledge on the bay side of the almost-island, they built a great fire. It had to be started from a new spark because their carry-fire had not survived the night on the Kowmuxes' beach. Leaving Mahkalt to tend the fire, Atsah took the others to forage for clams and roots—a great quantity for a great feast. They found out-of-season but still firm sweet-bulbs by the lagoon, and Pahdow and Sierka killed two wintering geese there merely by letting them take cover in a brake from which they could not fly then pelting them with stones.

While they gathered their food, a low rumble, like continuous but very distant thunder, caught Aengus's attention for a moment. A waterfall deep in the forest, he thought, but Atsah was not close by to confirm his surmise. Later, after they had assuaged their sharpest hunger with spit-broiled clams and were waiting for the birds and roots to bake in leafy, steam-stone beds under the fire, Aengus heard the thunder again. It was a moment when, by chance, all were still and no one was speaking. The rumble caught everyone's attention. They did not at first realize that it had been there all along, waxing imperceptibly louder all through the bright middle of the day. It seemed to be a new presence. Aengus's immediate thought was: "Earthquake!" for no other sound he had ever heard resembled it more nearly. But then he recognized it as an increase of the sound he had heard earlier.

"Atsah . . . ?"

"Come with me," she told them.

She led them across the narrow isthmus and then back over a corner of the forested almost-island to a ledge overlooking the narrows: a half-mile breadth of swiftly coursing water, a surging river of the sea. Though the current tore viciously at the rock-bound shore beneath them and broke into frustrated turbulence around unyielding boulders there, farther out the surface was smoothly uneven, like a furrowed and worn paving stone—a vast paving stone with a huge undulating dome at its center: a mountain of water thrust up by a sunken reef. Ribbons of foam swirled out from the oily smooth prominence and spread downstream, outlining whirlpools and upwellings.

It was not that strange sight, though, that gripped them and chilled their blood. It was the sound it made. Less heard than felt, it seemed to come from below the world, penetrating even the rock ledge where Pahdow lay belly down.

"I can feel the vibrations," he said with awe. "They go right through me."

The others merely stood or sat in spellbound silence. As the tide-driven current increased during the hour they were there, the great fluid dome collapsed several times into crashing turbulence. Slowly it would grow again to a height impossible for water, and then higher. The sudden airborne racket that startled them each time it fell would as slowly give way to the subterranean rumble.

Aengus looked toward Mahkalt, who leaned on a smooth beach stick he had picked up to make walking easier. The older man's lips were moving, but no one could have heard him even if he had shouted. Aengus saw that Sistohka was mouthing silent words also, as if she and Mahkalt were communicating in some secret speech that could penetrate the din.

When they had returned to their fire, Pahdow was the first to speak. "What is it? What makes the water climb up to make a hill like that?"

"An island was there once, when the world was first made," Atsah replied, "but the rushing water has worn it away so that now there's just a huge, smooth rock left. It can be seen only at the very lowest water, just under the surface. Sometimes young men stand on it. They bring rocks out in their canoes to brace their feet against and to hold in their arms for weight. They try to see who can stand the longest before the rising current sweeps them away."

"Oowah," Pahdow whispered with a broad grin of appreciation. He imagined himself out there with other young fellows, screaming and yelling at each other in wild exhilaration at first, then grimly leaning into the powerful current, and finally, desperately, clawing at the shifting rocks with their toes, striving to be the last to be lifted and flung downstream by the torrent.

"It's a kwal-k'washa place," Mahkalt murmured.

Aengus leaned toward him to hear what more he would say, but Mahkalt's thoughts were focused on some inward vision.

Sistohka said, "He means that it's a special place where the kwal-k'washa spirits and the wills of men, if they're strong enough, can come together to accomplish what neither could do alone. In the story of our people, extraordinary events have happened at such places."

"Then this could be the place where we stand against the Wayabuks," Aengus said. "But I wonder whether they'll come this way if they know about the narrows. They might believe it's too dangerous for the Serican ship. Atsah, you said that there was wide water if we had gone the other way from Muklanogh's village—up the other side of the tongue of land. Would that be a better route for the ship?"

"No. This is the safest route. North of that other wide water, there are twisted channels and narrow places, too. The rapids and whirlpools there are worse than here."

"You've seen Wayabuk canoes take this route before?"

"This is the way to their country," Atsah insisted.

"Then they surely know about this place," Aengus said. "They must know they would have to pass through the narrows at quiet water. And it would have to be high water, just before the current flows northward. At low water, they'd be swept back into the narrows again as soon as the tide began to flood."

Sierka said, "That means they'd have to come this far—to this bay—on the earlier ebb and then wait for high water."

"Yes. A long wait," Aengus replied. "It should be time enough. . . ."

"To do what?" Pahdow asked impatiently when Aengus had seemed to pause too long.

"Somehow we'll have to separate them. When our numbers have been equal, we've outfought them. But it will have to be more than that," Aengus mused. "More than us killing them one by one. The narrows . . . the narrows . . . how can we use the kwal-k'washa place?"

"When will they be here? During dark or daylight?" Sierka asked. "It would make a difference."

Hoping that she had useful information, Atsah said, "The noise is less now. The water will be at its highest soon—about midafternoon or later."

"Well, they're not here now," Aengus said, "so they won't go through the narrows today. Tomorrow's high water will be later. To be ready for it, they'd have to come this far in the morning, as we did. The same for the next day, and maybe the next."

"But there's another high water during the night, isn't there?" Pahdow asked. "And the moon's almost full. And the sky's clear now."

"Yes," Aengus conceded. "They could come then. But, unless they're being pursued or have some other reason to come by night, I don't imagine they'd risk it with the ship in tow. They'll be here soon, though. They never stay in one place—they just keep moving. They must have completed the evil deeds they planned for this country by now."

"They'll come by night." Mahkalt had been silent. The others had assumed that pain and weariness drew his thoughts away from their discussion. Now they stared at him in surprise. "By night," he repeated.

"How do you know?" Sierka asked.

"I don't know how I know," his uncle replied. "It's just in my mind that they'll come by night. But I do know *why.*"

"Why?" several voices asked.

"Because it will be best for *us* if they come when it's dark—so the kwal-k'washa will see to it that they do. If the Wayabuks have to wait here in the dark, we can do all kinds of mischief. We can make our numbers seem equal to theirs. If they camp ashore, we can break their canoes or set them adrift. Then they wouldn't be able to follow us if we stole the ship and pushed it into the current with our own canoe. And that current would carry us back down the channel."

"But they'd leave men on board to guard the ship," Pahdow said.

"There'll be killing again," Mahkalt replied simply.

Even Chehassa, who rarely spoke, was engaged by Mahkalt's speculations. "What if they have the children ashore?" she asked him.

"Then we must scatter the children into the woods like mice. Send them in all directions and collect them later, after we've dealt with the Wayabuks in some other way."

"The children will not likely be taken ashore," Aengus said. "It would take too long to unload and load them. And they'd have to be watched lest they run away. They've probably been kept on the ship since they were captured."

In a voice almost too quiet to be heard, Chehassa asked, "Are they suffering much? The little ones?"

Aengus replied, "Their older sisters are with them."

Chehassa, and the others, too, were unsatisfied with that answer. They waited for some more adequate response. Under the focus of their gaze, Aengus's mind was forced at last to picture the close, dark spaces within the floating dungeon: to see Kwetah, Kwetah, whose suffering made his heart ache; to see Leeaht . . . to see Leeaht . . . Could Leeaht truly love him? Certainly not his time-ravaged face, his exotic coloration . . . but she loved him, she did love him, and suddenly he let her love rush into his heart.

He saw Kwetah and Leeaht huddled together in fetid

261

darkness, standing in accumulated seepage and ordure. Because young people could be quickly fattened later to be made presentable as gifts, he saw them already thinning, fed only enough to keep them alive through their journey. Tears sprang to his eyes.

He saw Mowbit's two little nephews also, four and five years old, standing together, past terror and stoic now as befitted little princes, for that is what they were. With Pugahlkuthl dead, the people of Hokodah had put aside all that was his, including the headman who had yielded to him in everything. Mowbit's sister's husband, scion of an earlier noble family, had been made chabotta, and his two solemn sons, already darlings of the villagers' eyes, became authenticators of their choice. All this Mowbit had told Aengus three nights ago. Now Aengus saw them: a glowing presence amid the filth and blackness of the ch'uan's hold. He saw other children, too, whimpering for solace from the other girls, themselves half-mad from unrelenting dread and horror.

Aengus's eye turned from within to the anxious faces around him. He could not describe his vision to his friends. He would have to bear its torment alone, although he knew that they must have visions of their own, equally terrible. But the time for sharing such fearful images would be after the rescue—or before the exaction of vengeance if rescue should come too late. Now, haltingly at first because the picture so long repressed would not release its grip on his imagination, he described for them, instead, the children's prison.

"Ch'uan—that's what Sericans call their ships—aren't made from single logs as your canoes are. They're made from great planks fastened together. You saw that, Mahkalt, and said that they wouldn't be safe in rough water, but the planks aren't loosely held together like the walls of your houses. They're fastened tightly to strong ribs, fastened even more closely and firmly than the bowpieces of your canoes. Inside, they build walls from one side of the hull to the other and so divide the space into separate rooms, perhaps ten or twelve of them, or twice as many if they run another wall the length of the ship as they sometimes do. Those walls are as thick and strong as the hull and as watertight, also. If a hole is driven through the hull in one place, only that compartment will flood. The ship won't sink."

To fill a pause in Aengus's description, Sierka said, "So the walls of the ship protect the children. But what about those in the most forward room? If we rammed the ship against a rock or the shore, wouldn't they be crushed?"

"No, there are no children in that space. That first one and sometimes the last one at the stern of the ship are made free-flooding: holes are drilled through the hull. That's so that water taken over or through the bow won't accumulate as dead weight. They store heavy cargo there. Sometimes fresh water in jars. But they wouldn't keep people there. All the *top* part of the ship—the house where some of the Sericans live, the masts and railings, the part of the stern that sticks out—all of that's added after the hull is built. A great storm could sweep it all away. But the hull would remain sound and wouldn't sink."

"So, however badly we handle the ship after we steal it, the children are safe," Mahkalt stated, partly as summary, partly as question.

"From drowning," Aengus replied. "But if they were thrown about, they could be injured that way. And I don't think even that hull could survive a collision with the water-mountain and the reef under it."

"Then you must watch out for other places, also," Atsah said. "Near the mouth of the channel is one." She pointed back toward Muklanogh's village. "That's where Muklanogh's son was drowned."

"I thought Quaquolos killed him," Aengus said.

"Quaquolos were chasing him. They were in canoes. We think Muklanogh's son and his friend lured the Quaquolos into the bad water there. They probably thought they knew better than the Quaquolos how to get out of it. But all of them drowned."

"I didn't see any bad water there," Sierka said.

"It's not there all the time," Atsah told him. "Only

when the wind comes from there"—she pointed to the southeast—"and builds up great waves in the open water. Then, if the current is flowing strongly out of the channel to meet them, the water becomes confused and the waves break sharply. Even the largest canoes are swamped when the water is at its worst."

Their talk continued—talk of weather, talk of what Wayabuks and Kowmuxes and Quaquolos would do if certain things happened—but no sure plan came from their talk. That plan, they realized at last, would have to come from what the Wayabuks would do when they arrived, and what opportunities the kwal-k'washa would provide.

Aengus took the first watch that night. Of the seven, he had rested best the night before while he waited on the Kowmux beach. Their fire was hidden from all approaches except through the woods across the little cove, so he kept it built up to warm the sleepers. He stayed away from its light as much as possible lest his eye be spoiled for dimness. Soon, though, the moon was high enough above the trees that he could see far down the channel through which the Wayabuks would come, and, as he prowled the circumference of the almost-island, the shorelines across the channel's pocket and across the narrows seemed to become close and familiar.

A quiet was upon him, but not drowsiness, so he did not waken Sierka for the next watch. He kept it himself. He settled finally on the ledge from which they had first observed the mountain of water above the hidden reef. The tide was in its ebb now, its current flowing northward and just past its greatest flux. The pile of water seemed different, frothier under the moonlight. The noise, also, was less oppressive, although he could still feel vibrations through the rock. Moonlight and solitary contemplation combined to make the strange spectacle less ominous.

He sat there an hour, trying to imagine a chance happening that could be turned to their advantage, or a scheme that would force the Wayabuks into disaster. The water raged against and roared over its own obstruction and told him nothing. In the end, he left the making of plans to the kwal-k'washa and roused himself to return to camp and relinquish the watch to Sierka.

As he stood up, the kwal-k'washa screamed their response through his skull: "Alien! You dare call on us!" From around the curve of the island, close in to shore and almost upon him when he saw it, the great Serican ship reeled and leaned in the mad race of water. He stood above the level of the deck as it swept past him; he could see frantic men grasping stanchions, ropes, and masts to keep from sliding overboard. The Wayabuk canoes swirled by close below, all but one of them held to the ch'uan by lines, but able to do nothing to control it in the impetuous current. One was whipped toward the bold rock bank just beneath Aengus. The Wayabuks threw off their line and paddled furiously to save themselves. Had he been quick and a large rock at hand, he could have holed their canoe. But they were past him before he could do anything or even begin to think of doing anything.

As he watched in utter dismay, the ch'uan swirled into the center of the channel, safely downstream from the reef, and began a slow rotation that would have wound the canoes up to its sides if the Wayabuks had not cast off their lines to drift freely with the ship. Aengus could hear nothing but the roar of the water, but he caught moonlit glimpses of some of the Wayabuks standing in their canoes and rocking them from side to side in maniacal glee while others waved their arms overhead wildly. He imagined their screams of exhilaration at the success of their audacious dash through the narrows, at their escape from the country where they had wrought such terrible desolation.

Only minutes after his first sight of them, he turned away to carry the appalling news to his companions.

XXIX

Frantically, the men carried and dragged their canoe across the isthmus while the women threw their few things into it. In minutes they were afloat and away from the shore, but they saw neither ship nor Wayabuks. To their left lay a confusion of noise and moonlight; to their right, where the ship had gone, there was only a desert of blacknesses and no sign of men.

Although Mahkalt's conjectures about their engagement with the Wayabuks had not been a plan, they had underlain the group's expectations. Now, all of them felt forsaken by the kwal-k'washa.

All but Sistohka.

"Paddle!" she commanded the dispirited men.

All but Sistohka and Atsah.

"We haven't lost our chance. Not yet," the Didotah woman declared.

The women's resolve filled the void of despair and the men took life.

"Where are they?" Pahdow muttered.

"Don't worry. Don't worry," Atsah counseled him. "We'll see them soon enough. We'll have our chance. You'll see. You'll see." She began to paddle hurriedly with her awkward short strokes.

"What—" Sierka began.

"Hush! Paddle!" Sistohka ordered.

She had put her daughter in the bow of the canoe. The

girl stopped paddling frequently to peer ahead.

Several miles of shoreline swept by as they rode the swift current. The eastern shore dropped away for a while, then leaped out at them in a headland. Behind it, a string of whirlpools spun out across the mouth of a second wide bay. The paddlers pulled out to mid-channel to avoid the sucking currents.

"I see them!" Chehassa called out. The others strained their eyes, but only Pahdow and Sierka could make out the masts of the ch'uan.

"Keep them in sight," Atsah cautioned. "See where they turn in. It will be to the right."

And it was as she said. Minutes later, Chehassa pointed and cried, "There! They're going in now."

Though they trailed the ch'uan by several miles, the current was swift and they approached the turning-in place rapidly.

"Pull in here," Atsah instructed when they were still a half-mile short of that place.

They came onto a rock shore with the forest close against it. They worked the canoe along the shore carefully until they found a notch large enough for it to pass through and a place within where they could pull it up.

"Why here?" Sierka asked.

"To wait for the current to lessen," Atsah told him. "I don't know what's beyond the bay where the ship went in. If we let ourselves drift past, we might run into bad water there."

"But you've been *this* far before," Aengus said.

"No, never before. But the Quaquolo women we knew that summer I told you about—they told us where they lived: A large bay with islands in it and smaller bays off the end of it. They also told us that travelers always stop there on their way north or south."

"For women who spoke different tongues, you managed to say a lot to each other," Aengus observed good-naturedly.

Atsah looked at him sharply, but she saw his smile and retorted, "Didn't you know that about women?"

Then she continued, "It's a place where much trading is done. That's why I knew the Wayabuks would stop there."

"Trading?" Sierka burst out. "Would they trade slaves there?"

"I don't think so," Aengus put in quickly. "Not even one. The Serican told me that the Wayabuk chief came to take slaves. All of the slaves are for him. I think the Wayabuks would trade other things for safe passage and whatever goods they need—they wouldn't even let the Quaquolos know that they had any slaves aboard."

He looked to Mahkalt for his concurrence. Mahkalt nodded, then said to Atsah, "You said this place would give us our chance. How do you know that if you've never been here?"

"From what the Quaquolo women told us. They have summer camps around the large bay where the ship has gone, but in winter they retreat to the small inlets that lie at the back of the bay. If the big ship can't be taken into those small inlets, it may be left outside without many guards."

"Won't the Wayabuks raid this place like they did the others? Why won't they do that?" Pahdow asked as the others considered what Atsah had said.

"Too many people. Too many Quaquolos, I think," Atsah replied.

"And the ch'uan is trapped in there until the current out here is right for it," Aengus added. "Besides, they wouldn't want to make enemies of the Quaquolos if this is the best way to go north or south. The Wayabuks would want friends along such a narrow passage."

"We'll see. We'll see what happens," Mahkalt muttered quietly to himself. He had been deeply shaken that his earlier intuition had been made false by the kwal-k'washa. He was wary of trusting the spirits again too soon.

Later, they set three snaggy branches into their canoe to confuse its moonlit outline and put out to drift slowly across the mouth of the bay. An hour after that, on the new tide, they drifted back again to the same notch in the rock bank.

"You saw the ship?" Aengus asked, for he had not been certain that he had.

"Yes . . . yes," several replied, believing he questioned their eyesight rather than his own.

Aengus had seen that the bay's width at its mouth was more than a mile and that a chain of islets lay in its southern half, but to learn the location of the ship and the islets and inlets at the bay's far end, perhaps three miles from their drift path, he relied on clues from the talk of the others. Their sharper eyes, though, had not discovered the truth about everything. A white blur they had seen on the bay's northern shore suggested a fire to some of them, but Aengus, who had seen only its color, was certain that it was just moonlight on a shelly beach.

At last he said, "We can tell nothing for sure from here. Before the current's too strong against us, let's go into the bay. We can keep behind the little islands—maybe go ashore on one where we can see more clearly."

Their canoe moved along the shore and around the corner into the bay slowly, cautiously, the paddlers all too aware that the moon would betray them to any watchers ashore and yet leave those watchers hidden among the trees. Many water birds sheltered in the quiet waters among the islets, and their anxious whistles and calls stopped the paddlers several times, afraid that they would startle the birds into flight.

The last island in the chain, deep within the bay, was more than a mile beyond the first one, and it took them more than an hour to reach it. Sierka went ashore there to scout it for safety while the others waited in the canoe. He returned, whispering excitedly, "This is a good place. No one's here. The ship is just across the water on the other side."

During the remainder of the night and throughout the following day, they watched the ship. While darkness lasted, they took turns sleeping in snatches. The chill air began to drain them of warmth, so Sistohka returned to the canoe for two pouches of oil. Sips of the oil taken during their time of spying fueled them so that, like

269

lamps, they glowed warmly from within.

The Wayabuk canoes were tied to the ship, and the ship itself drew first toward the back of the bay on the great rope tied to its anchor and then ponderously swung around to draw the other way when the current changed before dawn. Although Sierka, Chehassa, and Pahdow said that they could make out figures sleeping in the canoes and on the deck of the ch'uan, they saw no movement.

Aengus saw other things. For all that he had been unable to form a picture of the captives in his mind when he had seen the ship six days earlier, now he was overwhelmed with visions of the children and young women—more than a hundred of them!—sleeping within that foul hull or lying in numb wakefulness. He wanted to scream across the water to them, "We're here! We're here to take you back!" He tried by sheer will to pluck Kwetah and Leeaht from among them, just to hold them against him until morning, to tell them that they would be with him forever before another day had passed.

Once during the night, seated against a tree with his thoughts turned in on his torment, he raised his head from his arms to see Pahdow watching him.

"When we have the children and leave this place, will we stop for Mowbit?" the boy asked.

"Yes," Aengus told him. "If we have to leave him at first to get the children to safety, I promise that I'll come back for him myself. We won't abandon Mowbit."

"Atsah says he's safe with Muklanogh. Do you think he's safe?"

"The chief regards him well. I'm sure he's safe."

With first light, two of the canoes left the ship. They made for the back of the bay and a narrow waterway there almost closed in by tall trees. Aengus and the others heard a dog bark, then many dogs. The sounds came from deep inside the inlet where the canoes had gone and across nearly a mile of open water to the island where the watchers waited. After a while, many canoes spilled out through the tight entrance and streamed across to surround the ch'uan. Throughout the morning, a great commerce of goods and visitations took place. Dark bundles that might have been ti-juk pelts and boxes that could have come from the raided villages were passed over the side, and baskets heavy with food, perhaps, were taken aboard. Canoes came and went. The activity became desultory around midday: mostly visits by women and children who paddled out for their turn to inspect the strange ship.

"They're through trading," Pahdow said. "They'll leave soon."

"No. The current outside the bay is against them all afternoon until almost dark," Mahkalt said. "They'll leave tomorrow morning."

"They may think now that they'll leave in the morning," Aengus said, a swell of new confidence in his voice as the time of waiting grew shorter, "but we'll be the masters of their ship by then."

Young Pahdow looked at him quickly. "How? Do you know what we're going to do?"

Sierka began a question: "The Wayabuks—"

"The Wayabuks," Aengus interrupted, "stayed with the ship last night because they didn't want to come into the village by dark. Tonight there should be feasting and celebration ashore to welcome the visitors. Am I right, Mahkalt?" Mahkalt nodded. "This place is better for us, after all," Aengus continued. "The village is hidden from the ship—I think it is. We'll have to check that. For now, we'll have to watch where lookouts will be posted along the shore. There shouldn't be many, if any at all. We'll take care of them after dark and then steal the ship. But we'll have to wait until the current draws it toward the mouth of the bay and then wait some more until the current in the channel favors us: almost the middle of the night."

"Will the Sericans stay with their ship?" Atsah asked.

"The Wayabuks don't trust them—that's what the one I questioned seemed to think. So they'll take them ashore to keep an eye on them—"

"Then who'll watch the captives?" Pahdow interrupted.

"They won't need to be watched. The compartments they're held in have hatches—lids that cover holes in the roofs—that are fastened from outside. There may be doors to inside passages, but they can be fastened the same way. No one can escape. There won't need to be many men left on board. Just a few watchmen there and ashore to make sure the Quaquolos don't become too inquisitive."

The Wayabuks posted three watchmen: one at the entrance to the inlet and two more on a headland that projected from the bay's northern shore. Those sentinels did not expect trouble from the food-bearing men and women who approached them openly from the woods behind after darkness had fallen. Using the Wayabuk knife that replaced the one Aengus had broken, Sierka swiftly and silently killed the first lookout. He and Aengus slew the other two as neatly. Each time, a low whistle afterward brought up the canoe, a dim, silent shadow moving along the shoreline.

That grim work done, Aengus looked toward the ship and drew a long breath. The ch'uan was pulling on its anchor rope toward the bay's mouth.

Sistohka said, "Any way we approach it, we'll be seen."

"Then we won't try to sneak up on it," Aengus said. "We'll seem to come from the village. Sistohka, you and Atsah sit together in the stern. Put Chehassa in front of you so she will be seen by anyone looking down from the ship."

They positioned themselves as he had directed, and Sierka stepped into the canoe to sit close to Chehassa.

"No, Sierka," Aengus said with a smile. "The women must sit alone. Come, sit behind me." To them all, he said, "We'll pretend to bring their share of the celebration to those who must stay to watch the ship. I'll be a Serican. Stay quietly in the canoe unless I call for you."

They paddled back along the shore until they could see a glimmer of firelight down the narrow throat of the inlet. As they drifted, that scintilla disappeared and another came into their sight, then another. The narrow pivoting line of their vision scanned the far shore within, seeing one fire after another of a sizable village.

"Now," Aengus directed, and they began to paddle toward the ship, making small noises of paddle against water and paddle against canoe purposely to see how many men would appear on the deck. There was only one head silhouetted against the sky as they drew up to the shadowed side of the ch'uan with the end of their canoe angled out so that moonlight would fall onto the women.

"Who is it?" a Serican voice called down.

Aengus was instantly relieved. "No Wayabuks," he thought, for surely a Wayabuk would have been in charge of the watch if any were aboard.

"Who is it?" the voice repeated.

Aengus affected drunkenness to mask his imperfect enunciation of the Serican dialect. "We've brought you women and drink. The chief said he would give us as many women as we want, so we brought three. We can bring more."

"Three is enough," the Serican replied, "except I don't want that fat one. The boy can have her. He needs a mama."

"And you'll have the boy?" Aengus snickered.

"What? Is that you, Ki? What are you wearing?"

"Clothes these people gave us because ours stunk too much for their noses. Aren't I a pretty fellow?"

Aengus kept his head down so that his rain hat hid his fair skin and beard. He busied himself pretending to untangle his feet from a line and a basket.

Suddenly suspicious, the Serican said, "Send the women up. Then you go back. Just send up the women."

Aengus replied irritably, "I'm going back, but I have to get something first. Now drop a line. My balls ache while I'm bantering east and west with you."

Grumbling, the Serican lowered a knotted rope that was already secured to something on the deck. Stumbling drunkenly and keeping his head tilted down, Aengus lunged for the line several times before he caught it. The thin rope bit harshly between his toes as he climbed it in the Serican manner until he could put his feet on the upper slope of the hull's barrel. The kneeling Serican extended his arm to help, but Aengus did not see it until the hand brushed the brim of his rain hat. He grasped the Serican's wrist, and the Serican's fingers closed around his. Bracing his feet on the whale-backed hull, Aengus leaned heavily backward and drew the startled Serican out from the deck above. The Serican's frantic efforts to keep from falling so occupied his mind that he probably was not instantly aware of the thrust of Aengus's knife into him just below his breastbone and up into his chest. If he did understand before he died, his paralyzed chest could force no shout.

Almost toppling, Aengus jerked out his knife and grabbed at the rope with his other hand as the Serican fell onto him, then onto the barrel of the hull and into the water. Aengus's rain hat followed. He leaped onto the deck and knelt there with his blanket shrugged up to hide his hair while his eye cast about for other men.

Something stirred in the shadow of the deckhouse aft.

"What's the matter out there?" a low voice hissed.

"Come here. Help me with this," Aengus called back in the same whispering tone.

Made incautious by Aengus's Serican speech, the man hurried over from the deckhouse, muttering, "What is it? What is it?"

Aengus rose from his knees and dispatched him as cleanly as he had the other.

Running into the house, Aengus found a young Serican, a boy younger than Pahdow, on his knees beside a pallet on which a still figure lay. A wick stuck into the neck of a jar burned fitfully on a shelf just above their heads.

"Don't shout or I'll kill you," Aengus told the boy gruffly. "Who's he?"

"The master of our ship," the frightened boy replied.

"What's wrong with him?"

"He's old. He's dying."

274

"Stay with him, then. If you show your face on deck, my men will kill you both."

The boy nodded. Tears started suddenly in his eyes, as if horrific Aengus was just the last of many terrors he had experienced and he could stand no more. He put his thin arm over the old man's chest and laid his head onto the pallet beside him.

Àengus made a rapid inspection of the ch'uan, then reported to his friends, "We have the ship. It's ours."

"Are you all right?" Mahkalt called up anxiously.

"Shh! Not so loud. We mustn't have our children recognize us yet . . . Yes, I'm all right. Why?"

"You were stumbling around. You were staggering down here."

"I was pretending."

The Kweneechekats and all of the other people of their country knew nothing of wine, of willful drunkenness, of lunacy by choice. Aengus did not try to explain.

"Go to the stern," he told them. "Take the rope I'll drop. Then I'll throw off the anchor line."

After dropping the end of a long line through the stern gallery, he hung two more from the sides of the ch'uan. Then, stumbling over spars, the wreckage of sails, and other rubble that the captainless crew had abandoned, he made his way to the bow. The shipboard end of the anchor line was thrown over a bitt, but the current drew the ch'uan so strongly that he was unable to cast the taut rope off. He sawed through it with his knife. The severed end fell to the water with a splash that he thought must be heard by everyone within miles.

XXX

Released to drift with the current, the vast old ship became as silent as an ancient tomb. Its loose parts no longer worked against their restraints; the chorus of rustles, rasps, muffled thuds, and mutters that Aengus had considered to be silence before, vanished when the struggle between anchor line and ship ceased. The stillness seemed like a hole in the world of sound; he felt that everyone must notice, whether ashore or below the deck.

He knelt with his ear against a hatch cover, listening again for any faint sound the captives might make. He heard nothing. He tried another hatch, then another. Nothing. He began to fear that the unconscious captain, the boy, and he were the only ones aboard. Again he was tempted to hammer on the hatch covers, to shout the good news, to discover if anyone was there; and once again he put the compulsion aside.

Atop the deckhouse on his way aft, he stopped abruptly. "The boy will know!"

But confused sounds and frustrated voices from beneath the stern gallery took his attention. That kind of Serican ship had a massive rudder hung within the framework of a false stern, and the line had become entangled in that structure as the ch'uan began to rotate in the current. Aengus scampered across to the transom behind the rudder and freed the line, then slid down it into the canoe.

"Let it swing," he said of the ch'uan. "We'll just keep it off the shore."

The men would rather have kept busy, would rather have felt that they were doing more to take possession of the ship than merely let the current deliver it for them. They waited and watched, then dropped the line and drew away from the ship to better gauge its motion, to see separately its drift and its slow rotation. All the while, the moon held its light steadily on them to betray them instantly to whomever would look their way.

"How far will we take the ch'uan?" Pahdow asked. "All the way back to Hokodah?"

"No. Just to the bay where Atsah said a path goes to Muklanogh's village," Aengus answered.

"Muklanogh?" Atsah squeaked.

"We'll need his help," Aengus explained. "The children will need attention. They're hungry and probably some are sick or hurt. Some of them are Kowmuxes. I'm sure he'll help us."

"He'll help," Atsah said. "He's not a cruel man." Her thoughts seemed not to be on the children.

"We can hide you from him and pick you up when we go home," Aengus said.

Atsah shivered at the thought of waiting alone somewhere in the cold, wet forest.

"Atsah, we also have to get Mowbit back from Muklanogh," Aengus reasoned with her. "We're returning Kowmux children as well as our own. And we've done him no harm. I'm certain we can convince him to give up Mowbit. And if we ask for you to help us take our young ones home, I'm sure he'll agree."

Atsah's round face bore a dubious expression.

"And if he doesn't," Aengus continued, "we'll say we stole you because you spoke our language—that you didn't run away from him. Then we'll come back for you another time. You've helped us. We owe you much. We won't leave you. For a while if we're forced to, but not forever."

Resignedly, Atsah said, "I want to see my Didotah home again. I know you'll help me when you can."

The current within the bay had slackened. The ship lay almost motionless at its mouth.

"Has the current changed in the channel yet?" Aengus asked the younger ones.

"Can't tell. . . . Can't tell," they answered.

"Let's pull the ch'uan over to the island"—he pointed to the outermost one of the chain—"and move around it if we can. It'll hide us."

This time they took the line that hung from the bow. The women had never watched closely how men maneuvered great canoe logs along miles of coastline. They were amazed that paddlers in a canoe could control a ship five or six times the canoe's length. For their part, the Kweneechekat men quickly realized that the ch'uan's tall masts and freeboard greater than that of any canoe or log meant little in their handling of it. They needed no instruction from Aengus; in fact, their adept performance guided his own movements.

Warily, watching both water and shore for currents and for their enemies, they tugged the ship a little this way, a little that, and carefully conducted it to the islet, then around to its far side and so out of the bay.

"Rocks!" Chehassa warned sharply from the bow of the canoe. Straining mightily, the paddlers swung the canoe toward midchannel. The bluff, flared bow of the ch'uan responded slowly. A dull thump, then several more, brought anxious expressions to the Kweneechekat's faces.

"No harm! No harm!" Aengus told them. "The hull can take that. It's barely moving."

Moments later, Chehassa spoke again. "We're going the wrong way! The current's taking us the wrong way!"

Mahkalt checked their motion against the trees ashore.

"Stop paddling," he said. "Don't fight the current. It'll change soon enough."

Slowly, slowly, the great ch'uan drifted northward in the channel until the paddlers could look back once again into the bay they had taken it from. The moon, a day from full, stood high in the sky, almost overhead. Its rays reflected brilliantly from the side of the ch'uan.

"They'll see us," Sierka worried. "They'll see us for sure, if any of them are looking."

"Even if they can't see us, they'll know where to look once they find the ship is gone," Mahkalt told him.

Eyes straining, Pahdow said, "If I went onto the ship and climbed one of the poles, I could see better."

"No," Aengus said. "We need you here. We've stopped drifting now. The current's reversing."

Within the span of a single breath, it seemed, their drift changed from northward to southward. Just before the small island again cut off their view into the bay, both Pahdow and Chehassa cried out:

"There!"

"There!"

"Canoes!"

"Where?"

"Away back."

"Past where the ch'uan was anchored."

"How many?"

"I couldn't see."

"One or two. Maybe more that we couldn't see."

"Let's attend to the ch'uan," Aengus cautioned.

They moved smoothly in the tide race, more rapidly as each minute passed. As long as they closely watched their towline and the sluggishly compliant ch'uan, they believed they controlled it still; but when they glanced toward the shore, shrouded in moonshade, and saw the dim rocks and stranded logs there racing by, they knew that the current was now master of both ch'uan and canoe.

"Paddle back! Against the current!" Aengus shouted when the ship swung ahead of them.

"We can't slow it down!" Mahkalt cried.

"No, but we can keep it off the shore."

It was as Aengus said. When they angled the ch'uan's bow away from shore and paddled hard to make the towline taut, the ship eased toward mid-channel.

"Not too far," Aengus called. He turned to explain to

Mahkalt and Sierka: "We want to miss the headland where we saw the whirlpools, but we want to pass on this side of the water-mountain, too. Otherwise we may be caught by countercurrents in that pocket beyond it."

The ch'uan's hull blocked their view ahead. Aengus almost wished that he had let Pahdow board the ship to be their eyes there. He pointed his paddle toward the eastern shore to tell the others to keep a constant distance from it. That shore, though, bent by imperceptible degrees to lead into the bay that had been guarded by whirlpools when the current swept their canoe northward the night before. The headland that formed the bay's far side angled back toward them like the point of a fishook. Sierka was the first to see its tip past the offshore side of the ch'uan.

"Pull out! Pull out!" he shouted.

Though they paddled fiercely, the ship responded more to contrary local currents than to their efforts. Aengus thought that whirlpools were grasping at them until he realized that now, with the current southbound, any whirlpools would be spun off the far side of the headland. But the ch'uan still refused to obey their will.

"We'll have to take the children off here—in this bay," Sierka shouted.

"No! No! Keep pulling," Aengus called back.

Long minutes passed—but only minutes—before they saw the ship begin to submit to their exertions. It aligned itself with the towrope; its bow began to follow them with ponderous docility. The headland, off to their left now as they pulled toward mid-channel, appeared to slide out of their sideways drift-course by inches, as if some giant gatekeeper was reluctantly allowing them passage.

But, in the end, the gatekeeper was too slow for the racing current. Just as it seemed that they would be swept around the blunt tip, the ch'uan's stern struck submerged rocks.

The ship heeled over. Its masts shuddered violently. With an ominous grinding of hull against rocks, the current swung the ch'uan's bow around and slammed it against the bold stone bank. The canoe whipped in a great arc on the end of its tether.

For an instant, the ch'uan slid forward over the clutching rocks, then it jammed fast and the line to the canoe snapped taut. The line had been wrapped once around the raised stern-piece of the canoe and then tied to the last thwart, the one Sistohka sat upon. The stern of the canoe dipped; the loop of rope slid up the stern-piece and sent its flat cap spinning into the air; the canoe jerked forward, and the thwart was snatched from its shallow sockets. Aengus had leaped up when the stern dropped. He charged past Mahkalt and Sierka, planted one foot on toppling Sistohka's shoulder, the other on the canoe's edge, and lunged for the rope. One hand caught the flailing thwart and pulled it toward him so his other hand could seize the rope. Then he was beneath the water and the canoe had swirled away and down the tide race.

The current pulled powerfully on his clothing, threatening to break his grasp. He shrugged, twisted, and released his hands one at a time to abandon his tunic and trousers to the torrent.

For an astonishing instant, the water seemed to course right through him, scouring, purging, every secret crevice of his soul—the sensation that Turfu had promised him at his baptism ages before but that he had not felt then.

Before the icy water could steal his strength, he began to pull himself hand over hand toward the ch'uan. At first, his body planed on the racing surface and he quickly hauled many feet of the rope past him, but, as he came up to the ship and the rope angled more steeply upward, his body hung more nearly upright and the current tore at him savagely. When finally he had heaved himself free of the water's grasp, he dangled below the flared bow and gasped for breath. Climbing again, the slipperiness of the rope hindered him, for it was not a knotted climbing rope. He paused once and twisted around to look for the canoe. The channel was empty. Moonlight on rushing water. Black forest. No canoe. No friends. Nobody.

He did not stop to wonder whether they had made shore where the narrows began or had slid through into more tractable water beyond. Doggedly, he pulled himself the last feet to the top of the weatherboard and slid over it onto the narrow deck.

He lay there for a moment, exhausted, until a sudden shift of the ch'uan brought him to his feet. The current was bearing the flood tide; rising water was lifting the ch'uan from its stony entrapment. But would the Wayabuks come before it was free? Had the hull been pierced? Would children in some of the compartments drown when the vessel had water beneath it to sink into? Those questions raced through his mind as he ran to the ship's side and then to the top of the house to see if followers came. Moonlight on the uneven water deceived him twice; neither time did those uncertain sightings resolve into any floating object.

"Is this how it's to be?" he wondered as he surveyed the empty channel. Was it to be a theft in the night, silent, furtive, followed by no clamorous battle, only timorous withdrawal by all contenders, all weary of strain and death? Was that what the kwal-k'washa intended?

He peered down through the sternworks to see what held the ship. He saw nothing but dark water.

"At least the rudder's up." Raised, he guessed, to make less drag when the ch'uan was being towed by the Wayabuk canoemen, for the anchorage had not been shallow.

The ship moved again. It slid forward a few feet. Branches of twisted redbarks leaning out from the high bank scraped on the masts. What would the young ones below the deck make of the strange noises and motions? They might believe they were going to die. Some of them *could* die if the ship began to sink. Aengus scanned the bank, the trees, the ship's deck, to see if there was any way to put the captives ashore quickly. But there was no way at all. He could not even begin to pull them from the compartments before the tide would lift the ship and send it careering down the channel again. They were safer where they were.

He jumped down to the deck and pounded on the nearest hatch cover. "Are you there?" he shouted. "Is anyone there?"

He looked up to see the Serican boy standing in the entryway to the house.

"Are the captives down there?" he demanded. The boy nodded, then withdrew into the shadow.

"Can you hear me down there?" he shouted again, using Kweneechekat words.

A few uncertain voices called back, "Yes . . . Yes."

His heart was wrung by the fragile, high-pitched utterances.

"We're taking you home again," he shouted, "but we can't let you out yet. There'll be rough water soon. Hold on! Hold on!"

Hold on to what? They would only have each other. They would be tumbled like stones in a jar if the ship rolled.

He went to the next hatch and the next, to all of them with the same message.

"Hold on!" he shouted through each one. "You're going home! Be brave!"

The Kowmux children must have been made more terrified by his rough shouts of words they did not know. Perhaps, he thought, they might sense the change in their fortunes from the behavior of the others in their black prison. If they could see them at all.

Suddenly the ch'uan pulled free so abruptly that Aengus fell to his knees. He ran toward the house, then stopped by a narrow center well in the deck that gave access to the after compartments. The well would be a safer place to ride out rough water than the flimsy house.

"Boy!" he called to the Serican. "Boy! Come here!"

The boy did not appear. Aengus turned his attention to the ch'uan's course. The flat-bottomed ship rotated slowly in the current so that he had trouble making out what path it followed. The whirlpools—if there were any—should be found between the headland and the entrance to the narrows, but he could see none. Relieved, he concluded that the ship's rotations had been started when the current pulled it from the rocks. The point of land that marked the beginning of the narrows, and the bluff just after the point, moved up and past, but they were farther from the ship than he had expected. Was it the eastern shore he watched or the other? No—the eastern shore still, but it was almost as distant as the one opposite.

He noticed the boy standing beside him now, his thin face drawn by uncertainty and fear.

The ship stopped rotating and was carried along beamward. The deck began to slant in that direction. Aengus looked ahead intently to see where the water-mountain lay. He could not find it. The current was not yet fast enough to thrust it up to any great height, he thought. The sky beyond had clouded over; against those moonlit clouds, he saw a low hill rising above the far shore of the pocket into which the narrows emptied. He watched the hill to see if they drifted to its left or right. It held its position dead ahead. And then suddenly it was not a distant hill at all but something close and louring—a dense blackness abruptly higher than the band of clouds. He heard the roar. He seized the boy and leaped into the well.

XXXI

Aengus sat tightly in the close well with his feet jammed hard against a bulkhead and his back against the one opposite. He groped with one hand and then the other for something on which to hold, but there was nothing, so he wrapped both arms around the boy.

The ship rose suddenly like a great bird taking flight. Aengus's stomach plummeted. He felt the floor of the well move separately from the heavy bulkheads; he thought the ship was breaking up, but, at the same time, refused to believe it. And then the ch'uan began to roll. It rolled back over its beam-ends, slid, slammed hard against water or rock, and spun sharply. It crashed, shuddered, and rolled again onto its other side. Above the clamor of dashing water and breaking masts, he heard the old ship's hull timbers groan and creak. Water sloshed into the well several times, then the well filled and was instantly quiet of all but rumbling noises. He clapped a hand over the boy's nose and mouth and held his own breath until the well emptied again and the racket returned.

Then it was over, and only then did he feel the boy's small fingers biting into the flesh under his legs like the talons of a hawk. The ship began a slow swirling motion, as if to soothe and reassure the souls it held. Aengus heard moaning behind the massive doors.

"We'll let you out soon," he called. "Be brave."

He freed himself from the boy and climbed onto the

285

deck. He found all the masts gone, snapped off; the house had been ripped away entirely; the stern gallery, the rudder, and the false transom behind it were gone; the deck had been washed clear of all the rubble that had been there. Nothing was left but the sturdy hull, and he was not certain that it would last very long. The ship listed alarmingly.

It drifted through the channel's pocket, following the outer whorls of one whirlpool and then another along great, sweeping arcs, but it was snared by neither. Aengus looked for his friends. They were nowhere to be seen. He saw the moonlit foaming crest of the water-mountain rapidly dropping behind, becoming smaller. He scanned the shorelines, as much as he could see of them on either side, but saw no one. Then the ship was in the long channel—eight or ten miles long—that spilled into the wide strait near Muklanogh's village. A gusty wind blowing up the channel did nothing to slow their drift. It was bringing clouds, though, clouds that threatened to extinguish his only lamp: the moon.

There was nothing left on the ch'uan that he could use to control its course: no masts or sails, not even loose boards to make any kind of paddle-sweep. He thought of releasing the children and, if the ship came close to a shore, throwing them overboard to swim to safety, but he knew that none would make it through the icy, racing water or survive for long on the winter shore if they did. No. They would have to stay below, boxed up, until the ch'uan was aground. The deck was steeply canted now. If the ch'uan turned over, only its sealed hatches would keep it afloat.

Holding on to the bulwark along the high edge of the deck, he pulled himself up to where he could see in all directions and waited. He waited for the kwal-k'washa to deliver the ship to wherever they intended; deliver the ship and him and some children—and how many corpses? He almost cursed the kwal-k'washa then for their rampageous handling of the ship, but he refrained. They were the only allies close enough to help him now.

He noticed that the boy had left the well and climbed up the deck to where he was. He was a thin boy, small, not much bigger than Kwetah but several years older than her. Maybe as old as twelve. He looked like a ship's mouse or some wild little storm-beaten thing from the forest.

"Where is my grandfather?" he asked.

"The shipmaster? Gone. He's dead."

The boy gazed around numbly. He asked no more questions.

After a while, Aengus said, "Your grandfather was going to show you an adventure, was he? Is that why he brought you along?"

The boy nodded.

"More adventure than he bargained for, I guess," Aengus said.

"It wasn't his fault," the boy retorted without much spirit. "The men—some of them—were bad. They turned against him."

But Aengus did not hear the boy's defense of his grandfather. His eye had caught a movement on the water behind them.

"There!" He pointed. "There. Do you see it? What do you see?"

"A boat," the boy replied, "with people, I think."

"One boat?"

"Yes. One boat."

Then Aengus could see it clearly himself. The Kweneechekat's canoe! And they had seen the ch'uan, for they were paddling furiously down the current to overtake it.

Soon he heard Sierka's strong voice: "Aengus! Are you there?"

"Yes!" He waved his arm. "Yes!"

He waited while they came closer. He would have to tell them that there were no towlines, that they would have to push the hulk to shore. But he had no chance, for suddenly there were more canoes—a horde of them that seemed to have burst that instant from out of the water. He could not believe that his friends had so riveted his attention that he had not seen their enemies approaching.

"Behind you!" he shouted. "Wayabuks!"

The Kweneechekats paddled desperately, but the other canoes had more men in each. They rapidly overtook the lone canoe. When the Kweneechekats were close enough to the ch'uan that Aengus could identify slender Pahdow and stocky Atsah but were about to be overtaken, they turned their canoe and charged their pursuers. As they closed, Aengus saw the three men exchange their paddles for whale-rib sabers while the women kept paddling. Mahkalt, Sierka, and Pahdow stood to strike into one canoe after another as they passed, to slay as many of their enemies as they could before they perished themselves.

Their chasers must have been astounded by such courage. And appalled, for Aengus heard their panicky cries across the water: "Friends! Friends!" Kowmux words! "Mahkalt! Sierka!" Mowbit's voice!

Sierka and Pahdow had begun to swing their sabers when sudden comprehension struck them. Unable to check their swings, they pulled their weapons upward to miss their targets. The two blades collided in the air as man and boy twisted awkwardly to maintain their balance. Pahdow fell into the water and, after churning the air wildly with his arms, Sierka toppled over the other side of the canoe.

Aengus saw the canoes converge. He could not see that Pahdow was pulled into one Kowmux canoe and Sierka into another while several Kowmuxes leaped into the Kweneechekat canoe to better man it. But he saw the knot of canoes separate and come toward the ch'uan again. He saw them form up along the side of the ship below him, their prows hidden from him by the swell of the hull as they pushed against it to drive it beamwards toward shore. He saw Chabotta Muklanogh shouting orders to his men and did not interfere to tell him that he should turn the ship to push it bow foremost. He saw Mahkalt fold a blanket into a tight bundle and hand it forward to a young man who threw it up to him. Aengus barely caught it, so slowly did he react. The wind was steadier now, biting

288

against his exposed body, and he had become chilled to dullness.

And finally, when he could do no more than point and shout unintelligibly, he tried to warn them about the Wayabuk canoes—Wayabuks for certain this time—bearing down on them. The Kowmuxes were slow to heed him, but Mowbit understood and tugged Muklanogh's arm to force him to look.

Muklanogh shouted a torrent of commands. His arms pointed now here, now there, and his instructions continued far longer than Aengus thought necessary for what the crisis demanded. And then his men seemed to ignore him. They applied their canoes again to the ch'uan's bulk.

As the Wayabuks came on, the clouds slipped over the moon. Aengus felt the cold more bitterly. He could no longer see the Wayabuk canoes under the sudden blanket of darkness. Mahkalt shouted. Aengus did not hear, or was too numbly intent on locating the Wayabuks to turn his head. Mahkalt tossed a saber up to him, but it clattered onto the deck and slid down a space between hatches and into the water on the ship's other side. Aengus hardly noticed. The boy's sharp fingers dug into his arm. Aengus did not feel them.

The Wayabuks burst out of the night, shouting fierce war cries. Muklanogh watched them coolly until they were no more than two or three hundred feet away. Then, at his sharp command, his canoes abandoned the ch'uan and his men paddled swiftly to put its length between themselves and the enemy.

The Wayabuks, now confused as to the number of Kowmux canoes they had to contend with, hesitated. Some of them came up against the ch'uan. Aengus carefully lowered the boy to the safety of the well, then followed him and lay against its sloping side, half-hidden there while he watched. Two of the Wayabuk canoes moved past the ship as if to pursue the Kowmuxes. When they paused, the Kowmuxes taunted them. The Wayabuks called for their fellows to join them, but one of those hanging back began to yell angry commands. Aengus could hear the Kowmux taunts and saw the uncertain reactions of the Wayabuks. Now a canoe or two would join those ahead of the ch'uan, then all would retreat; soon two or three more would come forward again, shouting their own threats.

The standoff continued so long that Aengus wondered at the lack of intelligence of the two chiefs. Battles are not fought with childish taunts and posturings and no joining. What could be gained by squandering energy and passion that way?

Finally, though they must now have known that they were outnumbered, all of the Wayabuk canoes quit the ch'uan and made for the tormenting Kowmuxes. Aengus heard Muklanogh's shout and saw several Kowmux canoes dart for the shore. Awkwardly, he climbed again to the high rim of the deck. Like a flock of startled birds, the Kowmuxes were scattering to as many different points on both sides of the channel as there were canoes.

"Cowards!" Aengus shrieked. "You cowards!"

The Wayabuks screamed their own cries of frustration and rage. Some gave tentative chase, but bellows from their leader dragged them back to the ch'uan.

The current was in full flood now. The ch'uan and the cluster of canoes beside it raced down the dark channel like things of the air rather than of the sea. And then, with no warning at all, they were plunged into a hell of breaking seas: great, sharply pitched rollers, an angry mob of them drawn high and close together, with tattered ribbons of spume flung like curses from their crests. A barrage of storm waves, piled up by the wind over a fetch of forty miles of open strait, slammed into the mile-wide eruption of sea-river at this place—this place where Muklanogh's own son had perished—this kwal-k'washa place.

The ch'uan nosed into the first ranks of the breakers, then swung broadside to them. Aengus slid down the deck and dropped into the well again. The ship shuddered as if it had been slammed against a wall. An erratic series of hammerings followed. The ship might have been sliding down a broken mountainside, from the pounding heard by those within. Aengus drew himself to the edge of the well again to see if the hull was breaking up. As he hung there, an empty canoe smashed onto the steep deck and the wreck of it slid off in the wave's wash. He returned to the boy and sat huddled with him while the kwal-k'washa destroyed their enemies.

A long while later, he became aware that the pounding had diminished. A new sound insinuated itself into his consciousness: a steady thumping. Lift—thump—lift—thump. They were aground.

From the top of the well and then from the high edge of the deck, he looked around to see where the shore was but could see none. The cold windblown rain hid distant places. He could see white-capped water stretching away in all directions, but only darkness lay beyond. He listened in vain for the sound of surf against shore.

"A shoal. We're on a shoal," he thought.

He retreated again to the well and sat with his head bent into his hands to wait for daylight. He tried not to hear the faint whimpers and moans that came at long intervals from behind the compartment doors.

XXXII

Strange shouts roused Aengus, but he did not understand them. He thought they had been made by people from a dream.

Then, from a greater distance: "Aengus!"

Was that Mowbit?

He eased the sleeping boy's head from his knee to the floor and climbed to the deck. The ship was firmly aground now and sat almost level on its flat bottom. The tide had dropped, although breaking waves still raced across the shallow water. And there, not a quarter-mile off in the predawn gloom, stood Muklanogh's high bluff and the stone guardians below it, most of them standing on a drying tidal flat now, gazing impassively out to the stranded ch'uan. A canoe was tossing beside the ship and two men were climbing over the bulwark onto the deck. Two more canoes angled across the shoaling waves toward the ship.

One of them brought Mowbit and Muklanogh. As Aengus reached a hand to pull Mowbit onto the ch'uan, the young man began to talk excitedly about the defeat of the Wayabuks, but Aengus cut him off.

"Is Muklanogh going to help us now? Have you made him understand?"

Mowbit stared at him oddly. "He *has* helped us. You saw what happened to the Wayabuks. He *intended* that. He knew about the bad water."

Aengus's thinking was slow and confused. "He fled. He left us."

"Only after he had distracted the Wayabuks until it was too late for them to realize their peril in time to escape it."

"You convinced him to help us, then?"

Mowbit said, "Men came from the village where we killed those Wayabuks. They told him what happened there."

"What do you think?" Aengus pressed stupidly, as if it was a time to weigh choices. "Can we trust him to help us with the children—with our own young people?"

Mowbit did not know what to make of his friend's uncertainty and became unsure himself. Perhaps Aengus had learned something about the Kowmuxes, perhaps the runaway woman had told him something. . . . Mowbit glanced toward the chabotta. "I don't know what he intends until he does it," he said. "I didn't understand what he was doing when the Wayabuks came until it was done." He paused, then said, "He seems to favor *me*."

Aengus's dulled mind was unable to find anything in Mowbit's words to dispel an obscure dread that Kwetah and Leeaht and Mowbit's nephews and the other children were not really beneath the deck or, if they were there, that they would be snatched from them again as soon as their prison was breached. He shook his head to clear it of chaotic fears, to bring present urgencies into focus.

He turned to the two Kowmuxes who had come aboard and showed them how to remove the lashings, pins, wedges, and bars that fastened the hatch covers. More canoes came up and more men climbed aboard. When the first hatch was opened, he lowered himself over its low coaming and dropped into foul darkness. His feet struck slime-coated floor timbers; he fell heavily and slid into pooled filth in the bilge. His body pinned a smaller one against the hull planking. When he turned to free it, he found that it was slippery with filth, bloated, and lifeless.

The stench was so powerful that he thought he would choke. There seemed to be no air to breathe. Nor any sound to hear. He looked along the bilge on either side of

293

him and into the murky corners of the compartment. He saw eyes first, incandescent in the darkness, and then dim huddled figures. He sidled toward them quietly, as if afraid they might scatter like sparrows and fly through the open hatch and be gone again. They shrank away from him.

"It's all over," he said softly. "The bad time is over. We're going to take you to your homes again."

They seemed not to understand him. Indeed, they may not have if they were Kowmuxes. He continued to speak gently, hoping that his tone would reassure them if his words could not.

The first child he lifted almost slipped from his grasp. His skin was slick with wet filth. When Aengus moved to position himself below the open hatch, he could neither brace himself against the slippery floor nor raise the child high enough for those above to grasp him. One of the men held up a hand to tell Aengus to wait. He left and returned minutes later with a net.

Aengus and Sierka were the last to leave the ch'uan. They had stayed to make sure that no forgotten child still hid in compartments that others had cleared, that no dead had been left behind. The water beside the hull was only knee-deep now. They bathed in it and scrubbed themselves with sand.

"Did you see Leeaht or Kwetah?" Aengus asked.

"I saw Leeaht. I saw her being put into a canoe."

"Being put in . . . ?"

"She was alive. She's all right."

"Kwetah?"

"I didn't see her. Or her body. But I was inside the ch'uan most of the time, just as you were."

"Did anyone else?"

"I only talked to Mahkalt. He hadn't seen her."

As they waded to the beach, they saw a line of Muklanogh's people, men and women, climbing the trail that angled back and forth up the face of the bluff. Each clutched a small child or led an older one.

On the ledge where the canoes were kept, Aengus and Sierka found Mahkalt, Mowbit, and several other men engaged in the doleful task of identifying the dead that belonged to their villages. Aengus anxiously scanned the nineteen small bodies and two older ones there, and then looked at each more closely. Kwetah was not among them. Nor were Mowbit's two nephews, although Mowbit found eight others who had been taken from Hokodah.

"So small," Aengus muttered. "Why would they take such little ones?"

Sierka assumed that Aengus expected an answer. He began to explain, "They're less likely to run away. They learn to live as slaves. They belong to their new villages and forget their old ones." But, before he finished, Aengus had picked up one of the bodies and was following other men who carried their own sad burdens along the beach.

The dead were laid behind a small copse above the reach of the tides on loose sand that had collected at the base of the bluff. When all had been carried there, they were covered with caked leaf mold, sand, and branches, and then with logs from the beach to keep scavenging animals from carrying them off.

The men cleansed themselves again and tried to lighten their hearts for the reunion that awaited them in the village above. But Aengus's spirit languished still. He waved Mahkalt and Mowbit to go on ahead while he followed more slowly. He was as reluctant to leave the beach as he had been to quit the ch'uan. If Pahdow or Sistohka—anyone—had come down to tell him that Kwetah had been found and was waiting for him, he would have bounded up the trail like a goat. But no one came, and he was afraid.

Cold rain still fell; people hurried past him as he trudged up the long incline. Some of them looked back with curiosity or concern at the tall man who carried his fouled blanket over his arm while rain filled his hair and beard and coursed down his pale body.

Soon he was alone on the path and would have felt all alone in the dripping world except that he saw a woman waiting for him far above at the crest. "Leeaht!" he

295

thought, and a surge of warmth passed through him; but he quickly realized that Leeaht would be with her brother, huddled close to a fire. He imagined the dazed girl, half-alive, staring numbly into the flames while Pahdow hovered over her with awkward solicitude. He wondered if she would recognize him.

"That must be Chehassa, then, or Sistohka. I've made them worry about me." He quickened his steps.

As he climbed the last steep rise, the woman removed a blanket from beneath her own, unrolled it, and held it up before her to drop around his shoulders. He tossed the one he carried onto a bush for the rain to cleanse and swept the proffered one over his back. And then he saw the girl's face—Leeaht's face.

"Leeaht!"

He wrapped his arms around her and crushed her to him. She lay against his chest quietly. She had scrubbed herself in the cold salt water and had rubbed herself all over with evergreen sprigs to remove the smell of ordure and death. She said nothing. She did not cry, although Aengus's eyes were full. And, later, it was he who first began to shiver from the damp chill.

"Where's Kwetah?" he asked.

Leeaht stepped back from him. Her face told him before she spoke. "She's dead, Akwahti."

He turned to ice inside.

"I looked at all of them," he protested. "She wasn't there."

"They threw her into the sea. Days ago. She tried to help all of us, but they caught her and threw her from the ship."

He turned to look at the remains of the ch'uan, a blur of darkness far out on the shoal flat. "Perhaps if I looked again. . . . Some compartment that was missed. . . ."

Leeaht took his arm and drew him toward one of the lodges.

The rain and wind increased to become a wailing storm that lasted for several days. The lodges were jammed with people. Ninety-eight children and young women had survived their dreadful trial in the ch'uan. How they had survived, the others did not know clearly during those days because most of the young people were so shocked that they could not speak of their experience.

There were Kowmux men from other villages in the lodges, too: men who had brought news of the Wayabuk attacks and who had appealed to their paramount chief for succor and vengeance. The first of them had arrived the very morning that Aengus and the Kweneechekats went up the channel to wait for the Wayabuks. By the end of the next day, Muklanogh knew the full extent of the Wayabuk terror, and he knew what the Kweneechekats had done for one of his villages.

The Serican boy was in Muklanogh's village, also, a lost and forlorn creature whom Atsah had found on the shore, walking away from the bustle and excitement where the children were being brought from the ch'uan. Perhaps he had thought he could find his way around the ocean and back to Serica. Atsah had gathered him to her and would not let him out of her sight.

Strangest of all Muklanogh's guests were two terrified Quaquolo youths. Curious about the events of the night that the ship was stolen, they had followed after the Wayabuks the next morning. Kowmuxes returning from the far side of the channel had caught them and brought them to Muklanogh. The chief was easily satisfied that the boys' intentions were innocent, but he held them under brief arrest so they would see that Muklanogh's lodges could accommodate as many guests as the Quaquolo villages; and so they would learn, also, the story of Muklanogh's utter destruction of the Wayabuks without the loss of a single one of his own men. He wanted the impressionable youths to carry word of Muklanogh's generosity, grandeur, and invincibility to their own irascible leader. But the storm had come and, neglecting to tell the boys that he was going to release them, he gave them into the charge of the women of his lodge.

The boys told the women, who told Atsah, who told Sistohka, about the fate of the Sericans. They were, in the Wayabuks' eyes, dubious accomplices. When they had found the ship gone, the Wayabuks' initial surmise was that the captain's illness had been feigned, at least as to its severity. It was a ruse, they thought, to enable him to remain on board unguarded and so be able to make off with his own vessel. Assuming that he had arranged with his crew to recover them at some other time and place, the Wayabuks slew them all, even those of the younger men who had seemed untroubled by evil deeds and had participated in them willingly.

"So that's why we had time to get as far as we did with the ship," Mahkalt said when Sistohka told her friends the story. "The time we needed was bought with Serican lives."

"They came a long way to die like that," Sierka reflected.

"Their gods must be powerless here," Mowbit said. "As feeble as the kwal-k'washa of the Wayabuks."

"Are the kwal-k'washa of the Kowmuxes and the Kweneechekats any stronger?" Aengus thought, picturing the dead children on the beach. "Do they heed any better those who call on them? Do they care at all about our world?" His sentiment sprang from anguish and bitterness; he kept it to himself. And, to himself, he asked again and again, "Why Kwetah? The only one from Appowad. Why is she dead?"

To be alone, he pulled a bearskin over his shoulders and went out into the storm. Leeaht joined him, and he was glad for that. Together, they went into a forest trail behind the lodges and found dry shelter under a thick tent of branches hanging to the ground from three canoe-tree cypresses growing from the same root mound. He wrapped themselves together in their two bearskins, then lay with her in a soft pocket between two buttressing roots and held her closely while they listened to the wind gust noisily through the treetops.

He soon gave himself up to the fragrance of her hair, the glowing warmth of her body, and loved her lingeringly, caressing her with gentle hands and kisses all the while. He felt her heartbeat quicken and her breathing grow deep and urgent . . . then subside, become calm and measured, as if she had fallen asleep.

And then, in the wistful aftertime, his thoughts returned to Kwetah.

Leeaht had not told him much, and he had not pressed her to relive her horror. She had said that Kwetah was convinced her Akwahti must be following the ch'uan. Somehow, the child got to the deck of the ch'uan with the intention of cutting or untying the ropes that were used to raise the sails. If those sails could be made to fall, she had reasoned, then Akwahti would overtake them sooner. But she was discovered almost immediately. Leeaht heard the men's rough shouts and Kwetah's shrieks of defiance. Apparently the Wayabuks had neither sympathy nor use for a troublesome captive, one whom they now saw to be lame as well. They threw her from the ship. Leeaht had followed her cries and childish curses across the narrow deck to the bulwark and then heard the splash.

Now, in his mind, Aengus saw Kwetah soon exhausted in the winter-cold water and sinking through layer after darkening layer until her soul was free at last to join her mother's for their journey to the land of the dead.

He glanced down and saw Leeaht's eyes on his face.

"Do you want me to tell you about her?" she asked. "About how she was brave?"

"Yes. I'd like to hear about that."

Leeaht settled her head onto his chest again and gazed over his arm, seeing not the massive cypress root there, but visions from a time that already seemed long ago. She took a while to reduce to order the confusion of what she saw, then began in a quiet voice.

"I told her to run into the forest when I went back to see what had happened to my sister, but she was still with me when I found her. I didn't know she had followed me until I felt her pulling on my arm, telling me to get up and run. And then the men were all around us.

"Two of them pulled me to my feet and began to drag me to their canoe, although I fought against them. Even then, Kwetah didn't run away. She could have, but she didn't. She pulled on the two men who held me, running from one side to the other to grab their arms or legs. When they swatted her away, she took up a stick and began to strike them, and when they snatched that from her, she picked up a stone as heavy as she could lift and tried to smash the foot of one of them. That man kicked her, kicked her hard and knocked her down. I tried to pull away, to get to her, but other men swarmed around us and I didn't see her again until we were inside the big ch'uan-canoe.

"The men were rough with us—very rough—until one of them, a Wayabuk, shouted something at them. Then they were not as rough. But they didn't let us climb down into the room where we were kept. They just pushed us into the hole. I was the first to fall, and then others as old as me came after. When the little ones fell, we tried to catch them, or at least break their fall when they pushed several down at once. I caught Kwetah. She had been crying, but she was not crying when I caught her. She clung to me and was very quiet.

"And then the men covered up the hole and it became as dark as night. We could see little cracks of light above, but that was all until our eyes got used to the darkness. Even then, we couldn't see much. There was nothing in that room to sit on or lie on except the wooden floor, and that was all wet and dirty.

"We stood until we were tired and the ch'uan-canoe began to roll from side to side. Then we sat in a tight group with the littlest ones in our laps so that we wouldn't slide around. Later we found that, if we sat along the front wall of the room so that we made a row from one sidewall to the other, we just rolled against each other and didn't slide."

When she paused, lost in her memories for a moment, Aengus said, "I tried to imagine how it was for you—you and Kwetah—inside the ch'uan with all the others, but a picture wouldn't come into my mind. All I could see was blackness when I tried to see you."

"It *was* blackness. That's all there was to see most of the time."

"Were you very frightened?"

"Yes. We tried to comfort the little ones, but we were as frightened as they were. That was at first. Then Kwetah said, 'Akwahti will come.' She said it so quietly that I had to ask her what she had said. She said, 'Akwahti will come for us.' I began to cry. Kwetah just hugged my arm and told me not to be afraid. Even though she was just a little girl, it made all of us feel better—less afraid—to hear her say that and keep insisting that it was true."

"Do you think she believed it, or was she just being brave?"

The question seemed to surprise Leeaht.

"Oh, yes. She *knew* you would come for us. I knew you would, too, but I think, if it wasn't for Kwetah, I would have begun to believe that I had only dreamed about you—that you didn't really exist."

Leeaht's words stirred a certain melancholy pride within him, but guilt too when he remembered his vacillations.

While he waited for her to continue, his thoughts left Kwetah for a moment as he considered how much Leeaht had changed since the first time he had held her so, in her people's river camp half a year before. Then, she had sparkled like a bright star. Now she was subdued, her warmth a promise, like a banked fire at night. Even her voice had changed: from a young girl's, whispering excitedly in the dark, to a young woman's, telling of things no woman should know. He loved her now beyond measure, but he was glad that he had known her then.

"We knew that other villages were attacked," she began again. "We heard captives being put into other rooms. We heard them screaming and whimpering. Each time, when it had become quiet again, Kwetah would say, 'I wish we could talk to them, to let them know that Akwahti will come for us.'

"One day—it was after the last attack—they uncovered the rooms. It smelled so bad inside that I think the Wayabuks thought we would die if they didn't give us some air. We heard the men working up above. We could only see the tops of two of the poles, but then we saw big mats being pulled up with ropes. When we saw them fill with wind, we knew that they were sails like those we use on our canoes to help the paddlers.

"That was when Kwetah thought we could slow the

301

ch'uan by cutting the ropes that held the sails up."

"Where would she get such an idea?" Aengus wondered to himself. She knew nothing of ships like the ch'uan. Certainly he had never described them to her. Was she just thinking furiously to stave off terror that threatened to overwhelm her mind? Or was she so confident of survival that she believed no harm would come to her whatever she did to hasten their rescue?

He asked Leeaht, "How did she get up onto the deck?" and was surprised when he saw that she was unwilling to answer.

He stroked her long hair and kissed her forehead to reassure her, and waited.

Finally she said, "I helped her up, Akwahti. She insisted that her idea was a good one, and some of the others took heart from that. When I saw her determination, I said that I would go because I was strong and could cut the ropes faster than any of them. But Kwetah said no. She said that she was smaller and less likely to be seen. She said that you had often talked about that kind of huge canoe, so she knew where knives were kept, what ropes to cut, and many places to hide afterward."

Leeaht paused, then turned her face up to his. "Did you tell her about the ch'uan-canoes?"

"I . . . We talked about many things. I . . . can't remember. She said I did, so I must have."

Leeaht saw through his awkward lie and began to weep.

"Don't cry, Leeaht. Don't blame yourself. Cutting the ropes was her idea, so she felt she should bear the risks. Kwetah could be very persuasive."

Her voice catching with suppressed sobs, Leeaht said, "Two of the girls my age got on their hands and knees and I stood on their backs and lifted Kwetah to the edge of the hole, then pushed on her feet to help her get out. Akwahti, I knew all the time that she didn't know any more about the ch'uan-canoe than I did. But I wanted to believe that she knew. She seemed so sure of herself."

She began to cry again, saying, "If I had only kept her with me, she'd still be alive."

Aengus caressed her face and arms, saying, "No,

Leeaht . . . no . . . no . . . You did what seemed best."

"But I was older than her. I should have said no. I let a little girl talk me into doing what I knew was wrong."

"You didn't know, Leeaht. You can say now that it was wrong, but you couldn't have known then what was the best thing to do."

Desperate to console the distraught girl, he said, "When the ch'uan rolled over that last night, when all of you were tumbled about so violently, she could have been killed then. Others were."

Leeaht said nothing.

"Were you frightened then, Leeaht? When the ch'uan rolled over. Were you hurt?"

"I knew that I *should* be frightened when that happened, but I wasn't. I heard you shout to us just before—that we were going home. I knew it was your voice. After that, all that mattered to me was that you were there. Even if I was killed, it didn't seem to matter to me because I knew that you had come for us."

Coloring at her profession of faith and love that he was still not confident he deserved, he asked again, "Were you hurt?"

She took his hand and placed it on the crest of her hip. "There, and down the side of my leg below, and my shoulder. But those were just bruises. *This* hurt more," and she slid his hand over the smooth roundness of her buttock until he felt a rough wheal. "That was a sliver—a big one—from the first day. Sistohka took it out."

Talk of her own experience had stopped her tears, but, in the silence that followed, her thoughts returned to Kwetah.

"Oh, Akwahti. Why did she have to die? I know that my own sister was killed too, but that was sudden and no one could have prevented it. It was different with Kwetah. She was alive and with me, and now she's dead because of what *I* did."

"The *Wayabuks* killed both of them," Aengus said. "You did what you thought best. *You* didn't kill anyone. The Wayabuks did."

While they had been talking, a dissonance was stirring

in the bottom of his mind, the beginning of an awareness of incongruity between Leeaht's words and his own perception of a gentle, passive Kwetah, overwhelmed by calamity. Now, abruptly, that dim feeling forced its way into his consciousness.

"Leeaht, you said that you heard Kwetah shouting when the Wayabuks took her to the side of the ch'uan and threw her into the water. What did she say?"

"The things that boys shout at each other when they're angry. Curses."

"Do you know if they struck her—injured or killed her—before they threw her from the ch'uan?"

"I don't know if they struck her. I know she was alive when she was in the water. After the splash, I heard her scream 'Ugly shit!' at the man who had thrown her."

Aengus's eyes shot up in astonishment and admiration.

Leeaht suddenly comprehended the tenor of his questions. "Akwahti, are you thinking she might still be alive? Oh, no . . . no. The water was too cold. She didn't know how to swim—only boys do that—and we'd been moving away from that last village for a long time. She'd had nothing to eat for days. They never gave us any food or water. . . . Akwahti, do you think it's possible?"

"She's like no child I've ever known," he replied.

He remembered his own hours in the sea after Semackul had given him to the whale. Hours in a winter sea. *He* had survived. It had been will, not physical strength, that had saved him. He thought of a Kwetah gritty enough to curse those who would kill her, and hope surged within him.

He got to his feet and lifted Leeaht to hers, and then into the air so that her head struck the branches above.

"Yes, it's possible, Leeaht. More than possible. I'm going to look for her."

XXXIII

The third morning after the filling of Muklanogh's lodges, there was a dusting of snow on the ground, a clear sky above, and no wind. The children were beginning to show signs of irritability, a welcome recovery from their morbid apathy. It was time to leave.

Aengus found Atsah and, with Mahkalt and Sierka, they sought out Muklanogh. The chabotta had kept to his lodge during their stay in his village, as if he was uncertain how he should conduct himself to maintain his dignity amid the multitude of his unusual and unprepared-for guests. Aengus and Mahkalt had concluded not to ask for Mowbit and Atsah. They would just take them, acting on the presumption that events had determined it should be so.

Muklanogh rose to meet them. He put on his severe mien, but was unable to hide the glint of curiosity in his eyes. Awkwardly, they told him of their gratitude. They said that they would tell all the people they met of Muklanogh's greatness, generosity, and wisdom in battle. Perhaps Atsah improved their ineloquent words. Awkwardly, he accepted their thanks. Atsah's translations seemed artless after all.

Later, people streamed down the cliff path. Some carried or led children; others brought blankets and food. From the top of the path, Aengus saw the ch'uan, now stranded high on the flooded tideflat. He imagined that, if

305

he were to return a year from now, he would find its timbers and planks in the walls and roofs of Kowmux houses, its few iron fittings made into tools.

On the beach, the children were packed closely into many canoes. There were twelve to be taken back to Hokodah. No, not to Hokodah, for Hokodah was no more. The children, most of them orphans now, would be distributed among the other Kweneechekat villages. Four Kowmux paddlers, displaced from their own canoes by the numbers of their children, sat among the Kweneechekats. The canoe, its proud wolf's head shattered from being pushed against the ch'uan's hull, was crowded, but the children had begun to chatter excitedly. Some even waved to new friends in other canoes.

Mowbit had avoided Muklanogh. He had not been convinced by his friends' assurances that the chabotta would let him go. But now he asked Mahkalt to wait. He had spied Muklanogh at the top of the path, as resplendent in his ceremonial raiment as when they had first seen him. Mowbit rummaged through the baskets in the canoe until he found the map. He looked to Mahkalt with a question on his face, but Mahkalt nodded.

Mowbit climbed the path in his awkward, halting way. When he neared the top, however, and paused to read the chabotta's expression, Muklanogh gestured to his four retainers and coldly turned away. Mowbit climbed the last few feet and watched the proud chief retreat to his lodge.

One of the women standing near saw Mowbit's gift and came up to him with her hand extended.

"For Muklanogh," he said as he handed it to her.

She nodded. "Muklanogh," she repeated.

A brave fleet put out from shore onto brilliant flat water under a brilliant winter sky. Aengus and Leeaht, in the small canoe that Muklanogh's men had said they could take, were the first to separate from the group. They stopped paddling when the stone sentries were only small black dots against the beach and Aengus could no longer make out the line of Kowmuxes along the top of the cliff.

The Kweneechekats only slowed their canoe to make their farewells; even with four extra paddlers, they did not want to fall behind the six Kowmux canoes.

"Will you come back to Appowad?" Mahkalt called, although he had already asked that question ashore.

"Yes," Aengus replied again.

"Even if . . . ?" Pahdow began the question that Mahkalt had intended but could not bring himself to ask.

"Yes," Aengus called across the widening gap. "Even if there's only Leeaht and me, we'll come back to Appowad."

To Appowad, where, according to Mahkalt and Sierka's diffident but frequent and hopeful hints, there was a place for him, a home to be claimed if he would have it, if he would be patient with the apprehensive people there.

Aengus's eye fell on Mowbit's two little nephews: sturdy, sober little fellows who sat together wide-eyed and solemn. Their faces were just as he had seen them in his vision by the campfire in the small bay near the water-mountain. Soon the little princes were hidden by the paddlers in their canoe as they dipped to pursue the other canoes. The Serican boy leaned out to look back past Atsah. Aengus raised his hand to him. The boy answered with an unsure half-wave.

Leeaht had said that Kwetah had been cast overboard the day after the last captives were taken aboard. The last village was on the east side of the strait, Atsah had told him. Soon after parting from the other canoes, Aengus looked to the southwest and was reassured to see that another canoe had left the fleet, its course roughly paralleling their own but diverging to make shore farther south from where they would begin their search.

Before long, Aengus and Leeaht were alone. Their companions of the morning had become mere sun dapples in a mountain-girt world of sea and sky. To the north-west, a thin bright band disclosed the cliff that fronted Muklanogh's village. But, of all the people the world held, there was no sign.

Release from Muklanogh's crowded lodges—that and

the monotony of steady paddling—freed Aengus's mind. Those worries that had made him fretful and peevish when he could do nothing but wait now seemed to belong to a vague and troublesome dream, the kind that holds a waking man in sleep against his will. He could recall only bits and pieces of that dreamtime now. He remembered worrying that Muklanogh's hospitality might wear thin. Atsah told him that would never happen. She explained that *Kowmuckthwaybsh* meant "people of the land where no one goes hungry," as much mandate as name to the proud chief. Mahkalt and Sistohka had tried to disburden him of other anxieties—about unremitting bad weather, about illness among the children—knowing then as he knew now that his worries were just an exhausted mind's barricade against dread over Kwetah's fate. Now clear sunlight dispelled that dread. Clear sunlight and the kwalk'washa would lead them to Kwetah.

His thoughts returned always to the girl who sat in front of him. When he had suggested that she should return to Hokodah or Appowad with the others, she said, "No. I have no one there any more. No one except Pahdow. Pahdow and you and Kwetah are my family now."

Her words had reassured him then. Now, in recollection, they astonished him. Beautiful Leeaht, bright and sweet-tempered, caught everyone's eye and everyone's admiration. How could she believe that there was no one for her but her brother, a little girl, and a half-blind, world-weary outlander, soon to be half-old like Mahkalt, and then, before Leeaht would be half-old too, he would be old. Did she believe that her people had given her to him irrevocably that night in the river camp? Her manner did not suggest any such persuasion. Her choice of him seemed to be freely and eagerly made.

Suddenly he remembered something else and was surprised that he had not thought of it before.

"Leeaht, was that you on the path when I hid my sack in the forest?"

Leeaht stopped paddling. She did not turn to face him immediately. He could not tell whether she was embarrassed by his question or afraid that he was angry with her.

"Leeaht, it's all right."

So quietly that he had to lean forward to hear her, she said, "I used to go there to watch you. . . . I went there a few times. I wanted to go down to your house, but . . ."

"You could have come to see me. Did Kwetah say you should stay away?"

Leeaht turned quickly. "Oh, no. No. She said some things that time when I did come to see you, but I knew afterward that she was only afraid that I might come between you and her. She was an anxious little girl. And then she came to see me just before . . . just before Hokodah was burned. When I saw Sierka bringing her to our lodge, I knew why she had come, and I cried. Then Kwetah cried and ran into my arms. We didn't need to explain anything to each other. We've loved each other since then."

"But those other times when you came to Appowad, was it *me* you were afraid of? Is that why you stayed on the path above?"

"I wasn't afraid of you. I was afraid you might not be pleased to see me. I was afraid you might tell me to go away. Then I thought that if I came to you at night, you would be happy to see me"—Aengus reddened at that— "so I didn't go home to Hokodah one night; but that was the night you climbed up to the trail and hid your bag. I didn't know what to think then. I watched you. And then I didn't follow you to your house because I didn't want you to know I had been watching you."

"So you put your comb in my bag then."

"Yes. I began to think you were preparing to go away. I thought that, if I put my comb in your bag, you would find it and bring it back to me before you left. I thought that, if you came to Hokodah, I could talk to you more easily there. And if you didn't come to see me, then something of mine would go away with you. You said you liked it, so I thought you would keep it with you and not throw it away."

Leeaht had lifted her feet over the thwart as she spoke and now sat facing Aengus, holding her paddle across her lap. Her eyes glistened.

Aengus was embarrassed by the girl's disclosures—embarrassed and humbled, as he thought of the half-hearted reception he had given her the one time she *had* come to his house.

"Leeaht, I didn't think that I could stay in this country then. I was afraid to love you. And you're so young. I thought you were too young to really know. . . ." He took a deep breath. "I thought you only felt a young girl's fascination for someone different, and that it would pass. I'm still afraid that you will wake up some morning and see me as something . . . hateful."

Leeaht put her paddle in the bottom of the canoe and came to sit by his feet with her arms folded across his knees. She looked into his face, then put her hand on his arm and said, "When I was a little girl, I asked my mother where I would find someone like she had found my father. She told me that the man for me would come from the sky, from the land of the sun. I used to ask her what such a man would look like, but she would only laugh and say that I would know when I needed to know.

"Often, while I was little, I used to imagine that the sun-man was my playmate. He would always be hot and fiery at first, but then he would become an ordinary boy, or sometimes a man, before he went back to the sky. I saw him in my dreams, too. He was big and glowing like the sun, with yellow rays all around him. I could never see his features clearly.

"Then my mother and father died, and there was only my brother and sister and me. We stayed in the same place in our lodge, right next to Mowbit's family, but I missed my parents greatly. They visited me in my dreams, though, and that helped me not to miss them so much.

"And then, just a few days before you surprised us in that meadow where we were picking lolowits berries—Do you remember? That first time we saw you?—a few days before that, I had a very strong dream. My parents were there, and the sun-man was coming from a great distance behind them. My mother told me I would meet the sun-man soon and he would look after me like a father and

310

mother and would love me like a wife. Then my mother and father moved away slowly and the sun-man came forward, step by step, closer and closer. I kept trying to see his face, to see what he looked like, but he just grew brighter and brighter until I could see nothing but brilliance. And then I woke up with the real sun shining through a gap in the wall of our summer lodge there by the river. It was right in my face. When I opened my eyes, it blinded me. But I was happy because I knew the sun-man would come soon and we would have a whole family again."

Leeaht's gaze had wandered to the distant horizon as she talked, but now she brought her eyes back to Aengus, as if she had said all that needed to be told.

"And I was your sun-man, then?" he asked.

"When I first saw you in the berry meadow, I knew you were. Your yellow hair—the way you wore it all around your face—and you were so tall. I ran away only because the others did—they startled me—but I knew I would see you again. And since then, it has been just like my mother said it would be. You've looked after me whenever there's been trouble—with Pugahlkuthl, with the Wayabuks. But, best of all, you've become a real man, just as you did when I was a little girl, playing with the sun-man."

Aengus was struck dumb. Before, his worry had been only that her girlish infatuation with a striking exotic would fade as she grew older and came to know her world better. Now he bore the weight of her mother's promise and her own childhood dreams. If he were ever to disillusion her, whether intentionally or through thoughtlessness . . .

Not knowing how to interpret his silence, Leeaht said in a voice now low and uncertain, "I've been waiting for you all of my life. I'll always love you. Always."

Aengus could only slide from the thwart and, on his knees, press Leeaht's head to his chest with both hands. The promise he made was as much to himself as to her: that he would make her "always" his own "forever."

311

XXXIV

They spent three days circling as many islands, looking for any sign, asking those they met if they had seen Kwetah. Most were disconcerted by Aengus's appearance and would have run off but for Leeaht, whom they found altogether more agreeable. No one had seen the child, or the Serican ship for that matter.

They made their way southward along the east side of the wide strait. They spent their nights in the lodges of those who would have them, or under their overturned canoe when they could find no better shelter. Bad weather followed good. Some days fierce squalls bound them to the shore. Aengus would sit, fretful and impatient, staring into the storm while Leeaht busied herself with hand-weaving small things from withes and bark strips that she collected when she could. One evening, in a lodge where they had spent a stormy day, he picked up a rain hat she had just finished and idly set it onto her head. To his surprise, the braided band inside was too snug to settle down over her brow. "It's not for me," she said quietly. Moved, he enfolded her with his arms. Her faith that he would find Kwetah buoyed him.

One night they made camp late. They turned into a long, narrow cove with sides so heavily forested that the trees blocked the last of twilight. Skirting a beach, Aengus looked up to the darkness beyond and saw scattered lines of light: firelight gleaming through chinks in the walls and roofs of unseen houses. They camped well beyond that beach, not wanting to disturb a strange village after dark. The next day, during the earliest gray of dawn, they passed the village again. Its houses were huddled against the gloomy forest, shaded from all but the highest summer sun. They seemed to belong to a dark phantom world. Carved figures of real and imaginary creatures were fastened to the buildings or stood free before them. The forms may have been colored once, but now winter moss and dimness obscured all but their outlines. The village seemed to be some mysterious, ancient growth creeping out from the bed of the vast forest. Aengus shivered and was surprised to feel a sudden, sharp longing for the bright, wind-scoured lodges of Appowad on the open coast.

About the tenth day of their search, a bright-cloudy, windy day, they were following the western shore of a large island, by now far south of where they had hoped to find Kwetah and as far in that direction as they intended to go, for they had decided to turn back the next day to another large island north of those they had already scoured. In the back of a broad bay, mostly a silty flat at low tide when they first saw it, they sighted a small group of lodges. They pulled their canoe ashore near the turn of land at the front of the bay and walked along the beach, wondering if they had found only another summer camp because they saw no one, the lodges appearing to be untended.

They called out as they approached, to announce their arrival as was the custom in that country. An old man and woman came out of the nearest lodge. When Aengus and Leeaht came close to them, the old ones' faces were suddenly horror-stricken. The woman ran inside and the man put up his arms to stop the strangers. Aengus spoke words that Atsah had taught him, words that declared their peaceful intentions and the purpose of their search. The man shook his head vehemently and retreated to his door.

Although Aengus did not understand their intense reaction against them, his curiosity was piqued. Ignoring

313

the man's protests, he went past him into the small house. Only the woman was there. Aengus reached through the doorway and pulled the man inside, then had him sit beside his wife on their sleeping bench. Aengus sat on the floor before them, below them to minimize the threat they perceived in him.

He did his best to learn what distressed them: he explained their search; he sketched a picture of a child, although he knew and had used the Kowmux word for "little girl"; he said Kwetah's name and even Muklanogh's. To all of those, the old couple shook their heads, waved their arms against him, and repeated, "No, no, no."

Leeaht, who had stood behind him during the first part of his interrogation, was attracted by something on another bench. When she had gone over and examined it more closely, she interrupted him with a soft, "Akwahti."

Hearing that name, the old woman gave a squeak and clutched her man's arm. *He* looked as if he might collapse from fright. Aengus went to Leeaht to see what she had found, and almost laughed in recognition and relief. On a board was drawn a face. Held in place by raised splinters were straggly clumps of moss to represent a beard and hair. Dead, yellow moss. And the eyes: a slit for the right and a circle for the left, a grotesque and staring eye.

"Do I look like *that?*" he asked Leeaht.

"No," she replied mischievously. "Not that beautiful." Clutching his elbow in her delight, she added, "Kwetah must have made this."

"Yes, and these people misinterpreted her meaning. Kwetah was showing them whom she was looking for, or who might come looking for her, and they must have thought it represented someone from whom she was trying to escape."

Leeaht's complexion was darker than Kwetah's, and there was nothing between them that could be called familial resemblance, but they chose to identify Kwetah to the old couple as Leeaht's little sister. That claim and Aengus's readiness to admit that the caricature represented

314

him—he held it up beside his face for them—finally persuaded them that they might have misunderstood the child's story. Their doubt was overcome, but only slowly.

With gestures and words, most of which were still foreign to Aengus's and Leeaht's ears, the old ones admitted at last that Kwetah had stayed with them for many days. They had first seen her on her hands and knees, crawling across the wide mud flat toward their lodge. She was exhausted, cold, and hungry, but not hurt or ill. They cleaned her, fed her, cared for her, and, it seemed, came to love her as a gift to them from the sea. Their story, told hesitantly at first and then in a torrent of words, ended with tears. She had left them. She resisted all their entreaties, their poor gifts, their caresses. She explained to them her reason for leaving, but they understood only that it had to do with "Akwahti": a demon with dead hair and a horrible, glaring eye.

When had she left? Yesterday, they said. Which way had she gone? Southward, along the shore.

Almost trembling with emotion, Aengus said to Leeaht, "It's early yet; we can find her today. Come."

Stopping him, she turned him to look closely into his face. "No, Akwahti. I'll wait for you here. I think you must see her first. I'll wait. You go."

Not quite understanding her reluctance, but assuming that, in the way of women, she was sensitive to things that he was not, he hugged her and left.

He did not find Kwetah until late afternoon. He spied her first as a dark spot far down a long beach. Paddling faster, his heart pounding in anticipation, he soon detected her slight limp and saw that she carried a long stick, twice her own height, which she was using as a staff. He called her name, but she was too far away to hear him.

When he was nearly upon her, he called again, but she did not turn around. Uneasy now, he paddled up abreast of her and spoke her name once more. She turned then and walked down to the water's edge, showing no more enthusiasm than if they had parted moments before.

"Hello, Akwahti," she said politely.

His canoe still floated just offshore. He said quietly, "I've come to take you home, Kwetah."

"I know, Akwahti. You tell me that every time."

"What times?"

"All these days. You told me last night. You told me this morning. But you always go away without me." With a sigh, she concluded, "I'm going home by myself because you can't seem to really find me. Maybe *I'll* find *you*."

She turned again to continue walking.

Saying no more, he brought the canoe to shore, stepped out, and knelt before the child. Gently, he wrapped his arms about her, then pressed her head to his shoulder so she would not see his tears. She did not resist, but neither did she respond with any emotion as he lifted her into the canoe, where she sat between his knees as he paddled away from shore and northward again.

After a while, she turned her face to look earnestly up at his for a long moment. She turned away again and slipped an arm around the lower part of each of his legs. She laid her head against his knee, and he felt the warmth of her tears.

"It's really you this time, isn't it, Akwahti?"

"Yes, Kwetah. We're going home."

"Are we going back for the others first? There are lots of children in a big canoe in dark rooms. I got away, but I was the only one."

"No. We've found all of them. Mahkalt and Sierka and some other friends and I took them from that boat. They're on their way home—except for one whom we're going back for now."

"Will the men who took us come back?"

"No. They'll never come back or hurt anybody ever again."

"They're all dead, then."

"Yes, Kwetah. All of them, except for a boy that belonged to them."

"One of them shouldn't have been killed, Akwahti. He pushed a piece of wood from the end of the big boat for me

316

to hold on to after I was thrown into the water."

"More than that one shouldn't have been killed, little one, but we didn't know that in time. They were killed by the Wayabuks, not by us. I'll tell you all about it sometime."

She was silent awhile then. The delusions that had possessed her mind, the fantasies born of fear and suffering, of loss and longing, evaporated only slowly. The end of her ordeal was too abrupt, it seemed, for her to trust immediately that it was real. Finally, though, confidence came. She stood in the canoe then and wrapped her arms around Aengus's neck; she clung to him as she had done in their forest home when he had returned from the river camp of Leeaht's people.

They camped ashore that night. The next day, on the high tide, they came into the shallow bay where he had left Leeaht. Kwetah had not asked who awaited them nor where they would find her. When they turned into the bay, Kwetah brightened and said, "I know the people here."

"They told us how to find you," he replied.

As Kwetah helped him to beach the canoe in front of the lodges, Leeaht came out and called to her. Kwetah squealed delightedly and ran up the long slope to meet her.

They stayed a month with the old couple. Those two were not the only inhabitants of their tiny community, but they lived alone in their lodge and, being only a remnant of a family lone gone, were mostly ignored by the others. They knew nothing of the Wayabuk raids or the full horror of their guest's sufferings, so those were not talked about and soon began to recede in the girls' minds. Talk and play and foraging and handiwork occupied the young ones' hours. They sought the old couple's advice and approval for many of the things they did and listened attentively even when the answers to their questions seemed disconnected.

One day the old woman learned the meaning of

Kwetah's name. "Oh," she cried. "A *hummingbird* you are. I know about a hummingbird-girl. Sit. Sit." She leaned over and patted the top of a large box that stood on the floor near her bench.

Kwetah understood enough of her words to know that a story was being promised. She climbed onto the box eagerly.

The old woman's story was of a mother who was blessed with a fine little daughter but was cursed with a choleric husband who ill-treated her and their child relentlessly. The mother appealed to the kwal-k'washa to preserve her daughter from her husband's wrath. The spirits' capricious response was to transform the girl into a hummingbird. Within days, before the hummingbird ever learned that she must follow summer southward, a bitter winter descended on their land. While the poor bird took what shelter she could find behind their lodge, her mother sought blossoms for her along frozen woodland paths and ice-rimmed streams. She searched through brambly thickets and deep into forests haunted by wolves and bears. She returned to her lodge late each day with nothing more than torn and bleeding hands to show her daughter. When she raised those cupped hands and turned her head away to hide her tears, the little bird's bill found what her mother knew nothing of: blood that had become like nectar from the love that filled her mother's heart. During all the days of lashing rains or frozen stillnesses that made up that terrible winter, the mother remained unaware that it was the forlorn display of her hands that sustained her little one. Every one of those days, she gave thanks to those whom she believed were responsible for her hummingbird's miraculous survival: the kwal-k'washa. The kwal-k'washa, abashed at last by that undeserved gratitude, hastened the crimson currant bushes into an early flowering for the bird-girl that year, an extravagant blooming that banished winter in a day. Thereafter, they never ceased to show special favor toward her. And so they have done toward all hummingbirds ever since, even down to this day.

The woman told the story with such continuous gesturing that her old body moved like a young woman's, dancing. Kwetah's eyes danced, too, with the delight of recognition. Though most of the Kowmux words were still strange to her ears, she glowed when she saw the familiar uplifted flower-hands.

"I thought my mother just made up that story for me," she said to Leeaht later. "I didn't know that other mothers told it."

Aengus watched all of this. He saw a Kwetah markedly older than the child he had first known. Her leg grew stronger every day, but there were dark stillnesses in her spirit now, somber pools that lay below her natural buoyancy. When at last she asked about her mother and Aengus told her that she had died, Kwetah did not weep. She let him hold her on his lap, and she leaned against his chest with her two arms wrapped around one of his for several hours while her dark eyes gazed into the flames of the evening fire.

At other times, he noted with pleasure the affection that had grown between Kwetah and Leeaht. He thought of the first time he had seen them together: Kwetah beset by jealous fears; Leeaht hurt and bewildered that her first offering of womanly love was not cherished. As long as he had believed that he was only a sojourner in their land, it could not have been otherwise. Did Leeaht accept that explanation for his behavior then? She seemed to have put the unhappy episode entirely out of mind.

A softness in the air, the first hint of spring, at last called them away; the booming surf and sea mists of the open coast and the wild cries of the seabirds there commanded their return. The old couple did not want them to go, but became reconciled to this separation as they had to others. They were consoled by the promise of another visit in another year—if the time left to them would be measured in years, Aengus thought sadly.

The three put out from the shallow bay on a high morning tide. Aengus sat on the stern thwart, paddling strongly, his heart swollen with pride and confidence.

Leeaht, his beloved Leeaht, was a herald of spring, for Kwetah had twined colored strands and leaves into her hair, and into her own and the old woman's, to make their farewell less bleak. Little Kwetah—little sister, little daughter—sat between them with her own small paddle, trying to match their strokes with her own.

They crossed the strait and threaded channels between islands. On the fourth day, they rounded the southern end of the great island and turned westward toward the ocean. Homeward. To Appowad.